OUT THERE

Frankie McGowan

HarperCollins*Publishers*

This is a work of fiction.
Any similarity to characters
living or dead is purely coincidental.

HarperCollins*Publishers*,
77–85 Fulham Palace Road,
Hammersmith, London W6 8JB

Published by HarperCollins*Publishers* 1994
1 3 5 7 9 8 6 4 2

A catalogue record for this book is
available from the British Library

ISBN 0 00 224466 7

Set in Sabon

Printed in Great Britain by
HarperCollinsManufacturing Glasgow

For Peter, Tom and Amy
with love

Acknowledgements

Writing this book was made considerably easier and unquestionably more enjoyable because of the input and support of a number of good friends and colleagues in New York and London.

Most particularly, thanks is owed to two special friends, Avril Graham (Brown) in New York and in London Melanie Cantor, whose knowledge and insight into the world of PR has been invaluable.

Special thanks also for their generous advice and expert help to Keith Schilling, Jillie Murphy and *Chic* magazine and the support of David Graham in New York. Not least I am, as ever, indebted to the talented team who in their various ways helped pull this book together, Rosemary Sandberg, Susan Opie and Imogen Taylor.

My love and thanks to you all.

Prologue

She knew there was going to be a row when she arrived at the triplex he occupied on Park Avenue.

Sleeping with Howard had been a mistake. She still didn't quite know why she had. Her future wasn't in New York, it was at home. Even if that was without Roland.

She allowed herself a wry smile as she watched the indicator light silently slide past each floor, whisking her to the top of the building.

What was the point of being one of the best PRs in the business, promoting other people's images, smoothing their path, making sure they were seen in the right company, featured in the right papers and protecting them against scandal, if your own life looked more and more like an exercise in how to self-destruct?

The moment when Howard's interest in her had stopped being exclusively that of a man knowing his public image was in her capable hands was approximately twenty minutes after she had accepted the job, nearly eighteen months before.

'One thing, Judith, before we sign the deal,' he'd said, detaining her with a smile and holding out a drink to her.

'What's that?' Judith had smiled, accepting it as Howard dropped into the opposite armchair.

'You must promise me you won't sleep with any of my friends.'

Judith regarded him thoughtfully. So that was the name of the game. When they said he was a womanizer, they didn't also mention crass.

'Mr Dorfman,' Judith began, her tone pleasant, her expression puzzled as she set down her glass on the table between them and leaned across it to smile right into his face. 'Tell me, are your friends all like you?'

'Most of them,' Howard smiled encouragingly back, his face about six inches from hers.

'Then you have my word for it,' Judith said serenely. 'I wouldn't dream of it. And to be doubly sure,' she went on, picking up her bag and getting to her feet, 'I suggest you give the job to someone else.'

For one split second Howard looked incredulous and then to her surprise he fell about laughing, not remotely offended. But then, neither was she.

'You're going to be great for my image,' he'd chuckled. 'But lousy for my ego.' And the deal had been struck. Judith was to reinvent his image to the satisfaction of the shareholders and the relief of the board of Dorfman Industries.

She liked Howard; she admired his business skill. But when you're trying to put the pieces of your own life back together again, emotionally you're anaesthetized, immune to anyone. Then it had all changed.

Judith had needed an intimacy and comfort that she had not felt for nearly two years – not since her relationship with Roland, but that was another story and one she preferred to forget.

So it was easy, when it came down to it, to have allowed her name to be added to Howard's conquests. So very easy.

The day had been long and fraught, starting at dawn, but by ten that evening Howard Dorfman had acquired a chain of companies that had seen his place on the Forbes list of America's wealthiest citizens shoot up a few more notches.

Howard being congratulated and fêted was a sight Judith had grown used to in her time as his PR, but not one that she wanted to participate in. Instead she waited patiently for him to decide when to leave the hotel suite at the St Regis, hired as neutral ground for the negotiations, and head for his triplex on the Upper East Side.

'Hey,' he said, as they rode in the back of his car through the dazzle of lights that lit up Manhattan. 'What is this?'

He pulled her face round to his. 'Nothing, Howard,' Judith protested. 'Just a long day. It's been terrific. Well done. Can Nico drop me off?'

'You're kidding,' he said. 'You're coming up and I'm going to pour you a drink and . . .'

'No, really, Howard,' Judith insisted. 'You're flying to Dallas tomorrow and I would really rather get back . . . honestly, Howard . . . How . . . ard . . .'

Ruthlessly clutching her arm, Howard pulled Judith out of the back of the limo and steered her across the carpeted lobby into the lift and up to his apartment. Conchita, the house-keeper, was waiting for him.

'Where's Jorge? I want champa . . .' He stopped and looked at Judith's weary face. 'No. I want tea. Good English tea. Me? Jesus, no!' The horror in his voice made Judith laugh. 'No, not me . . . I'll make do with a Scotch.'

Just for a brief second Judith was interested. Howard think-ing of someone else? Tea? Sympathy? It was a cliché.

'Okay, let's sit you right here,' Howard said, pushing her firmly onto one of the spacious and restful white sofas that made up three sides of a square and gave an uninterrupted view through glass doors over the skyline of New York. 'Then you can tell me what the face is about. After which I call up Oprah and say I have a case of executive abuse which needs a national airing . . .'

Judith laughed and relaxed. Sipped her tea. She let him massage her feet, mostly because it seemed churlish to refuse, and the rest because she found it comforting.

Somehow sitting there in the soft light of Howard's apart-ment she had, at his insistence, told him about the married man back in England, the loss of her job, and how she missed her family around her all the time. Maybe she felt it more because she'd just got back from a Christmas visit home to Yorkshire. New York was great, but there was never any sense of home, of belonging anywhere.

'Poor baby,' Howard had said. 'Poor kid,' and it had been so long since someone had been that kind to her that to Judith's shame she had felt tears starting to well up and Howard had held her in his arms and kissed her hair.

Her sense of humour was proof against the abrupt rudeness of New York taxi drivers and waiters. She could handle with her customary warm charm the pushy intrusiveness of the most persistent Wall Street journalists who daily tried to breach the walls of Howard's financial empire. But kindness? Kindness finished her off.

Then Howard had kissed her neck and pushed her over so that he was lying on top of her, and all the while he talked and soothed and stroked her legs and breasts until sheer need and longing and loneliness spun in her brain. For the first time in a long while, she felt needed.

Within days there had been a subtle shift in their relationship.

Howard had called Judith from Dallas to arrange dinner and arrived an hour late, bringing one of his cronies whom she loathed. Judith had called a car and gone home.

With Howard, business came first.

Their explosive relationship became the talk of the town. Judith's best friends in New York, the gossip columnist Jed Bayley and the television producer Ellie Carter, both urged her to believe them when they told her that Howard was bad news.

She agreed. But then Howard would phone and make her laugh, and laughing for Judith who hadn't laughed with any-one in a long time was good news. And for a few days they would once again be charmed with each other. It was what they had in common, charm.

But not a harmonious meeting of minds. She slammed the phone down when he interrupted meetings and he sulked if she rang to say she would be late. She gave away tickets to a Pavarotti Concert to two students standing in line at Carnegie Hall as the first act was about to start and left him hammering on her door at midnight when he found she wasn't waiting for him at his apartment when he finally showed up.

Howard was seen dining out at the Café Carlyle, flirting outrageously with a redhead who clearly would have been more at home scouting for business in the lobbies of the big hotels on Sixth, simply because he knew it would irritate Judith who had refused to cancel dinner there with a financial editor to have dinner with him instead.

Next day Judith told Ellie over lunch that she was more

angry that Howard was wrecking the image she had so carefully reinvented for him than that he was with another woman, and privately began to make her own plans.

Only Howard's threat that he was going to storm her apartment made her agree to go over and talk to him the night after she had heard from a chance remark dropped by his personal PA, Connie Mayerson, that far from being locked in a meeting three nights ago he had been in a club noted for its ability to cater to all sexual tastes. The night he was meant to be having dinner with Judith.

Annoyed that she had been phoned by Howard at three in the morning instructing her to cancel all his meetings for the next day, Connie had snarled his whereabouts to Judith as she met her in the corridor and swept on, leaving Judith struggling with a mixture of anger and surprise. Anger that Howard should have chosen a sleazy nightclub to punish her for spending the weekend in Connecticut rather than out in Long Island with him, and surprise that his usually discreet-to-the-point-of-secretive secretary had blurted out the truth.

When they had first met, Judith had found Connie's carefully mounted guard over Howard rather admirable, but as weeks ran into months and her friendly overtures had been snubbed, she agreed with the rest of the staff that Connie took her job just a shade too seriously. Great for Howard but frustrating for the smooth running of their jobs.

If Howard thought she was going to be just another Connie with sex thrown in, Judith knew it was time to disabuse him of that notion.

'I am not a toy, Howard,' she said, calmly ignoring his wrathful face. 'I have a life and I am not sitting around waiting for you to make up your mind whether we have a dinner date or not.'

'That's not the point, Judith,' he stormed, striding up and down in front of her wrapped in a short white towelling robe, running a furious hand through his hair, finally slumping down into a chair opposite her, slinging his tanned legs across the arm.

'Well?' she asked coldly, studying her nails. 'What *is* the point?'

He glared at her. 'The point is I pay you to be there when I need you . . .'

Judith knew that keeping calm was her only weapon. Lose it and you're lost on all fronts, she reminded herself.

'Goodnight, Howard,' she said, rising from her seat and starting to make her way out.

He was there before her, getting between her and the door. 'And where do you think you're going? Goddamn it, Jude, you just don't do this to me. What do you want me to do? Pay you to have dinner with me like some little tramp?'

'Now you're being ridiculous,' she said, attempting to move past him. 'And you're wasting my time.'

'Marry me then?'

'No.'

'You're fucking rude as well,' Howard said, folding his arms as he leaned against the door, preventing her from leaving. 'Okay, if you won't marry me, have dinner.'

'It's too late. I have to work for you in the morning.'

Judith reached behind him to open the door, but he wrapped her in his arms and began rocking her back and forth.

'Come to bed then?'

Chapter One

The grey dawn light just discernible through the blinds threw a ghostly outline around the understated elegance of the apartment Judith had chosen, the decor she had insisted on at the right address, the dressing room lined with clothes that she had selected for him, reflecting the lifestyle of the sleeping man beside her.

Getting Howard Dorfman's name past the severe and censorious board of residents in the uptown apartment block that housed half of the most prestigious names on the New York social register had been a feat not even the Dorfman directors thought she would pull off. The task of reinventing the image of the Chief Executive and major shareholder of Dorfman Industries from one of flash cash to stylish acceptability had been strewn with the moral indignation of the socially correct and the dismay of the easily outraged, who saw nothing of the Dorfman empire's founder in his son.

It was a fortunate thing, Judith thought grimly as she negotiated a new address for Howard, that his father had been well-liked and respected. That, plus the promise of a Canaletto to be donated to the art gallery of which the most formidable board member was a trustee, squeezed in Howard's acceptance by the skin of his even and very white teeth.

Howard's reaction, however, when he heard the price of admission to a part of town he wasn't particularly enamoured of, was as rich as it was lengthy. Throughout the tirade, Judith had simply sat perched in a window embrasure of his office, calmly surveying the traffic crawling below on Wall Street, ignoring him, just occasionally stifling a yawn as she crossed slim legs, encased in sheer black tights, into a more comfortable position.

A trip to the Madison Avenue addresses of Leonard Logsdail and Alexander Kabbaz ensured that his appearance would now be in the hands of some of the finest tailors in town, and when she ordered Howard's staff to donate his present wardrobe to the nearest thrift shop she had simply swept him aside as he furiously protested, reminding him that he was a businessman and not a rock star.

Within months he was to be seen playing tennis at the River Club and squash at the Harvard Club. Clothes, hair, decor and lifestyle gradually changed, until even his nightclub cronies were only too happy not to be seen in his company. Howard Dorfman, they said, wasn't fun any more. But Howard Dorfman businessman flourished. While Judith would never have found the old Howard attractive, it was odd how, now she had reinvented him, he seemed a more likeable proposition. The mistake she had made was to believe she could reinvent the man when all she had done was given him a more acceptable package.

Judith turned her head and looked at Howard's face – his mouth slightly open, his chin slack, the creases around his eyes the only evidence that he was nearer to forty-five than thirty-five – and wondered why he had cheated on her.

No, not that. Cheated implied a commitment he had never made to her, but one that he assumed she had made to him because he paid her salary.

It had hurt knowing, in spite of all his denials, that on one evening he had preferred the company of a hooker to hers – how could it not? That was bearable and forgettable, but the utter humiliation of finding she had been moved sideways in her job was not. No warning, no indication it was about to happen.

David Corrolla had been appointed over her, not because he was better, not because she hadn't done her job well, but because Howard Dorfman could find no other way of making Judith totally available to him when he wanted her. If her job got in the way, then the job had to be adjusted. To do that meant hiring someone who would take over the work that Judith did so well.

'And exactly what is he?' she had coldly asked the decidedly uncomfortable Personnel Director, minutes after she had heard about David Corrolla's appointment. 'Someone who reports to me . . . or what?'

'No, not exactly,' the man hedged with little conviction and even less truth. 'You're getting a promotion. You work exclusively for Howard and Dave – who is just great, Judith, we are *so* lucky to have him – Dave will take over the nuts and bolts of your present job.'

As promotions went, this was so thinly disguised as a sideways move that she could hardly speak. No discussion. Howard had simply made a decision because he owned the company and therefore believed he owned her. The one scenario Judith had vowed never again to get involved with, and here she was back at base. Well, no, not quite. This time she was better armed. This time she wasn't in love, not even in lust with the man; that had passed. But a more powerful and seductive force had emerged: belonging. However, belonging was beginning to blur with being owned. And for Judith the gap between the two was unbridgeable. Howard still thought it was the same thing.

Howard stirred in his sleep, his left arm lying heavily across her stomach, making movement impossible, unless she woke him. And Judith did not want him to wake, not just then. She wanted to collect her thoughts, to really understand what it was that she was going to do: something conclusive, no loose ends, no messy goodbyes.

Her feelings for him were uncertain, something hovering between loyalty and need but nothing strong enough to have pushed her over into hopelessness. Judith wanted out before the relationship reached that fragile moment when a parting would consume her for weeks and months on end. It would mean the end of her job – but that had changed anyway. And where was it written, she said to herself as her gaze took in the elegant bedroom, that life was easy for a girl who was still climbing?

Judith eased her arm from under the sheets and screwed up her eyes to look at the hands of her watch. Nearly five thirty. Down below on Park Avenue, the cross-town traffic had yet to start moving. In an hour or so the sidewalks of New York would be heavy with commuters striding out towards their offices on Madison or Fifth, into the heart of Manhattan. The bridges would be bumper to bumper as cars and taxis pressed their way over from Westchester and Riverhead and the midtown tunnel would be alive with the sound of horns and frustration.

It was time to go. Carefully she eased her body to the side of the cavernous bed. The sleeping man's arm, relieved of its resting place, dropped heavily onto the crumpled white sheets. Judith held her breath. Waited, motionless. He mumbled something in his sleep but his eyes remained closed.

Safe now. Sliding over onto the carpet, Judith straightened up and then gently replaced the sheets, standing for a moment to stare down at Howard's face for the last time.

Last night, there had been the familiar angry exchange, the weary acceptance that neither was going to win. Bed but no sex. 'I just want to hold you,' he had said. That's all she'd wanted; loneliness did that to you. Pride didn't even get a look in. And because he was exhausted and maybe because he couldn't bear to be rejected, he had done just that: held her and drifted into sleep.

In leaving him she liked him better than at any time in their stormy relationship. But it was no longer enough. Crossing the white carpet, she sat down at a small walnut bureau and dragged a sheet of paper towards her, frowned for a moment and then began to write. Rapidly as though a moment's loss of time would weaken her resolve, she scrawled across two pages. Then, folding the letter, she sealed it and propped it against the lid of the bureau where Howard would see it when he woke.

Judith rose from her seat and caught sight of herself in a long mirror which reached the ceiling and reflected the casement windows behind her, the view of tall grey apartment blocks soaring up into the already soft blue spring sky of another day in the city. Silently she gazed back at her reflection. She saw a tall slender girl, thin really, with a mass of dark hair pinned carelessly on top of her head; a pale oval face, with a beauty that came more from its laughing brown eyes, straight nose and high cheekbones than from conventional good looks – features which gave her in repose a solemnity she didn't really possess and a confidence she did not always feel. Hastily she turned her back on the mirror.

Nothing else to keep her there. In one hour, another day would begin for Howard Dorfman and by the time he had finished his breakfast he would be worth another half a million dollars on Wall Street. And Judith would no longer be a part of any of it. Sixty minutes in which to change her whole life. It was enough – it had to be.

As she sat in the cab, the familiar streets of New York that had been home to her for nearly two years flashed by in a blur. Down Park Avenue, right into 79th, past Madison and Fifth. The Metropolitan Museum of Art towered on their right as they sped through Central Park to Judith's apartment on the Upper West Side. For once the lights were with them and as they hit each set and sped through them, Judith gazed resolutely ahead. New York had saved her. And now she was going to save herself from New York.

Another ten minutes and she was in her own apartment, throwing a fresh jacket and make-up into a large leather Louis Vuitton holdall, snapping shut two already packed suitcases, checking her purse, wallet, credit cards. In the bedroom, ignoring Dorfman's regular car service, she rang for another company to collect her at precisely seven o'clock. Then she dialled Jed Bayley's number.

Jed was perceptive. He had once been her boss in London but he was also her friend. Because of him, New York had opened doors when she had arrived all that time ago. After that, her husky English accent, sharp intellect and easy charm had broken down walls. But Jed knew that under that cool English exterior, the one that had so enamoured and intrigued Howard Dorfman, there was a vulnerability that Judith went to extraordinary lengths to disguise.

The soft purr of the phone in Jed's town house in the West Village switched to his answer machine. Judith waited until the message came to a halt.

'Jed? It's me, Jude . . . Oh hi . . . Jed, stop swearing, it's too early . . . Jed, I'm leaving New York . . .'

The mists of sleep lifted from Jed's voice.

'What do you mean, you're leaving? Leaving what? Howard? *Howard?* Christ . . . what happened? Where is he? Hang on, let me get a pen, this I've got to record. Have you told anyone else?'

Judith almost laughed. 'Jed, you're a nightmare. Is everything just a story to you? It's okay, I've left him a note . . .'

Jed screamed. 'A note? You leave him a *note?* Is that all? He is going to be *so* humiliated. Why?'

Judith took a deep breath. 'You know why. Everyone knew except me. It isn't what he is, it's that he lied to me . . . that he thinks he can because he pays me . . . it's because he thinks he can re-order my life without consulting me . . . oh God, Jed you name it. I just feel like the biggest fool in the world and I am so angry that I allowed him to think he could do it. That's what hurts the most . . .'

'Jude, don't go. Come and stay here . . . he won't come here, he's never forgiven me for writing what his first wife said about him . . .'

'Thanks, Jed . . . but no. I'm not sure I could trust myself to stay in the US, let alone New York. I haven't even tried to have a conversation with him about Corrolla taking my job, or that he spent the night with a hooker . . .'

Jed interrupted. 'Listen, you don't know for sure that he did . . .'

'Oh, don't defend him. Connie is the *grave* when it comes to discretion, but he drove even her to dumping him in it. Anyway, it's Corrolla who hurts more, not a Seventh Avenue tramp.' She sighed impatiently. 'I don't want to talk to him. I don't want denials. I don't want promises he can't keep. I want to walk out on him before I'm taken out of his life and straight into a clinic. Do you understand?'

Jed did. What could he say? He had tried in his own way to tell her what most people knew about Howard Dorfman, something he had known from the moment he had encountered him in the kind of club where Wall Street financiers, politicians, actors and writers go to find pleasure in their own sex or sex that comes at a price and where their sexual proclivities will go unrecorded.

Men like Dorfman didn't change. He was in the scholarship

class when it came to exploiting those around him. Howard, for all Judith's efforts to improve his appearance and his thinking, could never alter what money had set in stone.

Two ex-wives and a string of not very bright but accommodating actresses and models had thus far filled his life with glamour and excitement of a kind. But Judith was different. She had given him something money couldn't buy. He had jeered at it, but in the end he couldn't resist it, or Judith. Bringing in David Corrolla to do her job was indefensible.

Quite clearly this wasn't the moment to be a mediator but simply to listen, so Jed did. Judith sounded calm and resigned rather than agitated. He whistled softly when she described her schedule for the previous four days: commissions completed, accounts wound up, no-one to let down.

'It's okay, I'm not leaving anyone in the lurch.'

'Not counting Howard,' Jed reminded her dryly. 'Are you sure you want to give up the apartment? You might change your mind, you have before.'

Judith winced. How many times had Jed listened to this? Who could blame him for being cynical? But this time was different. 'No. I know what I'm doing. Thanks, Jed. Listen, I must go, but will you call Ellie? Tell her what's happened. Ask her to organize the rest of my clothes and stuff and send them on to me. I'm going to stay with Rosie for a while – just until I get a place of my own.'

'Rosie?' repeated Jed. 'Is she in on this?'

Judith laughed. 'You know Rosie, she just said "Great" when I called. She's so busy restyling half the homes of England I just said I'd explain everything when I got there.'

Jed sighed. 'Of course. And take care, you understand? Jude . . . ? Take some advice, will you? When you get home, catch up with your family, that kid sister of yours and your grandmother. Get your old man to write his memoirs. Get some family back into your life, Jude, stop trying to prove to the world that you're a tough player. And call me. Call me the minute you get there, d'you hear? I don't care what time it is. Yeah, yeah, I know what I said. Don't be so smart. But when did you always mean everything you've ever said?'

She chose not to answer the last question but promised him

instead that she would ring when she arrived at Rosie's home off Kings Road, blew him a kiss down the phone and hung up.

Fifteen minutes until the car was due to collect her. Midday in London. She had to be right. This had to be the way.

The shrill of the telephone brought her out of her reverie. She stared impassively at the phone as it shrilled again. Judith backed away. Her suitcases were by the door. Ignoring the phone, she pushed them into the hallway, almost colliding with the doorman who had arrived to take her luggage down to the waiting car.

'D'ya wanna get it, ma'am?' He hesitated.

She nodded. 'Take the cases,' she said. 'I'll be down in a few minutes.'

A deep breath and she reached for the phone. Howard's irate voice hardened rather than weakened her resolve.

'Jude? Judith? Where the hell are you? What is this? Oh, c'mon, say something?'

Judith opened her mouth, but the words wouldn't come out. Anyway, she thought, what words? Nothing left to say. The words of the Tom Rush song 'No Regrets' came floating into her brain. How did it go? 'Don't want you back, we'd only cry again, say goodbye again.' Without a word she replaced the receiver, waited a fraction of a second and then picked it up. Pulling the receiver under her chin, she punched out the number she wanted and waited, hearing the familiar double ring of a London phone.

'Premier Publicity,' came the bored tone of the English receptionist.

'Spencer Drummond, please.'

Judith tapped her fingers absently on the bedside table while she waited for the girl to put her call through.

Slowly she walked over to the double casement windows with their elegant white voile curtains pulled back into shapely curves, offering a glimpse of tall apartment blocks across the street and way down below a sight which never ceased to fascinate Judith, the crawling New York traffic, yellow cabs, single-decker buses, the waves of energy that kept the city open twenty-four hours a day. A performance, she thought, that's what New York is. One helluva show. Definitely time to go before she was seduced by the whole act all over again. Or Howard.

'Hi,' came the familiar voice. 'Just back from your job on the way to the gym or whatever it is you do in New York at this hour?'

'Neither,' she laughed. 'Spencer,' she said, turning her back firmly on the view and coming straight to the point, 'I've decided to take the job.'

Chapter Two

The girl sitting behind the reception desk regarded Judith with a mixture of annoyance and mild curiosity. The fashion magazine that had been absorbing her was moved grudgingly and only fractionally to one side, just enough to give her access to the phone buried beneath, leaving it still open at the page to which she clearly meant to return as soon as she had unloaded the responsibility of the visitor onto Spencer's secretary.

She stabbed out Camilla's extension with the end of a well-chewed pen and, as she waited for the familiar clipped tones to answer, she wondered why Spencer Drummond, chief partner – these days, only partner – in Premier Publicity had asked to see someone so stylish who clearly wasn't a client. Before her stood a tall, dark, slender young woman in a well-cut wool jacket, its narrow lapels open to show a cream cotton T-shirt, with brown leather Gucci loafers just visible under the tapered ankle of the jacket's matching trousers. The girl knew the whole lot breathed money because the model in the magazine she had temporarily discarded was wearing identical shoes and they alone cost a fortune.

'Mr Drummond's secretary will be down in a moment,' she intoned, in a voice that sounded programmed to make that single announcement to whoever happened to turn up.

Judith, who had wandered away from the desk to study the photographs on the wall, turned, her hands thrust casually into her trouser pockets, and smiled her thanks. She watched, half amused, half exasperated, as the girl turned her attention back to her magazine, ignoring the arrival of a motorbike messenger with whom she was on familiar if bad-tempered terms.

'Ergint,' he said briefly, fishing clumsily into a battered leather jerkin for a screwed-up piece of paper. 'Sign 'ere, darlin'.'

Without taking her eyes from the page, the receptionist scrawled an illegible signature, groped in front of her for the package and threw it carelessly on top of a wire basket, already overflowing, perched perilously at the far end of the cluttered desk. This was her kingdom over which she reigned untroubled by the work she was paid to do, where urgency had no place and where her career as a fashion victim flourished, fuelled by an unrelieved diet of magazines.

Judith looked at the bowed head, the streaked cloud of pre-Raphaelite curls out of hell cascading down her back, the top layer pulled back and up from her thin face into a scrunched tartan band. The girl wore a tight long-sleeved sweater, stressed jeans and enough bangles to stock a market stall. A mass of silver chains fell mayorally from her neck while silver rings shaped like serpent's heads, Chinese dragons or fertility symbols were wedged so tightly onto every finger that Judith wondered if the blood supply to her brain was being constricted, which might explain the choice of baubled earrings that looked as if they could fell a navvy in one unguarded moment.

And she'll be on her feet and through the door at five twenty-nine on the dot. What *was* Spencer thinking of, wondered Judith, turning away to examine a blown-up photograph that had originally appeared in the *Daily Mail*. There in the centre was the charming, handsome Spencer welcoming the Princess of Wales to a charity premiere for ChildLife, a high-profile organization which raised money for underprivileged children. His arm was outstretched, drawing the Princess's attention to the familiar and endearing figure of Judith's old schoolfriend, Libby Westhope, the charity's indefatigable secretary.

Judith had been there that night. It had been a good night, one of Spencer's best promotions, and the society columns had vied with the news desks for the story. Judith smiled at the memory. There had been so many changes, including right here at Premier. So why was she suddenly feeling so uneasy? Premier was the best. Those who asked Spencer Drummond to promote their company, their product, their name, knew they were getting a man who could deliver what they wanted.

Ideas for publicity flowed out of him, leaving their competitors standing. Newspaper and magazine editors knew that, even allowing for hype, the fact that Spencer Drummond was prepared to throw the weight of Premier behind a company or a product was worth a hearing and precious space in their pages.

The top end of the market was where Spencer ruled over a dazzling parade of accounts from designers to jewellers, cosmetics to cars. Under his flamboyant and calculating expertise their names became as familiar to readers of high-profile society magazines and Sunday supplements as the array of glittering international names who bought them.

Judith gazed around. Something was not right. Last time she had been here, the reception of the elegant headquarters of Premier in a fashionable side street off Bond Street, fresh flowers had cascaded from strategically placed, vast balloon-shaped glass vases and the walls had been lined with a gallery of posters, a testament to the company's continuing success. Now the bouquets had been replaced with featureless green plants which did little to disguise the shabbiness of the beige sofas or the fact that the photograph of Spencer was at least five years old. Judith knew that nothing since had eclipsed Spencer's finest hour. And that was the problem.

'Miss Craven Smith?'

Judith swung round, her face already giving a pleasant smile.

'So sorry,' said the woman advancing across the reception area. 'Spencer was taking a call he's been waiting for all day. I'm Camilla O'Neill, Spencer's PA.'

Judith shook the proffered hand and moved with her towards the lift but just as the doors began to close Camilla, with a tsk of annoyance, pushed the door nearest to her, automatically stopping the mechanism, and addressed herself to the receptionist.

'Beth, *please* sort out that basket. Is that the Cornwallis file? Oh for pity's sake . . . excuse me.' She grimaced at Judith as she kept her finger pressed firmly on the 'door open' button. 'Bring it here. For heaven's sake, girl, I asked you four times to let me have it the minute it arrived.'

A sullen Beth plucked the last package in from the pile and handed it to Camilla. 'I can't do everything,' she grumbled. 'I can't be on reception *and* run messages. I'm not paid to . . .'

Her voice was lost as Camilla, ignoring her complaints, released the button to let the doors slide shut.

'Sorry,' said Camilla in her clipped accent, her eyes watching the floors gliding past. 'Too boring. Ghastly girl. But then if you pay peanuts you get monkeys. Through here, after you. Spencer's waiting.'

Judith followed her along the familiar route, strangely silent, just a handful of employees working quietly in offices leading off from the main wide corridor, until they reached the end and turned into an elegant office that housed the Chief Executive.

Spencer Drummond rose from behind an oak and leather desk as Judith entered his office, his arms extended, a welcoming delighted smile on his face.

'Jude, *Jude*. Come here. You look wonderful, *wonderful*. My darling girl, just the sight of you has transformed my day.'

Judith laughed, returning his hug, but while she continued talking and exchanging pleasantries, she saw that he had lost weight, the once piercing blue eyes were now tired and the visible signs of a man who was far from well clung to him.

Later she would come to it. Later she would find out where and how Premier had clearly lost its way. Later, when she had plucked up the courage, she would enquire just how many clients this once thriving company had left. There couldn't be many. What had she done?

Spencer was firing questions about mutual acquaintances, Jed, Ellie, Howard, and the latest gossip from Manhattan. Judith let him flow on. For the next few minutes she simply wanted to slow down the pace with the man who had been a constant contact for stories when she had worked for Jed Bayley in London on his gossip column, and who had been one of the first on the phone when he'd heard that shortly after her arrival in New York she had switched from society diarist to public relations, caring for Howard Dorfman's image.

Spencer Drummond was not at all surprised that Dorfman

had snapped her up. It was Spencer, sensing just how useful she might one day be to him, who had shrewdly made sure he kept in touch with her. It was in the end Spencer who had wooed Judith back home with an offer that seemed at once to be the career move she yearned for and the solution to an emotional existence that had threatened to wipe out the solid ground she had put between her old life and her new one. For that she would be grateful to him.

Spencer had once again eased his tall, spare frame back into his chair. Camilla, watching him silently, seemed anxious to screen his fragility from visitors. Judith waited. Camilla could have been any age from thirty-five to fifty, but what was it Jed had said about her? Younger than she looks, with the safeness of her navy straight skirt and carefully laundered white blouse, and her fawn-coloured hair, streaked with grey hairs she did nothing to disguise, pushed back from a high forehead with a velvet band. Totally unreadable.

Spencer, with enormous courtesy, gave Camilla a list of instructions but before she had even left the room he had turned his attention to Judith. Alone, they gazed at each other for a few seconds in silence. Spencer spoke first, elbows leaning on his desk, fingers pressed either side of his temples. He gave her a rueful grin.

'From socialite to bag lady, that's what you're thinking, isn't it? No, no. Don't deny it.'

Relieved that Spencer wasn't attempting to paper over the obvious flaws in his business, Judith relaxed. 'Why, Spence?' she asked, already suspecting the answer.

'It isn't as bad as it looks. This isn't the company I'm asking you to work for. It's the one that I envisage that will interest you.'

Reaching into his pocket, Spencer drew out a gold chain with a key attached and unlocked the top drawer of his desk. Withdrawing a slim buff folder, he handed it across the desk to Judith. 'Don't bother with all of it. Just the first page is all you need to know now. Clients three years ago. Clients now.'

Judith opened the folder and scanned the sheet. Listed under 'Then' was a heady cocktail of clients and accounts from travel to jewellery, banks to perfume. Her eyes crossed the page to the column marked 'Now'. It looked like a major amputation of a limb. Judith was shocked.

'What happened, Spence? You've still got the Masters account and de Vries, and what about ChildLife? Surely Libby is keeping it with you?'

Spencer shrugged. 'What happened? It's so simple, you'd laugh. I didn't delegate. I couldn't. You see, I *was* the business. When this happened,' he tapped his chest lightly, 'no-one knew what to do. Oh, sure, they could keep the day-to-day events ticking over, but the grand plan, the forward thinking, okay, the bullshit, was impossible without me.'

Spencer wasn't boasting. Judith knew that. Companies had been attracted to Premier because Spencer Drummond was a one-off. They wanted Spencer. Now it would seem they wanted anyone *but* him.

'What happened to Rik?' Judith asked, closing the first file and turning her attention to the section marked 'financial projections'. 'And what about Anneline? She was terrific.'

'Oh, they're around. Anneline came by yesterday. She works over at Dayman's now, looking after a couple of finance accounts . . .'

'. . . *Finance*? Annie? Good grief. She's couture, not corporate.'

'Worse,' he said solemnly. 'She nearly lost her hairdresser. She's in Broad Street and he's in Knightsbridge. Too far across town to get to him,' laughed Spencer. 'But you know Annie. She might have lost the accounts she wanted, but her hairdresser? No way. I gather he agreed to fit her in at eight or eight, depending which end of the day she was least busy.'

Judith smiled. Anneline Murphy could have persuaded Moses to drop the tenth commandment if the display had looked better with nine. She was a real loss.

Spencer continued to fill in the depressing details of Premier's star executives.

'Rik has teamed up with a couple of guys who used to work for Spartan,' he told her, referring to a company that had constantly bitten at the heels of Premier. 'Some of our clients went with them. You know how it is . . .'

Judith knew exactly how it was. She didn't need to go

back to the file to know where all Premier's accounts had gone. The ambitious and superficial Rik Bannerman, with half Annie's talent but nearly twice her salary, would have hesitated only long enough to collect his squash racquet from behind his chair before abandoning ship. Judith had never liked Rik, although she had wisely never made that evident.

'Anyway.' Spencer sounded weary. 'What does it matter? They're not here, nor are the accounts, but . . .' He hesitated.

'But . . . we are,' finished Judith dryly. 'Excuse me just for a second, Spence, while I flick through this.'

Judith hoped that her face did not betray her sinking heart as she read the brief financial report in the document. This wasn't what she wanted, nor what she had expected. Challenges were one thing, professional suicide quite another. Spencer's vision suddenly seemed very cloudy to her.

Time. That's what she needed. She had signed nothing and owed nothing to anyone. She was a free agent and freedom meant time to think. Yorkshire. That's it, go back home. Think. Get some space around her, bring some normality back into her life. Already she could see herself enjoying some bracing walks across the moors with her father, shopping in York with Alice, a long and longed-for talk with Laura, sitting on the terrace of the old farmhouse, gazing out across the familiar skyline of rolling hills and crags. She began to feel better. Impossible to believe she had left New York and a successful job only hours ago.

The board of Dorfman Industries had not been aware of the panic waves that had swept over her when she first joined the company. Nor did it seem to matter to them that, until then, her role had been to chronicle the lives of the Howard Dorfmans of this world, not protect them. Judith had simply captivated them. And Howard. Only Howard – in the end – hadn't understood.

So why didn't the thought of freedom, choice, a new beginning make her feel better about everything? Instead she simply felt sick.

Camilla reappeared with a tea tray and a correspondence folder, which had nothing of any real urgency in it since

Spencer simply signalled to her to place it on one side. She poured out tea for both of them. The orderly action irritated Judith. For all the deterioration around them, some things didn't change. The tea service was Royal Doulton, the brew Earl Grey and the lemon thinly sliced.

Briefly she compared this with what she would have been doing if she had remained in New York: using two phones at once, juggling meetings and interviews, lunch at Le Cirque and dinner at Le Périgord, crossing town in company limos and ordering her whole life to be delivered to her door – or Howard's. Keeping his image in shape had included making sure he was seen where the big players hung out, and it was her business to know where that was. Upstairs at Café Tabac, business lunch at the Four Seasons, Sunday brunch at Isabella's on Columbus.

Even when he entertained at his apartment, she insisted that the caterers he called were Dean and Deluca. His nightlife was a continual exercise in weaning him away from the nightclubs that pinned their profits on the attractions of topless dancers to the classy environs of Tatou on the Upper East Side. It had been a long time since Judith had lived without a constant wave of activity. She would miss it.

So what was going on here? Who did these people think she was? A bloody air ambulance coming to the rescue while they sipped afternoon tea? Her anger surfaced with everyone, including herself, for falling into this trap, anger that people she had allowed herself to like should have put her in such a position.

'Ask me anything you want to know,' Spencer offered, sipping his tea and beginning to look uneasily at his guest. Judith was a terrific girl. She was what he wanted. English to the back teeth but fresh from the best training school in the world: New York. The same girl who had left London nearly two years before, but . . . what was it? He studied her carefully. Yes, that was it. Same girl but a different mind.

Last time she had worked in London she was picking herself up after a disastrous love affair with her married boss and being made redundant. He remembered the defiant cheerfulness the day they had lunched at Lorenzo's when she had told him she was going to New York for a while. He'd given her a list of contacts, phoned a few of them as well.

When his heart attack had come swiftly, terrifyingly out of the blue, for days he had hovered uncertainly between life and death. Life had won but, lying in his hospital bed, Spencer had realized it was time to call in some credit.

Judith knew that at times in the last two years Spencer had helped her, but dear God, she had to earn a living, she had responsibilities to shoulder, bills to pay. Spencer was relying on her personal circumstances to draw her into a job that would have been rejected by any one of half a dozen candidates already working in London.

Glancing around the still pristine clean, but no longer elegant, offices of the Chief Executive of Premier Publicity, a panic wave went through her. Laura, Alice, Dad – there were all of them to think of. Sentiment had no place here. Spencer's lifestyle, his affairs and lavish entertaining had brought on his heart attack and downfall, not Judith.

'Okay,' said Judith, looking squarely at him, ignoring the tea so carefully poured out and growing cold in front of her. 'Let's be blunt about this, Spencer. What makes you think you can get this show back on the road? Secondly, what makes you think I can do it and, thirdly, what the hell makes you think I'd *want* to do it?'

There was the briefest of pauses. Spencer looked back at her steadily. 'Okay, Jude. Gloves off. I think this show can get back on the road because we still have a name, three major clients – forget the routine ones – and I'm not dead yet.

'I think you can do it because you looked after Dorfman. You got his image into shape, you virtually reinvented the man. Don't deny it, I'm too old a trouper not to recognize a skilful PR job. Lastly, because you once told me you didn't trust anyone to look after you, except yourself.'

He eyed her narrowly. 'Where else do you go from here?' he asked bluntly. 'Who's going to give you the money to bankroll your own company? No-one. But this way you get to have a big say and help run the company the way you want it. You're starting off with something you're an expert in – reinvention. Premier Publicity is fertile ground . . .'

'. . . And what about you?' Judith interrupted, irritated that Spencer should see her as someone in need rather than to be sought after. New York had not been wasted on her. She promptly lobbed the ball back into Spencer's court.

'What's your part in all this? I rebuild the company, get new clients, inject confidence into a – quite frankly – neglected operation, and you,' she paused with deliberation, 'you do . . . what?'

The cup Spencer was holding clattered sharply into the saucer. He was fifty-five years old, twice divorced, witty, charismatic, grey-haired and stylish. His face was still handsome in spite of the pallor his recent heart surgery had left him with. He was also vain. Judith knew it and used it. It worked.

'What I do is provide the good will. Keep the names, give you a smart address. You would never pull the same credit I can. The banks would laugh. My credit is still good. What's yours like? Still enough to pay your sister's school fees? Keep your old man from having to face reality?'

Judith got up from her seat and began to stroll around the room. Her grandmother, Laura, might be the wisest woman she knew, but she was over seventy years old. Her father's most recent book was not exactly walking out of bookshops and Alice's school fees were certainly a drain. Spencer was playing dirty. But so could she. Turning, Judith looked at Spencer, sitting calmly, enjoying his tea, confident that he had scored just the right amount of points. One phrase flashed into her head: disconcert him. Grinning, she rested her hands on the back of her chair and started to laugh.

'Spence, you are too funny for words. Last time someone spoke to me like that, it took delivery of two dozen roses every day for a week before communication was restored. And that was just for my lawyer. I don't negotiate. You should know that. So, while you get used to the idea . . .' She picked up her bag as she spoke and started to move towards the door. 'I am needed elsewhere now, so let's lunch some time.' With that she sauntered out of the room, waving a cheery hand in farewell as she passed the startled Camilla at her desk.

She had reached the lift when she heard Camilla behind

her. 'Miss Craven Smith, Judith . . . please, just a moment . . . stupid, stupid, man . . .'

Judith paused as the doors slid open. She raised one enquiring eyebrow as Camilla stepped between her and the lift.

'Don't go. Spencer didn't mean it. Oh, all right, I expect he did. But he does need you, really he does. Stupid of him to have said all that . . . yes, yes, I heard. I hear everything. Might as well get used to that. But he was so relieved when you rang from New York, he looked better than he has done for weeks. Just come back and talk again.'

They were standing in a carpeted corridor attracting attention from a bevy of curious secretaries and what looked like some junior account executives, all of whom were staring through open doors to the scene taking place by the lift.

Defuse the image and distract was Judith's first rule of operation. She smiled warmly and put her hand onto Camilla's shoulder. Quietly, smiling, she spoke rapidly to the anxious secretary.

'Just how sick is he?'

Camilla looked nervously around. 'Very. No, no. A lot better. Just . . . well, frailer than he was. Needs sleep. Medication. That sort of thing . . .'

Judith went on smiling and talking, her arm around the older woman, guiding her back down the corridor. The gaggle of observers, denied an angry exchange, lost interest and began to drift back to their desks. Telephones were picked up, conversations restarted.

'Are you staying on?' Judith asked the puzzled Camilla.

'Yes, of course. Why? I mean, why wouldn't I?'

'Would you stay without a salary increase for another year, work from eight to eight, increase your workload . . . ?'

'Oh yes, of course.' The other woman's face lit up.

'And work for me?'

Camilla stopped dead. 'You? Work for you? I couldn't. What about Spencer? What would he do? Oh, no . . . it just wouldn't be possible.' She was shaking her head in dismay.

Judith leaned her shoulders against the wall, gazed up at the ceiling and looked back again with faint amusement at Camilla.

'And where,' she asked gently, 'exactly do you think this company will be in six months, if you continue to work for Spencer, pouring his tea, fretting over him? In liquidation, that's where. And you'll be out of a job.'

Camilla glared stonily, silently back at her. Finally she spoke. 'You've mistaken loyalty for stupidity. I'm not daft. But Spencer does need someone.'

'I know,' said Judith. 'We all need someone. He needs me. I will need you. You need to make sure he stays out of trouble.'

Camilla sighed and then gave Judith a lopsided grin. 'He said you were persuasive. Provided you agree he can have someone to replace me and give me a title like, I don't know . . . Administration Executive . . .'

'What's that?' asked Judith.

'Same as I'm doing now. But it sounds like promotion. Won't hurt his feelings so much . . .'

Judith laughed.

'Camilla, thank you. In fact I've got a couple of titles I'd like myself. Deal?'

And in the corridor, grinning at each other, the two women shook hands.

'Deal,' said Camilla. 'Will you tell him or shall I?'

'No. I will. Hold the lift for me.'

Smiling, Judith walked swiftly back down the corridor and straight into Spencer's office. 'Forgot this,' she said, swooping up the file from his desk, enjoying his startled and bemused expression. 'Don't forget two dozen roses and perfect. I want to choose my own staff. I want to be consulted on everything from the postroom to the colour of the boardroom napkins. I'll start a week today provided the salary is more than you paid Rik – and don't try to kid me, I know what that was – and Camilla knows where to find me.' With that she blew him a kiss, laughed out loud at the look of pure fury mixed with sheer relief on Spencer's face, and strode back down the corridor to where Camilla was waiting. Judith gave her a broad wink and sped down to the ground floor.

As she passed Beth, the receptionist, she glanced at the girl reading her horoscope and dipping into a bag of crisps.

Judith stopped, surveyed her and walked quietly back to the desk. Without a word she leaned over and removed the crisps from the girl's hands, screwed them up and lobbed them neatly into the nearest waste bin, over her head.

'Here, just a second,' said the indignant Beth, making an ineffectual grab at the half-finished packet sailing past her highly individual taste in earrings. 'What do you think you're doing?'

'Doing?' repeated Judith, taking the magazine from the startled girl's hands and throwing it after the crisps. 'Believe it or not, I'm saving your job. Now listen to me. You will learn that I say what I mean. Take my advice. Clean up this desk and try to locate your job description. Learn it by heart by the morning. It may come as a surprise to you. It bears no relation to what you clearly think your job is.'

Beth sat motionless and open-mouthed in her chair. Trying to keep a straight face, Judith went remorselessly on.

'Exchange those jeans for a reasonable pair of trousers, and lose most, if not all, of that jewellery. If you insist on wearing nail varnish, invest in a decent manicure, cultivate a more agreeable greeting and spend your money on a hairdresser instead of crisps. Got it?'

Beth had recovered just enough to splutter, 'And who the hell might you be?'

Judith flicked her eyes over the outraged girl and sighed.

'You really must catch on a bit faster if you want to stay here. Mr Drummond is promoted to Chairman. I'm the new Chief Executive of Premier Publicity.'

Chapter Three

Howard called her, as Judith knew he would, as soon as she reached Torfell in Yorkshire. With a questioning look on her face Laura held out the phone as her granddaughter, on the point of leaving the house, hesitated between refusing the call or getting it over with.

Getting it over with won. She dropped her coat onto a chair and took the phone from Laura's outstretched arm. Waiting until her grandmother had tactfully left the room, Judith slowly sat down on the arm of a comfortable sofa. Taking a deep breath, she removed an earring and put the phone to her ear.

'Hi,' she said carefully.

'Hi yourself,' Howard said easily. 'Miss me?'

'Of course.'

'Enough to come back?'

'Yes.'

There was a pause. She heard him laugh softly. Triumphantly. She could see him, wrapped in a long white towelling robe, lazily sprawled in a cavernous cane chair in his penthouse, long tanned legs resting on the next chair, juice in one hand, phone in the other. His hair would be tousled from the shower and he would be shielded from the chill wind of a New York only just emerging from the whiplash cold of winter by a wall of sliding glass doors that stretched the length of the terrace.

Judith knew the sight so well. The tubs of flowers and foliage that she had organized would still be spread out in a gentle oasis of calm high above a city with a mission to keep moving at ever-increasing speed.

She saw no point in lying. Howard Dorfman was not a man you dismissed lightly from your thoughts. Glamour and charm were his obvious attractions, but his sense of humour was his most irresistible virtue. Judith knew he had no others. The rest, as she had told Rosie only the other night, were all vices.

'Why did you start an affair with him?' Rosie had asked.

'God knows,' Judith sighed. 'He made me laugh, he was there. You tell me. But I knew it wouldn't last. I was lonely, you know? Lonely in my head. He'd hate to hear me say that because it sounds normal, and he loves, just *loves*, to appear dangerous, especially to women. He believes in making them wait for him, while he hangs out with the boys. I once suggested we walk along the beach at Montauk, you know, on Long Island, just the two of us. Not because it was romantic but just to get him to have a normal conversation, to do something ordinary.'

'And did he?'

'Yeah, but he brought his mobile phone which rang the whole time.'

Rosie had fallen about laughing. 'Oh, poor Jude. Only you would try to disconnect a Wall Street legend from his power supply.'

Judith had laughed. But what she didn't want to tell Rosie was that it wasn't ordinariness she was trying for, but to be important enough in someone's life for him to have time for her, to make time for her. Someone who would be waiting for her once in a while.

Roland hadn't wanted to because he didn't care. Howard, she'd discovered, didn't know how to make time for anyone. She could pinpoint her need to withdraw from him from that moment on the beach, even if it had taken the appointment of Dave Corrolla to make it happen.

Now, through the lattice windows of the farmhouse, she watched her father and Alice getting into the Range Rover to drive the five miles into York. The house she had known since childhood lay a mile beyond the village, no longer a farm but a cheerful family home. It had been the haven of her school holidays, close to the cottage belonging to her grandparents, and it had been the shelter that had cushioned her and Alice, still only a baby, when her mother had died so tragically in America. Laura, now a widow, had moved in and the safety and security of her presence had done much to alleviate the grim toll the death had taken on them all. Judith could still sense her mother's presence in the house, but over the years she had come to realize that it was her grandmother's influence that gave charm and unexpected elegance to the family home.

She could see Alice was sulking outside. The night before she had commandeered a disused barn for what she termed a 'gathering' of her friends and what Laura had described, on seeing the chaos as she swung open the door that morning, as more like a direct hit on Beirut. Alice, home for a weekend exeat from her boarding school in Oxford, had been made to clear it up and no amount of appeals that she had exam revision to do worked on Laura.

It was the first sound Judith had heard as she opened her eyes, Alice and Laura arguing, then her father being appealed to. The sound of Alice's indignant voice wailing, 'But Dad . . .', was followed by Andrew's trailing off into the distance, urging her to be quiet and not wake Judith. A wide-awake Judith didn't know whether to laugh at the wonderfully comfortable familiarity of it all or wish she was back in Manhattan.

For one brief moment, now that Howard was asking her, she wavered. But the sight of Alice and her father, waiting for her to join them to go into York with them to shop meant that her answer was easy. Howard would never understand.

She sighed into the phone. 'Of course I miss you. Enough to come back but not enough to make me want to leave here. Does that make sense?'

Howard didn't seem that interested. 'No. Not a word. None of it makes sense. You don't make sense. You never have. What have I done that a thousand other men in my position wouldn't have done? Can't you see the difference between that and what we have . . . ?'

'Oh, please,' Judith interrupted impatiently. 'Spare me that, Howard. It doesn't even have the merit of originality.'

'For Chrissake, Jude, stop using words. Get feelings into this. What difference does it make what I say? I really need you, you need me. You're making a big mistake. You know you are. Listen . . . just listen to me . . .'

'Amazing, isn't it?' Judith said. 'Suddenly everyone thinks

I'm making a *big* mistake. Howard, the mistakes I made have nothing to do with taking or not taking a job, staying in New York or coming back to London. The mistake I made was not making myself known to you. I didn't need that wall you threw around me. I don't believe I'm no good on my own. That in order to have a relationship with you I had to compromise myself. I made that mistake once before. I don't intend to let it happen again, and it was beginning to.'

Judith heard a groan. 'Are you going to let one bad relationship rule your life forever?' Howard sounded exasperated. 'What happened to you and Roland Whittington is history. Okay, you made a mistake. You fell for the guy, he treated you badly. Big deal. If you would just let me take care of you, there wouldn't be anyone else . . .'

The conversation was too familiar. Howard was right, she wasn't the first woman in the world to have fallen for her boss, but the experience had been cataclysmic. She regarded it in the same light as someone getting over food poisoning: shaken and off the source of the damage for life. Whereas she knew now that Roland had been an addiction, not a great love, at the time she had misread every signal.

She had been tired of trying to keep everything afloat, tired of struggling to earn enough to keep Alice at school and her father from feeling guilty that his books were not making enough money. Afterwards, shaken and bruised and for a while physically ill at Roland's betrayal, she publicly shrugged off the termination of their much-whispered-about relationship. Stop it, she chided herself. Hang up on this phone call. This is Roland mark two. Get a life.

'Howard, listen to me. I'm going to stay here and put Premier on its feet. I know financially it's going to be tough, but I want to know I can do it, and believe me I can. All you want is for me to be there when you decide to come home and to create a fuss when my job keeps me late. It isn't enough. I want to have a relationship where money isn't the issue, where who holds the purse strings doesn't dictate the terms. Where the relationship is worth nurturing every bit as much as a job. Do you understand?'

Howard didn't. He said so. 'Get real, Jude. You're

successful and you need someone more successful than you in your life. Someone you can respect.'

'Oh, for God's sake,' Judith snapped. 'It's the quality of a relationship that counts, not the financial commitment. You sound absurd.'

'And you sound like something out of *Cosmopolitan*,' Howard retorted.

There was a silence. Finally Judith ended the conversation. 'Howard, I'll call you . . . sometime. Just wish me luck. Okay?'

She heard him swear. 'Okay. You'll come round, I know you will,' he shot back. 'Meanwhile, I'll even help . . . yeah, I might just do that. Take care, sweetheart.'

Judith looked at the receiver before hanging up. The odd thing about Howard was that he hadn't once berated her for leaving him with a lot of explaining to do to his friends and colleagues about why she had fled New York so abruptly. Nor, she reminded herself grimly, had he offered any explanation about why he was with the hooker that night. Connie Mayerson's accidental slip had caused Judith real pain. Accidental? She sighed. Who cared? Connie was quick and efficient and protective. But her motives didn't matter now.

Judith wondered if Camilla would do the same for Spencer, cover up for him, shield him? Probably. She grabbed her coat and headed for the door.

Armed with a list of errands to do for Laura, Judith, Andrew and Alice headed into the nearest car park as they approached the city centre and set off on foot for the shops. Alice slipped her arm through Judith's, affecting the slouch she currently regarded as cool.

'That isn't the end of you going to New York, is it?' she said. 'I mean, you will be going back, won't you?'

Judith regarded her with suspicion. She knew Alice well. All her questions delivered in that innocent tone had a hidden agenda that was also, usually, costly.

'Not for a while. Why? I thought you'd quite like having me home all the time instead of just every couple of months?'

'Oh, I do, yeah, it's great. It's just that your apartment is dead cool and Melissa said she would have come with me next time. I just thought I'd let her know if it's on or off.'

'Listen, you spoilt brat. It was never on. I do not remember asking Melissa to stay with us in New York.'

'No, I know,' Alice wheedled. 'But you said I should regard it as my home too, so what's wrong with that?'

They were crossing the square in front of the museum. On a Saturday mid-afternoon in early April, it was filled with the first tourists of the season and families shopping for the day. The beautiful town, mellow and historic, was to Judith a never-ending source of delight.

Alice thought it was boring. 'Don't know what you see in it,' she grumbled, getting nowhere in her quest to take her best friend to see her big sister in New York. 'Oh well, we'll just have to come and stay with you in London. You could get a house like Rosie's, yeah, that's it. Drop dead cool, then we could walk to Kings Road and be near all the cl . . .' She stopped, glancing quickly at Judith.

'All the what did you say?' Judith enquired severely, stopping Alice in her tracks.

Alice tried and failed to look nonchalant. 'All the clubs I've heard about,' she said defiantly. 'Well, you went to them. Why shouldn't I? Honest, Jude, it's so gross at school. I mean, it's not as though we're into drugs and all that . . . and anyway everyone else goes to them. Alex and Scott and Andy.' She reeled off a list of names of the boys currently in her orbit. 'They go to London *all* the time . . .' She exaggerated to make the point.

Thankfully at that moment her attention was claimed by the sight of a pair of heavy-duty boots in a shop window that left her convinced that her whole life would be transformed if they only had her size. Twenty minutes later, relieved that Alice had been distracted from the allure of London and some of its shadier clubs, Judith had bought them for her.

Alice was delighted. Even better, two minutes later they bumped into Melissa and Alice – waving her boots like a trophy – promptly sat on a wall and changed into them, stuffing her black Palladiums into Judith's canvas shoulder bag. With a promise to meet them at the car park an hour later, the giggling duo sped off.

'You spoil her,' grumbled Andrew Craven Smith, glad to have Judith to himself for a while.

'No, I don't,' said Judith. 'I negotiate. The price of a pair of boots is small beer if it bribes her into not creeping out of school at night with the dreadful Melissa. And where did she get that black dress?' she asked, gazing after the retreating Alice who had elected to wear a black tunic over a vivid red T-shirt, both worn over a long dark green skirt and now wrapped in a wool jacket made in Afghanistan and smelling strongly of untreated goat's wool, as she set off in great glee with her new Caterpillar boots.

Andrew Craven Smith had not really noticed what the resourceful Alice was wearing that day, or on any other day. The mysteries and complexities of the minds of thirteen-year-olds eluded him. In fact, most people who knew him would say that the complexities and compromises of modern life escaped him too. He was a decent and good man, with values to match, but which were mostly impossible to maintain in the face of increasing urban violence and a huge shift in the social order that had left him standing. The life of an army diplomat had instilled in him a regard for doing things correctly to the point where Alice simply saw him as a dinosaur and Judith found his standards unnecessarily burdensome.

'Everyone spoils her,' he insisted, refusing to see the force of Judith's argument. 'You were spoiled too.'

This was, in Judith's view, patently untrue – she had to refrain from saying 'bribed' was a better word in her case – but it was all a long time ago and much had changed since her mother had died all those years ago in Washington where Andrew Craven Smith was on diplomatic service and where Alice had been born.

'How's the book?' she asked, tucking her arm in his to distract him from Alice, who had been swallowed up in the crowd. 'On the Booker list yet?'

Her father frowned. 'Ludicrous really that decent, worth-while books are regarded as nowhere near as important as some instant trash peddled by a name that is here today and gone tomorrow.'

Biographies of army generals who had little to offer history but their titles were not exactly causing a stampede to the bookshops either, but Judith knew it was pointless to argue.

'Of course they are,' she said. 'It's simply that they sell more slowly but stay around longer. Your books will still be on the shelves in fifty years' time. Lurid romances won't be.'

Andrew Craven Smith shook his head. They both knew it wasn't true. But at least they were all together. It could have been a lot worse.

In mutual silent agreement they turned and began a brisk stroll towards the Minster. Judith could tell her father had something on his mind. He had listened intently when she had told him of her plans to put Premier back on its feet, but had said little beyond tossing her the odd abrupt question, mostly about finance.

'C'mon,' she said. 'I know that expression. What's the matter?'

'Well, obviously I'm concerned about this job you're taking. Naturally I am. You give up a well-paid job in New York to earn a fraction of that amount back home in England. I just want to make sure you know what you're doing. I mean, is anyone underwriting it? You know, insuring you against closure, that kind of thing?'

Judith looked surprised and felt a bit hurt. She didn't need reminding that Premier needed a shot in the arm, but she had plans to make it work without raising too much extra investment. Plans she knew would meet with Spencer's approval.

'Of course I know. I really believe I can make it work. You've always said aim high, and it's exactly what Mum would have said: go for it. You know she would.'

He frowned. She was right. The girls were both so like his late wife. For that he was grateful. There was such a lot to blot out, so much anguish, and in the end Lizzie, so determined that the birth should go ahead, never survived to see Alice grow up, or to see Judith make a success of her life. Catching the look on his face, Judith squeezed his arm.

'Dad . . .' she said hesitantly. 'It's all over now, all in the past. One day we'll find the right moment to tell Alice. She'll understand, trust me. Anyway, Mum would have been right behind me and come to that she would have been the first to buy Alice that dress. Come on, let's go and treat ourselves to a beer while Alice terrorizes the town in her boots.'

Judith didn't need anyone to tell her that her father was a broken man. But Andrew Craven Smith was proud, and he would have died rather than let the world know his circumstances were so reduced. Washington had delighted him where it had bored his somewhat younger wife. The life of an army diplomat suited him perfectly and he would have gone on enjoying it, but not without Lizzie. Judith had seemed to like it at first; what teenager wouldn't? Yet it had ended in disaster. Lizzie dead. Judith devastated. Alice just a baby. When Andrew had left Yorkshire all those years ago he had never dreamed he would come back again like this. That wretched heart attack on top of everything else.

He longed to be able to take the financial burden from Judith, but she had stubbornly refused to allow him to, even if he had been able. Just like her mother. Funny, that's what Judith always said when he raised the subject. 'Mum would expect me to. You've done more than enough.'

Chapter Four

Judith left Torfell three days later, arriving at Rosie's small terraced house in Chelsea late in the afternoon. There she found a note saying that Rosie would be back the following day after she had dropped her ten-year-old son Tom back at school. There was also a list of messages, mostly from mutual friends anxious to snap Judith up for dinner or lunch, having heard that she was back in town.

Judith glanced at the list, chuckled at some names such as Carey Templeton and Libby Westhope and groaned at others, feeling quite cheered that at least her social life was not going to be a problem.

Finding somewhere to live was, though. Rosie's little house was delightful and Rosie welcoming, but it was a short-term stay. Judith had given herself a week to get her new life underway before she started officially at Premier, but back in London she realized she would need to pack in more than she had expected. Finding a flat was not going to be easy. The next morning she rang Camilla at the office and told her to start calling estate agents and to recruit for Spencer's new secretary.

'How is he?' she asked, checking off a list in her notebook. 'Because I shall need you as soon as I start next Monday.'

'Okay,' Camilla replied. 'Better than I thought. He's lunching with Bill Jefferson from Masters today, so I don't expect he'll be back. Lot of messages for you, though. Most of them I can deal with, a couple I will need advice on.'

'Like . . . ?'

'Rik Bannerman suggested lunch . . .'

'Uh huh, no way,' laughed Judith. 'Let him find out the hard way what we're doing. And the other?'

'Well, it was from Hamilton Carew, you know the lawyers?'

Judith paused. She knew the name well. They looked after

Howard's European interests. Gray Hamilton was also a close friend of Howard's, although Judith had never met him. There had been no need. Connie Mayerson had dealt with all of that. 'What do they want?' Judith asked.

'Well, the call was from Gray Hamilton's secretary. She asked if you could make an appointment to see Mr Hamilton. Wouldn't say what it was about, just that it was personal.'

Personal? What was Howard up to now? 'I know who Gray Hamilton is,' Judith said, puzzled. 'But I've never met him in my life. I'll call them. Anything else?'

For quite a while after Camilla had hung up, Judith wavered between phoning Hamilton Carew and ignoring them altogether. Finally she dialled the number Camilla had given her, curiosity winning the battle.

The brisk, efficient and impersonal voice of Gray Hamilton's secretary betrayed nothing. Mr Hamilton had merely asked her to make an appointment with Miss Craven Smith. 'I believe it has to do with you relinquishing your role in New York and just tying up some loose ends.'

Judith breathed a sigh of relief. Of course. She had left in a hurry and Connie Mayerson would take great delight in pouncing on anything that could be construed as an oversight on Judith's part. But at least Howard had replaced Judith with a man, and a single one at that. That might, if nothing else, cheer bootfaced Connie no end. Reassured, Judith agreed to be at the solicitors' offices the next afternoon.

She spent the morning checking out some properties that Camilla had selected, and rejected all of them on sight.

The morning had been cold and blustery and while faded denims, boots and a navy pea jacket were about right to deal with a day geared to flat-hunting, they were not entirely suitable for an interview with an eminent lawyer. Still, she decided as the taxi dropped her outside his office, as it wasn't likely to be a memorable meeting for either side it wouldn't matter. But when the receptionist at Hamilton Carew announced her arrival, Judith began to wish she had worn something more formal. Her outfit suddenly seemed even more inappropriate in this imposing hallway.

A small, brisk woman, in a neatly tailored dress with grey-ing hair tied firmly back in a French pleat, appeared around the bend in the oak stairway that spiralled up through the centre of the lobby.

'Thank you for coming,' she said pleasantly and ushered Judith before her to the first floor.

The oak door ahead was ajar. Judith could see two secretaries behind desks piled high with documents and files. There was an air of efficiency coupled with a polite indifference to visitors that was strangely calming.

Judith was shown into a small and unexpectedly pleasant waiting room, which had bowls of fresh flowers, pale green upholstered chairs and a centre table with an array of serious-looking journals spread out among the current issues of the more upmarket glossy magazines. The walls had several impressive prints on them but before Judith could take advantage of a quick look in the mirror hanging above an empty fireplace, the grey-haired woman reappeared and smilingly asked Judith to follow her.

On a door at the end of a carpeted corridor was written: Gray Hamilton. Her escort opened it, standing aside for Judith to go in.

At first Judith thought the room was empty. She walked in and looked around uncertainly. Wooden French shutters framed two floor-length windows, which looked down over trees that were just turning from grey winter claws to pale green leaf. Floor-to-ceiling bookcases occupied two walls, while the others played host to a series of black-framed prints. The centre of the room was dominated by a highly polished rosewood desk on which stood a brass desk lamp and a couple of art deco silver frames displaying pictures of a smiling, beautiful blonde woman.

An imposing pile of files was stacked at one end of the desk. Those that were not in use had been thrown onto the floor. Behind the desk against one wall, a long pale green sofa was scattered with cushions.

Judith moved further into the room and leapt with shock when a voice from behind her enquired: 'Miss Craven Smith?'

Judith wheeled round and found herself staring at a man

who didn't look at all pleased to see her. Dark hair, with flecks of grey, tall, and clearly fit. Tanned and unsmiling, he was jacketless, and the cuffs of his blue striped shirt were rolled back. He was in the act of stepping down from a ladder that gave access to the books on the highest shelves.

'God, you made me jump,' she said, putting her hand to her throat. 'Sorry I didn't see you. Yes. I'm Judith Craven Smith and you must be Gray Hamilton.'

She smiled and extended her hand.

He shook it briefly and motioned to her to sit down. 'I won't keep you long. It's very straightforward.'

'Good,' said Judith briskly, not at all sure she liked being treated in this dismissive way. 'I was pretty sure I had left everything in order. So what mysteries do you want me to unravel?'

'I can assure you there is no mystery,' Gray Hamilton said, seating himself and pulling a file towards him. 'I represent the business and personal interests of Howard Dorfman in this country . . .'

'Personal interests?' Surprise made Judith blurt it out. 'What kind of personal things . . . ?'

'Miss Craven Smith, I am Mr Dorfman's lawyer. You must know I can't answer a question like that. Shall we get on?'

Judith swallowed hard. The man was unnecessarily rude.

He picked up a pair of heavy-rimmed glasses and put them on, flicked through the file and extracted a closely written sheet on which Judith could see the familiar Dorfman Industries logo.

'Mr Dorfman has told me to ensure that you have everything that is necessary to make you comfortable while you remain in London. To that end, he has instructed me to put at your disposal an income which will cover what I imagine he perceives as your necessary expenses.

'His instructions are that we take a lease on an apartment or house of your selection and free you from the necessity of financing it. Mr Dorfman will, through us, arrange all the necessary details once you have told us where this will be.

'He has left the level of finance to you. He says,' the lawyer paused to consult the document in front of him and then intoned in a dispassionate voice, ' "Judith knows her value and will exercise her own judgement as to the style and location of the house that she chooses, knowing my own taste so well and what I would wish for her".'

He got no further. Judith's face had changed colour to a deathly white and her voice shook with fury.

'Stop this. Stop this at once. What in God's name is this about?'

Gray Hamilton remained unmoved by her outburst. 'This is not an unusual arrangement, Miss Craven Smith. Mr Dorfman is merely ensuring that his protection of your interests is maintained while you are not living with him.'

'Living with him? *Liv . . . ?* Are you quite mad? I've never lived with Howard Dorfman. Did he say that? *Did* he?' She was on her feet, leaning across the lawyer's desk, her eyes livid with shock and embarrassment.

Gray Hamilton put the document down, loosened his tie and looked at Judith with a mixture of boredom and exasperation. She noticed he also flicked a glance at his watch.

'Miss Craven Smith,' he said, removing his glasses and patiently addressing her like a doctor talking to a difficult child. 'Please sit down. Your relationship with Mr Dorfman is your own affair. We simply act for him. Any queries you might have about defining your relationship with him would, I think, best be served by addressing them to him yourself, don't you? Now shall we get on?'

It struck Judith that this man was the personification of arrogance. He had decided she was nothing more than a kept woman and was delivering an intolerable insult to her.

'No, we won't get on, Mr Hamilton,' Judith said quietly, resuming her seat. 'We won't get on at all. Since you are acting as . . .' she paused quite deliberately and threw a disdainful look at him, 'Mr Dorfman's agent, shall we say, you should at least have the courtesy to discover whether I am willing to accept this offer and on its terms. You have assumed I find them welcome and to my liking.'

'I assume,' he said coldly, 'that you will dictate the terms yourself. Mr Dorfman has indicated that you must do so. I can't see where the problem lies.'

Judith thought she had rarely disliked someone so much in all her life. Howard must be mad to employ somebody like Gray

Hamilton and even madder to believe she would accept such an outrageous proposal. Gray Hamilton clearly thought she would. Well, she would give him something else to think about.

'The problem lies in the entire proposal being quite laughable,' she said, smoothing an imaginary crease from the sleeve of her jacket with a greater control than she felt. 'As you've gathered, I know Mr Dorfman extremely well. So well that I am one of the few people who is privy to the extent of his personal wealth. You too, as his ... whatever you are ... must also be aware of it.'

'Lawyer,' Gray Hamilton reminded her helpfully.

'If you say so. But we are talking real money here, Mr Hamilton,' Judith said politely. 'I'm sure you understand me.' As she spoke she held out her hand as though she were inspecting her nails and went on. 'I think I am worth a lot to Mr Dorfman. Much more than just a house, an income and a few er ... toys ... to keep me happy. Mr Dorfman's mistress – which I think is the phrase you were trying to avoid – must live up to his reputation, don't you agree?

'Now,' she said briskly, enjoying his surprised look, 'I am a very busy person. Please give my compliments to Mr Dorfman and my regrets that I can't accept his offer. And really I can't spend any more time here. In fact if I do I may be extremely unwell.'

Gray Hamilton had listened to Judith in silence. He rose politely as she did, shuffling the papers in front of him and returning them to the file.

'As you wish,' he said and crossed the room to open the door for her. As she walked past him, rigid with anger, he made no attempt to stop her but simply said, 'Just for the record, Miss Craven Smith, may I tell Mr Dorfman why you can't accept?'

Judith stopped, walked back and leaned insolently against the door jamb, pushed her hands into the pockets of her jeans and laughed contemptuously into his face.

'Why not? Oh, come, come, Mr Hamilton. You must know why not. The offer is simply not interesting enough or,' she paused, adjusting the gold bangles on her wrist, 'high enough. Good day.'

Chapter Five

Judith had never worked so hard or so long in her entire life. For weeks on end, sandwiches at her desk became routine – if she remembered lunch at all. Her day started well before eight and rarely finished before nine that same evening. The humiliating scene in Gray Hamilton's office and her outrage in its wake evaporated in the face of the more urgent need to get Premier into some sort of shape. Phone calls from Howard went unanswered; new leads had to be followed. Camilla had taken a message that a Mr Van Kingsley was anxious to meet her. But a series of disastrous dinner dates and foursomes organized by Rosie left Judith firmly believing that work was the most satisfying element of her life.

At Rosie's insistence, she accepted a dinner date from Dirk Hemmingway, a friend of Rosie's boyfriend, Piers Imber. Dirk met her at a restaurant and spent the entire evening saying that women like her were too expensive for him.

Rosie's musician friend seemed more promising, until he proclaimed that it was a proven fact that children of working mothers were more intellectually impoverished than those of mothers who stayed at home. There was the accountant who claimed he was an ardent feminist and who painstakingly divided the bill right down the middle to please her, the divorcee who complained about his access rights for four hours and told her he was not ready for another commitment, and the art director of an ad agency who was having a mid-life crisis.

Judith told her friend Carey, who unfeelingly laughed helplessly at her description of the dating scene in London, that she could now see the attractions of the celibate life. Which, she told herself as she climbed into bed, was just as well. Considering.

Even her business contacts were hard to read. Mike Sullivan

had been a good contact for years. Deputy editor of one of the more acceptable tabloids, Judith had been able to rely on him to be co-operative about placing helpful stories. Usually they lunched or had a quick drink after work. He was a good business friend, and was married with a family in Sevenoaks.

It had seemed too silly to hesitate when he suggested that they talked over dinner about her ideas for an interview for Bill Jefferson, who owned an exclusive men's outfitters, and was one of Premier's few prestigious clients.

'I just thought it would be easier, not to have to rush so much,' he said as Judith wavered at the other end of the phone. Dinner was so loaded. 'This week has been a real pig and I'd like to help,' Mike insisted.

It changed their relationship for ever. Over dinner Mike suggested that she wouldn't have said yes to dinner if she hadn't been inclined to agree that they moved on to a small hotel later. Judith suggested they called for the bill and went home — separately.

About a week after their chilly encounter in his office, Judith saw Gray Hamilton leaving the Savoy Grill with a woman who was clearly the subject of the photographs on his desk. Lightly tanned and vivacious, her fawn-coloured hair was fashionably cropped and expertly highlighted. The porcelain beauty she possessed would have turned heads if she hadn't so obviously been in a raging temper.

Judith, who had just enjoyed a highly successful lunch as guest of the urbane and hugely popular Bill Jefferson, was standing at the foot of the thickly carpeted stairs waiting for her host to finish taking a phone call.

She saw Gray before he saw her, and swiftly turned her back, praying that the arrogant man wouldn't notice her in the crowd. And he might not have done, if Bill Jefferson had not chosen that moment to return and, spotting Gray strolling towards them, cordially hailed him and offered a more restrained but courteous greeting to his companion.

Judith mentally raced through a selection of expressions she thought would meet the occasion appropriately and settled for cool charm; an effort which appeared to be totally wasted since at first Gray didn't seem to recall her at all.

'Oh, of course,' he said in a tone that implied it was not one of his more memorable moments. He shook her hand. 'Yes, we did meet, didn't we? Are you feeling better?'

'Better?' she repeated blankly.

'That's right. Didn't you say you felt sick as we parted company?'

Judith made a point of adjusting the strap on her shoulder bag and resisted a childish temptation to kick his shins. 'Much better, thank you. I think it was just that the air in your office was so,' she paused just for a fraction, considered her handiwork with her bag, appeared satisfied and finished with a bright smile, 'oppressive.'

'In which case I must remember to open the windows next time you come, to let some fresh air in,' Gray said softly.

'Too kind,' Judith purred, looking deliberately and enquiringly at his companion.

'Gray,' the blonde woman said sharply. 'We really must go. Goodbye, Bill, and goodbye Miss . . . ?'

'Judith. Judith Craven Smith,' supplied Judith.

'Lisa Hamilton,' replied the woman and moved away, followed by Gray.

They disappeared up the wide staircase towards the main entrance and out of view.

'His wife?' asked Judith, turning to leave with Bill towards the river entrance where his chauffeur was waiting to collect him.

'Ex,' he replied briefly. 'Messy divorce. But then lawyers always do. So much better at other people's. She still seems to be able to make him come running when she wants to. But I suppose that's because she was the one who instigated it. Problem is – or so I'm told by my wife – Lisa still wants all the financial and social advantages of marriage with Gray without the responsibility.'

'Well, she can't want him for his charm or sense of humour,' Judith remarked.

Bill hesitated. 'He's a changed man these days . . . but then the divorce hit him hard.'

'She's very attractive,' said Judith, as they emerged onto the pavement and saw Bill's chauffeur springing out of his seat to

46

open the door of the navy blue Jaguar parked just feet away.

'Not my type,' returned Bill. 'Prefer independent young women like you, who don't expect men to be at their beck and call. Now, when are you going to bring over those proposals? They sound good to me.'

'I'll get Camilla to call you,' Judith smiled, delighted that she had managed to persuade Bill to readjust some of the thinking behind Masters. It meant she would have something new to promote, not an exhausting exercise in persuading the style editors to write about the same old thing.

Masters' goods were beyond criticism, ranging from the finest tailored suits to handstitched shirts and a collection of accessories that could be found in the bedrooms and dressing rooms of the landed gentry the length of the country. Yet a younger, less reverent clientele wanted the traditional snob value of Masters mixed with the style and panache of Ralph Lauren or Calvin Klein.

It was a source of concern to Bill Jefferson that his customer profile was becoming elderly. At first more seduced by Judith's easy-going charm than her argument for change, he found himself for once moved to think that there could be no harm in listening to what she had in mind.

'By the way, Bill,' she said as he leaned to kiss her on both cheeks. 'Does the name Van Kingsley mean anything to you?'

'Kingsley?' Bill repeated, slowly shaking his head. 'Don't think so. Why?'

'Oh, nothing, only Camilla said he had phoned a couple of times while I was out and was anxious to discuss Premier taking him on as a client. She said he was some kind of financial entrepreneur. No? Never mind. Lovely lunch, be in touch soon.'

Collapsing into bed at the end of each long, mentally punishing day, Judith had little energy left to assess whether business was going well or taking on Premier was really an elaborate exercise in masochism. She made no attempt at all to unravel why she hadn't just explained to Gray Hamilton that he had misunderstood her relationship with Howard.

Nice to know someone could bring him to heel, she thought viciously, recalling how immediately he had reacted to his ex-wife's brisk command, but then, Judith would argue, yawning as the mists of sleep claimed her, how could she explain her relationship with Howard when she wasn't sure if she understood it herself?

At first her fury at Howard's complacent belief that she would agree to becoming a kept woman had nearly driven her to the nearest phone to call him, but the thought of dealing with the disdainful Connie Mayerson put her off. Then she decided that Gray Hamilton should have the pleasure of telling Howard. A thought which gave her enormous satisfaction as sleep finally came.

After a few days, when she had calmed down, she thought it had been a blessing in disguise that she hadn't erupted on the phone. No contact and distance was what she needed.

Howard made it plain he thought otherwise and at the end of several phone conversations ranging over the next month, followed by another two weeks' silence, he arrived in London. Rosie thought he was devastating. Judith thought he was outrageous. She was also appalled, relieved, angry and very confused.

This man had pulled the plug on her career to suit his own ends. He also pulled hookers. In this day and age of AIDS he risked his own health and that of others. There was, she told him firmly, no future for them.

'Bullshit,' Howard said when Judith finally accepted his call at the office. 'And you know it. You can be *so* prissy. When did I ever put you at risk?'

Camilla had brought in her tea at that moment. Judith paused, acutely aware that a telephone discussion on safe sex at three in the afternoon with an oversexed tycoon might be misconstrued, and Camilla listened to everything.

'That is not what I meant,' she hissed down the phone.

'Oh God, not again. I don't understand anything you say. I don't know what you mean. Baby, just come over here and see me. It won't kill you, but it might kill me if you don't and that must sound attractive to you, even if I don't.'

Judith refused but, threatened with an embarrassing abduction in Central London which she was fairly confident Howard would attempt, she agreed to just one drink. Not dinner. And certainly nothing else. Agreed? He agreed. She knew he was lying. Howard never stayed in a hotel. If he didn't possess a home of his own in whichever capital he had landed in, any one of a dozen people raced to put their own luxury house or apartment at his disposal while he was in town.

Quite deliberately Judith kept the car that he sent for her waiting, so that she arrived nearer to seven than six at the white-fronted town house in St John's Wood.

This house, she decided, was rarely used and probably owned by Americans. It was a case of Provence meets Rhode Island, and Rosie would have approved.

Pieces of French rustic furniture had been blended artfully with the cool sophistication of buttermilk walls and carpets, set off by antique cushions, an Aubusson rug and plump, deeply inviting sofas and armchairs in shades of rust and blue. French watercolours lined the walls of the generously pro-portioned drawing room into which a silent black-coated manservant led her.

'Mr Howard will be back presently,' he announced. Judith stopped dead. Back? She felt the anger rise to her mouth. Back? He had gone out? *Out?*

She did not sit down. She refused a drink. She looked point-edly at her watch. 'Please tell Mr Dorfman, when he returns, that I couldn't wait,' and she swung on her heel towards the door.

Howard caught her as she strode furiously into the hallway.

'Serves you right,' he said, pinning her to him. 'You kept me waiting.'

'Oh, for God's sake, Howard,' Judith stormed, pulling away from him. 'This is a very silly game.'

It was also a very familiar scenario. 'Whose house is this?' she asked, as he ignored her protests and poured her a drink.

'Friend of mine,' he said cagily, sitting next to her and pulling her against him.

'Nice taste,' she commented, preventing his hand from sliding any further up her skirt.

Howard looked around as though seeing the decor for the first time. 'Yeah, I guess. Bedrooms are great, come and look.'

'Nice friends, too,' she said, ignoring him. 'Handing their house over.'

'The best,' he agreed.

'Where are they?'

'Who?' he said impatiently, as she removed his hand from straying inside her shirt.

'Your friends. The couple who live here.'

'Oh yeah . . . he's in Paris. No idea where she is. What does it matter, sweetheart? I just said I needed somewhere private and discreet . . .'

'Obliging too, aren't they?' Judith said icily. Dear God, what kind of woman did his friends think she was? 'And of course such a waste.'

'We'll see,' was his only comment.

It was the only truly civilized exchange they had for the next hour. She would not, she told him evenly, be involved with a man who openly picked up hookers and tricks and instructed a total stranger more or less to bribe her.

'Bribe? What's so awful about wanting to give you a present?'

'You made me sound like a whore.'

'You're wearing a present from me,' he said, grabbing her wrist to expose the exquisite Cartier watch he had given her. 'You accepted that. So what's the difference?'

Impossible.

They glared at each other. They argued. He shouted. She refused to give in. Reluctantly she agreed to dinner, which was served by a pleasant but impassive-faced woman in a small dining room filled with bowls of unseasonal white roses. Double glass doors led to a pretty conservatory overlooking a generous, walled garden.

Later, when they moved back into the drawing room, Judith with coffee, Howard with brandy, the tranquil and restful atmosphere of the flower-filled house left them both in a mellower mood. Returning rapidly to their old, comfortable habit of exchanging gossip of mutual friends, laughing at old shared jokes, Judith forgot she was meant to be distancing herself from Howard and made no attempt to discourage him when he slipped his arm companionably around her shoulders, throwing back his head and laughing at her description of the scene in Spencer's office when Camilla had solemnly poured Earl Grey while all around Spencer's company was collapsing.

It was relaxed, sheltered. Judith felt the tension of the last few weeks slip away. Howard always had that effect on her. It was, she knew later, her undoing. She felt Howard take her hand, pull her silently to her feet. Her brain said, this is a mistake. Her body said, just one more time.

The house was silent as he led her up the curving staircase, along a thickly carpeted corridor. At the end he pushed open a door to a bedroom. You don't have to go any further, she told herself, taking in the soothing yellow walls, the George the Third four-poster with its blue-and-yellow silk hangings.

Howard was murmuring softly into her ear. 'We're the greatest, baby, the greatest,' he crooned as he felt for the zip on her skirt and slowly opened it. The skirt fell to the floor, she stepped out of it and slid her hands inside his shirt.

Howard always did things in perfect settings, she thought, glimpsing a nineteenth-century Bessarabian rug as she allowed him to push her gently back onto the sumptuous bed, lifting her arms so that he could pull her sweater over her head, wrapping her legs around his hips, feeling the familiar stirring in the pit of her stomach as his body became more demanding. Finesse, she remembered, was not Howard's forte, as he began to press himself urgently between her thighs, but then sex for sex's sake was rarely delivered imaginatively when there was a stronger need for instant gratification.

It was just as he was biting hungrily into her neck, her long dark hair cascading loosely over the edge of the pillow, that she glimpsed, upside down, the photograph in a silver frame on the bedside table.

Her eyes flew open. It couldn't be. Twisting, she abruptly pushed Howard's pulsating body away and sat up, reaching over to grab the silver frame. No mistake. All desire left her.

'Howard,' she demanded as he lay stupefied, staring up at her as she sat naked, clutching a photograph of a couple sitting on the sun deck of a yacht. A glamorous couple, a happy couple. 'Whose house is this?'

'House? For Chrissake, are you crazy? We're having a screw to end all screws and you care about who lives here?'

'Howard,' Judith said, her voice shaking with rage as she brandished the photograph under his nose, 'who is this?'

'For fuck's sake, Jude, it's Gray, of course and . . .' he squinted at the picture, 'and Lisa. Jude . . . Jude . . . for Chrissake, Jude, you can't leave me like this,' he moaned and Judith's last glimpse as she swept out of the room, after angrily struggling into her skirt, hopping on one foot as she pulled on her shoes, was seeing him slumped on the pillows with only his most prized possession still standing obediently to attention.

Chapter Six

Two days later Howard left for the States and Judith arrived home to a display to rival the Chelsea Flower Show. She picked up the card. It was simple: a battle won, but in his view not the war.

'Okay. Next time your place . . . or ours. Always. H.'

'Are you sure about this?' Rosie asked in wonder, surveying the mountain of lilies, roses and tulips that threatened to engulf her tiny sitting room.

Judith went into the kitchen, pulled a bottle of wine from the fridge and began searching for a corkscrew. 'No, no, no,' she sighed, returning to join Rosie. 'No, I'm not sure. He's amusing, attentive, generous, but I know he isn't really in love with me. I was never in love with him. But for God's sake, Rosie, in *that* man's house. I just couldn't.'

'Sure?'

Judith shook her head vehemently. '*Quite* sure. What the hell does he think I am?'

'The woman he's in love with?' suggested Rosie helpfully.

Judith shook her head impatiently. 'Not Howard. Gray Hamilton. Thinking I was the sort of woman who would screw in someone else's house.'

Rosie coughed discreetly.

'Not his house, anyway,' mumbled Judith. 'It must have been on his honeymoon. The picture. They're divorced now.'

'I know that. So what were you doing?' asked Rosie, beginning to arrange the flowers. 'You're not promiscuous, Jude. What is it with you and Howard?'

Judith slumped into an armchair and closed her eyes.

'You're right. It's just easy having sex with an ex. And sex with Howard was always okay. Don't tell him I never said, *in-cred-ible*, will you?'

Rosie's voice was heavy with sarcasm. 'Oh sure, hi, Howard, I hear your ego's bigger than your . . .'

'Rosie,' Judith giggled. 'You know exactly what I mean.'

'No I don't,' said Rosie frankly. 'Having sex with Rory *was* the problem – it stopped me getting to know him. I think I could do without all that again. Hand me those scissors, will you? Some of these stems need pruning.'

'I mean, it's safer – emotionally,' said Judith, getting up to fetch them. 'You both know what you're there for. I was in love with being cared for. But, Rosie, I don't need any man who makes me feel that without him I'm nothing . . . characterless . . . know what I mean? Howard is in love with someone who doesn't really exist.' Judith stopped and searched for the right words. 'He wants me to be me, but to also give up everything for him to be there whenever he turns up. But if I did that, I wouldn't be me any more. I'd be someone else, and he wouldn't understand what had gone wrong. He loves my independence, he loves the fact that I can do deals. He finds all that sexy . . . yeah, I know, but that's what he said. He likes watching me get the better of the guys he's surrounded with. It's a real turn-on, like watching one of those awful shows he goes to.'

Rosie began to rearrange the flowers, pulling open cupboards to search for vases and improvising with jugs and bowls.

'And is that what he's said, or what you think?' she asked, carefully slitting the stems of the lilies, giving Judith a sidelong glance to where she was pouring a glass of wine.

'It's what I know,' answered Judith, handing her friend a glass. 'So I stop doing the deals and stop being sexy . . . and then what? Sit around waiting for him to come home? Ignoring the hookers and the rumours? I've been down that road. It's stained with my blood.'

As May turned into June, Judith found an apartment in an established block just off Kensington High Street. Badly in need of renovating, but with an extra bedroom that would take two single beds and a small room she could use for an office, it was ideal for her needs and the crumbling decor had placed it within her price range. Judith's own bedroom with an en suite bathroom overlooked a garden square, as did the drawing room.

In the fading afternoon light and even with bare floorboards, the three sets of French windows with their wooden shutters reaching down to the floor were enough to let her see that, once decorated, it would be a stunning flat, particularly as there was a narrow wrought-iron balcony running its length, just wide enough to take a couple of wicker chairs to relax in when the weather made it possible.

Judith mentally redecorated as she wandered from room to room. A cosy dining room on the other side of double doors from the drawing room overlooked a quiet leafy street, and led into a modern kitchen large enough to be used as a breakfast room. Plenty of room to have Alice, Dad or Laura to stay and less than twenty minutes into the office.

Rosie was delighted, and offered to come up with some schemes to decorate. Meanwhile, Judith would continue to live with her.

At half term, Rosie took Tom to stay with his father Rory and then flew on to Paris with Piers for a fashion shoot. Laura came to London with Alice to shop and to stay in Rosie's little house with Judith – a trip which had served only to emphasize Alice's impatience to live there forever once she saw Judith's new flat, but had more beneficially made Judith pause for a couple of days. While she could have done without the interruption, it did at least mean she needn't feel guilty about not getting up to Yorkshire for several weekends in a row.

It occurred to Judith, as they stopped for lunch at Alice's choice of Beach Blanket Babylon in Notting Hill, that Alice seemed to be very familiar indeed with the interior. But it was Laura looking tired that claimed most of her attention and with a wince she remembered that her grandmother was over seventy and really shouldn't be carting a thirteen-year-old down to London. She must speak to Dad and see if Margie, the help from the village at Torfell, might be persuaded to come in a bit more often.

Judith was pleased that the decoration of her flat was

distracting Rosie. Halfway through her Paris trip, Rory had phoned to ask her to collect Tom.

'Bloody selfish Rory is the problem,' she said bitterly to Judith after she had tucked Tom in for the night. 'Tom adores him, but Rory just drifts in and out of his life when it pleases him.'

Meanwhile, Camilla had weaned herself out of Spencer's office but not out of his life by insisting that her replacement, a good-humoured, easy-going girl called Fenny, reported to her.

'Report what?' asked Judith, amused.

Camilla solemnly read Judith what passed for a lecture and possibly even a mild ticking-off at not understanding the pivotal role Spencer had in the company.

'He might not be able to – all right, all right, doesn't want to – play a big part in Premier, but his name and advice stand for a lot,' she said huffily. 'And at the end of the day he holds the purse strings.'

During a quick shopping expedition at lunchtime, Judith arrived back with a peace offering: a jumbo-sized box of Earl Grey tea bags, gift wrapped. Camilla's stern look disappeared and good relations were restored.

Which was fine for Camilla, but Judith was very conscious of the fact that Camilla was right. Spencer ruled while she slaved.

A brief look at the client accounts they held did not inspire Judith with good humour or with any great enthusiasm. Two were undeniably distinguished but were creaking with age.

Both were desperately in need of an overhaul but neither would be easy to budge. Glancing through the latest correspondence from the MDs of both companies made it clear that Spencer's confidence that they were much-sought-after accounts was bravado. Who, she sighed as she stacked the papers away, was kidding who?

At least Bill Jefferson had already conceded to Judith's plan that they leave Masters intact and open up a concession called Young Masters which would draw in a younger, sharper clientele without alienating his valued but conservative older one.

The walls of de Vries, on the other hand, were still to be breached. But for the moment they looked impenetrable. The legendary jewellers were, in Judith's view, now more famed for who they had once had as customers and were being overtaken by more youthful, more marketable companies.

Libby Westhope over at ChildLife was wonderful. But companies like Premier took charities on board more for political correctness than in any belief they would make a living out of them.

Each morning as she pushed her way through the front entrance into the reception area, Judith mentally revamped it and at the end of the first month, she called in the surly Beth and gave her a final warning.

The staff was another matter. The loss of Rik and particularly Anneline was worse than she had at first realized. The remaining three account executives were junior and hesitant without the guiding hand of a more seasoned campaigner. Each presented themselves to her, waiting for instructions on their less-than-demanding accounts. Judith sent all three away to do some thinking.

'Working here is a two-way experience. You come up with ideas, you don't bring me problems, you solve mine,' she said curtly. A bit too curtly as it turned out, when two of them promptly resigned.

'No loss,' comforted Camilla. 'Over-promoted secretaries really. Rik's fault.'

Judith pressed her fingers against her eyes, sliding them slowly down her face to look at Camilla, pausing in the doorway, who had as usual overheard the conversations.

'I know,' said Judith. 'But I should have found replacements before giving them the treatment. That'll teach me. Now I'll have to take on their wretched work as well. Although frankly I wouldn't mind losing Softdown.' She flicked through a folder in front of her to find the figures on the Softdown bed linen account. 'They expect every national magazine to be devoting pages to them and the damn stuff isn't available in more than three stores in the whole country. And none of it matches UK standard sizes. Lunacy. Honestly, they're using up time we could be devoting to another account. Their budget is so low it's totally unrealistic. Remind me to call that ghastly woman who runs it and see if we can get some sense going here.'

Before sense could prevail, Softdown's demanding MD had written a letter saying they were going to move to Rik Bannerman as he had been so instrumental in persuading them to give Premier their account in the first place and he understood the market so well. Camilla's reaction was to reach for the phone to ring the woman and give her a piece of her mind, since her recollection of events was that Anneline had done the persuading, not Rik.

Judith shook her head, restraining her.

'But we can't afford to lose the money,' protested Camilla. 'At least it pays for the stationery.'

Judith shook her head. 'Actually it doesn't. Look at the figures. Because they insist on a national mailshot, postage alone is money down the drain. It's costing us at this rate. Besides, a revamped company needs a new image. Losing some dead wood isn't such a disaster.'

From the ground floor to the top floor of Premier, account executives watched uneasily as their departments were trimmed or streamlined. A new financial director was brought in who Spencer insisted reported directly to him. Judith just shrugged. Within a month she had introduced a series of weekly board meetings where every account executive had their targets assessed as well as being given an opportunity to express their views.

Finally she told Spencer she wanted to appoint two group heads who would take on the day-to-day running of all the accounts, with account executives reporting directly to them.

He agreed but insisted on the final say in who she chose. Judith suppressed an exasperated sigh.

The surprise of the week was the appearance of Beth, who had asked if she might see Judith.

'Right, Beth,' said Judith, glancing at her watch. 'What's the problem?'

Beth sat awkwardly on the edge of the chair in front of Judith's desk, looking nervous. She's going to resign, thought Judith. Oh well, no loss. But there was something different about her. What was it? Of course, the rings. They were gone, her nails were varnished in a clear pink, she was wearing a white shirt and a long petrol-blue jersey wool skirt that stopped just short of the rim of a pair of Doc Marten boots. The hair was still long and streaked but it was twisted into a clasp at the nape of her neck.

'Do I take it you're offering me your notice?'

Beth stared miserably down. 'Well, yes and no. Yes, I don't want to be a receptionist, because it is so boring, honestly it is, and no, I don't want to give you my notice because,' and the rest came out in a rush.

'Because I think I really could be useful to you, I know all the clients, I take all the calls, but that's it. I have nothing else to do all day and because I don't have A-levels or anything, it's really difficult to get the kind of job I want. I just thought if I could have a word processor I could help Camilla in between other things, I mean I could get a database going for mailshots and sometimes I have really good ideas . . .'

Judith threw up her hands.

'Whoa, hang on, Beth. Why the sudden change of heart? Surely those opportunities presented themselves before. Why now?'

Beth was clearly struggling with a need to tell the truth without offending anyone.

'C'mon,' coaxed Judith, curious about this sulky girl who clearly had a good head on her shoulders if she would only use it. 'Let's say this is a confidential conversation, okay?'

Beth looked up gratefully at her, swallowed hard and explained.

'When I came here a few months ago, I kind of assumed I might use it as a . . .'

'Stop gap?' supplied Judith.

Beth looked surprised. 'No, not a stop gap, more a starting point. When Mr Bannerman interviewed me he promised I would be moved on, but nothing happened. Only then you came along and at first everything began to change and you weren't very pleased with me . . . but you never asked me to explain why things were the way they were, you just assumed such a lot, just like Camilla does. I didn't think I looked awful but I can see it wasn't quite right for being on reception, so I've been working on my image.'

Judith felt touched by the awkward girl's honesty. But it was Beth's accusation that she had assumed so much about her that rankled. Hadn't she herself accused Gray Hamilton of the very same thing?

'You look great, Beth. A real difference.'

'Anyway, I really think what you're doing is needed and I can see it could be really exciting staying here, and I know there isn't a job for me up here, which is really where I want to be, but I *could* be useful, honestly. So I just thought I'd suggest a few things . . . and . . . and well . . .'

She tailed off, her prepared speech having come to an end, unnerved by Judith's silence.

Judith knew it took courage for a nineteen-year-old to say such things and while she didn't have much faith in Beth's belief that she could turn her job into something so useful, she did feel that such initiative should be rewarded.

'Okay, Beth,' she smiled. 'Why don't you have a shot at it. Talk to Camilla and report directly to her. Let me have a note of what you think you can do and we'll review the situation in, say, three months? Okay?'

Beth opened and then closed her mouth. Then she tried to thank Judith but it came out in a hopeless jumble. After which she got up and, bright red, shot out of the room to find Camilla.

When she'd gone Judith leaned thoughtfully back in her chair. Getting to be an old softie, my girl, she told herself sternly. It could all end in tears. We'll see.

She had no such difficulty in other areas of Premier's operations.

The remaining senior account executive, Clark Noble, came to see her and bluntly asked for the job of group head. Judith had not seen much of him since she'd arrived, but there was nothing wrong with his work.

'I don't want to hear what's wrong with Premier,' she interrupted as he launched into an analysis of the firm's problems. 'Without boring you by repeating myself, give me one good reason why I should listen to you?'

He gave her several. Most of which made enough sense for her to see he was worth holding on to.

'I'm a bit puzzled why you and . . .' she stopped herself saying 'Beth' '. . . why you haven't made this pitch before,' she finished.

'Opportunity didn't present itself,' Clark said briefly. 'I came here when Rik was MD. He wasn't looking for ways to broaden the company. He concentrated on the existing clients. I used to come up with ideas and possible clients. For instance, I have good connections in local radio, but Rik took the view if you didn't get the client on "Start the Week" or "Woman's Hour", it wasn't worth bothering too much about local stations. Yet out of London, local radio is very big and . . .' He stopped, looking sheepish. 'Sorry, you know all this anyway. But, for all kinds of reasons, it was difficult for him to pursue them.'

As hidden agendas went, Judith had no difficulty in recognizing what Clark meant. Rik sat on his backside, enjoying the comforts of a solid company, and baled out when the going got tough. Nor did he want anyone taking the shine out of his performance in front of Spencer. Ludicrous.

'So what made you stay?' she asked.

Clark shrugged. He was youngish, she decided, probably late twenties. His salary was clearly enough to buy good shirts and sweaters. She recognized Farley Cottenham's distinctive design in the open-weave jacket he was wearing. His hair was long, a rich brown that nature had no part in, and tied back in a pony tail. She liked him.

'I stayed because I hadn't been here long enough to leave when Rik jumped sh . . . I mean, was headhunted.'

'Jumped ship is fine,' smiled Judith.

'We had just lost Annie -- Anneline Murphy, you know her? – then I heard you were coming, and frankly I wasn't going to bounce in the day you arrived because I wanted to get your measure.'

'And . . . ?'

'I've got it. I think. I mean, probably.'

'Enough to want to stay?'

'If the price is right.'

'Which is . . . ?'

He paused and named a figure that was more than half the budget Judith had asked Spencer to allocate for two new account executives. She replied she would have to consult Spencer because it was far too high.

'Negotiable,' he conceded.

She looked at him. Nothing wrong with being in it for the money, but you had to believe in the accounts you handled, otherwise the company would head for disaster. Cynicism she didn't mind, but indifference was fatal. Passion and the product were inextricable, and she wasn't entirely certain Clark believed in it all. However, he was ambitious and worth hanging on to. She said she'd get back to him.

'By the way,' she called after him as he was leaving the room. 'How did you get on with Annie?'

He paused in the doorway. 'Fine,' he said. 'Great girl.'

That bad, eh, she thought, watching him go.

Spencer told her to leave Clark to him and just get on with running the show.

'Let me know what you end up paying him, won't you?' she insisted. 'I've got someone in mind for the other vacancy. I need to know I can at least afford them.'

A series of phone calls and short meetings unloaded small-budget companies with unrealistic expectations. But a patient, courteous debate on the facts of financial life with the indignant owner of an exclusive health and beauty salon, whom Judith was keen to keep on board but who wanted coverage in glossy magazines and the upmarket newspapers without offering anything in return, resulted in an unwelcome further reduction in Premier's dwindling client list.

'You must be prepared to do a reader's offer, a competition, be receptive to new ideas,' she pointed out to him during yet another angry phone call. 'You must find a way to give the beauty editors something to write about, not to mention complimentary treatments or a percentage off.'

'I know that,' Henry de Sholto shouted, thus rudely startling two of his clients relaxing in nearby treatment rooms where they had come to experience his much-publicized tranquil, stress-free atmosphere. 'But who is going to pay for *my* time? You are not doing your job properly. Let me tell you, Rik Bannerman has been after my business for months . . .'

A week later Judith walked into Quaglino's to find Rik and Henry toasting each other. Under her breath she quietly cursed. Henry was a bloody nuisance but he had just enough clout to be worth hanging on to. She waved cheerily at both of them as she swiftly took in the other diners. Confuse them, that's what this situation needed.

In an alcove she spotted the solution. Giving a silent cheer, she promptly took a detour which meant that Rik and Henry would get an uninterrupted view of her stopping to greet the European countess and socialite famed for her limitless glossy picture spreads and anodyne interviews of the good and the great which appeared regularly in the mainstream gossip magazines. She was lunching with Farley Cottenham, the rising star in the world of men's fashion, who was rumoured to be secretly signed up to bring his fastidious eye to the wardrobe of several members of the Royal Family eager to improve their image.

Judith's acquaintance with the countess had until then been confined to frustrating her many attempts to have Howard photographed in his penthouse in New York, his country home in Connecticut or, even better, his beachfront home on Long Island. All requests had been met with a polite, apologetic refusal. Judith had forbidden Howard to even so much as think of agreeing to ever being photographed again for a magazine or newspaper unless it was with the Queen of England, Hillary Clinton or Mother Teresa.

The countess, who never allowed such rejections to deter her for longer than it took to think up the next request, greeted Judith with feigned delight which was followed by the shrewd lady's insistence that she join them for a drink while she waited for her own lunch companion to arrive. Judith Craven Smith might have bitten off more than she could chew by taking on Premier, but it was common knowledge that Howard Dorfman was putty in her hands. On the whole, she was still worth cultivating.

The games we play, thought Judith, sitting down and paying

great and public attention to the young designer, who clearly regretted agreeing to this entire episode and who therefore greeted her with more enthusiasm than he might have done on another occasion.

Anneline Murphy arrived a few minutes later to join Judith, who had the satisfaction of knowing that Rik and Henry were paying little attention to their food and even less to each other while this scene was played for all it was worth. With a promise to lunch soon, she moved Annie to their own table.

'Good heavens, Jude,' breathed a curious and agog Annie. 'What are you up to? Bill Jefferson would abandon Premier if you even suggested that woman interviewed him and as for de Vries . . . are you out of your ever-loving mind?'

Judith, taking a quick glance at Rik Bannerman already beckoning a waiter to send a bottle of champagne over to the countess compliments of Henry, just smiled.

'Rik Bannerman,' she said dryly, 'has all the judgement of a cabinet minister leaping into bed with an out-of-work actress. He'll be so busy figuring out how he can get the countess interested in the ghastly Henry, he won't even wonder why we're lunching, will he?'

Annie took a sip of her mineral water, dabbed her lips with her napkin, ran a beautifully manicured hand through her artlessly arranged red curls and studied the menu.

'And why are we lunching, Jude?' she asked, without taking her eyes from the task in hand.

'Do we have to have a reason?'

'No. But I know you. There is an economy of activity about you that I've always liked. You don't waste time. I've never known you to have a social lunch midweek.'

Judith laughed. 'Annie, what a great girl you are. Tell me about Dayman's.'

'Thought as much,' Annie chuckled, checking the menu once more. While they delivered their orders to the waiter, Judith took stock of the girl opposite.

Twenty-eight years old, unmarried. Annie's days were filled end to end; even her weekends seemed to be an extension of her working week, which was swollen with people who were currently considered to be politically right-on in design and writing.

And she loved style. Happiness for Annie was being with people who understood the importance of detail, and she would spend hours fretting over anything and everything to do with her job, from the design of an invitation to the correct way to address the son of a second son of a duke or even, as she had been known to do, spending a week working in a dye factory so that she would understand exactly how her client – a leading fashion designer – achieved the brilliant colours for which he was world-renowned.

Nothing was too much trouble for Annie. Frequently her intense need to get things right drove people around her to screaming point, but Annie sailed blithely on. Judith, however, had always liked dealing with her even when they were on opposite sides of the fence. She knew that Annie's clients were charmed by her.

Annie's base was her tiny terraced house in Camden, filled with her friends, a mixture of style gurus and ex-lovers, and always, always a disastrous love affair on the go.

'His name,' she said soulfully when Judith dutifully enquired on the state of play, 'is Marcel Proubert. He is drop-dead gorgeous, talented, loves me and is so sensitive. No money of course. He really feels it that he can't take me to expensive restaurants or buy me perfume. And he gets so cross when I buy something to cheer us both up that it's difficult to know what to do.

'So we end up eating at cheap bistros or not eating out at all. Mind you, I've started lying a bit,' she admitted guiltily. 'Since Dayman's got the Extra Special account, I tell him I get the clothes for nothing and that grateful clients give me theatre tickets or that I can buy dinner on my company expenses.'

She looked defiantly at Judith, who as yet had made no comment at all even though Extra Special, which dealt exclusively with rich, overweight women, was hardly Annie's style.

'It might sound ridiculous to you,' Annie went on. 'But I can't hurt his feelings and sometimes I think I'll go mad if we don't have some fun.'

Judith had set out to woo Annie back to Premier with no

money to offer, no clients to dazzle her with, just a percentage of the profits when they came, if they came, and a title that sounded great but would do little to pay the rent. Blast Marcel. To hell with all of them, she thought irritably. And most of all with Gray Hamilton. For some reason she was more angry with the man she had met for a mere twenty minutes than she was with Howard.

But that could wait. For the moment Annie was the problem to be solved. Annie had moved on to Dayman's and her work seemed fine, if not overwhelmingly creative. Her accounts were long-established names who required little more than someone to maintain their reputation.

In return, Judith made her own plans for Premier sound vague. Even to someone as trustworthy as Annie, revealing the more precise details was a risk she wasn't prepared to take. So far she had allowed only Camilla to be a party to those. Sufficient for now just to ignite Annie's interest in returning to her former company. Easily, fluently, injecting just the right amount of optimism into her description without exaggerating the projection for success, Judith noticed that Annie was paying keen attention to what she was saying and very little to the food before her.

'No money of course,' Judith confided cheerfully, forking up the salad she had ordered. 'But it isn't every day you get the chance to rebuild a company, bring in fresh faces, new ideas.'

Annie listened carefully, asking a question now and then and just at the point when she was beginning to join in with eager suggestions, Judith looked at her watch.

'Annie,' she exclaimed. 'Just look at the time. I'm so sorry . . .' She craned her neck to catch the eye of their waiter, still talking as she reached into her bag for her cheque book. 'I'm going to be really late . . . but we must do this again.'

Annie silently gathered her things together and as Judith signed the cheque, she said hesitantly, 'Who are you getting to replace Rik?'

Judith looked blank. 'Rik? Oh yes. I've already got Clark Noble – you know him, don't you?'

'Clark? Oh yes. Great, great,' said Annie. Oh dear, thought Judith.

'Anyway, he's terrific,' Judith said firmly, zipping her bag shut. 'So I must have someone who will complement him. I'll start to put out feelers next week. The point is, whoever it is must come with ideas and commitment and not expect an expense account that includes lunching here every day. Lovely seeing you, Annie, I'm so pleased Dayman's is working out . . .'

As the taxi took off she leaned forward to wave to Annie, still standing on the pavement gazing thoughtfully after her. From her bag, Judith plucked her small mobile phone and called the office.

'Camilla? Hi. Me. Yes. Think so. Give it about an hour. Fingers crossed. She might change her mind.'

By the time Judith had arrived back from a plodding, screamingly frustrating meeting with Jacob Frankenheim, the Senior Partner of de Vries, Annie had phoned twice.

It was five o'clock. Judith waited until six and, just as she was about to return Annie's call, the phone rang. Camilla's voice betrayed nothing as she announced, 'Annie on the line, Judith.'

'Annie, hi. What's the problem?'

'Don't give me that, Jude,' came Annie's sarcastic voice. 'When can I start?'

'Start?' Judith feigned surprise.

'You know what I mean,' said Annie, her voice breaking into laughter. 'God, do you know how to sell something!'

'Are you sure?' said Judith, suddenly serious. 'There's no money in it.'

'Oh well, that should please Marcel, then,' chuckled Annie. 'But the salary will be the same as Clark's, won't it?'

Judith gave a silent wave of delight to Camilla who had been listening anyway, and agreed to talk to Spencer.

'Anyway,' continued Annie, 'not much I can do about it now. I resigned an hour ago.'

'I'm beginning to forget what you look like,' Rosie yawned from the doorway of the kitchen, barefoot and still wearing

67

pyjamas as Judith, briefcase clutched under one arm, downed black coffee after a glass of juice and, looking frantically at her watch, started to whirl out of the door.

'You can talk,' retorted Judith. 'I'm the one who won't be seeing you for a few days. Enjoy Rome.'

'Don't forget dinner next Wednesday,' Rosie called after her. 'I mean it. I will put your suitcases on the doorstep if you don't show. Piers is relying on us for moral support.'

'I promise, I promise,' Judith called and slammed the door behind her.

Sloane Square tube was a ten-minute walk. As she strode briskly down Kings Road, Judith mentally rearranged her diary, having completely forgotten Piers was holding a dinner party to celebrate his father's sixtieth birthday the following week. Thank God for once it wasn't another one of his and Rosie's attempts to fix Judith up with a man.

She had been back in London now for nearly three months and it had taken her just one to realize that when it came to men, London was as impoverished as New York.

'Honestly, Rosie,' she had grumbled as they arrived home from a dinner party where at least two of the men were in their thirties, allegedly successful and available. 'The minute you say you're running your own company, the glazed look comes down, the defences go up. Annie's absolutely right. London's full of bloody Marcels, quivering with sensitivity if you can afford a taxi and they can't. It might be less threatening if you said you were drug running.'

'Dear me, what that would do for their finances,' Rosie remarked tartly, punching in the code for the house alarm and yawning. 'We'd have them beating a path to the door. Problem is they say one thing and secretly want another.'

'A vamp in the kitchen?'

'Yup. Someone who is successful, but not threatening, someone who earns a lot but not more than them, someone who understands that their work is more important . . .'

'So what are we looking for?'

'He hasn't been invented. Compromise is the name of the game. Pretend, dear girl, it was ever thus. God, I'm whacked.'

Judith hoped Rosie was wrong. But all the evidence so far

showed that she hadn't misread the signs. One thing was for sure, *she* was not compromising any more. Those days were over.

Anyway, she thought, slotting her money into the ticket machine in the foyer of the station and then making her way to the escalator, love and sex are not on the Premier business plan.

She reached the office twenty minutes later and as she dumped her briefcase on her desk, Annie, who had now been with her for two weeks, whirled through the door.

'All set?' she asked. 'Van Kingsley, here she comes.'

'Sure,' said Judith, distantly looking down at the messages that Camilla had left the evening before. Her eye stopped and she stiffened at the last name on the list.

'Please call Gray Hamilton. He would like to arrange lunch.'

Chapter Seven

The lobby of Colby's was bustling. A breakfast meeting with Van Kingsley had been his idea, and one that Judith had leapt at.

Frankly, as Annie pointed out, they were one armchair short of credibility as far as the decor went at Premier, and trying to pitch for a new account on their own premises would be doing them no favours, given that the office's appearance didn't match their ambition. Not yet.

'Don't worry,' Judith reassured her. 'I've got plans for this.'

'You wouldn't let Marcel loose on this lot, would you?' Annie had asked Judith on her first morning at Premier, waving an arm around the reception area. 'All this and your office and, I have to say, my own little kingdom could do with a touch of imagination.'

'And Clark's too,' reminded Judith.

'And Clark's, of course,' said Annie lightly.

Judith wasn't at all sure that the combination of Annie and Clark was going to work. Both were fiercely competitive, both the same age, and both jealously guarding their relationship with Judith. Scoring points had become a daily ritual. Camilla thought they were tiresome. Judith just said, give them time. Annie and Clark she was prepared to nurture. Annie's sulking boyfriend was something else.

Judith paused on her way to Spencer's office. 'No, I wouldn't,' she said in answer to Annie's question. 'I couldn't afford him. Thing is, Annie, I have got some pretty clear ideas myself how it should look. Would Marcel listen to me? And as usual . . .'

'No money,' finished Annie. 'But you know, Jude . . . have you thought of asking him about the design for Young Masters? Now, listen. I know I'm prejudiced but I'm not the only one who thinks he's brilliant. Besides, he's feeling a bit insecure about me doing all this. I just thought if he was involved in some way he wouldn't feel so threatened. What do you say?'

There was quite a lot Judith could say, but she confined herself to a bright smile, a sympathetic nod and agreed to Annie bringing Marcel in for a preliminary discussion.

Meanwhile Van Kingsley had agreed to see her at eight A.M. at the hotel where he was staying before flying on to Paris for a few days.

Judith saw him immediately, threading his way easily through the crowded restaurant. She rose as he approached her table, which was by the window leading onto a long white terrace filled with flowers and ornamental bushes.

'Hi,' he said comfortably, swinging into the vacant seat opposite her. 'Sorry to get you here so early, but I've a pretty crowded schedule to get through. I guess you have too? So let's talk.'

Judith liked him immediately. Easy-going, direct, with the American habit of getting to the heart of the business, which she admired. Howard had had a similar approach. 'Charm to disarm' had been his motto. It might well have been Van Kingsley's too.

Within minutes he had made her laugh. By the time fresh coffee arrived, he was already outlining his business commitments and projections, and broke off only to ask the waiter for a very large cup.

'I am an advocate of early starts to the day, but my head doesn't always agree,' he confessed and smiled, showing even white teeth, and lines crinkled around his eyes as he explained that the night before had been a business dinner that included too much wine.

It would probably have been easier to say what was wrong with him. But from his well-cut grey linen jacket, streaked blond hair and, as Judith noticed, manicured nails, the flaws in Van Kingsley, if there were any, were well-disguised.

Judith, inured to the charms of good-looking men, was not immediately beguiled by his easy manners but she liked the fact that he was clearly at ease with women and comfortable about allowing her to order for them both.

Making no more than the necessary courteous protest, he acquiesced immediately when Judith made it clear Premier were paying. When she had tried to pay the bill at the Savoy Grill, Bill Jefferson had nearly had a cardiac arrest. Even though the lunch had been at her request, he had controlled the entire event. Van Kingsley seemed to expect her to order and pay. For her part, she merely wondered how she could find out who else was after his account. Knowing the competition, she would be on surer ground with her pitch for his business.

Bill Jefferson had rung Judith back a couple of days after their lunch to say that a stockbroker contact on Wall Street had called on Van Kingsley's behalf, asking him to be helpful if he could.

'Might be interesting to find out what he's got his eye on over here. Let me know first, after all I'm a client too,' chuckled Bill.

Now Judith's potential client was describing his work.

'Seeligman Ventures, whom I represent, have business interests in the States and in Geneva, mostly financial, but a little property and some interests in age rejuvenation techniques through some Swiss clinics,' Van explained as he downed his second cup of black coffee. 'My interest is purely to protect their interests as investors and I am not concerned with becoming involved in the day-to-day practicalities of these organizations. They pay me well to develop new ground for them,' he gestured to their surroundings, 'and I don't have to worry about their present obligations.'

Judith didn't bother to take notes. She was more interested in checking out her instincts about him. For once they were blurred.

'Judith, are you quite comfortable in that seat?' He suddenly broke off. 'Let me adjust the blind, here . . . that better? Good. I was saying . . .' Thoughtful. She had a sudden mental image of Howard doing much the same thing, but Gray Hamilton would not even have noticed.

Van meanwhile was describing in detail what he did and what he wanted.

'I know London well, I was born here as a matter of fact,

although I've lived in the States all my life. But it's a long time since I visited here. I am not even sure with the present financial climate that it's worth broadening our interests. I've said as much, but I simply do as I'm told,' he said in a tone that was easy-going and not entirely dismayed at having been over-ruled. 'Right now, I have limited time, which is why we thought getting involved with a company like Premier would speed things up. I need to get the feel of the city and to discreetly get to know the kind of people that might be useful to me in the future. In short I need an excuse to meet the right contacts in a non-business context without arousing speculation.'

It crossed Judith's mind that he must have very extensive backing, and she began to do some mental calculations as to just how much this account might be worth. When he told her his budget she tried not to blink.

'It's initially for three months and your concern is only to make the necessary introductions and create opportunities for me to meet the right contacts. The companies I represent will then reassess the situation with a view to a larger ongoing role for whoever I work with over here, if it all turns out satisfactorily.'

'A larger role?' Judith broke in. 'What does that mean?'

'But first,' he gently interrupted, 'first I need to make sure you guys know what you're doing. I need to know about you too.'

'Oh, of course,' stammered Judith, momentarily thrown. 'I thought you knew about us. That's why you're here, surely?'

Tough, she decided. Don't take the charm at face value. Silly mistake that. You're selling, not buying. He's the client.

Van Kingsley was counting off points on his fingers.

'I know you've taken over Premier Publicity because Carla Pevrocini let us know, and said you had done a great job in New York. I checked out your clients and I like the stable. Masters, de Vries, good names. You clearly have the right kind of clientele and a reputation in New York that carries weight.'

He was, Judith guessed, around thirty-one or -two. Single. Educated. He was clearly ambitious. But with the allotted hour nearly over, she had to move fast to make sure the impression she created was sufficiently strong to overcome the competition that he would inevitably be seeing later.

It would also be a departure for Premier. Until now they had been involved purely in corporate or product promotion. While this was a corporate account, it was heavily loaded towards the personal. To make it work she had to like the man, believe in what he wanted.

'Obviously,' Judith said, sliding into her pitch, 'we would like to have the account, but you must admit it is new ground for Premier, although my own track record in personal PR in New York is extensive. What I would like to do is draw up some proposals for you, let you see what we could do to help you achieve your needs, but off the top of my head I can immediately see one or two areas that would create the right opportunities for you.'

Rapidly she described a brief outline of what she had in mind, which was not off the top of her head, but the result of a think tank last night with Annie and Clark.

Van Kingsley was listening attentively and agreed that some concrete ideas from Premier would be welcome before he made a decision. He was, he said casually, seeing only two other agencies and Judith had to swallow very hard not to ask who they were.

Instead she smiled and rose to go, holding out her hand and saying, 'Mr Kingsley.'

'Please, Van,' he insisted.

'Van, I am so confident that you will like our ideas, I don't even want to know who they are. Shall we say by the time you return from Paris?'

'Great,' he said, rising and moving with her to the door. 'Have them delivered here Monday morning. If they're what I want to see, I'll buy you lunch. How does that sound?'

Judith smiled confidently at him as she shook hands.

'Sounds,' she said lightly, 'as if you'll be buying me lunch.'

Chapter Eight

Judith was elated when on Wednesday morning Premier won the Kingsley account. She was, however, slightly surprised that Van Kingsley appeared not to have seen anyone else and had made such a swift decision.

Spencer was inclined to think that he had done so because he fancied Judith. Judith thought that Spencer was placing himself just this side of being murdered for those remarks, while Annie tried to placate both by saying that a great proposal delivered by an attractive woman was bound to get the contract. But the same proposal delivered by a frump would eventually have got it anyway. After all, looking good just speeded up the process, and surely if they were in the business of making their clients look good to get attention, they could hardly then turn round and say looks didn't matter?

Both protagonists heard Annie out in silence, but neither was really listening, simply waiting for her to pause before they each delivered an even more convincing argument of the merits of women in business using all their assets. Fortunately Camilla buzzing through at that moment for Judith to take an urgent phone call broke the meeting up and left the matter unresolved.

At least Spencer agreed with her plans, Judith thought as she strode back to her own office.

'Who is it?' she asked Camilla as she passed her desk.

'Gray Hamilton.'

It was not a good day for Judith. Her temper, fanned by Spencer's sexist remarks, seemed to topple over into cold fury. She stopped in her tracks, her first instinct to refuse to take the call, which was one she had been avoiding since the previous week, when winning the Kingsley account had eclipsed everything. Well, perhaps not quite everything.

It was weeks now since Howard had returned to New York

and she had begun to think Gray Hamilton had simply been a passing, if nerve-racking, incident. All in all she was managing to put the whole unpleasant encounter behind her.

The phone call late last week had unnerved her, no doubt about it. But now curiosity, and a desire to put him in his place for colluding with Howard on the grand seduction scene, overcame her initial reaction to ignore him. Judith wasn't entirely certain you could be seduced by someone you'd already had a six-month affair with, but it had definitely been set up. And Gray must have known.

'Gray Hamilton is not on the urgent agenda,' she threw over her shoulder as she headed for her own office, for once kicking the door shut behind her so that Camilla wouldn't hear.

'Judith Craven Smith,' she snapped into the phone, and was thrown by a female voice.

'Mr Hamilton would like me to arrange lunch with you. Could you tell me which of these dates are suitable?'

Judith almost choked. Her grandmother would have been very surprised to hear her reaction; Rosie would have stared in disbelief.

'I'm sorry,' she said coldly. 'What makes you or indeed Mr Hamilton think I have time to personally arrange a lunch date? Please deal with my secretary. I warn you now my diary is very full and I doubt I can accommodate any of the dates you suggest,' and with that she replaced the phone.

Furiously she buzzed for Camilla to come in. 'You said it was Gray Hamilton on the line. It was his secretary. Bloody typical. Important man gets his female secretary to phone head of a company but she however is a mere woman and therefore can't possibly have anything nearly important enough to do . . .'

Camilla stood transfixed. 'But Judith,' she protested. 'You often arrange your own lunch dates, in fact I'm always telling you it causes confusion. I mean, you're the one who loathes that sort of grandeur . . .'

'I know, I know,' said Judith, irritated by her own contrariness. 'It's just the assumption by that ghastly arrogant man that I am on the level of a . . .' She tailed off.

'Go on,' said Camilla dryly. 'A mere secretary.'

'You know I didn't mean that,' said Judith, going red. 'I just meant . . . oh damn you, Camilla, you know exactly what I meant to say.'

Camilla looked exasperated.

'Actually no, I don't. You can be very confusing, Judith. One minute you're arguing that good secretaries are vital for their bosses to work efficiently, then when one does try to be exactly that, you behave as though it's the greatest impertinence in the world. I'm not sure who you're most angry with. Me for allowing you to take the call – although I have to say I assumed from her tone that she was simply getting you on the line for him . . .'

'Even that is arrogant,' exploded Judith. 'He will deign to take the call once I am on the other end. People like that are megalomaniacs, it's simply another way of putting someone in their place.'

Camilla threw up her hands. 'I suppose it's useless to point out that he had simply given his secretary an instruction – as you do to me – and she misled me into thinking that he himself was on the line?'

Judith, beyond being placated, wondered why she had become so informal with Camilla that her own secretary could talk to her like that. In her fury she mentally made a note to become more distant.

The phone ringing in the outer office put paid to any further discussion and by the time Camilla returned bearing coffee and the post Judith had begun to feel ashamed.

'Ignore me,' she invited with a rueful grin.

'I have,' returned Camilla calmly. 'I've also arranged for you to have lunch with Mr Hamilton. Don't worry, he's had to rearrange his plans. Happy?'

Judith laughed. 'God, I'm getting petty. Well, it's better at any rate. While you're at it, could you call Van Kingsley and arrange for me to see him ASAP?'

'It's done. He rang to confirm lunch on Friday. He sounds nice.'

'He is. Has Rosie phoned? Piers is having a dinner party at his house tonight for his father's birthday, Rosie's hostessing, and I've got to go. It would just help if I knew who the others are and what I should wear.'

In the event Rosie rang and instructed Judith that it was euphemistically tiara time, ignoring all Judith's pleas for something more relaxed.

'Sorry,' said Rosie firmly. 'It's not exactly Piers's dinner party, and you know what his father's like. With the exception of me and you, all the others are his father's old fogey friends from the City, so no, you can't wear trousers even if they are Armani. And we mustn't let Piers down.'

'Oh, shit,' groaned Judith, replacing the phone. 'What is Rosie thinking of? Just the kind of evening she knows I loathe. And making me dress up like a peacock to please Piers and his father.'

Annie, walking into Judith's office at that moment, looked surprised.

'But you know Piers is like that. He might be a fashionable photographer but at the end of the day he's very establishment. What else can you expect with his father being knighted and practically living in the Chancellor's house? Piers was brought up expecting women to look . . . you know . . . flirty and feminine rather than executive. Rosie does it to please him.'

'But all Rosie wants to do is relax when she's off duty. I mean, she isn't a lady who lunches and has nothing to do all day except plan supper and what to wear. She's the best style editor in the business. And that's because she works from dawn to dusk all week. Her job is every bit as demanding as Piers's,' snapped Judith, knowing that under any other circumstances she would not be making such an issue of it and she was just being churlish because the day wasn't going well.

Annie raised a surprised eyebrow. 'But she'd rather have Piers. And if he wants someone to play the little woman at the end of the day, she's prepared to compromise. Remember, they've only just got back together again and Rosie is trying hard because she has Tom at weekends and seeing Piers is difficult.'

Half of Judith wanted to tell Annie that it wasn't Tom being around that was the problem, but Piers's refusal to give any ground. But the other half remained loyal to Rosie, whose private life she never discussed with a third party.

Even if she had developed a penchant for the establishment. The establishment? Hold on a minute. Judith gazed thoughtfully out of the window. Van Kingsley might well find such a dinner party useful, and it would mean she could leave Friday free to go up to Yorkshire. Hastily she redialled Rosie at the studio where she was on a shoot.

'How difficult would it be for your arrangements if I brought someone with me . . . a new client? Good-looking, works for financial interests in the US and wants me to help him get a portfolio together of possible investors his clients can work with over here.

'I might even,' she added as Rosie hesitated, 'be persuaded to wear that chiffon skirt with my hunting jacket instead of trousers . . .'

Rosie laughed. 'Blackmailer. Important to you? Okay, I'll square it with Piers but for that you'll be placed next to his father.'

'You wouldn't, would you? Okay, it's a deal but wake me if I fall into a coma. Give me ten minutes to ring Van and make sure he's free.'

Van's hotel said he had left instructions to expect him at around three off the afternoon flight from Geneva. Judith asked them to get him to call her the minute he arrived.

At ten to three Van phoned, saying he had planned to work on some papers for a series of meetings, but if Judith thought the dinner would be useful, he would be happy to come. She did, and arranged to meet him at his hotel at six for a drink so they could sort out the details of the contract between them before going on to Piers's address in St John's Wood.

She began to feel that her dreadful day was turning the corner, but it didn't last. Within ten minutes Annie sauntered into her office to show her Marcel's design ideas for Young Masters.

'They're terrific,' enthused Annie – a little too heartily, thought Judith, but put it down to Annie's quite ludicrous view of her boyfriend.

And Judith had to agree that they were wonderful if she

had wanted a decor that would not have shamed a unisex boutique with changing rooms that looked like a rock star's bedroom, with leopard-print chairs and abstract nudes. Oh good grief. Perfect for Sixties refugees. Utterly useless for a company selling itself as striding purposefully into the future, taking the next generation with them.

'Very interesting,' she said admiringly, turning to face an apprehensive Annie. 'How would Marcel feel about coming in to discuss one or two small changes? Nothing drastic.'

Annie's smile was uncertain enough for Judith to guess that she knew the designs were horribly wrong. 'Okay,' smiled Annie. 'I'll ask him to come in later this afternoon.'

Judith's own plans for their own foyer and offices were nearly complete. One weekend she had dragged Rosie and Tom over to inspect the place and got Rosie's view. Between them they had put together a scheme that was at once both energetic and calming.

Rosie had said it would be cheaper to start again and with the help of Farley Cottenham, who was her slave since she had tipped him for great things at his first collection three years before, and who also had an unerring eye for design. Together they transformed the whole area with streamlined high-tech chrome and glass, softened with glass bowls filled with armfuls of green foliage.

'Keep the flowers to white,' instructed Farley. 'It's when you start mixing the colours it goes wrong.'

Rosie and Judith solemnly promised to do just that.

Down came the posters depicting an era now gone. In their place – since they were short on clients – Judith asked Farley somehow to arrange displays of Masters accessories and de Vries jewellery in slim glass cases pinned to the walls.

Beth went out on the first day of viewing her new surroundings and blew all her salary on having her hair cut to chin length and gently blow dried.

As Annie had said, what a difference a wave makes.

Marcel arrived unannounced at five o'clock and the signs were not good. Clark, seeing Annie hovering anxiously in the corridor, did little to help matters by making a slitting movement across his throat as Marcel disappeared into Judith's office.

Inside, Judith was bringing every ounce of tact to this difficult meeting. Their first encounter, when Marcel had swept aside all her suggestions, was fresh in her mind. He was not without talent but completely devoid of commercial sense. And it showed.

'Perhaps,' Judith said with a smile, 'if we went over them again, I might find it easier to explain what I want.'

'It would help,' he said curtly. 'But I would rather speak to Spencer.'

That was it.

'I am the Chief Executive of Premier.' Judith's voice was cold but very even. 'Speak to Spencer by all means, but he will take my advice and it seems to me a waste of time.'

'But surely Spencer *is* Premier,' said Marcel with an expression of such bewilderment on his face Judith had to admit she was enjoying his discomfiture. 'You report to him, don't you?'

'Eventually. But decisions at this level are mine. Frankly, Marcel, that is hardly what is at issue here,' she said, folding her arms on her desk and staring straight into his eyes. 'You're not the first or the last designer to have to negotiate with a client.'

Marcel's face was transparent. It was like dealing with Alice when she was being ticked off. He must be great in bed, thought Judith, otherwise how on earth could Annie put up with his sullen temper?

'This is the bottom line, Marcel. Every day of my life, and Annie's too, come to that, I have to see the other person's point of view. Do you know what my dream is? It's to dispense with the client's view and just promote them the way I see fit. But they are the clients, it's their money and I have to keep this company on its feet because I have everyone's salary to think of. I don't have the luxury of that choice.

'Now I broke off a very important meeting to come and see you because I think the design of Young Masters is vital. But it must be done in a way that combines what I want with your expertise interpreting it properly. I must get back, let me know what you decide to do.'

She shuffled the papers in front of her, tossed them into her out-tray and moved towards the door.

Startled by her sudden change in mood, Marcel rose and said he would think about it and let her know by the end of the week. Judith stopped in the doorway. Why did it have to be so fucking hard to get guys like Marcel to accept women at the top?

'No, I don't think so, Marcel. Tomorrow morning. Latest. Nice seeing you,' and she swept out.

By the time she reached Colby's to collect Van Kingsley, Judith was in a dangerous mood. To please Rosie, she had changed into a hip-hugging black velvet riding jacket which had a deep V neck, trimmed with gold braid, worn over a floor-length chiffon skirt that floated in soft clouds of palest yellow, matching the cuffs of her jacket. All of which belied her frustration with the day that had been, in her terms, a pig.

Van Kingsley was waiting for her in the bar and rose to greet her with a warm smile. She noted with approval that he was wearing a well-cut dinner jacket that was so understated it must have cost a fortune. He looked like something out of a Ralph Lauren advertisement. She made a mental note to introduce him to Farley's designs. A good-looking American client would not do Farley any harm. Not for the first time since she had suggested he came to the dinner party she wondered how such a stylish and handsome man would fit in with the very staid, formal group that Piers had assembled to celebrate his father's sixtieth birthday.

As she reached him, he held her shoulders in a light clasp and kissed her on both cheeks, smiling mischievously down at her startled face.

'I don't kiss every new colleague, just the ones that deliver the goods and don't drag their feet getting the show on the road.'

Spencer's assessment of why she had landed the contract floated back to her.

'What on earth do the men say?' she asked lightly, sitting

down as he summoned a waiter. 'When they er . . . deliver the goods and get such an affectionate greeting?'

'No problem. I just tell them I was brought up in Russia. Americans can't tell the difference between any culture outside of the US. Works every time. Although of course it may not work in the UK. Do you think I might get arrested?'

Judith laughed back at him, not believing a word of it, and tried to ignore how ridiculously pleased she felt at his immediate understanding of how his gesture and remarks could have been interpreted, and the fact that he obviously found her attractive had nothing to do with her pleasure. Nothing at all. Too silly to even contemplate. Much too silly.

Straightforward and businesslike, it was Van who introduced the subject of contractual obligations. Judith was impressed with the fluency with which he enumerated the details, presenting her with a slim folder in which were the principal names she might need to contact if she was unable to reach him.

'But mostly I'll be available, so it's unlikely you'll need to. We'll pay you in advance for three months and if there are any outstanding expenses at the end of that time, we will adjust the balance for the second three months of the contract.'

How could she argue with such terms? The cheque would be with her by the end of the week and what was there left but to enjoy the evening? So she allowed herself to be cajoled into accepting his openly flirtatious manner more easily than she would have done normally.

Most of the men who were her dates out of hell when she first returned to London were puzzled by her lack of response to their compliments. Van on the other hand had no trouble getting a teasing comment back.

One of them had listened politely but noncommittally to her views on the bank's base rate going up half a point, but Van engaged her in a vigorous debate on Maastricht, which ended when, collapsing into laughter, both finally confessed they hadn't a clue what any of it meant.

By the time they reached Piers's white double-fronted town house at quarter to eight, Judith's dangerous mood had switched dramatically to her more recognizable witty good humour, bathed in a heady glow of delight that Van Kingsley was not only good-looking but had not once questioned her equal status, openly admitted it was a relief to be with a woman who didn't keep looking to him to take the lead, clearly felt extremely comfortable with business women and had made no attempt to seduce her.

She also forgot that Piers lived two roads from Gray's house which she passed without so much as a wince.

The door was opened by a pony-tailed out-of-work actor earning a living as a butler. They followed him across a square hall furnished in a surprisingly pleasant mix of old and new.

Judith had guessed from her previous visits to Piers's house that he was content to leave such matters as decor to Rosie, who had used family heirlooms and pictures deftly arranged against a backdrop of pale green-and-blue swagged curtains to counteract the leaden feeling such family objets often brought. The whole effect was of old money, which all the contemporary thinking in the world couldn't disguise.

Just as she was about to follow the young butler into the drawing room, Piers emerged and greeted her.

'You look wonderful,' he enthused, kissing her on both cheeks. 'Rosie?' he called. 'Jude's here.'

He broke off as Rosie appeared from the kitchen where she was supervising dinner, looking ravishing in a black silk jersey dress. Judith introduced them to Van.

More like a great friend than a business acquaintance, she thought, watching Van shake hands with Piers and give Rosie a charming smile and thanks for including him at such a late hour.

While Van was sharing a mild joke with Piers about which accent he should play up amongst such very English company, Rosie rolled her eyes expressively at Judith. 'Wow,' she mouthed and, as Judith moved ahead of her to join Piers, she whispered, 'This is *business*?'

'Strictly,' Judith murmured severely, which didn't fool Rosie for a second.

'Nice business,' she drawled.

The drawing room was already filled with a dozen or so

guests exchanging pleasantries, the odd burst of laughter relieving what was potentially a very stiff gathering.

'Come and meet my father,' invited Piers, beginning to thread his way across the room to where a tall, silver-haired man holding a whisky glass was deep in conversation with a couple who halted Judith in her tracks.

The woman caught her attention first: a willowy, vivacious blonde who Judith had last seen dragging her ex-husband out of the Savoy, now smiling brightly from one man to the other. Clearly she was bored witless by the conversation, but her easy acceptance into the discussion by two powerful men appeared to be ample compensation.

Judith stood still, startled, as the woman's identity sank in. Then her eyes slid to the man laughing at something Piers's father was saying. Piers was urging her forward, Van was charming Rosie, all around there was a buzz of conversation and banter, but all she could think was what on earth was Lisa Hamilton doing here? And, even more mystifying, why was Gray Hamilton with her and how could she get herself out of here?

Chapter Nine

Afterwards, Judith decided it could all have been a lot worse. After all, she might have found herself sitting next to Gray, which would have meant feigning some totally transparent excuse about a headache and leaving early. Seated safely between Piers's father, John Imber, and her old friend Carey Templeton, the newscaster who was also John's godson, Judith found herself in charming and immensely good company.

A fact that was ruined when she happened to glance up to find Gray watching her. His expression wasn't so much disapproving as that of someone who had decided that her ambition peaked at being little more than a rich man's plaything.

To her horror Judith found herself blushing, and so she began subtly to encourage Piers's father to converse with Lisa Hamilton, who was seated on his right. In the course of the next few minutes, Judith was treated to an exercise in how to charm an old man off his feet. The beautiful socialite flatteringly deferred to his every opinion and thought.

Judith wondered how John Imber could stand it. Lisa was clearly a bright woman, but to her surprise he didn't seem to find her unqualified approval or unchallenged view of life at all irksome. It occurred to Judith that he was actually enjoying himself.

John Imber safely and courteously occupied left Judith free to talk to Carey Templeton, whom she had barely seen since returning from New York.

'I saw more of you crossing the pond once in a while than I do now you're home for good,' he teased.

'And you, I take it, are available at the drop of a hat?' she replied sarcastically.

'No, at the drop of a dinner date,' he grinned. 'Let's run

away one evening next week and pretend we're business. Lots of gossip. Who, by the way, is your blond friend?

Judith glanced down the table to where Van was sitting between Lisa and a prominent banker's wife to whom he was listening attentively, his head slightly bowed and turned towards her.

'A new client of mine,' she said briefly. 'Works for investment bankers.'

Carey took a sip of wine and, feigning interest in the gold chain bracelet Judith was wearing, asked her casually if Van was American.

'His accent has an East Coast edge . . . good-looking guy.'

Judith looked sharply at Carey. She knew from Jed Bayley that he was gay but, unlike Jed, he never acknowledged it. He had been linked, as glamorous good-looking newscasters inevitably are, with a string of equally glamorous women, but whenever he was asked why he hadn't married, he would laugh ruefully and say it wasn't off the agenda but his job made it difficult to keep relationships going. No-one doubted him for a second.

He featured regularly in magazine celebrity interview spots, bringing an extra measure of interest with him as the son of a high court judge. His lean, dark, handsome features grinning boyishly out of the accompanying photograph usually brought resentment from his colleagues while his fan mail doubled. He had thus far been successful in keeping his relationships out of the public eye, although Judith was aware that he had of late been seeing less of the manic and imaginative designer, Brendan Harman, and the rather donnish but immensely likeable art historian Josh Mengies had recently been included in supper parties at Carey's home.

Now Judith thought he was wasting his time. 'Van's half English. He was born here but brought up in America or at least his working life has been almost exclusively there. I must ask him. You're right, though, he certainly likes attractive women,' she concluded, hoping that the casual slip might save Carey an unnecessary excursion to nowhere.

Carey turned back to his meal and simply said lightly, 'He's doing well tonight. Arrives with you, Lisa Hamilton's already got his phone number and Marjorie Fulton has clearly marked him out as a highly desirable extra man. Now your turn. Who are you interested in?'

Judith was seated across the table and two to the left of Gray. So far he had made no attempt to talk to her, contenting himself with a brief handshake when Piers had introduced her to him. Judith had smiled thinly. Lisa Hamilton had not ignored her any more than she had any of the other women in the room. Still, why they were together bemused her. Bill Jefferson had told her they had gone through a messy divorce. It was a strange relationship.

Folding her knife and fork onto the plate and without discernibly changing her expression or tone, she took up Carey's offer.

'The Hamiltons,' she said. 'They're very close for two people who had a very painful split.'

'Mmm. You're right. Strange. He's as tough as old boots and if it wasn't for John Imber, he wouldn't be here and that's a fact. But the word is that he's still in love with Lisa and that's why he still sees her.'

'But why get divorced if they like being together?' asked Judith, puzzled.

'You tell me,' said Carey with a shrug. 'Lisa started proceedings and by all accounts was adamant. Some say she thought it would bring him to heel. He's a complete workaholic and Lisa likes to have fun. Trouble is he puts work first and fun second. It's rumoured that she became so lonely she had an affair, awful scenario – some golf instructor or other – and that brought it all to a head. Gray was incensed and moved out. She filed for divorce for some peculiar reason, thinking it would bring him back.'

Judith thought this a bit far-fetched. She had met the man briefly but in that short time it had become abundantly clear that he wasn't into emotional blackmail. Surely Lisa, who had lived with him for six years, must have known that? In fact she doubted Gray was into any emotions. Nothing seemed to move him, but plenty seemed to bore him. And something else about him puzzled her.

He looked expensive; plainly he was reasonably wealthy.

Lawyers always were. But she had a distinct feeling there was more of a street fighter about his character than his present appearance suggested.

But now boredom seemed to be his problem. Gazing straight ahead, he was making no attempt to respond with more than a slight nod or a bland 'really?' to an animated authoress who was currently occupying the number one slot on the bestseller lists. On the other hand he easily gave his attention to her husband, sitting immediately opposite him, who had recently chaired a government committee on penal reform. What was wrong with the man? He's a misogynist, Judith decided, but as Gray's gaze happened at that moment to travel across to her, she turned hastily away, hoping he hadn't imagined for a second that she was remotely interested in him. Good God, what a thought.

A far better idea was to ignore him completely, which she managed to do with such stunning success that, as the first guests began to leave with Judith and Van following shortly after, the lawyer told her gravely that he was looking forward to lunch and hoped she would by then have thought up topics for discussion, since none had arisen that evening.

'How considerate,' she smiled back. 'I shall instruct my secretary to compose a list for me and fax it to yours before we meet.'

In the cab taking them first to Van's hotel to drop him off and then on to Rosie's, Judith was frowning.

'I do hope that ferocious look isn't for me?' Van said, watching her profile.

'Oh, I'm so sorry, Van,' she replied hastily. 'No, certainly not for you.'

'That guy Hamilton?'

Judith was tempted to tell him exactly what she thought of Gray Hamilton, so judgemental, so irritatingly indifferent to anyone he thought unworthy of him. But discretion got there first.

'Not at all,' she lied. 'Just wondering if the evening was useful to you? Was it?'

'Great, nice people. Not sure about connecting with them, but I'll follow up Marjorie Fulton's invitation to dinner – with you, incidentally. Sorry I didn't have time to consult you, but strictly business,' he grinned. 'You will come with me? She's quite ferocious, is Marjorie.'

Curiously enough, Judith didn't mind. Van's company was a relief. She enjoyed his attention, he understood their relationship and, more importantly, she hadn't wasted his evening.

'Terrific. Of course I'll come. Anyone else?'

She suppressed a yawn and gazed out of the window to see where they were, which was just as well because it stopped Van noticing the flicker of alarm on her face when he next spoke.

'The guy next to you, Carey Templeton. I thought he might be worth getting to know.'

Judith swallowed hard. 'He's a fascinating man, a newscaster. I wouldn't have thought he would have the kind of contacts you need. He reports on them rather than deals with them.'

Van seemed to accept what Judith said and they talked of other things until arriving at his hotel.

'Come and have a nightcap,' Van invited.

But Judith declined. 'You've had a long day and I don't want one of my clients too exhausted to live up to my plans for them,' she teased.

'Ah well,' he smiled, briefly kissing her on the cheek. 'Dinner on Friday?'

She hesitated, remembering the dreadful Mike Sullivan. But Van solved her dilemma.

'I know,' he confided conspiratorially. 'Lunch is business, dinner is something else, yes?'

He *was* nice and so refreshingly upfront. 'Sorry.' Her voice was apologetic. 'Is that what you thought was going on in my head?'

'No, didn't think it, I knew it. But then I'm American and I keep forgetting over here, it's still viewed like that, isn't it?'

'I'll say,' she agreed.

'Okay, lunch, how's that?'

Judith had begun to feel a bit silly, apart from which she had not expected him to want to see her again so soon. It was only two days away and she had wanted to go up to Yorkshire to talk to Dad about getting more help for Laura. Oh, hell. Have to rethink that one. Business came first.

'Dinner is fine,' she smiled and made a mental note to switch her plans.

She had booked Friday as a day off to start moving into her new home. This was a relief in more ways than one. By Thursday night she was barely speaking to Spencer; Annie was not speaking to him at all. Only Clark was still on reasonable terms with everyone else.

It had come as real news to Judith to discover that Annie was being paid less than Clark when Annie herself had virtually pushed Camilla aside to come into Judith's office. As rages go on the Richter scale, Annie was in orbit. At first Judith refused to believe it. She'd seen the figures herself.

'I'm damn well not making it up,' stormed Annie. 'It's just not bloody on, Jude. I mean it.'

'How do you know? Did Clark tell you?'

'Clark?' she scoffed. 'Clark wouldn't tell me anything. I got it from Charles Holland – works with Rik – I met him at a preview last night and he said that Rik had tried to get Clark to go over there but he couldn't afford him. And he told me what the figure was. It's a helluva lot more than I get, for doing the same job – and better – and I'm more experienced than he is. How could you do this to me? You said you would match his salary, you actually *said* it.'

Judith winced. Of course she had said it. She had meant it too. But, fool that she was, she had left it all to Spencer. Once she had agreed figures, she had simply assumed that was the end of the matter. Emotionally she was totally on Annie's side, but if she said so she would have a battle on her hands with Clark. Practically speaking, she would have to try and keep everyone happy.

Annie was nearly in tears. Judith knew it was anger but she didn't want Spencer to see her like that. Bloody Spencer. Old world charm, old world notions. Old world thinking. The immediate point was to stop Annie shouting at her. Salary disparity or not, Judith was her boss. She said so.

'I don't take that from anyone, Annie, not even you. Not even if every word you say is true. If you want to discuss it with me, fine. If you want to shout, reconsider your position.'

Annie looked at her in disbelief. Shook her head slowly from side to side, and then slammed out of the room.

Judith groaned. A quick check with Camilla proved that Annie had got her facts right. Spencer was unrepentant, even indignant.

'I hold the purse strings. I decide who's worth what. If Annie doesn't like it she can look for another job,' he said furiously.

'She may well do just that, Spencer, and I wouldn't blame her. And what's that going to look like for Premier? We just lure her away from one company and she resigns. Get real, will you? Anyway, what the hell did you do it for?'

'Clark's great and I agree, Annie is every bit as good. But he wouldn't have stayed for less. Anyway, until Charles opened his mouth Annie was content with her salary. I don't see she's got a point. She had every opportunity to negotiate with me, just as Clark did. She chose not to.'

Judith slumped into a chair.

'Spencer, *do* something. We have enough problems without those two fighting . . .'

'It's the first I've heard that Clark's fighting . . .'

'Oh, give me a break, you know what I mean . . .'

Recognizing that he was on a winning streak, Spencer moved remorselessly on but was stopped in his tracks by Judith rudely telling him to shut up.

'I want a solution, not point scoring . . . What is it, Camilla?'

'I couldn't help overhearing, but would it not be possible to give Annie some kind of bonus to make her feel a bit better and then give her a bigger increase at the next pay round?'

Judith looked at Spencer. 'Well?' she demanded. It was the obvious solution.

Camilla looked levelly at him. 'I know how I would feel if I heard that Fenny was getting more than me,' she said pointedly.

With a workload that was greater than usual to deal with,

Judith was in no mood to pursue the subject. She leapt to her feet and headed back to her office. 'Perhaps you two could discuss this and resolve it, before I lose half my staff.'

On Friday, Rosie and Piers came over to help her move and at lunchtime Carey, who was not on the rota to newscast that day, turned up with a couple of bottles of wine and a picnic basket, the contents of which they devoured sitting crosslegged on bare boards since the carpet had yet to be laid.

By six the curtains were in place, primrose with a piping of dark blue, softly draped back by dark blue swags. Piers took a picture of Judith with one draped Roman style around her. The carpet, a haze of cornflower blue which Rosie had correctly insisted would look great, was fitted by five o'clock.

Ellie Carter had sent two Tiffany lamps straight from one of her favourite shops in Greenwich Village in New York, which Rosie regarded with envy, saying how very Ellie they were. And from Jed in Bel Air came a riot of country flowers that he knew Judith loved, which had to be dumped into buckets when Judith ran out of vases.

The bed had arrived and been ceremoniously made by Rosie and Piers with their own flat-warming present to Judith, a mountain of lace-covered pillows and cushions.

'Now all I've got to do is pay the mortgage,' announced Judith, leaning happily against the doors leading onto the terrace.

'Easy peasy,' drawled Carey, lying full-length on the floor, balancing his glass of wine on his chest. 'Just sell your soul to the highest bidder.'

They were all laughing when the entryphone buzzed. Expecting the delivery of some kitchen furniture, Judith strolled to the intercom.

'Flowers for Ms Craven Smith,' came a muffled voice.

'Come on up,' she said. 'The bath it will have to be,' she went on as the door buzzer sounded and she went to open it.

What appeared to be a tree confronted her. Two in fact, marguerites in satisfyingly chunky earthenware pots.

'Wow, what is this . . . ?' she breathed.

'I thought they'd look great on your terrace,' said Van, appearing round the side of the miniature bushes.

'*Van*. How did you know where to find me?' she exclaimed, welcoming him in as he leaned over to kiss her cheek. 'This is too kind of you. Do come in.'

He followed her across the newly carpeted square hall and into the drawing room where Rosie, Piers and Carey were gazing expectantly at the door.

'I think you know everyone,' she said, standing aside to let Van go in first. Piers and Rosie greeted him warmly, lavished compliments on the marguerites which they insisted on immediately placing on the terrace. Only Carey remained silent.

'And Carey you met briefly,' said Judith, a tiny pang of doubt crossing her mind. But she dismissed it at once. Carey couldn't have known Van was coming. They hardly knew each other, and also Carey hadn't known until today that she was having dinner with Van later.

Carey rose in one graceful movement from his position on the carpet and held out his hand.

'Hi, nice to see you again. Judith, I'll run along, your dinner date won't want to be kept waiting.'

'No problem,' said Van easily. 'I thought I'd surprise Judith, so I'm a little early. Don't let me drive you away.'

Judith racked her brains. She remembered perfectly well arranging to meet him at the restaurant, but how did he know where to find her? She could have sworn she hadn't mentioned her address, just that she was moving.

'Absolutely not,' agreed Rosie, overhearing Van's last remark as she emerged from the kitchen where she had gone to rinse the damp earth off her hands. 'Where are your manners, Carey? Pour Van a drink.'

How it happened, Judith could never quite explain afterwards. But after a glass of wine, amid much hilarity as Van described moving into his own apartment in New York when he had misjudged the size of a sofa and had to have it hoisted up by crane, taking out a window in the process, it seemed the most natural thing in the world for all five of them to have supper together.

A flash of uneasiness shot through her. Van was business. After Howard, she had vowed never to mix that with pleasure again. It simply didn't work. But what could she do?

Make sure it didn't happen in the future. In a week or two, Van would be too busy with his business interests; he had to fly back to New York for a briefing with his company, and he would have to find an apartment for the rest of his stay in London. It'll be all right, she reassured herself, you're just overreacting, that's all.

She noticed that Carey didn't protest at the suggestion and, bathed in Van's undeniable charm, became his usual witty, urbane self.

For some reason, as they settled into the booths of a restaurant Piers had said was absolutely the place to be but one that none of them had heard of, Judith felt uneasy. She couldn't pinpoint what it was; just that something was threatening her peace of mind. Don't be ridiculous, she admonished herself. It's sheer superstition because everything seems to be going so well.

On the other hand, how did Van know she had a terrace? You couldn't see it from the front of the block and she knew for a stone-cold certain fact that she'd never mentioned it. Not once.

Chapter Ten

Bill Jefferson declared himself delighted with the new designs. Guided by Judith, leaned on by Annie who had hinted quite untruthfully that Judith was terrified he would turn her down, Marcel had produced a more relevant theme, one that would lure clients in rather than embarrassing them into walking straight past.

They would also give Bill Jefferson personal credibility, whereas the previous ones would have given rise to speculation that his understanding of the market had evaporated.

Gone were the stark colours and bizarre prints of the rock-star boudoir and in came leather chesterfields, dark green wall-paper, blazing fires and oak-and-brass fittings. The impression was of a highly desirable bachelor pad. Added to this was the brilliant collection of jackets, trousers, jeans and shirts that Farley Cottenham had produced, putting paid to any possible belief that Young Masters was anything but the only place to shop.

Even Annie sighed with relief when the decision came and, while nothing was said between her and Judith, both used Camilla as a go-between to let the other know how pleased she was at the outcome.

The subject of Annie's salary remained a sore point until she received a buff envelope from Spencer with a generous cheque for securing Farley Cottenham as a client. It had actually been Judith who had won his confidence but after the initial contact, Annie had been let loose on the young designer and, apart from giving Marcel a sleepless night or two since his insecurities seemed limitless faced with any hint of competition, she had thrown herself with such enthusiasm into promoting Farley's designs that Judith privately suspected she would have forgone any amount of bonuses just to get her hands on the young man's work.

The opening of Young Masters was only days away. Annie was exhausted, but buoyant. Camilla, and the dynamo Beth had turned into, rarely left the office before seven. Judith refused all invitations to lunch or dinner, knowing that her energies had to be concentrated on keeping all her other clients happy while getting the first night for Young Masters just right.

Sometimes Van would drop round with a bottle of wine to listen to her woes, claiming that an invitation to the opening of Masters would be compensation for not having his adviser at his beck and call. Not once, however, did he attempt to move their relationship onto different ground. Judith was both relieved and puzzled, but had no time to analyse the situation more closely. Later, when she had five minutes to call her own, she would. But Lord knows when that would be.

Press releases were drafted and redrafted, radio shows scanned for those that would be a natural setting for Bill to appear on, making sure he was presented as a serious business-man and not chat-show fodder. Judith had seen at the outset what was wrong with the way Masters was being marketed – frivolous and lightweight, and with only Bill to represent them, he was being seen in the same light.

Farley, young, gregarious, a perfect foil for Bill Jefferson, had the right image for magazine programmes and TV. Clark was dispatched to persuade the Forward Planning depart-ments of the radio stations and the breakfast TV com-missioning editors that the launch of Young Masters was not just another opening, but a new departure in dressing men.

The workload kept the lights burning late in Judith's office and the feud between Clark and Annie well stoked.

If anything had come out of her night out with Van and Carey, Judith had no time to give it more than a passing thought as she dialled the direct line of the *Sunday Post*'s city editor to arrange for him to lunch with Bill at his club in Pall Mall.

That night when they had all had dinner together had passed off so well that Judith had decided she was being para-noid. Van and Judith had dropped Carey off at his house, where Van, looking enquiringly at Judith, had declined a nightcap.

'I'll call you,' she said, giving Carey a swift kiss as he alighted from the cab. Next day when he called to confirm dinner for the following week he never even mentioned Van. Judith breathed a sigh of relief.

Spencer too was benefiting from the energy Judith had generated in the company. His old cronies were reviving an interest in having him join them for lunch and most days he would disappear around midday to various watering holes the older generation had made their own. Ignoring all Judith's and Camilla's pleas to remember his health, he sallied off to more of these invitations than they thought was good for him, but surprisingly seemed to thrive.

The only time Judith ever felt really irritated with him was when he lunched with Rik Bannerman. Sometimes she had the feeling that if he'd had a choice, Spencer would have tried to lure Rik and his bloody squash racquet back to Premier. Even more strongly did she believe that Rik would not hesitate to accept. No doubt about it, Rik was courting Spencer with a vengeance. But Judith had little time to concern herself too deeply with their burgeoning friendship; the broad plan for Premier occupied most of her waking hours.

Pleased with the way both Annie and Clark were handling the day-to-day running of the accounts, and resigned to their bickering, but still nurturing Van's progress in London herself, she got used to Spencer hinting that at this rate Judith would soon be offered a partnership. Yet she noticed he still insisted on meeting every new client to sign the deal that she herself had thrashed out. Not for a second would Spencer admit his input was not needed. Nor did he allow a deal to go through without making at least one alteration to the details, usually so slight it could have been classed as petty. Spencer would simply smile kindly and say it was the tiny details that made all the difference.

Infuriating, but Judith knew Spencer could not be unaware of her ability to handle it all. This was ego talking and she just shrugged. Ego got in the way. So did Rik Bannerman.

And why shouldn't she feel proud of herself? Masters was on the verge of being revitalized. Farley was the darling of the style gurus and de Vries were slowly but encouragingly beginning to think about their own image, even to consider sponsorship.

'Not polo,' Judith had said quickly at her last meeting with the austere board. 'Overdone now. Anyone can go. Something much more exclusive but with strong socially minded overtones. Ward off accusations of simply the rich at play. I have some ideas to bring you together with ChildLife.'

Jacob Frankenheim, whose ideas for the company had been undisturbed for the past twenty years and who resisted change with a vigour that would have delighted Victorian England, had surprised Judith with a handwritten note after one particularly exasperating encounter, saying, 'It seems only courteous that we should at least see what you have in mind. Perhaps you could write it all down and let me see your suggestions.'

Judith grinned as she tucked the letter away. Getting there.

The opening night of Young Masters left Annie and Judith, as Van laughingly whispered in her ear, looking ready for the home for bewildered PRs. In the scrum trying to thread her way through to find Bill Jefferson for an interview with the *Daily Express*, she hadn't noticed Van in the hubbub of fashion editors, photographers and style editors who had crammed into the new premises next to the original Masters. Nor did she see the photographer standing behind her. Judith had just flashed Van a smile as the photographer captured the moment on camera.

It was doing her no harm having Van as a client. His name was being circulated by the hostesses who mattered. His ready charm and willingness to adapt to any situation made him much sought-after. And Judith too. But that, she decided, was a drawback. She liked Van enormously, no-one could be more entertaining, but wherever she was invited Van would come too, either because her clients asked her to bring him, or because he openly admitted he adored the company she kept.

But the picture that appeared in a gossip column the next day was of Van whispering into her ear, Judith smiling at what he was saying, his face hidden, hers full to camera, rather than of her client for that night's event.

The words left her choking at her own stupidity.

Last night's glittering opening of millionaire Bill Jefferson's newest creation, Young Masters, based on an idea by his attractive and much-admired Public Relations Advisor, Judith Craven Smith, was wall-to-wall celebrities.

But the word among the *tout monde* is that the stylish American, Mr Van Kingsley, newly arrived in London for a short visit to the UK investigating business opportunities for multi-conglomerates in the US, is working hardest on becoming more than a good friend to the high-profile Public Relations expert.

Still mooted as the girl most likely to become the third Mrs Howard Dorfman, the US Wall Street financier, friends say Chartbury-educated Judith, who is totally discreet on these matters, is still tipped to succumb to Dorfman's open pursuit of her, but Van Kingsley is rarely far away from her side while he is in London as our picture shows. Watch this space.

Judith threw the paper back onto her desk in fright. This simply was not true, and was not good for Premier. It was certainly not good for her. The item was about *her*. Bill Jefferson paid her good money for the press to talk about *him*. Oh Lord.

Nor was she looking for anything other than friendship with Van. What she wanted was the opportunity to build up the business for Spencer; financial security for herself that wasn't dependent on the good will of an older, influential man; and someone who would just be there for her. Someone who would understand her erratic hours, not caring that she earned more or had a higher profile than him. Was it too much to ask?

Apparently it was. Van rang early and laughed at her attempts to apologize for dragging him into such a story. By mid-morning three newspapers had phoned her. Two wanted a quote about her relationship with both men and one to see if she would be included in an article featuring what successful women wear to the office.

To the first two she delivered a good-humoured but crisp, 'no comment', and the third she turned down flat, irritated that successful women were still being seen as a freak species.

'Only if you're also describing what successful men are wearing,' she said calmly. Features like that trivialized what she was doing. And good grief, wasn't it hard enough without fuelling the popular image of women as ornaments in the workplace, not serious contenders for business? She longed to be phoned by the city pages or one of the business magazines. What a shame she couldn't do a PR job on herself, but without the aid of a paid image-maker she had to rely solely on her own behaviour and public persona.

And it would be today, when she was meeting Gray Hamilton. For a brief moment she flirted with the idea of tipping off one of the papers that had phoned her to say she would be lunching with him. If nothing else he did have the right air of seriousness, his client list was forbidding and he certainly looked good.

Cheap stroke, she counselled herself. Far better to let the lawyer see she was to be reckoned with on her own merits. Left to a newspaper, the introduction of a third name into her life would have them writing her off as a man-mad airhead.

More apprehensive than she cared to admit, Judith turned up just two minutes after the appointed time to meet Gray Hamilton for lunch. She had even dressed particularly carefully to avoid any impression that she was very aware of the fact that she was lunching with an attractive man: a dark rust round-necked linen jacket severely buttoned to the hips, worn over a plain white T-shirt with matching knee-skimming linen culottes and flat leather pumps. Under her arm she carried a soft black leather briefcase.

It gave her an air of efficiency and distance, she thought, as she surveyed herself in the mirror that morning before she left her flat.

Unfortunately, it also made her look incredibly feminine. Her mood was not helped by meeting Rik Bannerman en route to the Savoy Grill, who leered suggestively at her accompanied by a growling sound which made his companions laugh. Judith gritted her teeth.

'Impersonating a man again, Rik?' she smiled pleasantly as she walked on, wondering if she could keep her jacket on all through lunch to disguise the entire outfit.

If Gray noticed what she was wearing, he made no mention of it. Good, thought Judith, shaking hands politely, and wondered why she had been ready gracefully to accept a compliment on her appearance and so disappointed when none came.

'Knowing what a busy person you are, I have ordered my car for two fifteen,' he began.

'Excellent, mine will be here at two,' she smiled back, planning to leave by the River Room since she had no car to order and keeping her fingers crossed that Gray's car would be at the Strand entrance.

'Now,' she said briskly, picking up the menu and beginning to study it. 'I believe you wanted to talk to me?'

'Well, to be precise my client does, but he's having trouble pinning you down, I gather.'

Judith slammed the menu down with just enough force to attract the attention of the diners on either side of them.

'Really, this is too much. I've already made myself perfectly clear on that score. I do not discuss my private life with anyone. I am not remotely interested in what Howard has to say now or ever . . . in fact . . .'

He ignored her and instead began ordering lunch from a hovering waiter.

Judith had no appetite at all. The hour ahead was going to be a nightmare.

'Now,' Gray said, as the waiter disappeared. 'Let's try and have a reasonable discussion. I am simply Howard's lawyer in Europe. What he does in his private life is nothing to do with me. You left me specific instructions to convey to him . . .'

'I did *what*?' gasped Judith. 'Where did you get such an idea?'

'Why, from you. I have a note of it right here.' With that, he reached into a briefcase and selected a blue folder. Taking his glasses from his pocket, he ran through a sheaf of documents and drew out one that Judith, reading upside down, could see was on headed paper from Hamilton Carew.

'Yes . . . right here. You said, I quote, "The offer isn't high enough".' He looked over his glasses at her and she noticed he had amazingly deep brown eyes.

'What? Oh God, yes, I did say that, but I didn't think you were going to repeat it to Howard. And anyway that was before . . .'

'Before?'

Judith took a deep breath and attempted a look that she hoped was at once disdainful and indifferent.

'Before I last spoke to him,' she said, settling for an approximation of the truth. 'Anyway, what did he say?'

Gray looked at her and thoughtfully removed his glasses, tapping them against his mouth. 'What a very confusing person you are. Less than a minute ago you said you weren't remotely interested in anything my client had to say now or . . .' He paused as though trying to recall her exact words. 'Yes, that's it, you definitely used the words, "or ever". Now you want to know what he said.'

Judith wondered if there was any way to unsettle him.

'I don't, but since I thought the matter was closed I'm surprised you've raised it again.'

'I didn't. I can't see any mileage to be gained from that. This is an entirely different offer.' He looked at her face, which was aghast and fearful of what was now to come. 'Howard wants to buy you your own business. Set you up as your own PR agency, if that's what you want, but provided you employ a Chief Executive and don't work all the hours that God sends.'

He paused and she had the strongest suspicion that Gray was having difficulty trying not to laugh. The offer was ludicrous: a toy for her to play with, nothing serious, just a little diversion to keep her entertained until Howard came home.

The waiter arrived with their first course. Judith looked helplessly at Gray. She'd left Howard behind. No great love affair, just a period of madness. She felt very vulnerable, what with the morning newspaper linking her with Van, being chased by the people she normally courted, and now this. Wasn't she ever going to be allowed to move on?

Her head was bowed, resting on one hand, the other held a fork, pushing her food desultorily around her plate. Finally she pushed the uneaten food away, and realized that Gray had not spoken a word. He was sitting back in his seat. Waiting for her. Giving her time.

'You know, it isn't at all what you think,' she said wanly. 'I don't know why Howard keeps this going. And I could have done without you helping him.'

She looked defiantly at him. There, she'd said it.

He shrugged. 'I use his house on Long Island. He uses mine on his rare visits to London. I thought you knew that.'

She looked down at her hands fiddling with her napkin. 'No. There's a lot about Howard that I don't know. I looked after his image. His business affairs were conducted by a stream of other people. The lawyers I knew were the ones in New York. I didn't know what you did. I suppose . . .' She hesitated. 'It's what I keep trying to explain to everyone. I'm not that important to him. Just something he can't have . . .'

'He must have some reason to think you're important to him. The newspaper this morning seemed to think so as well. Half New York thought so. It would appear the only people who don't are you and your friend Mr Kingsley.'

'He's not,' she said indignantly. 'I mean, Van's not a friend, well, yes he is, but he's really a client.'

'Of course. But then so was Howard. And I act for him. So really this isn't getting us anywhere. Let's try and focus on what matters. Do you want to accept any offer from Howard? A simple yes or no will do,' he added hastily, seeing her prepare to launch into another explanation.

Judith realized it was hopeless. 'No,' she said flatly. 'No offer of any kind is welcome to me.'

Gray scrawled some comments into the file.

Judith looked at him curiously. 'This is a very odd business for you to be involving yourself in,' she remarked. 'It seems so trivial for a man of your reputation to be bothered with.'

Gray remained unmoved. 'I couldn't agree with you more,'

he said without glancing up. 'However, Howard rarely asks for anything unless it matters to him. In which case I have to make it matter to me.'

'But you don't think it is, do you?' she said bluntly.

'What I think is irrelevant,' he replied. 'All that matters is that he is my client and I happen to like him. Now, as we still have some time to go before your car arrives, shall we talk of something else?'

'Of course, I know my manners,' Judith said, glad to have got off so lightly. 'That was a pleasant dinner party a few weeks ago, did you enjoy it?'

'I'm fond of John Imber and I like Isaac Wentworth. So yes. Did you?'

'I'm fond of Rosie Monteith Gore and I like Piers Imber. So yes,' she mimicked.

Gray smiled. It made his eyes crinkle. His eyes were nice. Warm, sort of sexy . . . oh, for heaven's sake.

'And Mr Kingsley?' he added, which she didn't like quite so much.

'I've told you. Van is a client. He also happens to be good company.'

'In what way?'

He might as well hear it. 'Well, Van actually *likes* women. He has time for them. He doesn't expect them to be there when he gets back from work . . . you know, that "hi honey I'm home" routine.'

'How do you know?' he interrupted.

'He's told me, but you can tell, you just know. His general view of women who work. I mean, he loves his job . . .'

'What *is* his job?' Gray asked curiously.

'He advises and networks for several multi-national companies. While he's in London he needs to be given opportunities to develop new interests for them . . . can I go on?'

Gray nodded. 'Of course. You were chronicling his virtues.'

Judith realized that she was making Van sound like every career girl's dream man. But she couldn't lie either.

'I don't know about virtues, maybe attitude is better. He listens, doesn't patronize and doesn't get into a flap if you insist on paying for dinner or a drink. Very refreshing.'

'You've made him sound like a tranquillizer,' said Gray in a bored voice. 'You know, makes you feel good.'

'And what's wrong with that? Just because he believes that women's careers demand the same sacrifice from a relationship as men's do? Don't be ridiculous,' she scoffed dismissively. 'If more men like Van, just once in a while, decided their partner's ambitions were every bit as important as their own, and didn't sulk if the women weren't home before them to get the dinner organized, there would be a lot more happy couples around.' She stopped.

'Like you and Mr Kingsley, I assume.'

'Exactly like me. But not me and Van. We are not an item,' she said crossly. 'I told you that. I'm trying to explain that someone like Van knows what I want.'

'And that is what?' he asked, looking curiously at her.

Judith sat back, absently carving a pattern on the white cloth with her coffee spoon. 'Not much. A chance to build up Premier. Something that would give me independence and eventually a relationship with someone who didn't feel threatened by my independence. You see, I know you find it baffling that I wouldn't throw in my lot with Howard, but that was the problem. He resented me wanting independence. He wanted me to be successful, but he was always irritated if my job got in the way of anything he wanted to do.'

'Like what?' Gray asked, who appeared to be watching her closely.

'Well, if he wanted to leave early to go up to Cape Cod for the weekend, or suddenly to take off for Aspen to ski, I had to be there for him. But he didn't have to be there for me. I once had tickets for Pavarotti at Carnegie Hall and Howard insisted on coming with me when I had planned to go with other friends. He didn't show up. I was very annoyed and he just spread his hands and said, "What do you expect me to do? Tell an urgent board meeting I can't make it, I have to go and see a fat Italian sing?"'

Gray laughed out loud. 'Typical Howard,' he said.

In spite of herself, Judith laughed too.

'If I had wanted a lasting relationship with him, I could see myself ending up leaving work and becoming dependent on his good will because he held the purse strings. And when he tired of me because I was no longer the person he had found attractive, I would be up the proverbial creek. It simply wasn't worth it.'

'Why not? The divorce settlement would have set you up for life.'

Judith decided an open restaurant was not the place to slap the face of a well-known lawyer.

'Mr Hamilton . . . You have clearly led a sheltered life. When you have responsibilities as I have, my family for instance, you do not treat such matters lightly. But mostly I owe it to myself to have the peace of mind and not to have to compromise all the time. Life's a big enough compromise as it is.'

Gray gave her an apologetic smile. 'Sorry. Lawyers don't lead sheltered lives. I see too many divorces for it not to seem a viable proposition to some women . . . no, no, I didn't mean you,' he added hastily, seeing her gathering her forces to defend herself. 'Tell me about your family. Howard says your mother died and you and your sister went to live with your grandmother . . . Yorkshire? Is that right?'

Judith became wary. She rarely talked about her family. Too complicated. Too vulnerable. 'Sort of. My father joined us permanently about three years later, from the Diplomatic Service. We were living in Washington when my mother died. Alice and I came home.'

'I've seen your father's books,' he said. 'They're good.'

'They don't make money though,' she sighed and added quickly in case such an admission would invite even further questions, 'He was invalided out of the diplomatic corps. We all pitch in. Alice is still going through school.'

For a moment Gray looked silently at her. She had the impression he was going to say something but thought better of it. Finally he asked, 'And your family is why you need independence, not just for yourself?'

'It's not that simple. I want it for them, but even if that weren't the case, I would still want it for me. Van understands that. He says, it's really that we all need someone who will let us be what we want to be, but also have time to just walk on the beach.'

'Walk on the what?'

She stopped abruptly. She hadn't meant to say all that and certainly not to Gray. It had all tumbled out so easily. What made her think he would care or understand? And, really, he didn't have to take everything she said so literally.

'What he meant is, if you really care for each other you will make time just to escape, be together, forget the world. Something someone who is a workaholic like yourself would never understand.'

'I see. And that's what Mr Kingsley offers, is it? I've never understood what all that means. It sounds like Californian claptrap to me. No-one can forget the world. You can reduce the pressures of the world by not expecting too much of it, that's all.

'Let me put another point of view which I agree might burst that idyllic bubble that you and Mr Kingsley live in but it might also let in a little common sense. There are far too many women around who want to blame men for all their problems, who want the trappings of success and then complain that that very success is getting in the way of what they really want. Frankly, if a walk on the beach is the answer to not getting divorced, the entire coastline of Britain would look like Blackpool on a bank holiday.'

They stared silently at each other. Hopeless, thought Judith, utterly hopeless. They were poles apart. No wonder he was Howard's advisor. They were like soul mates.

The waiter appeared at Gray's elbow while they were still staring at each other.

'Your car is here, Mr Hamilton.'

His car. Oh God, it must be two fifteen. She hadn't noticed the time. And she'd lied about her car. Where could she say it was?

Gray signed the bill and looked politely at Judith. He also looked as though he were suppressing a grin.

'I expect your driver's got held up in traffic,' he said politely.

'Not at all, he's been here since two,' she said with convincing confidence. 'I simply didn't want to appear rude and interrupt what you were saying. Being a man, that thought would not have occurred to you.'

'I do beg your pardon,' he said with what sounded like genuine contrition. 'I thought we'd said all we had to say on the subject of relationships and . . .'

'Mr Hamilton,' Judith said smoothly, 'men like you and Howard wouldn't recognize what makes a real relationship work if the whole of Relate counselled you.'

She rose as she spoke and held out her hand. 'Thank you for lunch.'

'My pleasure,' he said politely.

Judith had not counted on his manners. He insisted on escorting her to her car.

As they went through the revolving door out onto the fore-court of the hotel, Judith had decided on her only face-saving course of action. Walking straight up to the nearest uniformed chauffeur, she announced in a voice loud enough to be heard by Gray that she had left her scarf in the restaurant and would be back in a moment.

Turning, she smiled at Gray, who had hesitated before getting into his own car, saying, 'Please go ahead, I'll be a few minutes.' And with that she disappeared back into the restaurant until she was sure Gray was out of sight and then ran out to call a cab, leaving the bewildered chauffeur scratching his head looking after her.

Chapter Eleven

Premier celebrated the conquest of de Vries's antipathy to change by cracking open champagne at the unusually early hour of ten thirty in the morning.

Jacob Frankenheim himself had phoned Judith, gruffly agreeing to nearly all of her proposals; but they would prefer Clark to run their day-to-day affairs rather than Annie.

'We want you personally to handle this,' he'd said, and Judith didn't know whether to be pleased at their belief in her, furious at their sexist attitude, or to put her foot down.

'That's just fine,' is what she said, but not what she meant.

Six long months of putting Premier back on its feet were taking their toll and she longed for a break. But now that de Vries was back on board with a vengeance, the chances of escaping were remote. Yet somehow the sheer pleasure she got from walking through the reception each morning, seeing Beth guarding her new territory like a lioness, making her way down a freshly carpeted corridor to her office where glass and chrome had replaced fading chintz, she knew that the leap of faith that she had made on the day Camilla had stopped her at the lift had been worth it.

Judith's office was crowded as everyone from Premier pushed their way in to offer congratulations. Sitting on the edge of her desk, casually swinging one leg and holding an untouched glass of champagne in one hand, Judith caught Camilla's eye across the room and they raised a silent toast to each other.

Judith knew that for all Annie's talent, Clark's inventiveness and Spencer's renewed, revitalized pulling power, Camilla had been her strength. It was Camilla who had stood by a boss who watched while his friends shook his hand with a reassuring smile and behind his back made throat-slitting movements and who had done what Spencer never would have. She'd put her pride on the line and pleaded with Judith to come on board.

This was the company where two major account executives with reputations created exclusively by Spencer had baled out before the predicted crash caught them in its wake, where the bank had tried to pull in credit and clients had stopped taking calls from Spencer while they secretly negotiated new contracts with Premier's rivals.

It was Camilla who had made Spencer swallow his pride, forced Judith to turn back and take on Premier. Of all of them it was Camilla, the hard-working secretary, who deserved much of the praise for what followed.

Masters, de Vries, ChildLife had remained loyal and had been well rewarded. Farley Cottenham Couture had been a real coup and both Annie and Clark had spared no pains in vying with each other to bring in major new clients. Annie pulled in Circe Hooper and Clark got the surprising account of the Harcourt Hotel. This was a small, exclusive establishment that played host to a stream of household names who were concerned only that their visit to the capital went unnoticed and undetected. But with fear of terrorist attacks in Europe affecting business, the Harcourt management were aware of the need to attract more corporate entertaining.

They were not immune to the advantages of playing discreet host to the likes of Jacob Frankenheim or Bill Jefferson and over dinner with Clark, who had pulled Judith in to meet them, they had found themselves asking this charming duo to handle their affairs. If the price of getting corporate customers into the exquisitely pretty dining room that would have done justice to any hotel in the world was to have that vulgar but curiously talented old harridan Circe decorating the place, it was a price worth paying.

Circe, who was as magnificently grand as the florists she had made into an international name, but who needed more frequent attention than the award winning arrangements that had become a fixture at every society event of any note, was the trickiest account of all, and only Annie could really handle her properly.

It was rumoured – possibly by Circe herself, thought Judith

grimly as she returned a pleasant 'no comment' to a newspaper – that two of England's more fashionable princesses were among her clients.

'They won't deny it, they *never* make any comment, do they?' said Circe with smug satisfaction when Judith had met her for her first exclusive magazine article for *Tatler*, sinking with her impossibly tangled layers of silk scarves, jackets and skirts into the plumpest, largest and most public sofa she could find in the foyer of the Harcourt Hotel. 'So who's going to say anything?'

'Well, me for a start,' Judith told her bluntly. 'It's so unnecessary to do it . . .'

'I will be the judge of that,' Circe returned grandly, attempting to freeze Judith into submission which, had she known Judith better, she would have realized was a waste of time.

'Circe,' Judith urged her. 'Think of all the others who claim the Royals, particularly the princesses, as clients. All those fortune tellers or whatever they call themselves. They end up looking really cheap and tawdry. And your other clients, the ones who make you money, will start to feel uneasy if they think you gossip. Don't you see? It could backfire on you.'

Circe, who Judith had discovered had been christened with the perfectly nice but straightforward name of Joan, bristled.

'At least I wouldn't be an insult to their name. And I cer . . . tain . . .ly,' she emphasized the word, 'would not confide their secrets to the *Sun* or the *Stars* whatever they're called.'

'I know that,' Judith began placatingly and with more patience than she dreamed she had, but was stopped by Circe who had more to say on the subject.

'I doubt you do,' Circe said, with a malevolence Judith had always suspected she possessed. 'I know how to conduct myself. I am, as they say, a class act. Unlike you, I wouldn't want to be plastered all over those pages with one man after another.'

Judith itched to get up and walk out. Only the knowledge that the magazine's photographer was walking towards them accompanied by a trail of girls bringing make-up and even more flowing dresses stopped her. Smiling and rising to greet them, she shot one more warning at Circe. 'The photographer is related to half the royal family, just bear that in mind. Hamish. How nice to see you,' she said warmly as the floppy-haired young man reached her and kissed her on both cheeks. 'I don't believe you know Circe.'

'Young man,' beamed Circe, shooting a triumphant glance at Judith, 'many of your relatives are well known to me. I say no more,' and to Judith's horror, she gave the startled young photographer a broad conspiratorial wink. So much for class. Judith closed her eyes in despair.

And she had had dinner with Gray Hamilton the night before.

Quite by chance. Not planned at all. Well, to be truthful, a drink that turned into dinner. Her feeling of well-being was not, if she were to be entirely honest with herself, completely due to the successful conclusion of a business deal. Farley Cottenham and Bill Jefferson had asked her to join them for dinner after a late-afternoon meeting that had gone on longer than any of them expected.

'I'll meet you there,' Bill had told them. 'Just got a couple of calls to make.'

Judith would have preferred to have gone home to change, but at nearly twenty past seven and on the other side of town from her flat, it was all a bit too much.

She left Farley to order a drink in the bar of the restaurant while she whisked off to the cloakroom to study the effects of an exhausting afternoon diplomatically explaining to Farley and Bill that they had to meet each other halfway over publicity. Farley thought his designs were vital on the style pages of glossy magazines and upmarket newspapers. Bill, glowering at Farley in his unstructured jacket and state-of-the-art glasses, pointed out that his credibility in the City was of paramount importance and the occasional interview for the City press equally vital.

And all because Judith had warned that they were in danger of overkill if they accepted every single request for an interview.

Bill had become accustomed to talking for Masters on everything from design to shares. Judith had spent too many long, careful hours nurturing him in the less obvious but vital City pages to let Farley ruin it by insisting on appearing in every magazine that showed an interest.

'Sometimes,' she explained to Camilla when yet another squall erupted between the two valuable clients, 'it's keeping them *out* of the papers that will do most good. Farley is getting hooked on fame – God help me, I'm convinced he'll be on game shows next.'

Whether the truce she had achieved would last, she hadn't a clue. Certainly she had to talk Farley into accepting dinner with Bill as a measure of his good will.

Rejoining him, she thought that at least Farley couldn't find fault with Bill's choice of restaurant.

'The trouble is,' he complained sullenly, 'I don't recognize anyone.'

'That,' she said dryly, 'is the whole point. The hidden message is that real class is somewhere where you don't find *le tout monde*.'

'Bill's lawyer isn't what you would call *le tout monde*, is he?' asked Farley absently.

She couldn't think of a less likely description and, sipping her drink, said so.

'That's probably why he's here then,' said Farley vaguely.

'Here?' Judith swung round to look at the point on the opposite side of the room where Farley was indicating with his glass. No mistake. She hadn't seen him since they had parted company over lunch. She could not, however, say she hadn't thought of him. Right at this minute she wished she had gone home to change.

She turned back to Farley, hoping that she didn't look as flustered as she was feeling. 'So he is,' she said and, pointedly looking at her watch, switched the subject. 'I wonder what's holding Bill up?'

Bill's message that he could not join them after all arrived five minutes later. Farley and Judith exchanged groans.

'Okay,' he grinned at Judith. 'Let's be straight. Do we want to sit with a whole crowd of people we don't know, or get the early night we both want?'

Judith liked him. Temperamental and talented and tricky.

But in the short time they had worked together, they had developed a good rapport and laughingly they exchanged a high five as they got to their feet, feeling no need to argue the point.

All of which, not unnaturally, made several heads turn in curiosity.

Judith caught his eye almost immediately and he smiled in recognition. Hell, now what? Leaning over, he said something to his companions, a man and a woman, who both glanced in Judith's direction as Gray rose to his feet and made his way to their table.

'Hi,' he said easily. 'You're a long way from home.'

'A bit,' she acknowledged. 'How are you? You two know each other, don't you?' She looked from one to the other.

The two shook hands and Farley, assuming she would want to stay and talk to the distinguished lawyer, addressed Judith.

'I'd like to go back to the studio and pick some papers up, so if you two will excuse me . . .'

'Of course.' Judith could hardly say anything else. Hang on, don't leave me with this man who never agrees with a word I say and is my former lover's lawyer as well, did not seem appropriate.

Gray, however, seemed unaware that she was having any kind of conflict. As a matter of fact he seemed to be making an effort to be quite charming. No, that wasn't right either. He wasn't making an effort. He *was* being charming, quite effortlessly.

'Mary Carew – Steven's wife . . . sorry my partner – she's a great fan of Bill's and Young Masters. I was just giving you all the credit for dreaming up his resurgence,' he smiled.

Credit? Gray Hamilton giving her credit? This she had to hear. Judith hesitated, looking expectantly at Farley who simply grinned and said he'd had quite enough for one day of hearing how great she was.

'I pay her a fortune already,' he said to Gray. 'Any more of this and I'll be bankrupt.'

'Any more of that,' she said severely, 'and I'll fix up an interview with the *Investor's Chronicle* and make you go alone.'

'Have you got a few minutes?' Gray asked her.

'She has now,' said Farley. 'We've been excused duty for the rest of the evening.'

Impossible for her to refuse without seeming rude.

A quick hug for Judith, a handshake for Gray, and with apologies he was gone. Gray looked at her. 'You'll like them and – it will please Bill.'

She hesitated.

'And of course, it would please me, too,' he added with a straight face. 'Honest.'

Quite impossible.

'Thank you, I'd love to,' Judith smiled back at him. 'It's been a long day . . .'

'I can imagine. Don't tell me you actually tried to get Bill to agree to anyone else's view but his own?'

'Tried,' she grimaced. 'Don't think it worked.'

By this time, talking easily like old friends, they reached the table at the other end of the bar where Gray's companions were waiting, clearly delighted she was joining them.

They were nice, enthusiastic. Steven was older than Gray, Mary a year or two younger. Judith, sitting between them as the waiter brought their drinks, felt at ease. Gray too she noticed laughed more in their company. All three were genuinely interested in what she did. A drink led to dinner and all Judith's protests were squashed, since neither Steven or Mary wanted the foursome to break up.

'But I'm not dressed to have dinner here,' she wailed, looking at Mary's black silk shirt and crepe skirt. 'They'll chuck me out . . .'

'You look great,' argued Steven, signalling to the waiter to bring menus. 'Well, go on, man,' he prompted Gray. 'Agree with me. Don't let her run away. Tell her she looks wonderful.'

Judith looked quickly at Gray, waiting for some teasing comment.

'Judith doesn't need to hear me say she looks wonderful. She knows I think that anyway.'

Judith knew nothing of the sort. Judith wondered why her knees suddenly lacked the strength to support her and why had the muscles around her mouth become immobilized? And, oh God, what did that look that had just flashed between Steven and Mary mean? And why was she suddenly breathless?

Fortunately she wasn't required to answer any of these pressing questions as Steven swept an arm around her, saying, 'So that's settled,' and all four made their way to the restaurant.

Dinner was an animated affair. It turned out that Mary had been Steven's secretary until they had fallen in love, married and produced two children, both of whom she confided to Judith were heaven but she longed to return to work.

'When they're older,' she said hastily. 'Okay, I'm lying. I never want to work again in an office. These two here put paid to that.'

'And to think we bought her all that wonderful new technology to improve her performance,' complained Steven.

'I knew it was a mistake when we found tippex all over the screen,' Gray said solemnly as Judith fell about laughing and Mary threatened him with expulsion from her home for ever more.

Lisa's name came into the conversation, but nothing that was said could give Judith any clues about the state of their relationship. Mary and Steven went home first, leaving Gray and Judith to linger over coffee. It was in fact nearly another hour before they left. Afterwards Judith could not recall exactly what they said, but they had swopped family histories, glossed over his marriage and her relationship with Howard, and laughed at his particularly wickedly accurate anecdote demonstrating the full extent of Marjorie Fulton's ruthless social mountaineering. Only once did the relaxed and leisurely atmosphere between them threaten to collapse.

'She is, however, a tireless worker for ChildLife,' he said, pushing a silver dish filled with a selection of chocolate mints towards Judith. 'And very genuine.'

'I know she is,' Judith agreed, inspecting the dish. 'She's an old friend of the family. But Van says she's out to make sure Becky Fulton marries the right man.'

'Does he?' said Gray politely. Judith paused. 'And of course, he would know,' he finished.

'No,' she said candidly. 'He wouldn't. But Marjorie has made a beeline for his company, you have to admit, and she got him to take Becky to the opera.'

'I'm a lawyer,' he said, signalling to the waiter for more coffee. 'I admit nothing. Except,' he finished, 'I meant what I said earlier. You always look wonderful.'

Later Gray drove her home and after such an easy-going evening when more than once Judith had to remind herself that this relaxed, amusing man was the same one who had treated her with cold indifference and her views on relationships with impatience, it seemed quite natural to ask him in for a nightcap.

Only she couldn't bring herself to do it.

'Well, thank you very much,' she said, turning to smile at him as he pulled in outside her apartment block. 'That was such a nice evening. Steven and Mary are lovely people.'

'They enjoyed your company,' he replied, swinging the driver's door open and walking round to open the passenger side. 'So did I,' he added, putting his hand lightly under her arm as she stepped onto the pavement.

'Yes, of course,' she said, flustered and not knowing why. 'It was kind of you to drive me home, so far out of your way, it isn't necessary for you to see me in, honestly. I'm sure you must want to get back . . .'

'I know,' he said, guiding her towards the doors to the lobby. 'At this time of night too.'

Judith looked suspiciously at him.

'And to think I'm taking the trouble to see you right to your door, as well,' he went on, accompanying her into the lift.

At her door, he waited until Judith had turned the key in the lock and switched on the light before leaning forward and kissing her lightly on the cheek. 'Ample reward,' he smiled, clearly waiting for her to go in.

Judith was annoyed with herself. If it had been Van, or Carey, she would have automatically invited them in for a drink. This was ridiculous. Ten to one he'd refuse anyway.

Gray did.

'On the other hand,' he said, as he pressed the button for

the lift, 'I hope you won't refuse to have dinner with me again some time?'

Now, surveying her packed office celebrating the de Vries conquest, and knowing the hard work that would come next to put together what Judith was determined would be the social event of the year, she felt she owed herself a moment of congratulation.

Absurd to think her good humour owed itself to anything else.

Even Clark and Annie seemed to have buried the hatchet, if only temporarily, and were being pleasant to one another. Beth, released from the front desk, was transformed. Judith hardly recognized her from the sullen girl she had met the day she'd waited with such sinking spirits in the front reception. The addiction to fashion was more considered if still clinging to her, but the stout boots and black tights visible under the swirl of a full-length jersey skirt were absolutely right for her age and ambition. Moreover, she had received the ultimate accolade from Alice who had told Judith after she and Laura had come for lunch one day and had been duly shown around, that Beth was the only one who had *any* idea at all.

Contentedly Judith looked around the small army who had lifted Premier back to where it rightfully belonged. But again and again her eye travelled to Camilla. What was the matter with her?

Camilla was answering everyone in a mechanical way, but Judith could see that what she was really doing was carefully watching Spencer reducing the likeable but talentless Fenny to flirtatious giggles. Judith knew that Camilla regarded Spencer as a respected elder statesman but she had a shrewd suspicion that Camilla deeply regretted not having put her undoubted talents to better use.

On paper she was still the same as Fenny. But in reality she had the administrative side of the entire company firmly in her grasp.

Many times Judith had wondered about her home life. She had never married, elderly parents lived somewhere in South

London and not since Judith arrived had Camilla taken so much as one day out of the office.

Judith could talk to Rosie late at night, or Ellie when she called from New York, or Libby Westhope when they would meet for dinner – in fact any one of her friends – about their relationships, but Judith's very tentative opening gambits to try and discover the state of Camilla's heart had been gently rebuffed.

Everybody's were. Except for Van's.

Van had charmed Camilla from the day he had turned up unannounced and whisked her off to lunch when Judith, half laughing and half exasperated at his unexpected arrival, had told him firmly she had to work.

'You're no fun,' he grumbled. 'But you won't deny me Camilla's company. I have to have someone to listen to me.'

And a flustered but flattered Camilla had accepted his offer of lunch at The Ivy.

On reflection Judith decided it must have been Camilla who had told Van about her new apartment and the terrace that now housed his present and thought no more of it, relieved such a simple explanation had presented itself.

Some time, she decided, watching Camilla begin to remove the glasses and gently encourage the Premier staff back into their own domains, she would get to the bottom of it. Time. There was simply not enough of it to absorb the amount she had to do, and even if Gray had phoned to take up her agreement to dinner, it would have been difficult to fit into such a schedule. Difficult? Knock it off, she reprimanded herself. But as he didn't phone it wasn't a problem she was asked to deal with. But it still occupied a lot of her time just thinking about it.

Once Van was established, she had suggested that Clark take over the day-to-day business of looking after his account.

'I'd keep an overall eye on what's going on, Clark would discuss everything with me, so it wouldn't be as though you were losing sight of me.'

He had shaken his head. 'Sorry, Jude, I work only with the top. My company spend that kind of money knowing they've got the best person on the case. 'Fraid it's a non-starter.'

'Of course,' she'd said politely, not attempting to argue further. Privately she wondered if she cut out two more hours' sleep, got to the office at seven, she could handle all of this more successfully.

Van's progress in London was gaining ground. Judith had worked tirelessly to effect introductions to the right people. He had invited John Imber to lunch, who had in turn invited Van to play a round or two of golf. Bill Jefferson had invited him to drinks in the boardroom. Spencer had arranged for him to tour the state-of-the-art laboratories of a chemical company whose chairman was a friend of his.

Marjorie Fulton phoned Judith to ask her to a dinner party that was as powerful as it was impressive, to welcome an Australian diplomat to London.

Van told her that the Australian was someone whose name was heard a lot at board meetings in the States. It would be great if he had the opportunity to meet him. Judith rang Marjorie, knowing full well she would be only too happy to include Van in her plans.

'For you, my dear, no problem. Sweet man. Of course it will mean finding an extra woman . . . I know. Becky will just have to join us.'

Judith solemnly agreed it was the only course left open to her.

As she had suspected, Gray Hamilton was among the guests, the first time Judith had seen him since they had had dinner with Steven and Mary. Being a close friend of the Fultons, she had suspected he might be here. This time he was without the beautiful Lisa, and although his greeting to Judith had been pleasant accompanied by a polite enquiry after her business life, she had not missed his indifference to Van. After which he made no further effort to talk to either of them. Van, however, had enjoyed himself immensely, and informed Judith that they were both joining Marjorie at a charity gala in the near future. Judith felt an irrational wave of annoyance that she was being commandeered in such a way, and made a note to try and introduce Van to a few eligible women who would act as an escort. She really must get her client to distinguish between business and pleasure.

The fact that Gray had seen them together and clearly thought there was more to their relationship annoyed her even more than the fact that he had not phoned her again after that evening with Steven and Mary.

Van seemed to be oblivious to her feelings and it was difficult to know how to make him see the corner he was pushing her into. Premier's fee was paid promptly and Van was not costing her money, yet Judith knew something was unorthodox about this relationship. It was no longer strictly business, was professionally totally ethical and certainly not sexual, but definitely consisted of more than was written in the contract.

Her humour was not helped by a note from Gray a few days later, which she eagerly tore open, recognizing the logo on the envelope, only to find it was a request from Howard to pay for her to visit him in Long Island where he had planned to spend two weeks.

Angrily she scrawled a note back to Gray, saying her views on that subject were unaltered.

'I think I mentioned on two occasions,' she wrote furiously, 'that no offer from Howard is of interest to me and even less when it's done through his lawyer. If I turned down his previous offers, do you really think a first-class ticket to a country I visit frequently under my own steam is a better inducement? I think not.'

The reply she got was three lines from a member of his staff.

'Dear Miss Craven Smith, Mr Hamilton has asked me to say he has passed your letter to Mr Dorfman and any further communication on the subject will be handled by myself. Please don't hesitate to call.' It was signed by a junior partner in the firm.

The humiliation of being dealt with by Gray Hamilton was bad enough. But somehow being passed to a junior member of staff irked her more. In Gray Hamilton's eyes, she was not worthy of higher attention.

But at least Howard was in another country. Van was practically living in her pocket.

*　　*　　*

Judith was suddenly asked to make an unexpected flying visit to New York to meet up with Jacob Frankenheim, who wanted to introduce her to the US board of de Vries and to link up with their Public Relations office – an event which quite naturally got to Howard's ears. He met her very publicly at the airport.

'I am not interested in discussing any offer you may or may not have made to me via your lackey in London,' Judith said coldly, having agreed to let him drive her into Manhattan. 'I don't want the subject raised ever again.'

'Okay,' he said meekly and made absolutely certain that on the one evening during a five-day trip that she had agreed to have dinner with him the subject was not mentioned.

They were photographed entering and leaving The Four Seasons. Fortunately the fact that Judith did not sleep at her hotel that night went unrecorded. Judith blamed months of celibacy. Howard said she knew damn well it was not and, sleepily smiling, watched as she struggled into a pair of his jeans and pulled on one of his sweatshirts, because, as she pointed out, she would attract less attention arriving back at her hotel at eight in the morning dressed like that than if she was still wearing the black crepe cocktail dress she'd had on as she left at eight the previous evening.

After a successful meeting, Jacob Frankenheim, who had been a schoolfriend of Howard's father, told her gruffly that she was the very thing for that wild young man but he would appreciate being told if she was leaving Premier.

In the UK such a high profile for a PR would have been suspect. In the US it simply added to Judith's prestige. In London the *Daily Mail* ran a picture announcing that the romance which had appeared to cool was definitely on and that friends predicted marriage before the end of the year. Camilla rang and told her.

Judith smilingly assured Jacob she was committed to the company but sadly not to Howard. It was just so difficult to persuade the gossip columns there was nothing in it.

To Howard she displayed a very different attitude.

'You might think it amusing to play games,' she said as they met at Isabella's at Columbus Circle for brunch on Sunday,

123

the day she was due to fly home. 'But it nearly cost me a client.'

'Bullshit,' he retorted amiably. 'The one thing that will keep you firmly in his eyesight is if he thinks you'll marry me.'

Once she would have swept out of the restaurant at such an arrogant remark. Now it made her chuckle. One night of sex with Howard had undeniably been fun and could have caused complications but for Judith it had finally resolved something.

'How low can you go?' she asked, swiping the last muffin as he made a snatch for it.

'Oh my God, is that the Pevrocini woman?' he hissed. Judith whirled round in alarm, her eyes sweeping the room for the dreaded gossip.

'Where . . . ?' she demanded urgently, turning back in time to see Howard take a bite into the muffin that seconds before had been on her plate.

'Lower than you think,' he said innocently, ducking as she threw a mock punch at him. 'Anyway, who says you won't?'

'Won't what?'

'Won't marry me in the end?'

'How-ard . . .' she said warningly. But she knew in that moment he was beginning to doubt it and they had slipped over the edge into becoming old friends.

'C'mon, let's walk this off,' he said, signalling for the check.

'You? Walk?' she mocked. 'This I have to see,' and they strolled out into the pale New York sunshine, more relaxed with each other than they had been in the whole of the three years they had known one another and certainly more than for the six months when they had been lovers.

There was a sharp wind as Howard's driver pulled into the kerb and ten minutes later dropped them outside the Plaza. New York in October was a time Judith had always enjoyed; the stifling heat of the summer was over, the freezing days of winter yet to come. What Judith loved about New York was that the people used their town. How many parks in London would be this full on a chilly but sunny autumn morning? She wrapped a long red scarf loosely around her neck and pulled the collar of her jacket around her ears, slipping on some sunglasses against the light, enjoying her last few hours in her favourite city before Howard drove her out to JFK.

'So how's Gray?' he asked as they strolled companionably around the lake. 'Still pining after the beautiful Lisa?'

'No idea,' she said briefly, dropping her arm from his while some small children rollerskated between them. 'Is he?' she echoed as they linked arms again. 'Still pining after her, I mean?' No reason for Howard to know about her dinner with Gray.

Howard shrugged, casually kicking a pile of leaves. 'Who knows? We all pursue the most impossible women. That's half the fun. Except she pursued him at the beginning.'

'How do you know?'

'He was over here for a few weeks, just after they met, and she turned up. Unannounced . . .'

'But surely not unwelcome,' interrupted Judith, not quite buying the idea that someone would travel three thousand miles unless they had been encouraged to believe it was the right thing to do. She nearly said so, but since Howard had done that very thing not long after she had fled back to England, she could hardly say the cases were different. She could hardly say anything at all.

'Not exactly that.' Howard paused, screwing up his eyes against the autumn sun, trying to find the right description. 'More surprised . . . flattered, I guess. No idea really. They were married over here six months later. I was best man.'

Judith looked startled. 'You? Gray never told me that.'

'From what I can gather, you don't give him time to tell you anything. You gave him a rough ride . . .'

She pulled her arm out of his, and he immediately yanked it back again. 'Aw, c'mon. What did you expect? He's my lawyer, I love the guy.'

'I'm not surprised,' she said dryly. 'Not when he does exactly as you ask.'

Howard was puzzled. 'Gray Hamilton? Does exactly what I ask? Get out of here. He does the reverse. God, haven't you got to know him at all?'

Inside Judith felt a small lurch of shock. Got to know him? Why should Howard assume that? And if Gray always did

125

the reverse of what Howard wanted, whose idea was it to treat her like some cheap kept woman?

'Oh, sure, we bump into each other from time to time. But we don't "see" each other, if you get what I mean.'

Howard stopped and pulled her round to face him. 'No, I don't "get what you mean".'

'We don't go out on dates,' she said, startled. 'I see him at dinner parties, that kind of thing. Howard, let go of my arm, you're ruining my jacket. Besides, we're in Central Park and you can get arrested for less.'

He dropped her arm and scowled. 'He just does his own goddamn thing.'

'Howard,' she protested, exasperated, 'what is this? What is Gray not doing for you, apart from stopping me from murdering you from time to time?'

Howard dug his hands into his pockets and they resumed walking. 'Seems crazy now, but when you did your feminist act, I thought it would help me to know you were okay with that insane business deal you had going if he kept an eye on you. You know, dinner occasionally, lunch. Huh. Does what I say? Are you kidding?'

He turned his head and looked at her as they strolled along. He looked at her for a long, long moment, mistaking the sudden quietness for surprise.

'I just wanted you back,' he said simply.

In all the wild, tempestuous time they had been together, the fights and the reconciliations, the accusations and the fury, Judith had always known she was never 'in love' with Howard. It had always eluded her, but the safety of being part of someone had seduced her.

But she knew now for the first time that she did love him. Oh, not in the way he wanted. Not to clear her life of everything to make him the centre of her universe. He was crazy and funny, impossible and spoilt. And, as Annie would have said, a great, if selfish, tumble in the sack. A dear man. And not for the world would she have insulted him by saying such a thing. He would hate it. Instead she took his face between her hands.

'It wouldn't have worked. You know it. I can't handle

people like you. You're larger than life. But you will always be my dearest friend . . .'

'Your what?' He almost howled the words out. 'God, you don't expect me to believe all that crap, do you? Larger than life? Jeee-suz, listen to you,' and he collapsed laughing against a tree and slid down until he was convulsed in a heap on the ground. 'Can't handle people like me,' he gasped between gulps of laughter.

Judith stood staring down at him. Of all the gratitude when she had been trying to let him down gently.

'Howard, get up,' she hissed urgently as a crowd began to gather. 'Stop it, Howard.' She smiled valiantly around at the knot of curious spectators as Howard rolled around, howling with mirth.

'Primal rebirth,' she announced to the crowd. 'It's okay, he's in therapy. That's it, Howard,' she encouraged him loudly, kneeling beside him. 'Big breaths, let it all out.'

Thank God it was New York, she thought as the crowd nodded understandingly and began to melt away.

'H . . . han . . . handle me?' he nearly sobbed. 'You? Oh, my God. Let me tell you, I sometimes get on my knees at night and thank God you left for England . . . all right, all right, don't get mad. But after you turned me down and I came to London and then you wouldn't do the deal . . . I sat one night with Gray, who said the only sane thing in the whole goddamn mess.'

'Really,' she said icily, hugging her knees. 'And that was?'

Howard retrieved his sunglasses from where they had fallen and came to sit beside her, pulling her arm through his and taking her hand in both of his. 'He said I would end up doing time for you. And he was right. You handle me? You just made me so nervous, I used to spend hours before I called you figuring out every argument you could put up about our relationship. I would deliberately not call you for two days, to try and make you miss me. I was on the biggest emotional rollercoaster since my first wife told me she was screwing the attorney who was handling our divorce.

'Gray said, it was a lunatic relationship and he couldn't imagine anyone finding you easy to live with, let alone me.

You see, I need someone to be there for me. I don't want to have to come home second guessing if every remark I make is politically correct, or stifling your ambitions . . . all of that crap.'

'Okay, Howard, I get the picture. But the one thing the fount of wisdom known as Gray Hamilton didn't mention is that I have a family in England and for a little while longer they need me. Political correctness has sod all to do with keeping a family together.'

'Yeah, I know all that stuff. I told him all about Andrew and Alice, and I came up with this plan that you would have your freedom but I would still be a part of your life until you got it all out of your system. I even thought of offering your old man a huge advance on one of his books so that he could pay your sister's school fees instead of you.'

'You didn't tell Gray that, did you?' Judith asked anxiously.

'No, of course not. But if he had just bought the goddamn house, set the account up like I told him to, you would have just had to accept it and you might have come back. But oh no, he had to insist you were asked first. And then I say, keep an eye on her until she comes to her senses, and you tell me you never see him. What the fuck's the guy doing?'

'I think,' said Judith, feeling ridiculously happy, 'he's doing what you said he would do, the reverse of everything you ask of him,' and for no reason at all she gave Howard a big hug in the middle of Central Park in front of everyone milling past, which both delighted and puzzled him. But Judith saw no reason, as they strolled on their way, that she should confide in him that she wished it had been someone else.

Chapter Twelve

Van broke the news to Judith that he was quitting his job about six weeks after she returned to England.

As it happened she saw very little of him during that time. The separate trips he made to the States and a couple of business meetings in Geneva following within days of each other meant that discouraging the idea that was rapidly gaining ground around town that they were an item lost its urgency. In fact the more she thought about it, when she had time of course, the more she was inclined to think that she had been entirely at fault and had become oversensitive.

If Van had tried to seduce her or his feelings were quite obviously in danger of being wounded, it would have been different. But he continued to appear content with simply being in her company, a careful listener, a considerate host, a thoughtful man who understood her ambitions and didn't make her feel guilty if she kept him waiting more than an hour if Premier meetings held her up, and indeed even if she had to ring at the last minute and cancel altogether.

'Poor you,' he would sympathize. 'Why don't I drop by and drive you home?' Sometimes he would simply be waiting for her in his car when she emerged from a darkened Premier office and, while she was sometimes aware that she was doing little to discourage him, she had to admit it was comforting having someone there at the end of a very long, often fraught day just to unload to.

In fact, the perfect friend.

Such perfection could sometimes, of course, be mildly irritating. That was only natural, she argued with herself. But such moments lasted only long enough to make her feel a heel to have even allowed the thought to arise.

Van had become a frequent visitor to her apartment and beyond making sure that evenings with him were also shared with close friends such as Carey, Rosie or Libby, reserving solo outings for what were quite obviously business commitments, she let go of her worries.

Her guidance had made Van's professional life an obvious success and since his commitment to London was nearing its end, she was unprepared for the shocking news on his return from New York that he had severed links with his companies and was planning to set up on his own in England.

His announcement abruptly put paid to Judith's plans, which had been to enjoy a rare evening just crashing out on her own and to consider whether she should accept Gray Hamilton's invitation to dinner. So, okay, it wasn't out of the blue and Libby had really made it impossible for him not to ask her. So what was the big deal?

Judith's plan for de Vries to sponsor a glittering charity ball culminating in a fashion show rather than the usual cabaret and auction as the central attraction, with all proceeds going to ChildLife, had been gleefully accepted by Libby.

But by the time Jacob Frankenheim's wife had been congratulated by half a dozen of her friends on de Vries's understanding how the excesses of the Eighties were over and the nurturing Nineties were absolutely right, and were already planning what to wear to be introduced to the Duke and Duchess who had agreed to grace the occasion, Stella Frankenheim was perfectly happy to let everyone believe that she had been the one to urge her husband to agree to Judith's plans in the first place. Judith breathed a sigh of relief. Libby, who was ecstatic at the kind of money and coverage that ChildLife would get, readily invited Stella Frankenheim onto the organizing committee.

The amount of work the project was generating was formidable. But Judith saw no point in relaunching de Vries with anything less than something by which all other charity events would in the future be measured. De Vries had the money, ChildLife needed the cash. Stella Frankenheim had a contact book to die for and Libby Westhope enough integrity and an established reputation which the wives of the many captains of industry invited to donate to the fund via the ball would find useful.

Stella Frankenheim, too rich to notice the cost, so vain she firmly believed such an event would not be possible without her personal support, too powerful to care what anyone thought anyway, rapidly became the scourge of both Judith and Libby's lives.

'God, she's a monster,' Libby told Judith over the phone. 'But she will sell every one of those tickets. Did you know Lisa Hamilton is on the committee too?'

Judith didn't.

'Something Gray asked Bill Jefferson to fix with Stella.' Libby sailed blithely on, oblivious to the silence at the end of the phone. 'Anything to keep her happy, I suppose. Which reminds me. I want a favour of you . . . Jude? Are you there? . . . Jude?'

The dusk of the early December afternoon had already descended on Judith's office. She reached out and switched on the lamp. Ridiculous woman, she chided herself. What was it to her if he was still involved with Lisa? Getting over someone took time. Gray was the same as anyone else. That is, if he was trying.

'Sorry, Libby,' she lied. 'Someone wanted to attract my attention. Yes, you're right, anything to keep her happy. What's the favour?'

'Well, Lisa thinks Gray should be roped in to protect Child-Life's interests in all this – you know how tough the Charity Commission are about making sure every penny goes in the right direction.'

'So what's the favour?'

'Oh, I said you would fill him in and because it was in your own time, he should at least buy you dinner.'

Dear God.

'That won't be necessary,' Judith said quickly. 'I can do it over the phone . . . fax him. A report, anything. No need to trouble him.'

'Must dash,' said Libby. 'People waiting. Don't be daft. Good-looking bloke, not out to pounce. Better than Va . . .'

'Lib-by,' Judith said warningly. 'Don't you go buying that story. Van's a client.'

'So he is,' agreed Libby cheerfully. 'I forgot.'

'And Gray Hamilton is still wrapped up with his ex-wife, you forgot that too.'

'Did I?' Libby sounded vague. 'Oh, perhaps you're right. Anyway, must dash. He's going to call. I made him promise . . .'

'Lib . . .' But she was gone.

Half a dozen times during meetings that day Judith found herself with her mind on anything but the business in hand.

Gray was a strange man, attractive when he cared to be, but at the same time she wasn't sure she wanted to spend too much time with Howard's lawyer. Or anyone come to that. Premier had become her companion, her apartment her haven.

He might not even call.

By the time she left Premier at just after seven thirty he hadn't, and she read that as a sign that he too was silently cursing Libby for rail-roading him into a dinner date he could have done without. Who could blame him? First Howard pushing him to invite her out and now Libby. Honestly, her friends.

On cold December evenings such as this after a gruelling day she craved nothing more than to close her own front door behind her, call Laura for a gossip, catch up with Alice and her father and maybe beans on toast in front of some trashy film on television. Perfect.

She was planning to take off for York a couple of days before Christmas, combining a well-earned break with the festive holiday and, as the tube rumbled through Gloucester Road and halted at High Street Ken, her mind was dwelling pleasantly on the prospect of long rambles with her father and Alice and certainly their annual walk on the moors on Christmas Day, leaving Laura to rule supreme in the kitchen.

Kensington High Street was already well cranked up into Christmas mode. Coloured lights and flurries of snow in shop windows vied with each other for shoppers' attention but were usurped by two competing Father Christmases on opposite sides of the street. The strains of 'We Wish You a Merry Christmas' issuing from an amplifier on the corner of Church Street drifted faintly on the night air through the roar of the traffic.

For the fifth time that week Judith resolved to do something about presents and maybe even get a small Christmassy 'something' for Gray, as a humorous offering. Should he call. Premier would be giving all their male contacts an extravagantly wrapped gift from Masters and the women would be receiving a small plain silver bar brooch in one of de Vries's distinctive white-and-scarlet trimmed gift boxes. Of course Gray wasn't a client, but he was ... Go on, a small voice asked accusingly. He's what?

A light drizzle was being whipped around by a cold wind as Judith dodged late-night shoppers heading towards the tree-lined side street that led to the haven of her apartment. The pavements were already wet enough to reflect the lights from the street lamps and at nearly eight o'clock both sides of the road were filled with parked cars. She bent her head against a gust of wind, digging into her pocket for her keys, oblivious to anything but reaching the double glass doors of her apartment block.

Dimly she was aware of a car door opening and slamming behind her as she hurried past. Footsteps followed her into the entrance. For a moment she froze as she felt rather than saw the figure of a tall man closing in.

'Hi,' came a muffled voice as she spun round, turning to push the door open with her back.

Shock and fright kept her immobile for a few seconds.

'Van,' she exclaimed angrily. 'You frightened the life out of me. I thought you ... I mean, I wasn't expecting you ...'

'I know,' he said, kissing her swiftly on the cheek. 'You were caught up when I rang. Camilla said you were going straight home. Can I talk to you for a minute?'

'Of course,' she said readily, trying not to care that her longed-for solitary evening was not to be and planning to throttle Camilla for not warning her. 'C'mon up. I'm drenched. Here, hold this lot while I unlock the door.'

It was only when she had deposited her case, kicked off her wet shoes and returned to the drawing room with an opened bottle of wine, two glasses and a towel draped around her neck with which to dry her hair that he told her he had resigned.

Resigned? Judith thought he was joking, but in the same moment realized he wasn't.

Gradually she lowered the towel and gazed at Van in disbelief.

'Resigned? But Van, why? What's gone wrong?'

Slowly she sat down on a small footstool opposite him, her mouth still slightly open at such startling news.

'Oh, not a lot. Nothing desperate,' he said, giving her a rueful grin, running a hand distractedly through his hair. 'One minute you're up there and it's all working and the next you can't take another day of making money for someone else. You know how it is, you've done it yourself.'

Judith knew she had done no such thing. Nor could she remember ever having given Van the impression that she had. Their circumstances were wildly different. After all, Van had no family to support. Their only common link was that both were unmarried, but she *did* have a family to support and could never have had the luxury of simply abandoning one job when it became boring or stressful.

Premier had been waiting in England. Otherwise she would have hung on in New York. She would have had no option.

It flickered across her mind that maybe he had been made redundant, but he seemed to read her mind and she blushed, rushing to explain that it had once happened to her and it hadn't been the end of the world. In fact it had focused her mind very much on what she wanted out of life.

'Nothing like that.' He reached down and kicked his shoes off, stretched his legs out comfortably before him and yawned. Judith was torn between relief that he didn't seem to be over-concerned and bewilderment that he had given no hint of his dissatisfaction with his employers at any time during the previous few months.

It wasn't that she expected him to confide company secrets, but his whole demeanour had been that of a man riding the crest of a wave, in a job that both stimulated and interested him. Not a word. Not a single clue. The whole thing was so sudden. And it didn't make sense.

'But why now? Did something happen in New York?'

'Well, yes and no. I was getting a bit out of touch with

the office and decided to go over. I was just concerned that developments over there that should have been well under way were a bit slow getting off the ground and I went to check out the plot.'

'You mean a kind of promotion?' Judith felt that some-where along the line it was she who had lost the plot.

'Yeah, I guess you could call it that. Anyway, let's just say London suits me better for a while.'

'What will you do? I mean, have you made any plans?'

'Don't look so worried,' he soothed. 'These things have a wonderful way of working themselves out. I'll take a week or two to have a break and then start looking for an apartment and thanks to you,' he smiled, stretching out a foot to rub it gently against her knee, 'I have made some wonderful contacts over here.'

Ridiculous to feel it was anything more than a friendly gesture. Then why did she feel so uncomfortable?

'So,' he yawned. 'Who knows what might happen?'

Judith was puzzled. She had always assumed that once Van's tour of the UK was over he would go back home to New York. She couldn't keep the surprise out of her voice.

'You're going to stay here?'

'Why not?' he said easily, picking up the bottle of wine and refilling their glasses. Judith felt a faint sense of unease. If it had been Carey or Piers she wouldn't have noticed. With Howard she wouldn't have given it a second thought. But Van made that simple action seem more familiar than she cared for.

More important to her, but not something that she felt she could raise with him right then, she had to think of Premier. Was this the end of the account and, if not, would they be sending someone else over in his place?

Van didn't seem inclined to want to discuss the company any more. Judith remembered how she had felt when the magazine she had once worked for had let her go. Maybe, like her, Van was putting a brave face on things. Maybe he had been forced to resign. All at once she felt sorry for him and abandoned her own concerns in the greater interest of making Van feel he was among friends.

'Look, why don't I call up Carey and one or two others and let's go and celebrate the beginning of your new life,' she suggested, eagerly jumping to her feet and reaching for the phone.

Van looked contented. 'Great idea, but nothing too extravagant. I'm not a corporate man now.'

Judith felt a rush of sympathy. 'Hey, listen,' she said, reaching over and squeezing his hand. 'You've got friends, remember? This one's on me.'

The phone rang as she went into the kitchen to call Rosie, leaving Van zapping channels on the TV and sipping wine.

'Bad moment?' asked Gray.

'No, no. Of course not,' she said, and for an inexplicable reason pulled the towel off her head, trying to push her unruly hair into some sort of order.

'Will you have dinner with me?'

No preamble, straight to the point. Heavens, is this what all lawyers are like?

'Er . . . sure. Yes, I mean this is about Libby, um . . . Child-Life, you know, the charity? I heard your wife, I mean ex, that is Lisa . . . mentioned to Mrs Frankenheim . . .'

'God, you don't want all of them along, do you?' he cut in. 'I meant me and you and possibly a waiter hovering, but if you would prefer more people, naturally you only have to say . . .'

She was laughing. 'Don't be silly, you know perfectly well what I meant. And yes, dinner sounds a good idea.'

'I'll pick you up tomorrow. Eight o'clock?'

Tomorrow she and Carey had arranged theatre tickets and then supper. Damn the man, assuming she would be free, just like that.

She took a deep breath.

'Look forward to it,' she said and replaced the phone.

'Something nice?' Van's voice from the kitchen doorway startled her. She'd thought he was in the drawing room. How long had he been standing there?

'Business,' she said briefly. 'But yes, nice too. Van, would you excuse me? I just have to call Carey.'

'Go right ahead,' he said, swinging himself onto a kitchen

stool and flicking open the evening paper. 'Do you fancy a movie? There's nothing on TV.'

Judith looked startled. Since when could Van command that kind of familiarity?

'Maybe,' she said, despising herself for her weakness in not seizing the opportunity to put the situation straight, but she really had been caught on the hop. 'Let me just call Carey.'

Van remained seated within earshot while she explained the situation to her friend about the following evening.

'Gray Hamilton, eh? Sure, this is business . . . all right, all right, I was just joking. No problem,' he said easily. 'I'll ask Rosie and Piers if they want them and we can go another night.'

'Lovely man,' she said gratefully. 'By the way, are you doing anything right now? Only Van's just resigned his job and I thought we might take him out to supper? You can? Great. Half an hour, then. We'll meet you there.'

Since Van had overheard every word it wasn't necessary to repeat the details and he smiled his approval.

'Great guy,' he said. 'Howard doesn't object to you seeing other men other than for business?'

Judith stood very still.

'Van, please don't take this the wrong way,' she began slowly and carefully, making no attempt to mince her words. 'I never discuss Howard with anyone except my very closest friends and even then only on a limited level . . .' She got no further.

'Oh God, Jude, sorry, sorry, sorry. It just slipped out. None of my business. But I would have to be blind and deaf not to know about you two.'

'Know what?'

'Oh, c'mon. Know you have something going between you. You can't seriously believe I wouldn't have tried to cut him out, if I'd thought you weren't involved. I saw all that stuff in the papers when I was over there . . .'

This was ludicrous.

'As I said, Van, I don't discuss Howard and I'm free to see who I like in London, socially or professionally.'

'Sure, I know that. I just never know which is which. Carey

is social, but I don't think you find him attractive, but that guy Hamilton . . .'

'Van,' she exploded. 'Please stop this. Carey is one of my oldest and closest friends and for the record I think he is very attractive. Gray is Howard's lawyer. So can we drop this? Please. I don't mean to sound abrupt, I'm just not into discussing my friends in this way.'

To her surprise, far from being offended, he apologized.

'You're right. It's probably why I like you. You're so discreet. C'mon, let's go and find Carey.'

Over supper and a glass or two of wine, Van did much to restore himself to Judith's favour. Even when he mentioned what good reviews the play that Carey and Judith were going to see had got, and Carey said, why didn't he go with him now that Judith couldn't, he was suitably appreciative, which she was sure was genuine.

What wasn't genuine was his claim that the only reason he hadn't tried to make a move where she was concerned, was his belief that she was tied up with Howard. As she sat removing her make-up later that evening, after much mental debate she was sure of two things.

The first was that, almost without a doubt, Van was at the very least bi-sexual. The second, more worrying, was that she was looking forward to dinner with Gray Hamilton more than she knew was good for her.

Chapter Thirteen

Hopeless. Completely mad. That's what you are, Judith told her reflection the morning after she had had dinner with Gray. He doesn't agree with a single thing you say. You have no chance of changing his mind once it's made up. His wife knew what she was doing when she left him and no-one in their right mind would agree to see him again.

Had she?

There was no immediate answer to that. Except she had a hangover that had nothing to do with drink. And all day she had tried to pretend that she didn't care every time a call was put through that wasn't the one she was expecting. Not that he'd said he'd ring. But what man did these days?

Van had called. Judith signalled to Camilla to say she was out and although she noticed the surprise on the other woman's face she was too absorbed with her own problems to take too much notice.

'You mustn't neglect him just because he's no longer a client,' Camilla said reproachfully when she had to put him off yet again. That time it was genuine. Judith had taken both Clark and Annie out to a working lunch to discuss the Child-Life fashion show.

Alice at her most unreasonable was less work. Both account executives could see the kudos of being involved in what would arguably be the social event of the year, but neither wanted the task of staging it by persuading the great and the good to donate much of the structure of the show for nothing.

'We'll never be in a better position to do it than now,' Judith insisted with a weariness that was totally lost on both of them. 'I promise you. We did this in New York for a charity that Howard Dorfman sponsored. Believe me, more people giving smaller amounts is easier. Now, let's just accept that and work out a strategy for raising that kind of interest. No, no wine, Clark, just mineral water.'

At four o'clock she took Van's call. 'Hi, I was beginning to think you were avoiding me.'

There was too much truth in what he said for her not to blush. She swung round so that Camilla would not see her face.

'Van, I'm sorry. How was last night? Did you enjoy the show?'

'Terrific,' he enthused. 'Carey's a great guy. We went to a club afterwards so we're feeling . . . I mean I'm feeling a little the worse for an ouzo or two. Hey, listen, Jude, can I talk to you? No, not now. I'll pick you up from the office and drive you home, we can talk on the way. If you're feeling like me you'll want an early night.'

Carey. It had to be about Carey. She groaned. If her suspicions were correct, this was one conversation she didn't want. Maybe Carey was the reason he had wanted to stay in London – all conjecture of course, but Van sounded different. This was no casual conversation coming up, but at least he wasn't planning to spend the whole evening at her apartment. So she forced a friendly note into her voice and agreed.

'Sure, Van, no problem. In fact a lift would be welcome.' And she thought a little reality around here wouldn't come amiss. Gray Hamilton was someone she should never even have contemplated getting involved with. But then last night had changed all that.

The small French restaurant he had chosen, within walking distance of her apartment, was crowded, bustling and casual. Clearly it placed more emphasis on service and food than plush surroundings and, having decided that her nerves would prevent her eating a single thing, Judith found herself sampling almost everything that was put before her.

Gray had arrived at her apartment looking similarly relaxed and low-key, wearing a plain navy crew-neck sweater, which she thought must be cashmere, under a dark grey wool jacket that she knew came from Masters and justified its expensive price tag if only for the cut, which was faultless. She thought twice about telling him he looked incredibly sexy, deciding it would confirm his suspicion that she thought of nothing else. And anyway what was the matter with her?

It was a sharp, cold evening with more than a hint of frost and while Judith wasn't keen on arriving anywhere with a shiny nose and windblown hair, she was less keen on appearing a wimp. Besides, he made no attempt to offer to drive her there. Gamely she pulled the collar of her coat around her neck and, exchanging pleasantries on the neighbourhood, the parking problems and debating which of the two Father Christmases was the fake, together they strolled to the restaurant.

All she knew was that she had spent the evening dining with a man who alternately made her almost cry laughing and then outraged her with his opinions – someone who had raised more questions than he'd answered.

One minute he was almost unbearably kind and thoughtful, just letting her talk about Laura and her concern that she was getting too old to have charge of Alice, even though it was only during the holidays; the next, he was dismissive when she told him how Van was now jobless and she would have to try and help him.

'Why?'

'Because he's a friend.'

'Take my advice. Save your energies for things that matter. Laura, your sister.'

She was stung by his abruptness.

'I would but I can't afford it.'

'What?'

'Your advice,' she said lightly. 'You're an expensive lawyer, remember?'

'It was free.'

Judith inclined her head in mock thanks. 'I still can't accept it. I do put my family first, always, every time. But friends need help. He's a bright guy. It won't take him long to decide what he wants to do, and I think it's great that he had the courage to get off a track that was taking him nowhere and explore new areas.'

'You sound like a travel brochure and he sounds like a man who is prepared to drift in the wake of someone else's success.'

Judith felt triumphant. 'And what is wrong with a man doing that, when it's okay for women?'

'Depends on whose wake they're trailing in. If you're married or have a relationship, you work these things out between you. It doesn't matter a damn whether it's correct or not. If it makes the two people involved happy, that's it. But then I'm being presumptuous, perhaps you and Mr Kingsley have worked that one out.'

'Don't be ridiculous,' said Judith crossly. 'Van is a friend and he isn't following in my wake or anyone else's. I'm surprised at you taking that view. You seem to think he can't be ambitious or serious about work, because he's having a rethink. Van's ambitions are obviously more tied up with the quality of life, rather than scaling an unfulfilling corporate ladder.'

'And presumably you're now going to guide him through this as you did his corporate existence.'

Judith groaned and pushed back her chair in exasperation. 'You simply aren't prepared to understand, are you?'

Gray shrugged. 'If there was any reality in it, I might be. Life isn't like that. You have all these bizarre ideas about relationships and walking on the beach and you talk about "quality" as though the rest of us have deliberately sacrificed it.

'So if that is true, you could have had a great deal more quality in your life if you had accepted Howard's offer. You could still have had Premier or something like it, but when you closed the door at night, you would have had the luxury of not having to worry about where the next penny is coming from. So why didn't you?'

She had been startled into listening to him in silence. It was so blindingly obvious to her why she couldn't do such a thing that she shook her head helplessly, totally puzzled that he should even question it.

'Because I'm not in love with him. I couldn't love someone who wants me to be something I'm not.'

The waiter cleared their plates. Judith had not meant to discuss Howard with Gray. She wouldn't with Van. But Gray was different. Why she couldn't say, but she desperately didn't want another relationship that was shrouded in confusion about where she was coming from.

Relationship? Hell. To all intents and purposes, this man was still married. The coffee was set down and with it she changed the subject.

'Do you like all things French?'

'What? No, not all. Why?' He had been frowning, miles away.

'Because this,' she said, indicating the restaurant as she poured coffee for both of them, 'is clearly a favourite restaurant of yours. You speak French and your house is . . .' She didn't finish the sentence. But he did, easily, giving her plenty of time to recover from the slip.

'Full of stuff from Provence. But it's also very American in its influence. I like both. But that's because my mother is French. A lot of my work is bound up in one and we . . . I try and holiday in the other.'

It was Judith who put an end to skipping around Lisa's name; it was silly to pretend she didn't exist. 'It must be tough,' she said, 'going through a divorce. No matter what the reasons. And don't give me that bullshit about it being easier for the one who brings the case. Any relationship that breaks up has got to be painful. Hasn't it?'

She made sure that her tone was practical. Gray wasn't a man to be drawn into emotional soul-baring. And besides why should he? He really didn't know her all that well.

He gazed silently into his glass and then lifted his eyes to look at her. She gazed steadily back.

'Yes,' he said simply. 'Very painful. I'm not sure that you ever do get over it. You can divorce someone, but that's a piece of paper. It's the rest that is so unexpected. Selling a home, starting again.'

'Are you selling your house? It's so pretty.'

He looked puzzled. 'Selling? No, this is my new house. Lisa's taste is far more ornate.'

'Well,' she said frankly. 'I'll say this for you, you have great taste.'

He smiled at her and to her surprise reached out and gently stroked the side of her face.

143

'Howard is a fool,' he said. 'But I can see why.'

The muscles in her face were immobilized. Such a simple gesture. She tried to smile and succeeded only in swallowing hard.

'Shall we talk about ChildLife,' she said hurriedly, her gaze locked into his.

'ChildLife?' he repeated. 'Oh yes, that.'

On the way home, he took the huge, soft, grey scarf he had knotted loosely around his neck and wound it around hers. 'It's as well I like your perfume,' he smiled, still holding both ends, his face smiling down into hers.

'I'll give you some for Christmas,' she grinned and, laughing, he kissed the tip of her nose and then the smile faded and everything changed.

The wind was whipping leaves and papers along the pavement, swirling around them. A door on the opposite side of the street opened and a laughing, joking crowd piled into a parked jeep and roared off down the road. The street lamp flickered as a flurry of sleet and rain began to fall.

Drops of rain trickled down Judith's face, soaking Gray's hair as he bent his head and kissed her. And because it was cold – what else? – she slipped her arms inside his jacket and they stayed like that, not wanting to move because if they did one of them had to make a decision that neither was ready to make.

Chapter Fourteen

'Well, yes, of course. But I thought you'd be going back to New York for Christmas . . . to your family.'

Van and Judith were driving through the rush-hour traffic when he asked if he could move in for a few days. For a man who claimed he had been on the town until nearly dawn, he wasn't looking too wrecked, but she was certainly feeling it. Which afterwards she realized was the only reason she did not properly think through his request. He did, however, seem nervous, not his usual confident, assured self.

He'd been explaining how the apartment he'd taken a lease on was in a mansion block near Albert Bridge. Nothing fancy, just a couple of rooms with a spare room he could use as an office. Great view of the river. She'd love it and he would really appreciate some help fixing it up.

'Love to, Van,' she yawned. 'You should pick Rosie's brains. She's the design freak.'

He took the next corner a bit too sharply and braked to avoid a car that was turning in front of him.

'Wow,' Judith yelped, clutching her seat belt. 'Don't make me a statistic just yet.'

Really, he was in a bit of a state. She wondered when he was going to get around to what it was he was obviously trying to unload. She didn't have long to wait.

'Sorry, Jude,' he muttered. 'Listen, the problem I have is that I can't move into the flat for a week or so, and, well, the hotel is a little heavy on my wallet, now that I'm not a salaried man.

'I just wondered if I could use your spare room, until you get back from York. You know, just until I can get into the flat? The couple in it had a problem with their plans and can't vacate the place just yet, so you know how it is.'

Judith was so unprepared for his request she found herself saying, sure, okay. Fine.

'And you must let me pay you,' he said, glancing at her as he took the turning leading up to her apartment.

Judith protested. 'Don't be silly, Van. I wouldn't dream of it. It's only for a few days. When do you want to come over?'

'Well, I thought maybe this evening. Tell you what, why don't I collect my cases, pick up a takeaway and then neither of us will have to cook?'

This scenario, she decided, needed slowing down. A guest staying for a few days was one thing. A flatmate she did not need.

'Oh, Van, that is sweet of you. But really all I want is a shower and bed. But you go ahead. I had a working dinner last night, you know how it is?' she finished, with not even enough conviction to fool herself.

Van gave her a sympathetic look. 'Poor you. Personally I can't stand the guy. Too sure of himself. Judgemental, know what I mean?'

Since they pulled up outside her apartment at that moment Judith didn't need to reply. What on earth had he got against Gray? He hardly knew him. Still, Rosie had welcomed her when she came over from New York with nowhere to go; she felt a little ashamed that she didn't want to extend the same welcome to Van. Oh well, it was only for a few days.

'I must get you a key,' she said as she unlocked the door, picking up the mail from the mat, glancing through it. A card from Alice on a school trip to France, which she stuck on the board in her kitchen. Bills. A couple of invitations and a square white envelope, which had been hand-delivered. She didn't recognize the writing.

'Want a drink?' Van asked, helping himself to a Scotch. Normally he only drank wine. She decided he must be feeling nervous.

'Er . . . no,' she said, absently throwing the bundle of letters into a dish. 'Careful . . . you've still got to drive.'

Van looked at the drink in his hand, shrugged. 'It's been quite a day.' He tossed the drink back and, saying he would be about an hour, let himself out of the apartment to go and collect his luggage.

Judith checked the spare room, called Rosie to tell her the

latest developments and took a call from Carey. He sounded about as nervous as Van. What the hell had those two been up to, she thought grimly.

'I tried to reach you a couple of times today but I've been involved in a story and couldn't get you before you left the office.'

'What is it, Carey?'

'Oh, just that Van stayed over last night and mentioned that he was going to suggest moving in with you until he got his flat sorted out and, well, I know you like the guy, but I wasn't sure if it was what you would want ... I don't want to interfere, but I didn't know what to do for the best. In the end I decided to call you.'

There was something odd about all this. The fact that Carey admitted Van had stayed overnight simply made her heart sink. She was touched by his concern but he could have left that message with Camilla.

'Don't worry, it's only for a few days. I'll be up in Yorkshire for Christmas, so we won't get in each other's way. Anyway, did you enjoy last night?'

There was a pause. 'Yes, terrific. Jude?'

'What?'

'Jude ... are you going to be okay there with Van? I mean, you don't feel awkward?'

It was the first time she had even thought about the impending visit from that point of view. Curiously, she was not at all worried about the sex of her house guest, just that at the moment she preferred her own company.

'Oh, Carey, Van isn't remotely interested in me. I think he's more ...' She stopped herself and changed what she was going to say from 'more interested in you' to, 'He's more concerned with not having to pay any more steep hotel bills. After all, he's sort of unemployed. But thanks.'

There was a silence. Really Carey was being over-dramatic. 'Honestly, Carey, I'll be fine. Anyway I'm off to York the day after tomorrow and when I get back after Christmas, Van will be practically throwing a house-warming at his new flat. Have you seen it?'

Carey hadn't, and they talked for a few more minutes until

Judith heard the door open as Van returned. He deposited his luggage in the spare room before joining her in the kitchen, where he told her he would be eating out after all.

He'd run into an old friend, he explained as he helped himself to coffee that Judith had brewed in his absence, who might be a good contact.

'For a job?'

He nodded, taking a gulp of coffee. 'I have a couple of ideas about starting up on my own . . . sort of an agency.'

This was new ground to Judith. 'What sort?' She was genuinely interested.

Van was vague. He'd tell her when he knew more, got the details worked out. She understood.

'I'll just take a quick shower and change. What are you going to do?'

'I'm not sure,' she answered, looking absently around. 'Tackle some of that post. Which reminds me . . . I wonder who that note was from?'

She sifted through the pile of envelopes until she found it, slit the envelope open and read the enclosed note twice, the second time turning her back slightly away so that Van would not see her face. Sliding off the stool, she walked down the passage to her bedroom and closed the door, leaving Van staring curiously after her. Sitting on the edge of her bed, she noticed her hands were not quite steady.

The thick white card said nothing about the owner. The handwriting was unfamiliar, but it was as though she had known it for ever even if she couldn't answer the question it asked.

'So what happens next? Happy Christmas, Gray.' What indeed?

Chapter Fifteen

Judith returned to London early in the New Year a day earlier than she had planned. The city was shrouded in a ghostly damp fog that clung to the streets, disguising familiar landmarks, muffling footsteps and the usual roaring clamour of life in the city.

Grey fingers of mist swirled eerily in the headlamps of cars switched full on in the middle of the day. The post-Christmas languor of deserted shops and offices only half-staffed was slowed even further by trains being delayed, buses unable to run and a security alert on three main tube lines which had virtually closed down the network.

Disgruntled passengers vied with each other for the few taxis prepared to struggle into the centre of town in such conditions. Most commuters abandoned their offices at midday and by the time Judith's train, which was two hours late, crawled into Euston, it was nearing four o'clock.

Any thought she might have had to check in at the office before going home was abandoned as she grabbed a trolley to push her luggage up the ramp and out onto the concourse in search of a phone.

Home, to the peace of her flat, to think without Alice or her father asking her what was the matter. Only Laura, watching her granddaughter who she knew better than anyone else in the world, guessed something was genuinely troubling her. In time, Laura knew, Judith would tell her, as she always did in the end. As she had when she'd come back with Alice from Washington after Lizzie had died. So vulnerable, so young and overnight so mature.

Laura paused where she was sitting by the fire and could hardly believe this was once the frightened seventeen-year-old who had insisted on going out to work, defiantly refusing to give in when job after job turned her down for being too young, with no qualifications, no experience.

She couldn't pretend she hadn't colluded with her grand-daughter when they decided to lie about Judith's age. Nor did they tell prospective employers that she lived with her grandmother, who cared for baby Alice, nor that her father, still in Washington, didn't approve of her going out to work.

Of course it looked dreadful. Andrew financed them from a distance, but since Judith had totally defied him by not continuing with her education when she returned home, grief-stricken and for the first time in his life faced with dealing alone with a daughter he really did not know at all, he had simply retreated and let her get on with it.

Who would have thought that five years later he would have cause to be grateful that Judith had defied him, when his heart attack had put paid to his life in Washington. A small army pension did not go far, even in Torfell.

Watching Judith wrapping presents on Christmas Eve and helping Alice trim the tree, Laura wasn't fooled by the ready smile and willingness to join in. She could wait, Judith wasn't ready yet. Give her time.

Alice had had a lousy school report. But then Judith had virtually been expelled from her school. She'd been a little older, of course, but talk about peas in a pod. Laura's gaze rested on Alice. In heaven's name, no fashion magazine in the world could have advocated what the irrepressible fourteen-year-old was wearing. Surely torn pink velvet over black leggings and boots was a mistake? Perhaps after a few shampoos those scarlet streaks in her hair would wash out? Both girls were exactly the same as Lizzie. They'd have to tell Alice, of course. But no point, yet. Plenty of time when she was older. That's what Lizzie would have advised.

Poor darling Lizzie. Those dreadful stories in Washington. Andrew's own fault, she decided, seeing her bewildered son-in-law trying to mend the fairy lights. Laughing as Alice with a sigh and exasperated, 'Dad-dy, you are hopeless,' took them from him and located the rogue bulb in seconds.

So stiff, that was his trouble. So conscious of reputations and such a horror of scandal. How on earth did Lizzie ever marry him? And what a pity he had never married again. Janey Woolcross would soon run out of patience if he didn't make up his mind. Money, he told her mournfully, how could he ask someone to marry him if he couldn't afford to keep his own family in the way he would have preferred let alone another one.

Laura privately thought Janey Woolcross was only too aware of the situation and since she was deeply fond of Judith and Alice, she would have willingly removed one financial burden from Judith's back. As she said to Laura only the other day, one day Judith would marry and then what?

But then would she? Silly girl still stubbornly believed she came with too much emotional debris. Who would want to take on her family as well? Laura thought it a great pity that Judith spent her life running away rather than pausing to find out.

Mind you, discreetly studying her granddaughter who was pretending to be engrossed in a book, not one page of which she had turned in nearly half an hour, Laura had to admit it would need to be someone special. Meanwhile there was Christmas to think about.

Judith found a phone box and called her apartment. The machine flicked on, as it had done all day yesterday. She was relieved that Van had obviously moved out, although she had left a couple of messages for him to call her and one to say she was coming home. He might have told her, she thought, but in the rush of moving he must have just assumed she would realize. He had said it would be straight after Christmas.

At the last minute, feeling a pang of guilt, she had suggested he join her in Yorkshire. But he had declined, saying if he needed company Carey would be back within a couple of days and the Fultons had invited him for drinks on Boxing Day. Besides, he had a mountain of paperwork to get through for this new idea of his, on which he still refused to elaborate. Judith's empty apartment was just what he needed. So he had waved her off, complete with a festively tied box which contained a Georgina Von Etzdorf scarf and she in turn had given him a black leather filofax. For his new life, she had explained, giving him a quick kiss on the cheek.

Replacing the phone she scooped fifty pence out of her bag and rang Premier, to find only a handful of staff, including Clark and Beth, still there. Camilla had been in earlier but by mid-afternoon the silent phones and the beginning of flu had driven her back home again. Spencer was still away in France, and Annie and Marcel would not be flying back from Marrakech until the next day.

'Go home, Beth,' urged Judith. 'This fog's a nightmare. Switch the answer machine on. I honestly can't imagine anyone will be calling now. Any messages for me?'

The last was said in what she hoped was a brisk, noncommittal voice, when what she really wanted to scream was, 'Has he phoned?'

Beth reeled off a list of messages, none of which needed immediate attention. 'Rosie rang and said she would call you tonight. Let me see . . . Carey Templeton . . . what did he say? Oh, yes. Call him before you go home. But that's when he thought you were coming into the office. What else? Libby Westhope says Mrs Frankenheim wants an urgent meeting with you. The *Guardian* and the *Independent* want interviews with Farley. Henry de Sholto wanted your home address to send you an invitation to his party.'

Judith, squashed into a small kiosk with one hand clasped over her ear to block out the noise of train arrivals, thought she must have imagined it. 'Henry? You're kidding? Oh ho, he's fallen out with Rik, I know he has,' she said gleefully. 'Don't give it to him, Beth, will you? I won't get any peace at all if he can phone me there. Er . . . anything else?'

'Nothing desperate.'

'I don't suppose Mr Hamilton called . . . about ChildLife,' she added hastily.

'Don't think so,' said Beth slowly, rechecking her list. 'Can't see it. Would you like me to call him?'

'No,' Judith almost screamed down the phone in alarm. 'No, no. I'll do it. Nothing urgent.' Call him? And say what? 'I can't think of anything else, until I know what "What next?" means. I have this silly breathless feeling, and would you please tell me what's happening to my brain?' Good grief, impossible.

Perhaps, she thought more rationally, he's left a message at the flat. Immediately she started to feel better. So instead she said, 'Beth, I'm going to go straight home, if I can find a taxi or a tube that's working. If Clark has anything urgent tell him to call me there, and you get off now. It will take you ages to get home as it is. See you tomorrow.'

Damn.

Slinging her bag across her body like a satchel, Judith picked up her case and lugged it across the forecourt where she willingly negotiated to share a cab with two complete strangers to Kensington.

Never had she been more relieved to get home. She turned the key in the door and pushed her suitcase ahead of her into the hall, and there to her surprise was Van, phone in one hand, glass of wine in the other.

He wheeled around as she came in and casually blew her a kiss, raising his glass in silent greeting. He appeared to be talking to a business contact, so she just mouthed 'Hi' and walked past him, glancing as discreetly as she could into the spare room as she passed and into the kitchen where she switched on the percolator. The flat was warm so he couldn't have been out. So why didn't he answer the phone?

There was no sign of Van moving out. His belongings seemed to be everywhere. She heard him wind up his conversation and forced a smile when he strolled into the kitchen.

'I didn't think you were here any more,' she said, turning her cheek to accept his kiss. 'How's the new flat?'

Van spread his hands in a helpless gesture and groaned. 'You wouldn't believe what's happened. They pulled out of the deal. It was such a shock.'

Judith looked at him in dismay. What a bummer for Van. But even as she voiced her sympathy, it flashed through her mind that he had nowhere to live except here. Oh hell.

She was right.

'I've been out all day looking at apartments, and yesterday,' he said, pressing his eyes with his fingers and dragging them slowly down his face in an exhausted gesture.

'Today?' Judith repeated. 'How have you managed to get around in this fog?'

'Nightmare,' he agreed. 'Took tubes most of the time. I finally gave up but it took me nearly an hour to get back. Traffic's awful.'

She knew he was lying but the sheer embarrassment of challenging him was too much for her. So she let it go. And if he really had been out, how many other days had he done so and left the heat on full blast? God, the bills.

Van poured coffee for both of them, rummaging in cupboards and drawers for mugs and spoons with a familiarity Judith didn't feel comfortable with. Rosie could find her way around this apartment blindfolded, Carey too, and she didn't give that another thought. Why did it bother her with Van?

'So what are you going to do?' she asked, sipping her drink as she leaned against the draining board, dreading the answer.

'Well, keep looking. The estate agents say there isn't a lot around at the moment, but straight after Christmas, the market shifts a bit. Fingers crossed.'

It amazed Judith that the subject of him continuing to live with her didn't seem to occur to him. He just took it for granted.

'So how long will you be staying?' she asked, refilling her cup. 'I was hoping to have Alice down before she goes back to school, you know, see a concert, a movie. Just let her loose in London, she's crazy about the place. But I only have the one spare room.' She said it lightly, almost playfully, hoping he would take the hint.

Van looked at her without comment.

'How old is Alice now?' he asked, frowning as though something had just occurred to him.

Judith paused. 'Fourteen. Why?'

'Oh, just wondered. That's quite a gap in age between you, isn't it?' he said, looking directly at her. The question wasn't even casual, it was probing.

She turned away and began to stack the empty mugs in the

dishwasher, wiping the surface next to the sink. She never discussed Alice or her family with anyone.

'Not particularly.'

'An afterthought, was she? Who was it told me?' He shook his head as though trying to remember. 'Oh I know, it was something I read . . . oh, way back when your father had a book published. Now what was it . . . ?'

Judith slowly sat down and looked squarely at him. That was as far as she was going with this conversation. She knew the interview he was referring to, in *The Times* just after his first book was published. It had mentioned his wife's death in Washington so soon after Alice's birth and how she had not lived to see the publication.

Not a subject that was anyone's business now except hers, her father's and Alice's. Only someone who was prepared to go to a newspaper cuttings file would have seen the very few interviews and even rarer reviews that Andrew Craven Smith merited.

'Van,' she said slowly, quietly. 'My mother died when Alice was just a few months old. She had cancer. We didn't know. It was all over in a few weeks. That time was painful for me and . . . and for my family. I just don't talk about it to anyone. I'm sure you understand.'

He shrugged. 'I'm sorry. It was just something Carey said . . .'

Intuition warned her not to take the conversation any further. Carey? Why would he draw Van's attention to that file? Just how pally had those two become?

'So,' she smiled, deliberately changing the conversation and the mood. 'What are your plans?'

'Well, I guess I'll have to impose on you for a week or two, maybe not even as long as that,' he said, following her into the drawing room where he flopped into an armchair and stretched out his legs, crossing one ankle over the other.

What else could she do, but say okay, fine, no problem?

'Any luck with a job?' she asked, moving around the room emptying ashtrays, picking up piles of days'-old newspapers, discarded nutshells and ferrying a bowl of decaying fruit into the kitchen.

'Well as a matter of fact, yes,' he said as she reappeared.
'Oh? Terrific. Tell me.'

For a moment he just smiled a pleased, almost triumphant smile. 'I'm going to go into public relations,' he said. 'Nothing demanding to start with, but I already have a couple of clients I could really promote. Of course,' he continued with a modesty that wasn't entirely convincing, 'I've learned such a lot just watching you, I reckon I could make a go of it.'

Judith looked at him in amazement. Van. A PR? On his own?

'Well, Van, that's terrific. I mean, if there's anything I can do to help. Where will you work from? Tell me more. Who are you representing?'

He made it all sound so easy. He would use his new flat as an office, work from home. His clients were a young soap star called Shade Morgan and a young actor called Vincent Perrereo.

Judith had never heard of either of them. For a while Van outlined a plan that was at times so weak she couldn't believe he had been so heavily involved in the companies he once represented. However, the worst that could happen was that it would fail. What did worry her was the number of times he introduced her clients' names into the discussion.

'I'm sure I could persuade Farley to rig Vinny out, so that he makes a better impression at auditions,' was one and later, 'All Shade needs is for someone like Annie to show her how to pull her image together . . . or you.'

Judith didn't like it one little bit. Churlish wasn't the word for how she felt when she was finally forced to say as lightly as she could, 'Well, Van, personally I'd be delighted to help with advice on that kind of thing but I don't know about approaching my clients. They can be tricky.'

She thought she saw a flash of annoyance in his eyes, rather like an over-indulged child being denied a treat. But while she was prepared to give him a roof for a few days, that didn't include sharing her clients.

'Yes,' he said thoughtfully. 'Yes. Anyway. It's early days.'

The phone ringing prevented either of them from continuing what was rapidly becoming a difficult conversation.

In spite of the fog, Van told her he would be out that evening, having dinner with some friends who had just flown in from New York. She was surprised that anyone would voluntarily go out on such a night but relieved because it meant she would have the flat to herself. There was a lot to do. The place needed a clean and if Van was staying he could jolly well help, she decided later, as she began putting her clothes away in the closets in her room, running a bath, checking her messages and the post. There was no word from Gray, and the few messages that had been left on the answer machine did not figure him among them.

Howard had called her at Torfell during his Christmas break in Aspen, before he flew off to Tokyo for some meetings. It was strange how she had gone through so many hoops with him and now they gossiped together like the oldest of friends. It won't be long, she grinned to herself, and he'll start asking me for advice on his love life.

Her own was very uncertain. Howard had included Gray's name in the conversation without any hint that Judith was seeing the lawyer in London. Her replies were noncommittal. All she knew was that he would be with Howard in Tokyo for some of the trip and out of the country for the better part of the month.

She had hoped there would be a message when she got back if only because she desperately didn't want to discover that she had read far too much into one kiss. Opening her bag, she felt in the back zip pocket for the plain white card that had arrived after their dinner date.

Why do this if it didn't mean something more than just another pleasant evening? She wished now that she had phoned to say thank you instead of losing her nerve and hastily sending by motorbike messenger a postcard of Renoir's 'Le Café', which she thought would amuse him, and a message which said: 'What next? Well, why don't we both have an especially Happy Christmas? Judith.'

Maybe he did this all the time. What if he hadn't got the card? Suppose he had lost her address and phone number, suppose he was ill?

You, my girl, she said severely, are beginning to sound like one of those neurotic women reeling off the qualifications for a date out of hell. Ill, indeed. She never saw a healthier man. And maybe he had already left for Tokyo?

And maybe you should stop mooning around like a teenager, she admonished herself, with which she carried an armful of laundry into the utility room, switched on the machine and followed it by vigorously hoovering the entire apartment.

Later, she phoned Carey.

The phone was answered by Josh, who greeted her with caution and first of all said Carey wasn't in. But within seconds of Judith replacing the phone, Carey himself phoned back.

'Jude, sorry. Josh thought it might be someone else I didn't particularly want to talk to.'

Judith laughed. 'Honestly, which frenzied fan is trying to molest you? And since when has Josh thought you wouldn't speak to me?'

Carey sounded as though he was forcing the laugh. 'No fans, and Josh misunderstood. Just a contact who's being a bit persistent. Listen, did you have a nice Christmas?'

They chatted on in this fashion for a few minutes exchanging Christmas stories. Carey had stayed in London instead of going down to Suffolk to spend Christmas at his parents' home, as Judith had fully expected.

'Oh, stuff at the studio. This flu bug was laying everyone out so they asked if I could be around. No problem.'

Judith glanced at the clock. It was just after eight and a movie she had thought looked promising was just about to start on television.

'Was there anything special you wanted, Carey? I picked up your message at the office, but I came straight home. Incidentally Van's flat has fallen through, so it looks as though I'm going to have him as a house guest for the next couple of weeks. Did you know?'

'Yes, he told me. I saw him a couple of times over Christmas. He called and we got together for a drink, dinner. No big deal. I just wanted to make sure you were okay.'

'In what way?'

'Oh, you know, you're not sort of . . . well, involved with

him, are you? I mean, I don't want you to get hurt. What I'm trying to say is Howard didn't work out . . .'

'Hey, hang on a minute,' she protested. 'He's only living here for a few more days. I think if he was going to pounce on me, he's had plenty of opportunity in the past. And incidentally, have you heard he's going into the PR business?'

Carey was apologetic and even more confusing.

'Sorry, Jude. Yeah, I did hear. Crazy, eh? Look, just remember if you need to talk or anything, I'm here. Okay?'

Judith was convinced Carey's interest in Van was now stronger than just friendly support for a loner in town. Van was certainly good-looking and, she had to admit, charming. She just personally didn't want a charming man with dropdead good looks sharing her flat. Her taste seemed to be driving her towards men who could be anything but charming.

What she didn't want was for Carey to get hurt. Curiously she wasn't concerned about Van's feelings at all.

'What makes you think he's interested in me?' she said, reaching over and switching on the TV, flicking channels to find the movie she wanted.

'Well, why shouldn't he be?' Carey sounded defensive. 'You're great looking, terrific company . . .'

'Ca-rey,' she protested, laughing at his earnest voice. 'Is this a proposal?'

Carey sounded tired and his laugh was half-hearted, embarrassed. 'Don't be silly. I just wanted to make sure you were okay, that's all.'

'I'm fine,' she said, touched by his concern. 'Listen, I'm now going to watch the man I really do love, Harrison Ford, so I'll call you.'

Frowning, she put down the phone and without taking in what Harrison Ford was saying to Kelly McGillis, sat staring at the screen.

No doubt about it, Van *was* interested in her. But she had the oddest feeling that it had nothing to do with attraction and, now she came to think of it, if Harrison Ford had darker hair flecked with grey and brown eyes he would look very like someone that she wouldn't mind just hearing from, let alone anything else.

Chapter Sixteen

After three weeks, Judith knew she would have to do something about Van. No longer was it just a question of having him in her flat, but without a home of his own he was launching his new career from her address. It was not the kind of career that she cared to be associated with.

Always he was suitably grateful, admired her for being so supportive, repeated over and over how he could not have done any of this without such a good friend. He told his friends so in front of her.

Glowing not so much with pleasure but embarrassment, her planned request for him to leave would die on her lips. Not that she would have admitted it for the world, but the very scenario she had so eagerly promoted to Rosie, to Gray, to anyone who cared to listen, that it was perfectly okay for a man not to earn so much, not to be so usefully connected as a woman for a friendship or a relationship to work, in reality was very different.

Maybe, she thought, if she had been involved with Van on another level, his attempts to launch himself as a PR might not get quite so much on her nerves.

But it was difficult to rewrite views so strongly held, so firmly expressed. She comforted herself that the activity in her flat must mean he was getting somewhere with his new company. Each night she arrived home unable to get into her own kitchen for the completely unknown people sitting around drinking coffee. The drawing room was similarly occupied. She had taken to going straight to her bedroom and shutting the door, which she hoped would be interpreted correctly and the hint taken.

It wasn't. When she would casually enquire how much business he was doing, Van would frighten the life out of her. All day, he claimed, he spent on the phone – which in itself made Judith wince, oh God, the bill – or else flat-hunting. And each evening he would spread his hands helplessly and say that the minute he found the right flat . . .

Judith even got Camilla to make some phone calls to find another apartment for him, but whatever she came up with Van rejected. Too expensive, too small, too far away, too big.

'The only thing he hasn't claimed is it's the wrong colour,' she snarled at Camilla when, after a phone call to Van, she had discovered he had been out at lunch until nearly four, had taken a cursory glance at the flat in question and rejected it. 'And not near enough to his favourite restaurant.'

Camilla looked uncomfortable. 'He is trying, Judith, it's just that it isn't easy for someone without a track record in England to get off the ground. I'm sure he'd like to be independent as well.' This was accompanied by a heightened colour and much fiddling with a pen she was holding, which made Judith wonder just how much sympathy Van had wrung from her.

'Certainly twisted you round his finger,' she remarked as Camilla headed for the door.

The explosion that erupted from Camilla left Judith sitting bolt upright in her seat. 'All right, all right,' she said, trying to calm her down. 'It was a joke, but you do defend him.'

Camilla's face was practically scarlet. Judith thought she was completely overreacting. 'Listen,' she said when Camilla had stopped protesting. 'I'm fond of Van. I totally support him in what he's trying to do, but if I'd wanted a flatmate I would have chosen Rosie, or Carey, who I've known for ever. Not someone I've only known for a few months.'

Camilla tried to smile, but only succeeded in looking more upset. 'It's just that he has always been so friendly to me, and I feel awful abandoning him, now that he's down on his luck. But when he calls for a chat, I don't always have the time to talk, and he was always prepared to listen if I had anything to say.'

Judith nodded sympathetically, surprised to hear that Van called Camilla as frequently as he clearly did. 'But no need for you and I to fall out over him, is there? Tell you what, call him up and see if he wants to have lunch. Put the bill in to Premier, okay?'

To her surprise Camilla didn't look all that enthusiastic. 'I've got a lot of work to do, but thanks. I'm sure it's too short notice anyway,' and with that she retreated to her own domain.

On another occasion Judith would have wondered more about Camilla's distress, but it was now nearing the time when she knew from Howard's last phone call that he and Gray would be back in London. And who knew what would happen?

In the back of the taxi that night taking her to Kensington, Judith knew she had to do something about Van, and soon. It was true. In the month since Van had moved in, he had rarely strayed from her side. The way Van put it was that the more people he met, the more chance he had of getting himself into a position where he could really get his business off the ground.

Too polite to disagree, she had put up little resistance when he turned up to meet her at the office and go along with her to any reception, preview or meeting she might have after hours. Always she introduced him as her friend and inevitably Van would charm everybody, so that as they left, she would frequently find herself being congratulated on having such a great boyfriend.

It was Rosie who first told her it had to stop. 'He's a great guy, Jude, but Piers says people are beginning to talk. This agency of his . . . what's it called?'

'Starlite,' Judith replied stonily.

'You're kidding? Seriously? Even more reason to cut loose. You don't need those people near your clients. I mean, Shade Morgan? Vinny Perrereo? And as for Maurice Allton . . .'

Rosie just raised her eyes in a very expressive gesture as she mentioned the deeply suspect leader of a Midlands city council, who could more often be found in certain nightclubs and on chat shows than looking after town planning.

'Piers says, Piers says,' exploded Judith. 'What else can I do? He's living in my house. I can't just abandon him. Besides, if it were me or you, Rosie, we'd be understanding. I think it's because it's not usual for a guy to be seen relying on a woman for help. And that's all wrong.'

Rosie looked sharply at her. 'Jude. Remember what you said about Annie and Marcel? She was holding him up. Well, that's what it looks like with you and Van.'

'But that's different,' protested Judith, feeling nervous. 'Annie is bonkers about Marcel. Van is just a friend.'

Rosie sighed. They were sitting in her kitchen, late on a Friday night. Tom was watching something totally unsuitable on television, relying on Judith, whom he adored, to keep his mother busy talking so that she wouldn't notice.

'Judith, listen to me. I know he is "just a friend", you know he is "just a friend" and so does Piers. But the rest of the world, not surprisingly, are getting the wrong impression. Now, if you don't mind, fine. But personally, I don't think it's doing you any good.'

'Why?' Judith asked abruptly.

'Because,' said Rosie carefully and deliberately, 'because I have to tell you I think Van is a freeloader. The charm is wearing thin. While he was your client, that was different.

'But you know last week he turned up on a shoot Piers was doing with that trashy Shade Morgan, and Piers said it was a real problem. Van hung around all afternoon trying to talk Piers into using Shade for the next shoot for *Focus*. Unbelievable. They stayed until seven and then he went off with Shade in her car back to London, the pair of them the worse for the two bottles of Krug they had swigged down.'

Judith was horrified and mortified. 'But why did Piers invite him?'

'Invite him? Are you crazy? You know Piers. He wouldn't invite the models if he could get away with it. He happened to mention it the night we were all at that book launch, and the next thing he knew, there was Van. He didn't turn him off the set because of you, my dear. Now do you see what I mean?'

Shade Morgan was a bleached blonde currently touting herself around most of the tabloids, having got a bit part in a soap opera on the basis that she was prepared to play a page three pin-up. Judith remembered she had crashed a party given by a visiting bestselling author. Shade and her photographer had managed to have a snatch picture taken with Leonora

Golding before Judith had intervened and asked Van to get her to leave. Judith suddenly felt sick. Rosie hadn't told her something she wasn't becoming increasingly aware of.

'Oh God, Rosie. What am I going to do?'

Rosie frowned. 'Tell him to find a flat. He seems to have enough money to spend on long lunches with that trashy crowd Shade hangs out with, he can easily spend it on rent and get his act together somewhere else. Next thing you know Premier will start losing clients if he keeps hounding them like this.'

As Tom chose that moment to shriek with laughter at a particularly offensive piece of dialogue, Rosie's attention was diverted to her small son. With a quick hug for Judith, he was ushered up to his room.

Over the next few days Judith was very conscious of Rosie's warning. It was true. Van's life revolved around hers. She hardly dared think what it was costing her since it was rare that Van bought anything for the flat in the way of food.

Wherever she went, he was sure to be there in her wake; her friends became his. At first she was indignant, but when she heard that Van was a regular visitor to Carey's flat, she drew her own conclusions and significantly she hadn't heard from Carey for a while.

But then Carey was hardly encouraging her to phone – quite the reverse. He had been photographed with Shade presenting prizes at a party hosted by Maurice Allton. Worse, Judith had been truly jolted to see Carey on the television interviewing the dreadful Maurice, who was implicated in corruption charges, and found him less than incisive, too prepared to listen, lobbing questions that lacked any fire.

What a pity Van doesn't move in with him, she muttered as she crawled into bed. Still, only another week before Howard gets back from Tokyo. And since when have you worried about Howard getting back from anywhere? she jeered at herself. It was knowing that Gray would be back in the country too.

For some reason she hoped that his arrival would help to alter the view that had rapidly become established in most people's heads, no matter what she said, that Van was the man in her life. Hard to argue the case when the guy was living with her, and off her.

About a week after her conversation with Rosie, she had planned to broach the subject about him moving, but it had been singularly unsuccessful. Judith had arrived home, slung her shoes off and announced she was going to sink into a bath and then go straight to bed. Van had looked astounded.

'I thought we were going to the Spielberg first night?' he protested as she flopped into an armchair and closed her eyes. The ChildLife fashion show was proving the inevitable nightmare. Steven Spielberg's latest blockbuster did not require her presence or anyone else's to ensure its success. She longed only for a night in.

Stella Frankenheim had fallen out with everyone on the committee and only the daily intervention of soothing phone calls and placatory lunches with Lisa Hamilton, all of which were billed to Premier, kept her from sabotaging the whole exercise. Libby was torn between the two, and Judith spent a disproportionate amount of time fielding phone calls from all three.

Mrs Frankenheim was imperious, but nothing compared to Circe, so Judith knew how to handle her. Flattery and gratitude worked wonders.

Libby she truly sympathized with, knowing it took a lot to reduce the ex-head girl to four-letter expletives. Libby had laughed, reminded of her schooldays.

'And to think,' mocked Judith, 'they said it was me who would come to a sticky end.'

'You,' giggled Libby. 'If you hadn't gone to Washington you know you would have, and look at you now. The girl most likely to . . . no, sorry, the girl who really has succeeded.'

Lisa Hamilton was brisk, to the point, polite, but regarded Judith as a receptacle for all her instructions and Premier as the machinery to execute them. 'I'll ask my husband,' was a frequent response when anyone enquired about a matter she could not answer herself, or, 'Please ring my husband's office and ask him to call me.' Never, Judith noticed, did she refer to him as her *ex*-husband.

Once when Judith had replaced the receiver after one such call, she looked down at her desk and was surprised to see that she had snapped three pencils during a ten-minute discussion.

Not surprisingly her temper at the end of another exhausting day was pushed beyond endurance to arrive home to find Van behaving like a spoilt brat having done little all day, expecting her to go out just because it suited his plans.

'Van,' she said with dangerous calm. 'I am so tired I could sleep for a week. Besides it isn't necessary for me to be there. None of my clients are involved and anyway Clark is going in my place.'

'Clark?' He sounded amazed. 'Clark in *your* place? What about me? I was really looking forward to it. There are people there I said I would meet up with. Don't you want Starlite to work?'

Her eyes flew open. 'Van,' she said wearily. 'This is my work. Not my social life. I'm sorry, I had no idea you were banking on going. Even so you couldn't go in my place. You don't work for Premier, Clark does.'

For a few seconds he had stood fuming in the doorway. 'You mean it, you're not going?'

'Van, please,' she groaned. 'I am very tired. Ring Clark, he might not be taking anyone.'

She thought that would stop him. But to her amazement, he stormed out of the room and phoned Clark's flat. The call was not successful. Minutes later Van appeared in front of her, this time more cajoling.

'Listen, sorry about that. Clark's taking a new girlfriend. C'mon, let's just go for half an hour, just to the reception.'

Judith's eyes remained closed. 'No, Van,' she said without moving. 'I am not going. I've had a helluva day.' She stayed where she was, listening to the door of his room open and then slam. A few minutes later she heard the door of the apartment open and shut behind him.

Where on earth had he gone? Not that she cared.

The next morning's papers showed a picture of Carey arriving at the premiere with Shade and, just at the edge of the shot, a blonde head that Judith recognized instantly.

She arrived home that evening and asked Van to move out.

'It's just that I want Alice to come to stay, and the flat is simply not big enough. I wonder if you could move in with one of your other friends for a while.'

It was a difficult speech to make. But he had been her house guest for nearly two months; it was not an unreasonable request.

'You mean, don't you,' he said, idly kicking his foot against the cupboard door, 'that Howard Dorfman is arriving and he might not understand about me being here?'

Judith froze. 'Howard has nothing to do with this. Nothing at all. He is a good friend of mine. This is to do with my family. Van, I think I have been as helpful as I can be. But I do need to think about other people now.'

'And where do you propose I go? And besides, I don't see what the problem is. You're out all day. We have our own rooms . . .'

Judith gasped in anger. 'Our own rooms? Just what do you think this is? You are simply a friend, Van. I own this flat. We are not flatmates.'

'But you don't pay for all this, do you? Howard does. Don't kid me. I know about you two.'

If Judith hadn't already been wide awake she would have thought she was dreaming. He was mad.

'Howard pays for nothing . . .' she started.

'Not yet, maybe. But everyone knows he's going to marry you.'

She had had enough. 'Van, my private life is my own. I don't discuss it with you, but I am not going to marry Howard.'

He simply stared at her. 'You should,' he said simply. 'You can't afford not to.'

Judith wasn't entirely sure if she had imagined it, but the look on Van's face was almost a sneer. 'Van, I think you should just go. Now. Book into a hotel, anything. But go now, before I really lose my temper.'

He went on sitting on the stool, swinging his leg against the door of the unit, kicking it shut as it sprang open. Kick, shut. Kick, shut. The movement tore at Judith's already jangled nerves.

She moved forward and slammed the door firmly shut. They

stared at each other in silence. Then with a shrug Van strolled calmly out of the kitchen into the spare room.

The silence between them was uneasy for the next few days and it was with relief that Judith told him that she would be away for the weekend with Howard in Torfell.

'Sure,' he said, hardly glancing up from the morning paper. 'Maybe I'll have resolved all this by the time you get back.'

For the first time in days Judith felt a sense of relief. 'That's great, Van. I'd much rather we were still good friends. I don't think we're cut out to live with each other.'

He said nothing. Simply smiled and went back to his paper.

Gray still hadn't phoned.

'Does he know you're coming with me to Torfell?' she asked Howard, staring out of her office window as she spoke to him on the phone, watching rivulets of rain streaming down the pane.

'I guess so. You mean, will he know where to find me? No problem. Connie has all my numbers. Can't wait to see the family who came between us, sweetheart. What do I wear for a weekend in Yorkshire?'

He pronounced it York-shyer and Judith, in spite of her well-disguised but intense disappointment that Gray had not even called her, had to laugh.

Laura adored Howard immediately. Alice thought he was dead cool, and even Andrew Craven Smith unbent enough to take him to the local pub for a drink before Sunday lunch.

'You know, sweetheart,' Howard said as they flew back to London on the last shuttle out of York, 'if I went for older women, I'd marry your grandmother. But your sister, hell, she makes you look reasonable. God help the poor bastard who hooks her.'

Judith, who was checking her diary for the following day, flashed him a grateful look. Torfell was not Long Island, but Howard had decided he was going to enjoy every second of it and genuinely had.

'You are a dear man, but,' she added hastily knowing his vanity, 'far too dangerous for the women of Manhattan let alone Torfell. How did you get such charm?'

'Easy peasy,' he announced smugly, leaning his head back on his seat and closing his eyes. 'Born with it and you would not be able to resist it if it weren't for that new room mate of yours . . .'

'What?'

Howard opened one eye and squinted at her.

'Who is this guy, Jude? All weekend I thought you would tell me. But I have to hear it from Gray.'

The light drone of the aircraft drowned her astonished gasp. Gray told Howard? Told Howard what?

'C'mon. I hear he's a great-looking guy and no-one can get near you, you're always with him.'

'He's just a friend, Howard. Someone who was a client, but he either lost his job or resigned, not sure which, and he's finding it hard to get back on his feet. That's all. He's moving out soon. How did Gray know?'

'Not sure. Some charity or other he's mixed up in. Lisa told him.'

How could she have believed it would not be misconstrued?

'All exaggerated stuff,' she said as noncommittally as she could. 'Anyway, I think the problem might well be over. Can't have my best guy getting the wrong idea. Silly of me, really. It never occurred to me that people would gossip.'

Howard yawned. 'But I bet you still won't come to Paris with me tonight?'

'Goodness,' she teased, leaning over and planting a kiss on his cheek. 'And there was me thinking all that York-shyer air would have worn you out.'

At Heathrow they parted company with an affectionate hug, Judith to head back into town and Howard to board a private plane to take him overnight to Paris and then to New York.

The minute she opened the door of the flat she sensed something was wrong. The door to her office was slightly ajar and there was a light on. She could hear a television in the background. Her mail was piled high on a small table in an unruly pile and newspapers were pushed roughly under it. Four days of them.

'Van?' she called, turning towards her office. What was he doing in there? 'Van? It's me.'

Pushing open the door, she walked right into the tiny room. It was empty but her usually reasonably orderly desk was in chaos. What the hell was happening here?

Anger was her first instinct and she called more sharply: 'Van? It's me. Where are you?'

As she spoke, she opened the door to the drawing room. It was in darkness but the television threw a flickering light across the walls. She groped inside the door and snapped on the switch. Light flooded the room. Slowly her gaze travelled around her once warm and inviting home. Cushions were strewn on the floor, the coffee table was littered with glasses and what appeared to be the remains of a takeaway meal. Ashtrays were overflowing and there was an ominous-looking dark stain on the blue carpet. An empty wine bottle was on its side where it had come to rest against the pelmet of an armchair.

Without a word, she marched down the hall to Van's room. Empty. The shower room attached was silent. No-one in the kitchen. Her bedroom. No, surely not? Not her bedroom. Not possible.

She wrenched open the door and as she did so, the lozenge of light from the hall behind her fell on her bed. There was a muffled stir and a more audible expletive from a voice she recognized immediately as Van's.

Furious and beyond speech, she snapped on the light. Van, unshaven, bare-chested, opened a bleary eye and heaved himself up in the crumpled bed. 'For Crissakes . . .'

Judith was rigid with anger. Her bedroom was littered with his clothes, a bottle of champagne was balancing precariously on the bedside table, and there was a sweet, sickly smell in the air which she did not have to be told was dope. But what she thought she would swing for was the sight of crumpled, blonde Shade Morgan lying next to Van, vainly trying to shield her face from the light.

'Get out,' she breathed. 'What the hell's going on?'

Van had simply raised his eyebrows when he had realized who she was and, clearly trying to keep her in focus, he giggled to his companion.

'See,' he said, reaching for the champagne bottle and

inspecting it through the top like a telescope. 'I told you she was stupid. Well, hi there. Little Miss Career returns from her family. Sorry we didn't know you were coming, otherwise I would have saved some of the champagne, but you see,' he swung the empty bottle in front of him, 'we had a good time. Okay, honey.' He turned to the sleepy blonde. 'Get your ass out of here. Miss Prim-and-not-so-Proper has returned.'

Judith thought she was passing through a nightmare. Why was he doing this? For the first time, Van frightened her. Before he had merely begun to irritate her. More recently she had come to believe what she had refused to acknowledge, that he was a freeloader with no ambition but to live off those richer and more influential than he could ever be.

But now he terrified her. She knew her knees were shaking, her mouth was dry. She was horrified to find that she was close to tears. Her first instinct was to ring for the police, her second and the one she acted upon was to get this nightmare couple out of her apartment.

Van had swung his legs out of the bed and pushed himself to his feet. Judith saw that he was completely naked. She simply gazed back at him, trying not to let him see that she felt repelled by this swaggering man, strolling insolently towards her, quite deliberately thrusting his lower body at her.

Her nerve cracked and she began to back towards the door.

'Van, please stop this. This isn't like you. Why are you doing it?' As she spoke she was moving into the hallway. There was an extension phone behind her.

'Van,' she said desperately. 'If you don't leave I'm going to call the police.'

His answer was to reach behind her and with a sharp, vicious tug, he pulled the cord from the wall. Face impassive, he began to laugh softly. 'Poor Judith,' he crooned. 'Get used to me, babe. I'm going nowhere.'

'Except out of here.' It was her last defiant remark.

He moved so fast, she was being propelled into the drawing room, her arm in a vicelike grip twisted up her back before the words had left her mouth. Terror gripped her. Her voice wouldn't come. With a thud she felt herself pushed into an armchair and Van was kneeling on the floor in front of her making escape impossible, his hands clamping her wrists to the arms of the chair.

The force of the shove he gave her as she landed had knocked the breath out of her. Her heart hammered painfully, her legs felt like rubber.

'What are you doing?' she whispered. 'Van, what is this?'

'I'll show you,' he said, sauntering over to his briefcase on the sofa. Out of it he extracted a white envelope and from it he took some photographs. Handing them to her, he cackled with laughter at her white face and her eyes round with horror.

'Where did you get these?' she whispered.

He shook his head, wagging a finger. 'No, no, honey. I have all the aces.'

Pure blackmail, of course. Judith listened in growing horror as he described in the kind of detail that only an eyewitness could have possessed what he knew of her family, of her. Of her mother.

Washington came flooding back in wave after sickening wave of revelation. Harry Jardine, his father Seth, Bradley Wallace and the whole promiscuous, loathsome social life of Ridge Harbour.

Names, dates, places. Nothing he said was inaccurate. Revulsion and nausea vied with each other as she watched his impassive features describe just what he would do if she upset the lifestyle he believed he was entitled to in return for his silence.

By the time he had finished Judith could hardly breathe.

He had a couple of photographs of her mother with Seth Jardine, taken at Seth's house; smiling, they were. Seth's arm was lightly around her mother's waist.

'It's not true,' she almost sobbed. 'You're mad.'

But she knew it was useless. He wouldn't tell her how he had found out, how long he had known. All she knew was that he had believed she was going to marry Howard and in return for a sum of money that was as laughable as it was ludicrous he would leave her in peace.

'Peace?' she whispered. 'You call what you're asking, peace?'

He shrugged.

'You've known all this ever since you phoned me at Premier. Why now? Why not straight away?'

'I would have done,' he said. 'Then I thought you were going to marry Dorfman. You still might. But I can't wait that long for you to make up your mind. But, I just have a feeling that even you might have pushed your luck. I hear he's on the loose again in New York.

'I agree we might both have misjudged that one. I waited too long. You may have lost the chance. But I do not waste my time, ever. There are still plenty of opportunities to be had here in London. Baby, you are still going to be very useful to me.'

She felt sick when he spoke to her. Just having him physically so close nearly choked her. He stood up, knowing full well that his genitals were only inches from her face. He laughed hysterically as she twisted her face away. Being degraded was, at that moment, the least of her problems.

Panic engulfed her. Someone must help. But who?

Van must have read her thoughts. 'No-one to tell, is there?' he jeered. 'Dorfman hired you to keep scandal away from his name. A fancy-shmancy lawyer like Hamilton couldn't afford to have any attached to his.'

Her eyes flew to his face. 'What do you mean?'

'You know what I mean. He couldn't afford to be associated with you with this kind of dynamite. And he doesn't want to lose Dorfman as a client. His wife likes his clients. He likes his wife . . . sorr-eee, ex-wife, but the whole town knows she's only got to go like that,' he clicked his fingers, 'and he comes running.'

Judith wanted to kill him. But the thought of touching him made her want to vomit. She knew Howard wouldn't give a damn about her past or her family's. Gray? As far as he was concerned, she was a momentary aberration. Lisa was still unfinished business.

'Tsk. Tsk,' he mocked, quite correctly reading her expression. 'Poor deluded Jude. Do you really think the eminently respectable Mr Hamilton would risk losing his biggest client for a quick screw with you?'

'Van,' she whispered hoarsely. 'Why? What have I done to hurt you? What has Alice or my mother or any of my family done to you to deserve any of this?'

'Me? Hurt you?' He sneered. 'I haven't done a thing. You people make me sick with your smart accents and classy backgrounds and enough dirt to start a pig farm piled in the closets. I haven't done a thing. I never asked any of you to behave as you did. I wasn't even there.'

'Van, I don't care for myself. If that's it you're wasting your time.'

'Hell, I know that.' He was shuffling the photographs like a pack of cards in his hands. 'It's a strange thing, Jude, there ain't no picture here of your father with Seth Jardine, is there? They all seem to be of your mother. Just like you, isn't she? Alice seen these? Or this one, the four of you?'

Judith didn't need to look. It was a picture of her mother and Seth and in front, trying to look cool and moody as only a couple of teenagers could, Seth's son Harry and herself.

It was taken the night before Harry died.

Judith pleaded with Van. He laughed. She tried to bluff it out. He ignored her. Exhausted, she asked him how long he planned to blackmail her.

'Just long enough to set myself up in London in the way I want to. I want to have a good time. I am so sick of those stiff-necked jerks you knock around with. Now I am going to have fun. And then you can go back to Torfell or Premier with your grubby little secret and no-one will be any the wiser.

'One thing you can be sure of. While you do as I say, and I am not unreasonable, I won't find it necessary to let this discussion go beyond these walls. Okay?'

She knew he was mad.

He pulled her chin sharply round to face him. 'I said, okay?'

She nodded. Tears were pouring down her face. She had never felt so frightened in her life.

Chapter Seventeen

Rosie was the first to ask her outright what was wrong. They were lunching in a wine bar around the corner from Premier, seated in a small alcove near the back. But even in the dim light, Rosie could see that Judith looked pale. Dark circles were quite pronounced under her eyes and she pushed her food virtually untouched around her plate.

'Is this Premier, Van or Howard?' Rosie asked casually, indicating Judith's strained look, as she removed her friend's plate and looked around for somewhere to deposit it.

Judith shook her head, and began to protest that she hadn't finished.

'No point, and you're driving me mad picking at it like that,' Rosie explained patiently, depositing the untouched meal on the next table. She turned back to Judith, having got her attention. 'That's better. At least you look like you're alive. I said, what is it? No . . . don't say, "nothing's the matter". I simply don't believe you. You've been like this for weeks.'

Bereft of a fork to fiddle with, Judith began to massage the rings she was wearing, twisting them nervously around her fingers. 'Just . . . um . . . just . . . well it's this ball,' she lied, pulling a rueful grimace. 'You know, the de Vries ball for ChildLife? It's all those women on the committee fighting.' She rolled her eyes in mock despair. 'Really, that's all it is,' she said, picking up the menu and making a creditable display of selecting from the desserts. 'Mmm. Maybe I could manage some pecan pie, though.'

'Liar,' said Rosie chattily, plucking the menu from out of Judith's hands. 'You don't think I'm going to sit through another charade of eating, do you? Now, *what is it*?' she hissed in exasperation, not wanting to attract attention from nearby tables.

For just a fraction of a second Judith wavered. Just Rosie,

no-one else. But even as the thought presented itself it was dismissed. Rosie would insist they told someone. It was pure blackmail. No two ways about it.

She cared nothing for what people might say about her. But she cared desperately for her father and her dead mother. And Alice. No, she couldn't put Rosie in such a position.

'Just tired. Christmas wasn't the break I was expecting and I can't get away until after this ball is over. If I'd known just one rotten fund-raising ball would take so long to plan and I'd have to deal with Stella Frankenheim making an absolute meal of it, I'd never have done it. Honestly, Rosie, I'd tell you if there was something really wrong.'

Rosie looked doubtful and reluctantly agreed to drop the subject.

'I know it's tied up with Van,' she muttered crossly. 'Why doesn't he just go and get another flat? You've really got to be firm with him, Jude. He'll stay there for ever if you let him. And your love life is suffering – when was the last time you had a date with someone other than for business? See? Not since Dirk Hemmingway and that was a disaster.'

For the first time Judith managed a ghost of a smile. 'Van wasn't living with me then,' she pointed out, refraining from mentioning that Gray Hamilton was business and that was the evening she remembered above all the others. At least Van couldn't be blamed for Gray not contacting her. It was now the end of February; next week it would be March. Nearly a year since she had quit New York. She had run out of excuses for his failure to get in touch. Except for one.

Lisa Hamilton.

'Is he driving you mad?' asked Rosie, pulling on her coat as they got to their feet.

Judith was too far down the road of perjuring herself to care any more. She took a deep breath, following Rosie through the packed restaurant. 'No, not at all. He's okay. I mean, I understand. He's just getting the business going. Anyway, you housed me for weeks when I came back from the States.'

Rosie briefly looked back. 'Yes, but you weren't running a business from my house and hanging around on fashion shoots and coming with me to previews, were you?'

Judith just stared back. There was no answer to that. 'I'll call you tomorrow,' said Rosie as they emerged onto the pavement. 'But honestly, love, you look completely whacked. Why don't you take a long weekend? Spencer will understand.'

Judith shook her head. 'I'll be fine. I wouldn't rest if I was away just at the moment. Besides, Alice is coming down at the weekend.'

Rosie sighed. 'I'd have thought organizing the de Vries ball was easier than Alice. Tell you what, Tom's with me until Monday, let's all have Sunday lunch. Okay?' Having got Judith's agreement, she hugged her and was gone.

Judith had never felt quite so alone. She just prayed that Van would get Starlite so well-established he would leave her in peace. But she knew it was a false hope. Van was on a rollercoaster, the apartment was no longer home and Camilla had twice enquired if she was going down with something.

Spencer had asked her for a breakdown of figures for the last six months and only because Camilla had discovered Judith hadn't done them and volunteered to work late two nights in a row had they been produced in time for the accountants.

Clark and Annie, who was having her usual bad time with Marcel, had taken to talking to each other for lack of input from Judith, which she thought was the only good thing that had come out of the miserable situation.

Even Beth had saved her from arriving at a meeting with a new client without any notes by leaping into a taxi, shouting at the driver to follow the one in front, and thrusting the file into a dazed Judith's arms as she was being greeted by the Managing Director.

'Last-minute information, arrived after Ms Craven Smith had left the office,' Beth explained breathlessly with a beaming smile, as the MD gazed in bewilderment at the human dynamo who had just flung herself through the swing doors while Judith closed her eyes in relief and grateful thanks.

How could she have been so fooled? The companies Van claimed he worked for existed all right, but the phone calls she had made over the next couple of days to check why he had really parted company with them left her with a longing only to resign from business life for ever.

'Mr Kingsley?' The personnel department at Seeligman Ventures recognized the name. 'No, ma'am. Mr Kingsley works out of London. He approached us last fall to explore possibilities of working for us in Europe, developing business opportunities, but the discussions have not as I understand it progressed.'

Judith called Bill Jefferson.

'Bill, can you help me with something? The name of your contact on Wall Street who asked you to help Van over here? Who was he?'

'Oh, you mean Walt Cromer? Nice fellow.'

And he was. But when Judith rang him, it turned out that he'd never actually met Van Kingsley. 'He called me before he went to London with a couple of ideas about expanding our opportunities in the UK. Problem for me was that he had more enthusiasm than experience.'

'Enough for you to call Bill Jefferson?'

'Well, it's a strange thing, but Bill's was the only name on a whole list of people Van asked me about that I vaguely knew. Played a couple of rounds of golf with Bill when he came over a few years back. Nice guy.'

Judith didn't have to ask who the rest of the names were. Spencer Drummond, Jacob Frankenheim and a number of others who were connected with or had once had accounts with Premier.

So easy. So plausible and convincing. The fee had been paid upfront, all communication was through Van. Stupid, stupid, pitiful woman. She wondered where he had got the money to pay Premier's fee.

She was staying later and later at the office and doing less and less work. If she went home, Van would frequently be there with the dreadful Shade and a handful of cronies who mostly had jobs as greeters at nightclubs long past their sell-by date, or were pop singers she'd never heard of who claimed they were big in Reykjavik. More usually he would be sitting in a smoke-filled room with some 'business' contacts who sniffed a lot and had white powder on their lapels.

'Hi, babe,' he would drawl unpleasantly. 'Just a few of the guys hanging out, we needed a little privacy,' and he would close the drawing-room door.

She no longer wept. She would simply either lock herself in her bedroom or turn round and go out again. It was not unheard of for Judith to see a movie alone and afterwards be totally incapable of recalling what it was about.

When Van wasn't 'entertaining', he was with her. His friends would come too. At first it was just the odd one that she could easily disguise at a first night or an opening party. After that, he became more reckless and it was not unusual to see him with not just Shade but also a dealer and on two occasions Judith was publicly forced into agreeing to have dinner with the tacky trio. It had to stop. But how?

Not wanting to face the office just yet, Judith decided to walk over to Piers's studio to see how the catalogue shoot for Young Masters was going. Clark had a careful eye on the whole account but it wouldn't do any harm to have a look for herself.

Slowly she made her way over to his studio. It was bitterly cold. She kept her head down, instinctively avoiding the press of lunchtime shoppers and office workers around her. She threaded her way through the back streets of Mayfair, emerging onto Piccadilly opposite the Ritz. She half ran, half walked through the congested traffic and arrived breathless on the opposite pavement as a gust of wind flattened her coat against her, whipped her hair across her face which momentarily obscured her vision, and collided almost head-on with Gray Hamilton just leaving the hotel with two male companions.

If she had been white before, Judith now resembled chalk. She hadn't seen or heard from him since the night he had kissed her under a street lamp but she had practised this moment over and over in her head.

At some point she knew she would see him again. Their lives touched each other's in odd ways and he was bound to be escorting Lisa to the de Vries ball. She had planned to smile, extend her hand, ask him civilly how he was and then as though in a hurry glance at her watch and, with a graceful smile, excuse herself, leaving him looking longingly after her.

In her imagination she was perfectly groomed, her hair a silky mane that she would toss becomingly. For some reason she would not be encumbered by a coat that was two years old and a generous scarf wrapped carelessly across her shoulders, but in some flattering jacket and slim skirt and she most certainly would not be standing there with her mouth open, running her hand distractedly through her hair, harbouring a dreadful suspicion that she might even have a spot on her chin and looking as though she hadn't slept for a month.

Which was very nearly true.

'Um . . . hi,' she managed, looking anywhere but at him. 'I didn't see you, sorry . . . I wasn't looking.'

'How are you?' he asked politely. He didn't look like a man who had given her so much as a passing thought in two months. He didn't sound like one either.

'I'm fine . . . just fine,' she answered, making a valiant attempt to glance at her watch and succeeding only in dropping her briefcase which she had tucked under her arm. It hit the pavement between them.

Oh shit. 'Well, I'm holding you up,' she started. He ignored her and bent down to retrieve the case as his companions stared curiously at her.

'No you're not,' he assured her, brushing the side of her case before restoring it to her.

She must look like some mad woman that had been prematurely released into the community. She took the bag and started to thank him, but he wasn't listening. He was talking to his companions, shaking hands, explaining she was a business acquaintance, sending them on ahead. He turned to face her. The wind was blowing his hair into a disordered tangle. His face was still faintly tanned and he was drawing her into the shelter of the hotel wall, out of the wind.

'None of my business,' he said, frowning down at her. 'But are you all right? You weren't paying much attention to the world around you.'

'Fine, just fine,' Judith nodded. 'I have a heavy workload and I was thinking something through. Business. Work. You know?'

She couldn't look at him. She made a vain attempt to pull

her hair into shape. There was a lump in her throat which made speech difficult. 'How are you?' she managed at last, forcing a smile. 'I hear Tokyo was very successful.'

He nodded. Still just looking at her.

'How's Lisa?' she asked.

'Lisa? Oh, Lisa. Okay, I think. She's working hard on the committee for the ball. She says she sees quite a bit of you and . . . your friend Mr Kingsley.'

Judith could have screamed.

'Yes,' she said. 'Yes. He's staying with me for a while. Just until he can get a flat.'

'I see,' Gray's voice was noncommittal. 'Well, I expect I'll see you at the ball. Can I give you a lift anywhere? My car is just here.'

She glanced at him, and saw contempt in his face. She couldn't blame him, but she did. 'No. No, thank you,' she said quietly. 'My next appointment is just across the street. Nice to see you again.'

This time without even being conscious of it, she did smile gracefully, and moved on, head held high. And, of course, feeling ready to die. What troubled her nearly as much as being so unprepared for bumping into him was the painful realization that he had thought better of their last evening together and had mentally moved on. So much for 'what next?', she thought bitterly.

Nor did she concentrate that hard on the shoot at Piers's studio. Like Rosie, Piers eyed her with concern but, unlike Rosie, he was tough. While the models were preparing for the next shot and Clark was occupied with the stylist, he propelled Judith into a corner and delivered a brutal assessment of the situation.

'You are living with a bullshitter and a creep . . .'

'Piers,' she protested. 'I'm not . . .'

'. . . don't care what you call it. What do you think it looks like? I believe you when you say you're not emotionally involved with him, but it's not what he's saying.'

Judith looked shocked and felt ill.

'What do you mean?' she said anxiously. 'What is Van saying? How do you know?'

Piers shook his head in exasperation and handed her a steaming mug of tea. 'I know because I was in Masters the other day and he was in there with that greeter he trails around with him and whatshername, the Morgan girl.'

'Shade?'

'Yeah, that one. He was ordering a couple of jackets and when it came to paying for them he told the guy serving him to call his girlfriend, Judith Craven Smith, the PR for Masters, and she would arrange everything.'

'But he didn't call . . . I don't remember that.'

Piers shrugged. 'Well, he called someone because he came back and Van left with the jackets. No, he didn't see me. Mainly because I walked away. Jude . . . Rosie is worried stiff about you and I've known you too long to believe you fancy this guy . . .'

She'd never wanted to scream so much in her life.

'Actually Piers,' she said, making a valiant effort to appear calm and lying through her back teeth. 'You're right. I don't fancy Van in the slightest, although I think he's got a bit of a thing about me.' She gave what she hoped was an embarrassed shrug. 'I should tell him to get his act together, but to be honest I've been frantically busy with this ball and one thing and another, and on top of that I am concerned about Laura. She's getting on a bit and Alice is such a handful when she's there. The problem I've got is that Laura is going to stay with an old friend for a week and Dad is researching his book, so I suggested Alice came down to stay with me while she's gone.

'I'm okay, just bitten off more than I could chew at a particularly hectic time. I mean, how would you like to keep a fourteen-year-old occupied for a week in London while working twelve hours a day?

'In fact,' she teased, thankful to see he was looking sympathetic, 'if you go on showing such concern I'll send her over to you.'

Piers promptly leaned forward and ruffled Judith's hair. 'No thank you,' he said. 'If you're sure that's all it is . . . I tell you what, why don't we take her to see Smashing Pumpkins? She can dine out on that for the rest of the term. How about it?'

She needed no second bidding. The chance to see Alice's

favourite group was not something to hesitate about, and it had mercifully diverted Piers from further questions.

'Brill,' she said. 'I won't tell her till she gets here. She'll be ecstatic and I'll be your slave for life.'

Shortly afterwards, seeing that Clark and Piers had the session well under control, she left for the office.

Camilla was racing through a report that Annie needed for a presentation to a new client later in the afternoon when Judith arrived back and simply waved an airy hand at her boss as she passed her desk.

'Sorry, Judith,' she called, frantically pounding away at her word processor. 'Be with you in a minute. Alice called.'

Judith removed her coat and sank down into her chair behind the desk which bore evidence that her morning's workload had still not been dealt with. She dialled Torfell and Laura answered.

'Hi, darling,' Judith said injecting a breezy note into her voice. The last thing she wanted was her grandmother concerned as well. 'I've just had a call from Alice. She *is* at school, I take it?'

The sound of Laura tsk-ing was unmistakeable.

'Just about,' she muttered grimly. 'She's trying to wheedle an extra couple of days holiday and wanted me to call the head and say you were getting married suddenly and she and her father had to be at the wedding tomorrow to give you away.'

Judith almost screamed in horror. 'And how did she think she was going to explain I hadn't?'

'Quite,' said Laura dryly. 'She said, I quote: "Easy peasy. Just say she was jilted and I had to stay to console her".'

It was too absurd for words, and both women were reduced to hysterical giggles.

'If it wasn't for the fact that you need a holiday, we should leave her there for the whole of half term,' Judith sighed.

'Are you sure it will be all right?' asked Laura. 'I mean, you're so busy, dear.'

Busy Judith could cope with. Blackmail was different. Between now and Alice arriving on Friday night she had to come to an agreement with Van that his friends would absent themselves and he would be pleasant to Alice.

'Not too busy for Alice,' she reassured her grandmother. 'Anyway, it will be fun having her to myself for a few days. You enjoy yourself and when you get back we'll talk about getting some more help at home . . . no, I insist. Don't look a gift horse.'

'I'm afraid you do enough already,' Laura sighed.

They talked for a few more minutes, arranging for Judith to meet Alice from the Oxford train at Paddington and for Laura to deal with Alice's phone call, which they both knew was designed to play one off against the other.

Camilla had of course heard her finish the conversation, and came in with a pile of letters and messages.

'Is that just today?' asked Judith, reaching for the bundle.

'Two days actually,' Camilla told her. She pulled a chair up in front of Judith's desk and sat down with a purposeful attitude.

'I promise this will take no more than half an hour to go through,' she said firmly. 'But there are several pressing questions that only you can answer . . . please?'

'Of course.' Judith gave herself a shake. This couldn't go on. 'Fire away,' and Camilla did, ruthlessly passing from one letter to another, giving Judith no chance to be distracted.

The messages were less complicated, although Camilla refused to permit 'I'll think about it' as a satisfactory answer. She was perfectly polite, but firm. Judith recognized the tactics and in a curious kind of way, while she found it difficult to show real interest, she did at least have the satisfaction of knowing that she wouldn't have to face it all tomorrow. There would be plenty of other things to face then.

Looking relieved, Camilla scooped up all her notes and made for the door. Judith stopped her.

'Camilla, remind me,' she said, making a big fuss about searching for a pen on her desk. 'Did someone from Masters call about some jackets for . . . for Van?'

She glanced up and saw that Camilla looked uneasy. 'Well, yes. It was Ben from the shop. He said . . . er . . . that Van was in the shop waiting to collect some jackets you had ordered for him, but he didn't have any instructions from you about them.

'I knew you must have forgotten to do it, because you've

been a bit tired lately, so I gave the go ahead and they'll bill it to you later. Was that all right?'

Inside her head Judith was raging. To Camilla, she simply smiled and said: 'Thank you, I'm afraid I did forget. Make me concentrate in future, otherwise I shall get into a dreadful muddle. By the way, Van likes to surprise me, so if he calls to see if I have any appointments, let me know. It's just that I'm so busy lately, I'd hate to hurt his feelings by having to let him down.'

Camilla nodded sympathetically. 'Actually, he has asked several times. He does seem quite smitten with you. Mind you, he's always been so understanding about your job in the past, I'm sure he wouldn't be too cross, he's not like that.' She hesitated. 'Judith?' She came back and sat down, her face slightly pink but determined.

'I've been meaning to mention this, and I didn't know how. It's just that Van asked me if I wanted to go and work for him, you know, organize all the business side of Starlite.'

It all came out in a rush. Judith stared blankly back at her.

'He said I was wasted here just being a secretary and the job he offered did sound exciting, but I don't want to work for that kind of agency. I just didn't want you to think I had approached him.' She stopped, staring anxiously at Judith who hadn't said a word. 'Judith? You're not angry, are you? I don't want this to be a big thing. Only I wondered if perhaps you had asked him to approach me because you wanted to get someone else in . . .'

If she could have seen what was going on in Judith's head she would have been shocked. 'Angry with you? Want you to go? Camilla. How could you think such a thing? The one thing on which I agree with him is that you've moved well beyond being a secretary, you could run this company.

'I'm just very surprised that Van asked you without mentioning it to me . . . I'm glad you said no. Perhaps Van misunderstood.'

Camilla studied her hands. 'It's my own fault,' she said quietly. 'I took to confiding in him quite a lot. A bit too much really. I expect he thought he was doing me a favour.'

'Depends what you confided in him about,' said Judith

gently. To her surprise Camilla's eyes were looking very tear-ful, and she was struggling to keep control. The door was still open. Judith got up and closed it so that no-one would sail in while Camilla was so distressed.

'I'm surprised you haven't guessed. I told Van how I felt about Spencer, I think he thought I would be better off not working for him. But when I said no, I would rather stay here, he said my secret was safe with him. Judith, he wouldn't . . . I mean, by mistake of course, he wouldn't tell Spencer, would he?'

You'd better believe it, thought Judith grimly as Camilla stared anxiously at her.

Poor Camilla, so obvious really. That's why she stayed. Fucking Van. She'd guessed that's where he was getting all the information about the invitations she accepted, where she would be at what time. Camilla, who had been charmed by Van, would not have suspected for a moment his more sinister motives, and Van must have made sure that the lonely older woman in need of attention would be putty in his hands.

'Don't worry. He won't. But, Camilla, have you ever tried telling Spencer how you feel?'

Camilla shook her head in horror. 'Oh, my word, no. Besides, it's stupid of me. Like a cliché. Falling in love with the boss. It's better already, just not being his secretary. Sorry, Jude. You don't need to hear all this, but I didn't want you to think I was being disloyal.'

After Camilla had departed, Judith was determined that she would confront Van when she got home. And for the rest of the afternoon she rehearsed over and over in her head how she would persuade him she needed a truce just for a few days.

The last thing in the world she wanted was to be publicly associated with a man with such a deviant mind. She couldn't however bring herself to confront the fact that the only man she had felt she could be linked with, wasn't remotely interested.

Chapter Eighteen

Since Judith could barely bring herself to speak to Van, it took a real effort and an uncustomary slug of whisky to confront him. It was therefore all the more surprising when he agreed relatively easily to hide his more exotic friends and the evidence of illegal substances until after Alice had gone back to school.

For once, his posse was not with him, although there were plenty of signs around that they must have spent the greater part of the day occupying her once-stylish apartment.

While Van clearly enjoyed living surrounded by Judith's tasteful choice of decor, he wasn't prepared to treat it with respect. Cigarette burns were visible on the carpet, the smell of stale tobacco was beginning to cling to the curtains. Every evening the kitchen would be a sea of empty glasses and bottles, the bin overflowing and the cupboards raided for food.

She had taken to locking her bedroom door each day so that Van would be unable to stage a repeat performance of his sexual gymnastics with the apparently willing Shade, but ever since the night Judith had found them together in her bed, she had lost her sense of security. He had laughed when she had stripped the bed of everything and thrown the sheets out, but just laundering them would not have rid her of the dreadful duo's presence.

Van himself had ceased to worry about his appearance. In the privacy of her flat, he was unkempt and slovenly. The guest room he occupied had rapidly turned into something that made a squat look reasonable.

Judith could have cried. The pleasant cleaning lady she had found shortly after she had arrived had had to be paid off, since she couldn't risk her finding drugs or worse, Shade and Van in bed, and Lord knows who else besides. All of which meant that the upkeep of the flat had been left to her. What was once a haven from the world had become a hated necessity, simply a roof over her head.

Tonight was no different. She found Van, as usual, sprawled in front of the television, phone in hand and the debris from a takeaway meal in front of him.

Judith swallowed hard. She no longer made any pretence of trying to get on with him. Over a month of living with his sneering remarks, his childishly petulant temper and the dreadful weapon he used to bring her back in line if there was the slightest danger that she might tell him to do his worst, a sly reference to Washington, had left her unafraid for her personal safety, just scared of the power he had to destroy so much.

She had long since abandoned any hope of tricking him into revealing how he knew so much about her. She racked her brains trying to recall if she had ever met him before. But neither Van's face nor his name evoked even the smallest clue.

She thought this in many ways was the most sinister aspect of this whole revolting business – she had become suspicious of all but a handful of people around her. Paranoia, of course. Knowing that he knew so much about her and she had never suspected. Someone, somewhere must have told him. But who?

And most enraging of all, this was the man that she had defended to Gray. A man, she had claimed, who understood about equality and the quality of relationships. What a joke. Walk on the beach, indeed. His only feeling for women was to exploit them and take them for the suckers he believed them to be.

He was blackmailing her and using Shade for sex and not even making any attempt to pretend it was anything else. Why Shade tolerated him was beyond Judith's understanding. But then, the bit-part actress was more street-sharp than bright. Her belief that being seen in the seediest of nightclubs and getting invited to rock stars' parties was the quickest way to appear in the newspapers was correct. That it instantly labelled her brainless and not to be taken seriously by any casting agent unless asked to find a trashy bimbo, completely escaped her.

Van, through Judith, was opening doors for her that might otherwise have remained shut. Shade needed Van and if in return some pretty third-rate sex and the increasingly unusual requests he threw in were the price, then it was just about worth it.

Alice's imminent arrival concentrated Judith's mind on the next obstacle to clear. So she leaned against the back of the chair and politely asked him to turn the volume down on the television while she spoke to him. She was going to gamble and he might, just might, bite.

He took his time, but he did it. Judith waited, used to this tactic too. He really was pathetic.

'Alice is coming to stay on Friday,' she told him. 'I would much rather you weren't here, but I suppose it's pointless asking you to move in with one of your friends for a few days?'

'Totally,' he agreed, smiling broadly.

She tried again. 'In which case I think I should point out that Alice is still only a child and, although in many ways she is quite grown up, she couldn't cope with the language or the lifestyle of people like Shade and what's his name? The one you dragged to Masters with you to pick up those jackets? Oh yes, Vinny.

'It's up to you, but if she suspects anything, and she's very bright, we both lose. She's not mature enough to remain silent. She'd be devastated, and once it's out you have no power over me any more, although I admit it is not the conclusion I want but for different reasons.' She paused and let her eyes flick over him knowing such a gesture unnerved most people. 'I really would have no control over her.'

She pushed herself upright and strolled out of the door. 'Think about it. And, Van, sorry to disappoint you but Camilla is staying put,' and she went into the kitchen to make some coffee.

Judith didn't see him again until the following morning when she was emerging from her bedroom. He was just coming in, dishevelled, unshaven and hungover, and followed her into the kitchen.

Judith regretted not having dressed first. Even in her towelling wrap, Van made her feel vulnerable. He pulled a chair out from the table and straddled it, flicking through the post, which incensed Judith.

Far too many people were writing to him here and it also meant he was aware of her own correspondence. She knew she was paranoid, but if she could have helped it she wouldn't have told Van the brand of toothpaste she used.

She ignored him. It was Van who spoke first, smothering a yawn.

'Not for the reasons you suggest but because I'm not keen on being around a fourteen-year-old for a whole week, I'll move in with Shade for a day or two . . .'

'No, a week,' corrected Judith, turning round to look at him from where she was pouring some juice. The coffee percolator was beside her and Van leaned past her to get it.

He paused, and with his free hand patted her cheek. It was not hard. But it held more menace than a fist could ever have done.

'A couple of days, okay?'

Judith pushed him away from her. 'Don't touch me,' she said dangerously. 'There's a lot of things I have to concede, but that isn't one of them.'

He simply shrugged.

'You have more to lose than me,' he said, pouring himself some coffee. 'And don't you forget it. You and the kid can move out if you want to. I'll be back after the weekend, sometime. Remember I have my job and a career to think of.'

'Career,' she echoed incredulously. 'What career?'

'Keeping secrets,' he said. 'Expensive business. You have to be on the case the whole time.'

'But I need your room for Alice,' she protested.

'That's okay. I'll sleep with you.' He was staring steadily at her and for once, to her horror, she knew he wasn't joking.

'Too kind,' she said sarcastically, revolted at the very thought. 'But I think you should keep yourself for Shade, don't you?'

'Maybe,' he said. 'Doesn't make any difference whether I screw you or not, half London thinks I do.'

Judith felt murderous. Her chair scraped noisily back and without another word to him she walked out and banged the door. She heard him laugh.

It was still only just after seven, but she had to get out of the flat, away from Van. Pulling on a black rollneck sweater over a long wool skirt, dragging on some lace-up boots, she grabbed her coat and fled outside.

A faint grey light hung over the streets; lamps were still alight. The icy cold grey dawn lingered as she walked hurriedly down the tree-lined road, the branches bare, very few lights on in windows. Car headlamps moved along the high street but shops and cafés were still closed at that early hour.

As she turned the corner, Judith stopped, depression engulfing her. What had happened? What was she doing at that hour of the morning wandering around half-deserted streets, shivering and at a loss to know where to go?

But a month of tossing the possibilities over and over in her head had left her knowing that any chance of calling Van's bluff was utterly futile.

No wonder Carey had been concerned. And Carey? Where on earth was he? She hadn't heard from him for weeks. I can't ring him, she thought dully, beginning to walk towards Knightsbridge. Supposing he really does fancy Van? What then?

Sharp fingers of frost began to numb her face. She pulled the black fur collar of her coat further around her neck. Her reflection in a shop window showed her a pinched face, a red nose and a woman who would do far better to go somewhere warm.

Breakfast. That's what she needed. She pulled back her sleeve and glanced at her watch. Twenty past seven. This wasn't New York, when she could have headed for any one of a hundred diners that would be open at that hour. A hotel it would have to be.

Glancing back along the road, Judith saw the welcoming sign of a taxi with its yellow light on. Within ten minutes she was walking into a small but exclusive hotel at the back of

Knightsbridge and ordering coffee and croissants. She'd taken the precaution of buying a paper to read to fend off any attempts anyone might make at conversation. From her bag she pulled her notebook and diary and laid them on the table, hoping to create the impression that this was business.

The table was in a corner partially obscured by an extravagant display of flowers so that Judith could see, but not be seen by, anyone coming in.

It was because of that protective screen that she saw, without being detected, Lisa Hamilton walking into the breakfast room just ahead of a man who for once wasn't Gray.

He had greyer hair, but he was shorter and carried more weight. Certainly affluent, judging by his dark, well-cut suit, but then she suspected that Lisa didn't know anyone who wasn't.

Judith had nothing against Lisa, and Lisa almost certainly regarded Judith with indifference other than when she needed her to solve a problem, but Judith didn't want to be seen and have to explain why she was breakfasting alone less than a mile from her apartment. And the last thing she wanted was to start her day with a stream of instructions about a ball that was genuinely driving her nuts. She also had reluctantly to admit it had something to do with Lisa's ability to get Gray to do her bidding. And Judith most certainly couldn't.

She'd been trying for days since she had run into him outside the Ritz to convince herself it didn't matter. But it did matter. He mattered. God, how did she manage to be such a victim? Roland, Howard and now Gray.

What did surprise Judith was the body language between Lisa and her companion. Usually smiling submissively and oozing sensuous charm, Lisa was clearly sulking. She had on the same look she'd worn the day Judith had seen her leaving the Savoy with Gray.

They sat at a table on the far side of the room so that Lisa was mostly obscured but the man was clearly visible. Judith silently berated herself for being so interested in them, but how could she not be? This was the woman who had charmed a besotted Gray into marrying her, and who only had to lift a finger and he apparently came running.

The first hint that this was not a breakfast business meeting was when Lisa shook her head angrily at the man. He leaned across to try and take her hand and she impatiently moved it away. Looking both ways, Lisa's companion then got up and moved to sit on the long banquette next to her and slid an arm around her shoulders, bending his head close to hers. After a few minutes he sat back, loosening his hold on her, and looked in despair at the ceiling.

Good grief. They must have been here all night. Judith felt like a voyeur and discreetly called for her bill.

The hotel lobby was reasonably full as Judith reached its safety, having remained undetected by Lisa. Heading for the powder room, she spent a few minutes slapping on just enough make-up to blot out the worn, strained look that had become her companion and, with a final cursory look in the mirror, she opened the door to crash straight into Lisa coming in.

Shit. For a split second the two women gazed at each other, neither thrilled with the encounter. Judith recovered first.

'Well, hello,' she said brightly, thankful she had at least put her eyes on. 'Nice to see I'm not the only one forced out of bed before it's light. I'm on my way to a breakfast meeting.'

Lisa looked briefly past her to see if there was anyone with her. Then she forced a smile. 'Really? Poor you. So boring first thing. My mother . . . she's staying here. I'm just on my way to collect her. Please don't let me detain you.'

She stood aside to let Judith pass, which she did, murmuring that she would no doubt see her at a committee meeting. They were poised half in and half out of the powder room. Judith didn't see Lisa's breakfast companion approaching, but Lisa did and with a muttered oath fled into the ladies' room, slamming the door in Judith's face just as the man reached it.

'Lisa,' he called angrily, banging on the door. 'Lisa, come out and listen to me. Lisa? Darling. Please. You know I love you, just give me time. Li . . . sa.'

Judith stood transfixed. With a groan the man turned and slumped against the door, instantly straightening up when he saw Judith.

'I'm sorry,' he said curtly. 'A stupid quarrel. It's nothing.'

Judith wasn't sure what the correct response was to a man

furiously trying to get an enraged lady out of the powder room at eight o'clock in the morning, so she settled for a small sympathetic smile, murmured, 'Oh dear,' and walked away down the corridor.

By the time she reached Premier she had given up wondering why Lisa had to stay overnight in a hotel with her friend when she was apparently free to entertain anyone she liked in her home, and had returned to her own more pressing problems.

The answer came from Libby who called to cancel a meeting because Lisa Hamilton was unwell. 'Not surprised,' she giggled. 'Her mother has taken up residence for a week, determined to get Lisa to come to her senses and have Gray back.'

'I thought her mother was staying at a hotel,' Judith said casually, despising herself for betraying such an interest.

'If only . . . No, she's moved into Lisa's house. Driving Lisa nuts.'

So that was it.

At least if she and Alice could have a weekend on their own it would be better than nothing. Mid-week she would snatch a day or two from Premier and make sure that they were out all day. She still felt uneasy that Van had offered even that small breathing space so easily.

The problem was that keeping Van was a costly business and any further expense entertaining Alice, except on a modest level, was going to result in one of those conversations with the bank manager that Judith desperately didn't want to have.

Thankfully Alice had a couple of school chums who lived in London and she had already said she wanted to spend some time with them. Rosie had phoned to say if she was stuck, Alice could always go and help on a fashion shoot and Piers, true to his word, had arranged tickets for all of them to see Smashing Pumpkins.

She'd get through it somehow.

Later that morning she put a call through to Carey's office only to hear that he was filming in Paris and would be home in a couple of days. She left a message, and to be on the safe side left one on his answer machine too. Just because he wasn't calling her didn't mean to say she should not call him, Van or no Van.

On Friday she arrived at Paddington ten minutes before Alice's train was due and strolled down to the platform entrance to wait for the Oxford train.

You couldn't miss her, even in the crowd of people surging up the ramp from the train. Not least because her case was being carried by a skinny youth dressed in a strikingly similar manner to Alice, but she was flirting outrageously with another boy, clearly the first one's friend, who was lugging a holdall that Judith recognized instantly as one her father had given Alice for Christmas.

For a while she watched Alice's antics unobserved. Happy, laughing, clearly wallowing in all this attention. No cares beyond which of her swains she should favour with her number. No, she couldn't allow Van to wreck those few precious years when Alice should be undisturbed by anything more than ghastly exams and what to wear to hang out.

Impossible.

Alice spotted Judith as she reached the barrier and began waving wildly. Her companions forgotten, not to mention her adopted air of sophistication, she hurled herself on Judith, shrieking with pleasure.

'This is brill. A whole week in London. Melissa has had to stay in York and she is so-o-o-o jealous. But I said I'd get you to phone her mother and see if she could come down just for a couple of days. You will, won't you?'

By this time the two hesitant bag carriers were trying to attract Alice's attention. Judith was relieved not to have to answer. With Van staying, it was going to be impossible for anyone else to move in. As it was, Alice was going to have to sleep with her.

She'd tell her in the cab once they'd retrieved her luggage. Alice was grandly allowing both boys to kiss her cheek, handing over Judith's number, indicating that they could ring her sister's London apartment at any time. Judith suppressed a smile. She was a complete case.

Alice didn't seem to care much where she slept. London

had been her goal for most of a particularly gruelling term at a school that she loathed because of the uniform. When Judith had suggested she moved elsewhere, Alice had declined, so no-one took much notice of her claims to be intellectually starved and emotionally stunted in such a place.

'Translated,' Laura pointed out, 'she means she isn't allowed to rabbit on about fashion and pop music and access to the opposite sex is severely limited in term time.'

Nor did Alice seem to be that interested in Van, particularly when Judith briefly mentioned he had been a client and was now looking for somewhere else to live.

'Cool,' was all Alice had to say on the subject.

Van had kept his word and disappeared for the weekend, but he had, to Judith's alarm, left a pile of American pop magazines for Alice and a note saying: 'Hi. Welcome to London. Looking forward to meeting you, Van.'

'Hey, these are fab,' enthused Alice, flopping onto the sofa in front of the fire and sorting through them. 'He's cool, okay.'

Judith just nodded.

They spent an energetic weekend largely designed to meet Alice's needs, including lunch at the Hard Rock with Rosie and Tom on Sunday and by Sunday night, not having had the constant pressure of Van's presence, Judith was beginning to feel stronger.

It didn't last long. Van arrived back midway through Monday evening and to her horror devoted the rest of the evening to charming Alice, which he did with an ease that frightened the life out of Judith.

Alice's favourite groups turned out to be ones he really rated. He admired her boots and her jacket of distressed denim. When she said she was hoping to buy a Walkman with all her Christmas money, he spent a good half hour advising her on which one to get and even offered to go with her.

Judith rapidly intervened. 'Thank you, Van, but I think that's asking too much. Alice and I can buy one when we're out tomorrow, I'm having a couple of days off.'

He spread his hands and said conspiratorially to Alice, 'I'm afraid big sister's word is law around here. Anyway, let me know if you get stuck. Now I must have a shower. Got some people to meet. It's a great restaurant, perhaps you two would like to come?'

Judith and Alison spoke in unison.

'Hey, great,' said Alice.

'Sorry, we can't,' said Judith, swiftly thinking up a reason to satisfy Alice who was looking reproachfully at her. 'We have an early start tomorrow and I know how you like late nights, Van. Another time.'

She looked him squarely in the eyes. He smiled his old charming smile, agreed it might be difficult, patted Alice's cheek, told her not to break too many hearts while she was in London, and left.

But not before Judith had seen a look of almost dog-like devotion on Alice's face and the triumphant look on Van's.

Dear God, now what was he up to?

Chapter Nineteen

The charming of Alice continued unabated until by Thursday Judith thought it only needed a ladder outside the younger girl's window to confirm that Van was the personification of Alice's dream man and a flight over the border must be on the cards.

Gone was Alice's previous notion of what made the perfect man – which included anyone wearing torn jeans, ripped T-shirts, any member of a rock group and preferably with a ring through each ear. In came highlighted hair, Armani jackets and all things American.

Van's behaviour was at least mercifully correct, but he left no opportunity unexploited to mentally seduce the impressionable young girl.

To be fair, Alice was a willing participant, responding with giggles and sharp banter to Van's overtures, switching to long heated debates on all her favourite subjects, rock groups, why marijuana should be legalized – not that they disagreed, just that Van wondered if harder 'recreational' drugs should be included – and the age of consent.

Finally she told Judith, who was frantic at the level of these discussions, that she couldn't understand why she hadn't snatched him up.

'It does appear to have been an oversight on my part,' agreed Judith, trying to laugh it off.

'But he's brill, isn't he? I mean, he really *knows* all about music and fashion and he said he could get me into any club I wanted.'

That was it. Judith rounded on her. They were walking through Covent Garden at the time, looking for presents for Alice to take back to Melissa, and Judith's nerves finally snapped.

Alice looked round-eyed and amazed as Judith, gripping

her shoulders, read her the riot act watched by some curious passers-by. 'If I catch you going anywhere with Van to any club, I will put you on the first train back to school so fast you won't know what's hit you . . .'

'But, Judith . . .'

'No buts. Do you understand? Van is a professional charmer. He is no more interested in you than the man in the moon. But he is interested in scoring points.'

'Then why are you living with him?' retorted Alice.

'I am not living with him,' fumed Judith. 'He is simply staying with me until he gets a flat of his own. He's already got a girlfriend, Shade Morgan.'

'Shade's his client,' Alice interrupted. 'I know, he told me. I know who she is too, she had a small part in "Carson's End". "Carson's End", Jude? You know the soap on television? Anyway, I don't care what you say, I'd love to meet her. I think you're being very small-minded. Just because Shade isn't like Piers or Rosie, you think she's beneath you . . .'

'That's enough,' snapped Judith. 'You don't know what you're talking about. You've let Van completely take you over. Now listen,' she went on, drawing a deep breath and trying to calm herself. 'I'm not going to discuss him any more. I know him better than you do. Alice, I don't want to quarrel with you, let's not fall out over Van. He's not worth it, honestly, love. Believe me.'

Alice didn't. Judith tried again. More bribery.

'I know, let's go to the Rock Garden for lunch. It's just over here. You'll love it.'

'Okay,' scowled Alice, the sullen look firmly in place. 'Whatever you want, Jude. I couldn't care less where we go.'

But she could and within a few minutes of getting a table and scanning the menu, Alice decided it wasn't such a bad place and the music was okay too. However, the unspoken difference of opinion hung between them.

Judith finally used her trump card. 'How do you feel about seeing Smashing Pumpkins?' she asked casually, piling salad onto her plate. Alice almost fell off her chair.

'You're kidding?' she breathed. 'See them? I'd *die* for them.'

'Don't be silly,' said Judith, who was used to Alice's over-statements. 'Then you wouldn't be able to see them, would you? Stop arguing ... Piers has got tickets for tonight although I'm afraid you'll have me and Piers and Rosie for company.'

Alice looked ecstatic. 'I don't care,' she said. 'I don't care if I have to go with King Kong. Wait until Mel hears this. And Scott,' she added meditatively. 'He'll be sorry he's started writing to that stuck up cow, Sarah.'

Oh very flattering, thought Judith and wondered on a scale of one to ten where she rated as a companion. But at least Alice was back in a good humour and, more important, Van had been relegated to the back of her mind.

Van showed every sign of being thrilled for Alice when he heard where they would be spending the evening, but Judith knew he was livid that his powerbase over the child had been eroded. Too bad, she thought viciously. He is completely corrupt and one day Alice will understand.

One day.

The concert was, according to Alice, completely crucial. Piers, who had secretly been wondering how he was going to explain to Rosie that he wanted to see a heavy metal group and regarded Alice as a heaven-sent excuse to do so, was in total agreement but Rosie decided she'd had enough excitement for one day and declined Piers's offer to take them all to supper.

Judith didn't blame her and said that she and Alice would see themselves home, stopping off for a bite to eat en route. Piers dropped them in Covent Garden.

'Okay, kiddo,' said Judith. 'Where shall it be? Quick, otherwise we'll get caught up in the opera crowd.'

Alice's first choice of a hamburger joint tucked away in a side street near Drury Lane, was full. Judith glanced at her watch, decided that it was too late just to wander, and headed for a small Italian restaurant that might not be Alice's idea of grooviness, but at least they took late orders.

By the time they turned the corner to head for the opposite side of the Piazza, the first opera-goers were spilling out onto the pavements. Cars and taxis vied with pedestrians for space in the narrow streets.

Grabbing Alice's hand, Judith began to dodge through the congested traffic, only to come to a full stop caught up in a surge of theatre-goers streaming out of Drury Lane.

Pulling a dawdling Alice after her, she stood back to wait until the worst of the crowd had filed past. She saw the man who had been with Lisa Hamilton first. Behind him, Lisa. Then the Fultons and then Gray. The rest of the group were unknown to her; they were standing in a loose knot half on, half off the pavement, comparing watches, clearly staying together but moving to another venue.

Judith didn't know which alarmed her more; seeing Gray again, or seeing Gray in the same group as the man Lisa was clearly having an affair with. What a nerve that woman had.

Too late to turn away. Marjorie Fulton had spotted her and as she exclaimed, 'Judith, darling. Oh my goodness, and Alice,' the whole group turned to see who she was calling to. Those who didn't recognize her turned back after a brief moment to resume their discussion. Marjorie hugged them in turn, exclaiming again at how changed Alice was since she had last seen her nearly a year ago.

'Charles,' called Marjorie. 'There's no reason in the world why we shouldn't take Judith and Alice with us, is there? You know Charles MacIntyre, don't you?'

Charles MacIntyre had moved forward at Marjorie's summons. Judith almost died trying not to laugh out loud and to keep a straight face. A look of sheer terror flashed between him and Lisa. They both shot a frantic look at Judith.

But the reason for their stricken looks had more to do with what Marjorie said next than alerting Gray to their affair.

'And Barbara MacIntyre, Charles's wife,' pursued Marjorie. Barbara was a pretty brunette somewhere in her late thirties, with laughing eyes and a warm smile.

'No, we haven't met Judith,' she said pleasantly. 'Have we, Charles?'

For the briefest of moments Judith caught his eye. He was holding his breath. Barbara was smiling, unaware. Happily married. Judith longed to say, as a matter of fact we have met, that morning, remember, the one when you were pounding on the ladies' door, shrieking away that you were in love with Lisa Hamilton. But who would that hurt most?'

'No,' said Judith, politely shaking hands with this nice woman who didn't deserve such a snake in her life. 'We haven't been introduced.' Which of course was perfectly true.

Charles MacIntyre breathed again. Lisa patted the back of her hair and smiled serenely around.

Marjorie was determined that Alice and Judith should come with them to Langans and Judith was equally determined they should not.

'I have work in the morning and Alice is spending the day with a friend. We're just going to have a quick snack and then home. But we'd love to another time.'

Defeated, Marjorie hugged them both, sent masses of love to Laura via Alice, and while her husband was doing the same, exhorting Judith to get that stick-in-the-mud father of hers down to London, Gray had moved quietly around the outside of the group so that he was standing next to Judith.

'Where are you going to eat? I'll drop you. Marjorie, I'll catch you up. I'm just going to drop Judith and Alice,' he announced without waiting for an agreement.

'Darling,' called Lisa. 'Don't rush, I'll hijack Charles to drop me home, if Barbara doesn't mind.'

Judith's mouth fell open and she glanced swiftly up at Gray, who was nodding in agreement. She was so surprised at Lisa's blatant manipulation of events it wasn't until they were gently ushered forward by Gray that she spoke.

'Honestly, it's too kind of you, but we're fine.'

'But I'm not,' he said. 'Alice, take pity on me. I need a hamburger, not steak.'

Alice, who had been largely silent and rather bored by the encounter, giggled at him.

'Are you dumping them?' she asked bluntly.

'Sort of,' he grinned back. 'Don't split on me, will you? I need an early night too. Charles MacIntyre will insist on a club afterwards and I have a day in court tomorrow.'

Alice looked him up and down. Judith held her breath.

'You're not dressed for hamburgers,' Alice pointed out,

indicating his bow tie and dinner jacket. 'But if you follow me in, no-one will notice. Just lose the bow tie,' she advised.

'Of course,' he said obediently and removed it. 'Is that better?'

'It'll do,' said Alice.

Gray looked suitably pleased and turned to Judith, who wondered why he was swapping Langans for hamburgers. He raised his eyebrows at her.

'I can see where she gets it from,' he said. 'She's just like you.'

'I suppose so,' answered Judith, ridiculously happy just to see him, but apprehensive too. This time she was on her guard. 'Well,' she said lightly. 'We appear to be having supper, so where shall we go?'

Unlike Van, Gray made no attempt to charm Alice, but without consulting either of them he piloted them into a small bistro that was lively enough for Alice not to notice that hamburgers were not on the menu. He chatted amiably to her, confessed he hadn't been to a rock concert in years and when for the third time he had to admit he hadn't heard of a group she mentioned, she seemed to lose all interest in him.

'What do you do?' she asked politely.

'I'm a lawyer. I know,' he said solemnly, seeing the bored look on her face. 'Very dull stuff.'

'Not necessarily,' answered Alice kindly. 'Divorces can be dead juicy . . . and libel. Do you do any of that?' she enquired hopefully, scooping up scampi provençal.

'Sorry, no divorces but some libel. Not much though. Mostly corporate stuff, thrashing out the details of mergers, business affairs of private individuals.'

Judith wondered how a brief sentence could make what he did seem so mundane.

Apart from Howard and Bill Jefferson, his list of clients included at least one princess, four captains of industry, three of whom were kept safe from bankruptcy by Gray Hamilton's aggressive negotiating tactics, and a newspaper proprietor so sick of Gray lifting millions from his empire in libel actions for his other clients against his newspapers, that he was currently trying to woo Gray into taking him as a personal client, the only effective way of stopping him.

Dull was not the word most people who knew him applied to Gray's job. But then Carey had once told Judith that Gray Hamilton's wealth was founded on making his job seem as interesting as waiting in a deserted launderette at midnight.

'The less everyone knows, the easier it is for him to operate,' Carey had said. 'You watch him, the minute the conversation turns to him, he deflects it. I'm not even sure Lisa really knew him, you know. He's just not into feelings or small talk.'

Judith remembered saying: 'But he rips into everyone else's feelings when he wants to. When it suits him.'

Carey had looked at her in surprise. 'Well, that's his job,' he said.

Looking at Alice and Gray and listening to them discussing why she found school so gross, Judith knew what Carey meant.

Gray rarely if ever discussed his job. But then he didn't discuss his private life either. Hard to know what he felt about anything or what made him tick. What on earth, for instance, had prompted him to join them for supper? No, *insisted* on joining them.

'Of course,' Alice was saying chattily, 'I've only been to two schools. The first one was dull because it was in Torfell and then Melissa – that's my best friend – her parents decided to send her to Manningtree and they persuaded Dad to send me too.'

Judith looked at her in astonishment. Alice's ability to rewrite history was impressive.

'You know we couldn't have stopped you going there if we'd tried,' she interrupted. 'I wanted you to go to St Bridget's, at least that way you would have come home every Friday night. But I seem to recall – now what was it?' She leaned her head on one side as though trying to remember exactly what it was Alice had said.

Alice blushed. 'Oh shut up, Jude. I know I said it was completely skanky – gross,' she said for Gray's benefit. 'And it is. It's all right for Jude, she went to endless schools, so she wasn't stuck with just one *and* she got to go to school in

America – but then Mummy died and we all came home.'

Gray looked at Judith, who had gone very quiet. What would Alice say next?

'Well, lucky for us you did. Otherwise I would never have got to know you both.'

His eyes held Judith's gaze for a brief second. A warning went off in her head. Don't make the same mistake again. She dragged hers away.

'Well, I suppose so,' conceded Alice, who was chatting to Gray as though she had known him for years. She was also displaying a great deal more charm in his presence than she had all week, quite naturally too. Unlike with Van, she wasn't interested in impressing him, but because she wasn't trying she was clearly succeeding.

'But then, everything is meant to be, isn't it? Mel and I were talking about it. You can't change anything, can you? It's all kind of laid out for you. Life I mean.

'I wasn't meant to grow up in America but it would have been dead cool. Mummy wasn't meant to have me as late as she did. I was an afterthought, you know.'

Judith choked.

Gray reached over and patted her on the back. 'Were you?' he said, looking at Alice with interest. 'Do you think that's made a difference too?'

Alice considered this. 'I don't know. It probably made more difference to Jude. It's funny, we just never talk about it much, do we, Jude? I don't remember Mum at all, I was only a few months old when she died. Everyone says I look like her, but then Jude does too.'

Gray looked from one to the other. Judith's glass was nearly empty. Gray reached over and refilled it and his own.

'Your mother must have been very beautiful,' he said, looking straight at Judith. 'Doesn't your poor father have a say in anything? Is he in London with you?'

Alice groaned. 'Oh, poor Dad. So fed up with all these women around him. He's stuck back home at Torfell and probably loving every minute of it, isn't he, Jude? Gran is in Scotland and I'm having a brill time here. Do you know Van, Jude's flatmate?'

Judith studied her plate. Gray didn't miss a beat. 'Not very well. I've met him once or twice with Judith. Why?'

Alice hesitated, sensing she had said something wrong. 'Sorry, Jude,' she mumbled. 'Nothing really,' she said to Gray. 'Jude isn't as keen on him as I am, that's all.'

'Really,' said Gray, draining his glass. 'You surprise me.'

'That's funny,' giggled Alice, scooping up the last of the sauce with a spoon. 'I thought lawyers weren't meant to be surprised by anything.'

'Ah, but you have to remember,' Gray said, looking at Judith, 'people often say one thing when all the evidence points in the opposite direction.'

Chapter Twenty

Camilla's office made air-traffic control at Heathrow look under-employed. Both phones flashed incessantly. Clark and Annie were in and out with demands, requests, questions.

Spencer had arrived at work before eight and by the time Judith showed up just past nine he had driven Fenny and Camilla into a rare show of unity with his shouted orders.

'What's his problem?' asked Judith, shedding her coat and nodding towards Spencer's office. As she spoke she automatically reached for the phone to call the first of the names that had left messages asking for her urgent attention.

'Anyone would think he owns the place,' growled Camilla. 'I've told Fenny to hurl a couple of tea bags at him and lock him in. Jacob Frankenheim was on this morning, and Harcourt. He wants to see you when you get in.'

'Goodness,' laughed Judith. 'Must be serious. Hey, leave that file,' she said, tucking the phone under her chin and holding out her hand. 'And get me Stella Frankenheim on the other line, what on earth can be so urgent for her to ring at this hour?

'Yes, Spencer,' she said as he picked the phone up in his office down the corridor. 'Do you want me to come down?'

'When you've got a minute in the next half hour. Before I speak to Jacob.'

She heard his phone go down and stared at the dead instrument in her hand.

'What on earth's got into him?' she asked Camilla with a startled look.

Camilla looked uneasy. 'Something to do with tickets for the ball, Jude. I think he wants to know who some of these people are.'

Judith beckoned for the list in Camilla's hand as she got through to Stella Frankenheim.

'Stella, good morning. It's Judith.'

At first Judith listened with a small frown on her face as the vociferous and hyperactive, socially demanding, class-conscious Stella Frankenheim reminded her about the agreement that the committee had reached about invitations to the ball.

'Judith, this ball is very prestigious. You understand? Yes? Only the very best are to be invited, yes? We want this ball to raise money and to be an evening where we can be certain that the Duke and Duchess won't feel compromised. Do you understand, Judith? Do you understand what I'm trying to say here?'

Judith rolled her eyes at Camilla, who was listening anxiously.

'Of course, Stella,' soothed Judith. 'The guest list is nearly full, but we expect to confirm the last two tables by the end of the week. Camilla and Libby are co-ordinating and updating each other the whole time. On Thursday they will check everyone. But the chances of getting tickets now are remote to zilch. Unless we put in another table, but . . .'

Stella Frankenheim was not in a listening mode. She was in a furious temper.

'No buts, Judith. The list Libby has sent me – and one I did not *dare* submit to the committee – contained names unfamiliar to me. Do you understand me, Judith? *Unfamiliar* names.'

Judith gritted her teeth. It could only mean that someone less than a Prince of the Realm had crept onto the list. She scanned the names in front of her. It read like a roll call from *Debretts*. 'The Duke and Duchess of course, the Earl and Countess of Deal, Sir Ian and Lady Mulcavey, the Hon Serena Michelson.' Her eyes travelled down. 'Sir John and Lady Imber, Mr Van Kingsley, Miss Shade Mor . . .' *What?*

Judith slowly slid into her chair. Mr Vincent Perrereo, Mr Maurice Allton. All Van's clients.

She took a deep breath.

'Stella, can I get back to you. I've just seen this . . .'

It wasn't good enough for Stella Frankenheim. Any threat to her social standing she regarded with the seriousness of the relief of Mafeking. Judith regarded it as professional suicide. Her own.

'Judith.' Stella Frankenheim was not mincing her words. 'I gave this ball my backing because I thought Premier was reputable. Why haven't you seen this list? It is your responsibility. I name no names, but at least one of these people has recently been in police custody. *Do you understand?*'

Judith looked at Camilla in dismay and spread her hands wide. Eventually, after much apologizing and pledges of an immediate enquiry, she put the phone down and slumped back in her chair.

Camilla was still standing rooted in the doorway. She didn't have to be told.

'My God,' whispered Judith, her hand across her mouth. 'What does Van think he's doing? All those people? Who gave them the invitations? I can't believe it.'

Camilla looked surprised. 'But you did, surely? Van called at least a week ago and said you wanted to reserve a table for eight for your own personal friends. I would have reminded you, only you weren't here yesterday when the list was faxed over to Mrs Frankenheim.'

Judith stared back at her. 'I said, Van, just Van.' She could hardly breathe. 'Vincent Perrereo isn't a friend, he's a . . . nothing.'

Mustn't let Camilla see. She swallowed hard. 'Van must have misunderstood. I said if we couldn't sell the tickets, and we needed to make up the tables, then he could invite his . . . his friends.'

Camilla had been joined in the doorway by Annie. It sounded preposterous; there was no problem filling tables. There was a list waiting for cancellations. Camilla must know she was lying. Annie and Camilla looked at each other.

'Don't worry, Camilla. I'll sort it out. Now, Annie,' she said briskly. 'What's the problem?'

By midday she had tried four times and failed to get Van. Spencer had been placated. Circe, who had been hired to do the floral arrangements for the ball, had pulled out and a whole hour had been spent coercing her back to doing it for nothing.

Clark had had Farley on the phone close to tears because the company hired to make up his special design for the waiters had mislaid the instructions and, while he was on, could he tell Judith that he didn't mind supplying Van with a dinner jacket because he was her boyfriend, but he was sorry he couldn't extend his generosity to Van's clients.

Judith didn't know whether it was Farley describing Van as her boyfriend or the breathtaking cheek he had wanting free clothes for himself and his dreadful clients that enraged her the most.

Annie was red-eyed after a particularly desperate row with Marcel and told Judith, who was nearly at screaming point herself, that she was seriously thinking of dumping him. Clark took her to lunch. And told her to do just that.

Another client rang with the dubious news that Rik Bannerman was now working as a freelance for, among others, Premier. It was the first Judith had heard of it, but Spencer was nowhere to be found when she stormed his office.

She didn't bother with lunch; she couldn't have eaten anything if she'd tried. It was going to be a long day. Thankfully Alice was with Ginny, her schoolfriend, and she wouldn't need collecting until late evening.

Where was Van? Last night when they had arrived home he hadn't been there. This morning his door was closed when they left the flat together, Judith having agreed to drop Alice at Ginny's in time for breakfast.

Ginny's mother worked so she was glad of the company for her daughter and also had a pressing dinner engagement in the evening. Judith had to admit that she too was glad Alice had someone to spend the day with. She loved having her around but the circumstances had made it wearing beyond belief.

She still couldn't decide why Gray had chosen to join them for dinner last night. All she knew was that she was glad he had. Very glad. Dangerously glad. On reflection, Alice's revelation that Judith didn't care too much for Van was not so bad after all.

It was very important to her that Gray should know that. In fact it was important that everyone should know it. But how, without angering Van into doing something vicious?

At three, Alice phoned to ask if she could stay overnight with Ginny. Some other friends were coming over and Ginny's mother had agreed they could phone the pizza home delivery and have a video as well.

Judith hesitated. Alice was due back at school on Saturday afternoon. She didn't want her zonked on her first day back.

'Please, Jude. Promise I'll get enough sleep. It's been a brill week and you're the best sister in the world. So please?'

Judith smiled wanly. 'Okay, you wretch. Let me speak to Ginny's mother, just to arrange a time to pick you up. I've got to go over to Libby's for a meeting so I'll be late getting home. But if you need me I'll be there after nine.'

'Brill. I left a message on the answer machine at home in case I missed you, so just ignore it.'

Since Ginny's mother was going to be back late, she was only too happy to have Alice overnight. 'Shall I drop her round to you? No? You'll pick her up at two? Marvellous.'

To be honest Judith was half relieved that Alice would not be staying at the flat any more. It also meant she could tackle Van about the de Vries ball. This could ruin her. Surely he must see that?

He didn't. He simply laughed in her face.

They were standing glaring at each other in the hallway. It was nearly ten o'clock when she came in, only to hear him announce he was going out almost immediately.

'You can have a ticket and sit at my table,' she said slowly. 'But that is it. Shade is a ludicrous bimbo that couldn't conduct a bus let alone a conversation. Vinny Perrereo is a drug dealer . . . yes he is. Don't deny it. Stella Frankenheim knows about him. Her brother is a judge, remember. Wouldn't surprise me if he wasn't the one who had sent Vinny down. And Maurice Allton? Are you serious? Don't you see, if you ruin me, I'm useless to you? And if you go on like this, I might just say do your worst.'

Van flicked his gaze over her and pushed his finger into her shoulder. 'That, honey, is your problem. You're a little gold mine to me. If Premier goes, you have other assets you can use. You have before and you know it.'

Without saying another word Judith walked into her bedroom and slammed the door shut.

There she stayed until she heard Van leave. The second the door closed she ran down the corridor and locked it, bolting it so that he couldn't return. She had the feeling that he wouldn't, not that night.

Wearily she sank down onto the bed fully clothed and just gazed up at the ceiling. In a minute she would have a shower and change and think, really think, what to do next.

The shrill ring of the phone woke her just after midnight. Drugged by sleep and still in her clothes, her hand fumbled for the receiver, switching the phone to her right ear as she struggled to sit up.

'Miss Craven Smith?'

'Mm. Yes,' she mumbled. 'Who is this?'

'Connaught Row Police Station, Miss.'

Police? Judith sat bolt upright. What in God's name had Van done now? She groped for the light next to her bed, grabbing the clock to peer at the time.

'What's the matter? What is it?'

'Sorry to disturb you, Miss, but are you Miss Alice Craven Smith's sister?'

Oh God. Alice. 'Yes, yes. Is she all right?'

'Yes, Miss. I'm sorry to tell you she's under arrest.'

Chapter Twenty-One

Judith reached the police station in thirty minutes. Stopping only to pull on some boots, thrusting her arms into a warm navy jacket, she grabbed a thick scarf which she wound around her neck as she raced out of the flat and into the street.

It was a bitterly cold night. Frost was already forming on the windscreens of parked cars, spreading diamond-sharp ice through hedges and trees. Not a taxi in sight. She set off at a run towards the high street, tearing around the corner, looking frantically each way for a familiar yellow light.

She was nearly at the junction of Church Street when she spotted a cab setting a passenger down and, with a sob of relief, she reached it before it moved away.

Alice arrested. What was she doing? Only then did she think of Ginny's mother. Where was she?

The policeman had been unable to give her any details on the phone, simply asking her to come down to the station where the charges would be relayed to her. Sitting on the edge of the seat, holding onto the door strap, she repeated what she knew. Alice was not injured or hurt.

As the cab pulled into the kerb outside the red brick building of Connaught Row, Judith was already thrusting money through the glass partition separating her from the driver and without waiting for any change, she wrenched the door open. She took the steps of the police station two at a time, heaving open the heavy swing doors and blinking around in the glaring light of the crowded reception.

A uniformed police officer was behind a glass-screened reception area dealing with a small queue of disparate people. From the outside the building was a monument to nineteenth-century imposing architecture but once inside, twentieth-century forces and needs had made sure that a warren of characterless, box-shaped offices erected in a self-assembly format, with frosted glass windows in plain cream wooden frames, had obliterated the original Victorian grandeur.

Two narrow benches faced each other below a pin-board of notices. A handful of people were scattered along them, gazing silently ahead, paying little attention to each other. A long corridor stretched away to the left, disappearing around a sharp corner at the end.

Judith ran her eyes rapidly along the faces of the motley crowd taking up most of the available seating. No Alice. A policeman emerged from a side door, calling a name from a list he held in his hand. Judith raced over to him, plucking at his sleeve as a young boy dressed in a heavy metal T-shirt was pulled to his feet by a pinstriped-suited older man in response to his name.

'Can you help me? Someone just called to say my sister had been arrested. Alice. Alice Craven Smith, she's only fourteen, I can't believe she's done anything. It must be a mistake . . .'

'Hang on, Miss,' he said firmly. 'Have you checked with the desk?'

'The desk? Oh, the desk. No, it's such a long queue, she'll be so frightened. Please can't you help?'

Near to tears, Judith gazed pleadingly at him. He looked at her for a second and then said, 'Take a seat. Craven Smith, you said? I'll see what I can find out. Let me just deal with this young man. Right, sir, if you'll come with me. And you are? Oh right, his father, are you. That's fine.'

Judith leaned weakly against the wall. A young girl perched on the end of the bench nearest to her, blonde hair like straw, heavily made up and wearing a skin-tight mini-skirt and high heels, drawing deeply on a cigarette, glanced curiously at her.

Where was that policeman? If she only knew what Alice had done she could get her a lawyer or something. But she couldn't believe Alice had done anything. Wild and irrepressible, Alice was still a very straight girl at heart. Simply fourteen.

Judith glanced at the clock on the wall. Fifteen minutes since she'd arrived. It was nearly one o'clock. Not wanting to make things worse for Alice by making a fuss, but knowing she would go mad if she did nothing while they took their time, she decided to wait just two more minutes and then to ask again.

But just as she sank back against the wall, she heard and saw a bustle of movement at the end of a corridor that led away from the reception. She glanced at the crowd of people coming towards her and stiffened. Shade Morgan was being escorted away by two men, one clearly a lawyer and the other, with his arm protectively around her, Vinny Perrereo.

They saw Judith as she saw them. A dreadful premonition gripped her.

'Oh, here's big sister,' mocked Shade as she drew level with her. 'Come to bail her out, have you? Right little raver she is. Bit like yourself, I gather,' she sneered as Vinny and the other man ushered her towards the door of what appeared to be an interview room.

'Shade!' Judith ran after her. 'Where's Alice, what's happened? Shade, you must tell me!'

'Tell you? I don't even want to *speak* to you,' Shade said contemptuously, not even pausing while she answered her. 'I'll leave that to your fancy-schmancy friends,' she called over her shoulder as a policewoman followed her into the room and the door shut behind them.

Judith gazed helplessly after her and then strode over to the reception. Van was behind this. How else would Shade know about Alice? She pushed her way through the knot of people, and placed herself squarely in front of the duty officer.

Surprise at her doggedness kept the rest of the queue quiet. 'One of your colleagues was going to find out about my sister, Alice Craven Smith, who was brought in earlier. *Please* let me see her. She must be terrified by now. I'm responsible for her. You must tell me where she is. She may need a lawyer.'

Maddeningly slowly the duty officer flicked down his list. Without taking his eyes off Judith's face, he reached for the phone and pressed a button.

'Jack? Yes. Craven Smith, Alice Craven Smith. Yes? Yes? I see. Right. There's someone coming down now, Miss, to get you. She's under age so no charges could be made till you got here.'

There was a bright light exploding in her head. Charges? What charges? The officer behind the desk had lost interest in her and had returned to the woman so roughly pushed aside by Judith.

'But is she okay?' persisted Judith. 'What's she been charged with?' She was irritating him but she had to know. 'Please,' she added.

He glanced back at his pad. 'Nothing yet,' he said briefly. 'She's a minor. I expect they're waiting for you or someone from Social Services before they do anything.'

Social Services? Judith pushed her way back through the crowd. It simply wasn't happening. At that moment Ginny's mother arrived.

'Judith,' Kate panted, gripping her arm. 'What's happened? Where are they?'

Judith had been planning to ask her the same question. 'I thought you would know,' she said. Kate was shaking with fright. She had been out to dinner with friends who lived in Hertfordshire, it had taken longer to get back than she had expected and she had found a police car waiting.

'They were in when we left. Ginny had strict instructions to stay there. How did they get mixed up in this?'

Judith shook her head, frightened. 'I don't know why they're here. I thought you might.'

'Oh God, hasn't anyone told you?' Kate's face was white with anxiety. Judith's remained immobile as the other woman sank against the wall, pressing her hands against her cheeks. 'The police told me they had been picked up in Chelsea at some party. Drugs or something. Porn videos. Someone must have tipped off the police because they were raided and Ginny and Alice got taken in along with everyone else.'

'Judith . . .' Kate's voice, already cracking up, sank to a whisper. 'What on earth has been happening?'

Drugs? Videos? What kind of videos? A half hope rose in Judith's head that there had been a mistake, only to be instantly banished.

Instead she swung around and looked towards the desk, searching for a phone. 'I'd better get them a lawyer . . .'

'They've got one,' Kate interrupted.

'*Got* one?' echoed Judith, feeling that the night could no longer hold any surprises.

But it could. Even as she was speaking, an officer called her name and Kate's and together they followed him along the corridor to a room at the far end. Kate, slightly ahead of Judith, uttered a cry of relief as her daughter sprang up from one of the chairs and fell into her arms. Alice was looking apprehensively at Judith, who was standing very still, trying to make sense of why Alice was here, and how come she was sitting with Gray?

Gray whispered something to Alice, who tried to smile, rose unsteadily to her feet and with a small convulsive sob ran across the room to Judith.

'Oh, Jude, it was awful,' Alice whispered as Judith hugged her. 'It all happened so quickly. I was so scared.'

Over her head Judith gazed at Gray. He looked tired, as, half sitting on the windowsill, he watched their reunion with interest. Clearly he too had been roused from his bed by a phone call. He was wearing jeans, a sweater and a leather bomber jacket. A tartan scarf was tied loosely at his neck. He needed a shave. He didn't look like a lawyer or someone who spent their life commanding the attention of men who ruled the square mile.

'How did you come to be here?' she asked him, still holding Alice. Ginny and her mother were talking urgently to each other a little distance away. Ginny was crying.

Gray rubbed his chin. 'She might have got herself into a mess but she did the right thing. As soon as she got here she asked if she could ring me because I was her lawyer . . .'

'*Her lawyer?*' Judith opened her eyes wide. 'Alice, why didn't you call me?'

Alice yawned, relief beginning to replace the fear on her face. 'You're not a lawyer. Gray is, and you said he's the best, didn't you? Well, I think he is, and I knew once he was here it would be all right.'

Judith glanced up at Gray. He gave a tired chuckle and strolled across the room.

'I wish all my clients had the same faith in me,' he said, ruffling Alice's hair.

'Anyway,' Alice went on, tucking her arm into Judith's, 'you would only have called him yourself, so I just saved time. Ginny was hysterical and Van had disappeared . . .'

'Van?' Judith grabbed Alice's shoulders. 'What's Van got to do with this?'

Gray interrupted her. 'Look, let's get out of here. I doubt there'll be any objection to both of them being released on bail until we can get all the charges dropped.'

Judith looked at Ginny and Kate and knew full well what they were both thinking. So too apparently did Gray, who went over to Kate and began talking to her in a low, reassuring voice, one arm placed around Ginny's shoulder.

'There is no evidence yet against either of them except that they were in the flat, but we don't know what Shade's story will be. She can't be relied on to say anything other than what will get her off the hook. I gather she's been held in the cells until they had an interview room free, so she isn't likely to be feeling sensible.'

'I saw her,' Judith told him. 'She was hysterical.'

Gray just shrugged. 'So for the moment,' he went on, addressing the matter in hand, 'I don't think there'll be a problem about them being released into your custody on bail until the police can arrange a hearing.'

'When?' Judith cut in, knowing her voice sounded more curt than grateful.

'A few days, a week or two. I'll let you know. But first we've got to hear what the custody officer has to say now that you're both here.'

The wait was longer than they had expected. It was a busy night at the station, but it gave Alice time to tell Judith what had happened.

Van had got the number of where she was staying from the answer machine. He knew she was anxious to meet Shade and he thought it would be a surprise treat. Ginny's mother had gone out and Van promised to have them back well before she got in.

'He said Shade was having a party at her flat and there would be some rock stars there. I knew if I rang you, you would stop it, and I thought it would be really crucial to tell

Melissa and Scott would be *so* jealous. Ginny was dead keen to go and you can't deny, Jude, that Van is a friend of yours. I thought it would be okay.'

Judith winced.

'When we got there it was fine and we met Shade – who's dead dim by the way – but she was trying really hard to be nice. But she was the only one we recognized. Van just said the others would be along later. Anyway we just sat on a sofa and listened to some music and then we noticed they were starting to snort cocaine.'

Judith was shaking inside. Alice was exhausted. Judith thought she would never have a peaceful night's sleep again.

'What did you do?'

Alice seemed confused about what happened next. 'Well, at first I thought it was okay, I mean they weren't doing anyone any harm. But then I thought maybe Ginny and I shouldn't be there. So I looked round for Van, but he wasn't there.

'Shade was in another room so I went to find her but she was . . . well, sort of um . . .' Alice looked up at Judith, who could see she was embarrassed.

'You can tell me, love,' she said, pushing Alice's fringe out of her eyes.

'Well, she was in bed . . . on the bed really with . . . it may not have been, but I thought it was.'

'Who?'

Gray, who had been leaning silently against the opposite wall, broke in.

'Alice never saw his face properly, so I've advised her not to think about it any more.'

Judith didn't need to be told. They were both trying to protect her from hearing it was Van. She couldn't recall when she had ever felt this humiliated. And it was over someone she loathed from the bottom of her soul.

'Quite right,' she agreed. 'Then what happened?'

'Well, I scuttled out and went back to Ginny who said that man Vinny was in the bathroom with a really awful woman and that they were so drunk they'd fallen into the bath together.'

'Pity they didn't drown,' remarked Gray. Judith knew she would have found great pleasure pushing their heads under water. What on earth would be the effect of this on two impressionable girls?

'Ginny thought we should just go and get a taxi home, but I didn't like to leave without telling Van, so I persuaded her to wait and then Shade appeared and said that Van would be back presently, he'd gone to collect someone and he would drive us home as soon as he got back, so it seemed okay.

'And then all hell broke loose, there was a knock on the door and someone started screaming it was the police. That man Vinny tried to climb out of the window and Shade was panicking like mad. The others were all trying to hide bags of cocaine, honest, Jude, you should have seen it, masses of the stuff.

'Anyway, we were pretty panicky ourselves but we thought it would be better to open the door, so Ginny and I did. We ran out onto the landing but they thought we were trying to run past them because we were so scared, but this policewoman caught us and made us go back. We kept telling her we knew nothing about it, but she wouldn't listen.

'After that we just had to wait until Shade had stopped shrieking – mostly about wrecking her career and suing them – and Vinny was found on the window ledge. Well, he wasn't found, I told them he was out there. Then we were all taken in cars to the police station and you know the rest.'

Judith was silent. This was Van's way of warning her just what else he could do. It had to stop.

Chapter Twenty-Two

Fifteen minutes later, a much-chastened Alice and Ginny had been interviewed separately. Alice glanced nervously at Judith or Gray while she was being questioned. The charges were alleged use of drugs, which Alice immediately vehemently denied, but the officer ignored her. And trying to resist arrest.

Judith gasped. Alice protested. 'I was trying to get away from that crowd, not the police, honestly ... Gray, tell them ...'

Gray motioned her to keep quiet. The police officer went on.

'You'll hear from us in due course once all the evidence and statements have been obtained. Meanwhile you are free to go, provided you stay at your sister's address, and in her charge, seeing as how your father is not in the country.'

A warning look shot from Gray to Judith, who promptly let the truth die on her lips.

'You can go back to school tomorrow but you will have to present yourself with your sister or guardian and a lawyer if that is what you wish, at a date you will be notified of.'

And then it was over.

Alice breathed a sigh of relief. Judith slumped back in her chair. Gray slid off the window seat, from where he had been viewing the proceedings.

'The main thing is to get the girls home. But can I just mention a couple of points ...'

They both looked at him. 'For some reason there are a few hacks at the entrance. If this is an obscure way for Shade Morgan to get publicity then we can lay the blame at her door, but I doubt it. Someone has obviously tipped them off. Walk straight out, keep it casual, try to talk normally to each other as you go past anyone who looks as if they're from a newspaper. Okay?'

'But why?' asked Alice. 'They don't know me from Adam.'

Gray glanced at his watch. 'I know that, and I want to keep it that way. Trouble is, your sister might not be instantly recognizable but she is known, and with not much else happening they'll be looking for almost any story to justify being here. And since I'm a corporate lawyer and am not usually involved in bailing teenagers on drugs charges, they'll wonder what I'm doing here at this time of night and smell a rat.'

Alice was appalled. 'You mean I shouldn't have called you?'

'Not at all, thank God you did. But it's better that it remains something between us three, okay?'

Of course, why hadn't Judith thought of it herself? So caught up in the relief of Alice being rescued, it had not until now occurred to her that Gray's own reputation was at risk. He wasn't actually saying it, but a lawyer of his standing would normally have recommended someone else to take care of the case, and the speculation that would arise if it got out that he was personally defending an unwise teenager would do him no good at all.

Why should all his hard work capturing the most prestigious clients in the country be tarnished by the hand of Van Kingsley? Nor did she want Van to rope anyone else she cared about into his sordid little schemes. Alice was bad enough.

Judith touched Gray's arm. 'I am so sorry. You're being dragged into a squalid case like this. It's entirely my fault. You mustn't be associated with this, it's simply not fair. Alice, I'll get another lawyer tomorrow . . .'

Alice nodded, trying to fight back the tears. 'I'm so sorry, Jude. I should have listened to you. Will you be able to get someone? I've got to go back to school tomorrow.'

Gray had listened in clear amazement to the pair of them. 'Bloody women,' he groaned. 'Do either of you ever listen to what is being said? I'm simply stating a few facts that are unavoidable and you both start behaving like a scene out of a soap opera. Another lawyer? Abandon you? Who the hell do you think I am? I am dragged from my sleep in the small hours after a helluva day in court and then you tell me, the deal's off. What kind of women are you? And,' he added, tragically passing a hand across his brow, 'what about my feelings?'

Alice giggled weakly, and both girls began to protest at once.

'Okay, you two,' Gray said, raising his voice enough to quieten them. 'Just listen. You,' he pointed a finger at Judith, 'might run a business and you,' he turned to Alice, 'might be Queen Bee at school, but for the rest of the night I'm the boss. Got that?'

They both nodded meekly.

'Right now, just do as I say. Go and join Ginny and Kate in reception, I'm going to see if I can find out who's representing Shade. I won't be a minute.'

Alice obediently made for the door; Judith paused. 'I am going, but you know what I meant, don't you?'

'No. I never know what you mean . . . or what you want. I don't understand you. But I'm a devil for punishment and willing to try.'

'I'd like that. Not now, not for a while. But one day.'

He looked at her for a moment and then reached out and touched her face. 'You're a strange girl. Howard always said he never understood what you wanted.'

Judith gave a low laugh. 'Odd, that, because I always understood perfectly what he wanted. And what I was trying to say was, I'll try to repay your kindness on another occasion.'

'Oh, is that all?' he asked in mock disappointment. 'In which case, I'd better think of a suitable reward you can offer. Go on, Alice is waiting.'

That's it, she told herself with determined cheerfulness as she followed Alice down the corridor. Just be friends, easygoing, no involvement. No future.

Anyway, men hated scandal touching them. Women were so much better at coping. No future there at all. The thought did not exactly cheer her up.

As Gray had predicted, a couple of reporters and a photographer were hanging around outside the station. Ginny and Kate had noticed them when they had gone out for some fresh air.

They hadn't been sitting in reception for more than a minute when Alice gripped Judith's arm. 'Look,' she hissed. 'It's Shade. Golly, doesn't she look awful?'

And she did. Her eyes were hidden behind dark glasses. She was wearing an outsize fur coat over leggings and little granny boots, she was smoking and at nearly two in the morning was attracting rather than detracting attention from herself. A summons to appear on drug charges in court was not what she had planned as part of her publicity campaign and she was nearly in orbit with fury.

It was difficult to avoid her, but if they had expected her to pass by without a word, they were soon disillusioned. Shaking off the restraining hand of the solicitor who was accompanying her and the two minders who were there to stop the waiting reporters from getting too near while they negotiated with the murkier tabloids for her story, she strode over to where Judith and Alice were sitting.

'You know what you are?' she practically spat at Judith, rage consuming her face and obliterating all reason, her hands on her hips.

Judith half rose as she spoke, but Shade shot out a hand and pushed her down so that she spoke right into her face. 'You are an A-grade cow. If you had any pride you would stop hanging onto Van. What kind of bitch are you, to shop complete strangers to the police – and your own sister?'

Alice leapt to her feet and pushed Shade. 'Go away, you horrible person. Leave my sister alone, do you hear? Leave her alone.'

Judith was shaken. Shade must be mad. What was she talking about? Shade's lawyer was pulling her away, but she shook him off. He looked round desperately for help. The whole lobby had come to a standstill. Shade hadn't finished.

'You'll get what you deserve when your sister ends up in jail. I know it was you who shopped us,' she screamed. 'You had us busted. Don't look so innocent, I got the whole story from Vinny. He knows, he's always said you were nothing but a cheap whore in designer clothes.

'You'd do anything to stop Van seeing me. What a cheap trick, ringing him to get him out of the flat so that he wouldn't be busted along with us. Listen, Miss Tightarse, if those guys out there want a story and I'm going to get done for this, they might as well have the whole lot and pay for it. How would your precious Mr Dorfman like that, eh? How would he like to hear you deliberately set us up so that you could get your hands on Van? Talk? You bet I'll talk. I've got nothing to lose, baby, nothing at all.'

Ginny and her mother were transfixed by the astonishing outburst. Alice had put both arms around Judith. Which is how Gray found them as he returned, having heard it all, in time to see Shade being dragged away by her lawyer, still shouting.

It took him just a few seconds to take in the scene. Shade's accusations were pouring out. 'Sit down,' he said curtly to Alice and Judith. Then, hands dug into his pockets, he strolled casually across the lobby to where the hysterical actress was surrounded by her entourage, preventing her from moving, and the duty officer was quietly warning her that she would be kept in the cells overnight for disorderly and threatening behaviour if she didn't calm down.

The threat of a return to the cells was all that was needed. There, unlike Ginny and Alice who because of their age had been kept in a side room, Shade had had to share accommodation with a hooker screaming profanities at anyone who passed, next door to a vagrant relieved to have a bed for the night, the smell of whom was enough to reform the most hardened criminal.

A shaken Judith saw Gray beckon Shade's solicitor from the group. The man, famous for his clientele of showbiz personalities, was clearly astonished at the sight of the eminent lawyer. 'Having trouble with your client, Arnold?' Gray asked pleasantly. 'What a very loud young lady she is. Shall we have a word outside? Say in about five minutes. Wait on the next corner.'

With that, he walked over to Judith and told her to stay where she was until he returned.

'What are you going to do?' she asked, white-faced.

'My problem. I now have two clients to think of. Howard is my business as well.'

Turning to Kate, he told her to leave with Ginny and Alice

225

and to wait in her car, which was parked on the opposite side of the road. 'I don't want all of us to be seen together,' he explained.

Once outside, Gray strolled undetected past the reporters who were busy on their mobiles, to where Arnold was waiting, shivering in the freezing night air despite a thick coat, scarf and fur hunting hat with earmuffs pulled down.

'Arnold, what a strange place to meet, but I'm sure you can help me with a problem or two. We now have at least a dozen witnesses who will be able to testify they heard your client's unprovoked and totally slanderous attack on my client, and I'm sure Miss Morgan doesn't need any more problems to cope with.'

In the course of the next two minutes Gray conveyed to an irate Arnold the fact that the Crown Prosecution Service would be invited to investigate the circumstances under which the two young girls were asked to the house, the natural inference being – as no doubt Arnold would realize – that they were to be drugged and then induced or forced to participate in underage sex.

'Minors?' Arnold's eyes rounded in disbelief. 'They've got to be sixteen at least. Shade said they were.'

Gray swung round and took his glasses from his pocket. He made a big play of studying Alice and Ginny standing on the other side of the road, waiting while Kate unlocked the car, looking exhausted and barely fourteen, let alone over the age of consent. 'Well, Arnold,' he sighed sadly, removing his glasses, 'I must be losing my touch because I wouldn't have thought they were a day over fourteen. Of course you're more experienced in these sorts of cases than I am, but I have to accept what my client tells me.

'Also, my client's sister – who is acting in the role of guardian – has a public duty to tell the press of the danger in which this woman placed these young girls. Those photographers can't get enough of schoolgirls and sex cases always sell . . .'

'Sex . . . ?' Arnold's scream was almost louder than Shade's. 'What sex?' he hissed. 'There was no sex.'

'That was not the information my client gave me. Of course,

being only fourteen she may have misunderstood and your client may have a perfectly reasonable explanation for what she was doing lying naked on a bed with a gentleman on top of her.

'Fortunately, my client was completely aware of the intention behind your client's invitation to two children to attend an adult party. But maybe I've read too many newspapers, and perhaps you can advise me, Arnold, but it seems to me Miss Morgan will have to explain why she specifically invited two fourteen-year-old girls to a house where a known drug dealer was present.'

'This is totally unethical, Hamilton, and you know it,' Arnold seethed. 'I could have you struck off for this conversation.'

The idea did not seem to have much effect on Gray, who simply smiled and said kindly that Arnold must do as he thought necessary, but perhaps if he explained to his client that were she to admit that the girls were there by accident, maybe even that she'd just arranged for a car to take them home when the police arrived, this might resolve all their difficulties. It might appear as though Shade had felt a responsibility for the girls.

Arnold looked as though he were in a bad dream. In the first place he had come to loathe Shade Morgan, in the second he had been astounded to hear who the kids' lawyer was and, thirdly, the mere sight of Alice and Ginny was bringing it forcibly home to him that any chance Shade had of winning a sympathetic hearing was lost, and was much more likely to bring further prosecutions hitherto unexplored in the hurried consultation in the cells.

That stupid moron Vinny Perrereo. Why didn't he say Gray Hamilton was at the station?

Arnold was furious at the cavalier way the whole case had been hijacked from him. He wasn't used to high-powered corporate lawyers patronizing him so early in the morning. Of course he could get Gray turned over for such blatant coercion but on the other hand . . .

'Ah yes.' Gray interrupted his reverie. 'And beyond a vivid and vindictive imagination there is not a shred of evidence for your client's quite outrageous allegations. All in all I'd say she'll be more in court than out for the foreseeable future. But of course you may think otherwise. It is up to you how you advise your client.'

'My client,' Arnold said through gritted teeth, as much to stop them chattering as to control his temper, 'will be advised to be truthful and state the facts as she knows them. If she wishes to help pay her legal bills by selling her story to a newspaper after all this is over . . .'

'She will have no career left if she does,' Gray interrupted. 'We are not talking here of a major actress who could survive a scandal. She might even welcome such advice as well as the fact that you could appear to be taking an interest in her future, Arnold – instead of just your own.'

With that, he wished him goodnight, and crossed the street to where Alice was hovering anxiously half in and half out of Kate's car.

'Okay,' he said, reaching her. 'I'm just going to get Judith and then we'll be off. Kate, could you drive up a couple of blocks and then when I catch up with you, Alice can hop out and get in with us.'

'Is that it?' Alice butted in. 'Aren't we going to get Shade to apologize or something?'

'No, not tonight. Maybe not at all,' Gray said, urging her into the car.

'Why?' she demanded. 'I want to tell them that she's a liar . . .'

'You will calm down and shut up,' Gray said severely. 'My life is about defusing drama, not creating it. Now into the car with you, and I'll see you in a couple of minutes.' Alice reluctantly did as she was told, watching him through the rear window as he disappeared back into the police station in search of Judith.

Gray found her still in the lobby, and sat down beside her. At first she hardly noticed he was there. When she did, she looked at him unseeingly. He leaned forward, hands clasped, elbows on his knees, staring at the floor.

'Do you feel up to walking?' he asked quietly when after a couple of minutes she still hadn't said anything.

'Yes, of course. And you must go home. You've done so much and that . . . that revolting woman will waste no time linking you to me . . . I mean us.'

Gray rounded on her in a fury. 'Don't be so bloody stupid. It's not my reputation I care about and you know it. Don't you understand that man is ruining you? Don't you care?'

Judith covered her face with her hands. 'Please, Gray, don't shout. I'm sorry, truly sorry. You have been wonderful and I will always be grateful to you. Now,' she said, trying to steady her voice, 'you want me to leave and join the others at the end of the road?'

He nodded. 'I'll join you in a few minutes and drop you back.'

Her stricken look stopped him.

'He's at the flat, isn't he?' he asked grimly.

She shook her head. 'I don't know, he could be.'

Gray muttered an oath. 'You can't take Alice back there,' he told her flatly. 'If he's implicated, no-one in their right mind would have allowed you to be given custody if he's around. Okay, here's what we do. Both of you stay at my place tonight and tomorrow I'll drive Alice back to school. That way she doesn't have to come into contact with him while she's with you.'

'I'm going to talk to Van,' Judith said defiantly. 'You don't honestly think I was just going to let the matter drop? What the hell do you think I am? What was it Shade called me – a cheap whore in designer clothes, is that what you think? Is it?'

She was close to tears. And so tired. All she wanted to do was sleep.

He ran a hand through his hair. 'Give me strength,' he muttered. 'You look ready to drop dead – I'm not far off it myself, but why don't you for once, just for once, do as you're told?'

'Why don't you answer my question?'

'I don't intend to. The question was neurotic. If you want to win an argument with me, try logic. You don't look or behave like a whore in any shape or form and you know it. You're playing on my conscience, transferring guilt. You now expect me to apologize for something I've never thought or even suggested. Now cut it out and do as I say. Tomorrow, when Alice is safely back at school, you can do what you like.'

Judith bit her lip. 'I'll drive Alice back to school, you don't have to put yourself out any further. Anyway, what would it look like, being driven back to school by a lawyer?'

'And you think that would be worse than hearing she was under the same roof as the same guy who tried to set her up? Oh, great, and your nerves are in such a state I wouldn't trust you to drive a three-wheel bike at the moment.'

'Oh fuck off,' she said and began to march out of the building.

'Eight o'clock start,' he called after her, unmoved by her temper. 'Or Alice and I leave without you.'

She stopped and looked at him as if he had lost the plot. 'I've told you. I'll take Alice back to school, okay?'

'Not according to Alice. Didn't she tell you? We arranged it all before you got here.'

Chapter Twenty-Three

By the time they reached Gray's house it was nearly three o'clock. Even Alice, who had dropped off to sleep in the fifteen minutes it took to get from Connaught Street to Gray's home, said she had to have some coffee before going to bed. Too tired to think properly, she had merely nodded when Judith had said that it would be better if she didn't see Van again, and was satisfied that between them Gray and Judith would sort everything out.

Exhausted, they drank in silence and it was only when Judith began to clear the cups away, Alice having once again closed her eyes, that Gray came and took the tray from her. 'Nice of you, but the housekeeper will do it in the morning. You look absolutely whacked as well.' He placed the tray on a side table, and stood looking down at her.

Judith studied the middle of his shirt and then with a small smile moved away to sit down on the sofa next to the fire.

'I'm not sure what I'm doing here,' she began. 'In fact, I don't know how to begin to thank you. I'm just so pleased that you had dinner with us last night and that Alice knew who to turn to.'

Gray pushed his hands into his pockets and leaned against the mantelpiece, looking down at her. He gave her a wry smile.

'Now you're pleased? You mean you weren't pleased at the time? And there was I thinking I was being charming.'

Judith smiled up at him. 'You were. And that isn't what I mean.'

'It's what you said.'

'Stop being a lawyer, you know what I mean and,' she glanced at the sleeping Alice, 'I should get her to bed.'

He followed her glance. 'Of course. There's plenty of Lisa's stuff around that you could both borrow for tonight and we'll leave early enough in the morning to stop by the flat to pick up Alice's luggage. And . . . well, it's nothing to do with me, but I think you need time on your own after that. Some space, you know, to think a bit about what you're doing.'

Judith could feel the lump in her throat.

'Although,' he said carefully, watching her, 'I suspect there aren't many walks taking place on the beach these days.'

Had she really said that about Van? Ludicrous.

'Too cold,' she replied lightly.

Clearly the joke left him cold too. 'So let's concentrate on Alice,' he said. 'She's my client. You're right, she must go to bed now.'

Alice stirred and opened one eye. 'Great idea,' she mumbled and promptly fell back to sleep. Gray disappeared to check the spare rooms while Judith made a vain effort to rouse Alice.

'Hopeless,' she said despairingly as Gray returned, moved around her and scooped up the sleeping girl in his arms.

'I thought you would prefer to sleep in the same room. It's a spare room, but Lisa always makes sure there are night-clothes and stuff, so just help yourself to whatever you need.'

'Thank you,' said Judith obediently. Lisa, eh? What double game was she playing, keeping all her options open, just in case Charles MacIntyre didn't come up to scratch? Vowing she would resist borrowing anything beyond the absolute necessities, she collected Alice's boots and straw bag.

It was a very odd feeling following Gray up the same staircase that she had climbed with Howard all those months ago. She wondered if the same thought had struck him; but if it had, he said nothing.

At the top he turned left instead of right and headed for a room at the far end of the corridor. Squeezing between him and the slumbering Alice, she pushed the door open and in the light from the passage crossed to the first of twin beds and switched on the lamp.

A soft glow suffused the room. Gray lowered Alice onto the bed, asked if she could manage and simply nodded when she said better than she had managed Alice's social life. His housekeeper would make sure they were called by seven. And with that he closed the door behind him.

Three hours' sleep was as much as any of them were going to get. Accompanied by much dozy complaining from Alice, Judith managed to remove her clothes and tucked her under the quilt in just her knickers. Then she swiftly undressed herself and climbed into the matching bed.

On another occasion she would have taken a moment or two to admire the pink-and-grey decor, delighted in the velvet-soft smoothness of the slate carpet and wallowed in the small but luxurious bathroom that led off from the main room. As it was, as she closed her eyes she knew that she would infinitely have preferred sleeping in another room in this house, one decorated in dark blue and yellow with a canopied bed and a delightful view.

Purely for the decor of course, she told herself as sleep claimed her. And a view of the garden. What else?

Of the three of them it was Alice who seemed to have suffered the least. Judith would have killed for a day in bed and Gray looked as though he would kill anyone who spoke before he had drunk a cup of coffee.

'Do you think it will be all right?' ventured Alice anxiously as Gray's housekeeper, apparently unperturbed at finding two extra house guests to deal with, placed a rack of toast on the table. If she recognized Judith from her last visit she made no reference to it.

'As long as you keep your head and do exactly as I tell you, I can do my best for you. I can't make promises,' Gray was saying to Alice. 'That would be unfair.' Judith reached over and squeezed the young girl's hand, smiling encouragingly.

Alice tried to look brave and failed. 'It's Daddy, Jude,' she said in a voice trembling suspiciously. 'He'd never survive this if it got into the papers. Shade is well-known. He couldn't take it, Jude, you know he couldn't.'

'But presumably your sister can?' said Gray dryly. Judith turned pleading eyes to him. It wasn't fair. This was all her fault. Van's vindictiveness was the culprit.

'Sorry, angel.' Gray smiled at Alice. 'Didn't mean that. Only Judith got a shock too. And it was rough on me getting pulled from my bed, much as I'm flattered you thought of me. And she can be quite fierce, you know,' he said conspiratorially, indicating Judith. 'What do you think she'd have done to me, if I hadn't got you out?' And he gave her a look of mock terror.

Greatly encouraged by his gentle endearment, Alice giggled and explained about her father. 'He hates anything like this. He's awfully sweet but the idea of "scandal" nearly kills him, doesn't it, Jude?'

Of course it did. Judith nodded and feigned interest in spreading butter on some toast which she left untouched on her plate. But not unnoticed by Gray, who said nothing, merely explaining to Alice what would happen when she was eventually called to the police station.

By seven thirty, it was obvious to them that Alice was in no state to go anywhere let alone school without a few more hours of sleep.

'I'll make sure Van isn't there,' Judith whispered to Gray. 'She needs normality for a little while.'

He shrugged, knowing she was right.

Judith just prayed she could get Van out of the flat. The idea of Gray confronting him was beyond even her imagination. She asked Gray if she could make a phone call, and got through to the answer machine. Judith spoke as quietly as she could.

'Van? I'm bringing Alice and her lawyer back with me. Please don't make a fuss. I'll talk to you later.'

The apartment was empty when they let themselves in. With a yawn, Alice went away to fall into bed in Judith's room while Judith checked her answer machine.

Rosie had called, and her father, and Libby to ask if she knew where Carey was. If only she did, but none of her calls had been returned. Curiously there were no messages for Van. Two more from friends asking her to dinner and one from Lisa Hamilton asking if she would call back.

Judith rapidly pressed the stop button but it was too late. The door to the drawing room was open; Gray must have heard every word.

Picking up the post, she flicked through it with as casual

an air as she could muster. 'Lisa called,' she said as she stacked the letters in a small walnut bureau. 'I expect it's about the ball.'

'Of course,' he agreed. 'Can I make myself some coffee?'

'Let me,' she said, hoping that the kitchen was not in the usual state, but Gray got up anyway and followed her. For once it was reasonably tidy. The thing that bothered Judith most was not so much the condition in which Van had left the flat, but why he wasn't in it at all.

All the plans she had been making to rid herself of Van had also taken a beating. Alice's artless but quite well-founded fears voiced over breakfast had put paid to them. Not just for her father, but for Alice too. The young girl had had enough for now.

Judith wasn't afraid, just disoriented. Fear might come later. So many things were crowding her brain. Gray had been right, she needed space. But not with him; her feelings for him were unresolved. Half of her wanted his attention, the other half desperately didn't want him focusing too closely on her private life. And for all kinds of reasons she doubted she had a future with a man such as Gray.

She knew she could not cope with another married man. And as he'd once said himself, divorce is just a piece of paper. In his head he was clearly still tied to Lisa. A rebound romance was not good news. Better to leave things as they were. Clearly he thought so too.

The older you get, my girl, she told herself as she watched him knock back a quick cup of coffee, the wiser you get.

And then of course perhaps it was exhaustion talking.

They dropped Alice at school at six o'clock, refreshed and feeling more optimistic about what the police would decide about her role in Shade's party. At nine that morning Judith had phoned the school to say a minor stomach upset had kept Alice in bed but they would be there by supper.

Once Gray had departed, promising to return by four o'clock, Judith had just accepted his part in their lives without caring too much about the consequences. Alice was his client, she reasoned with herself, not really believing that lawyers

235

put themselves out so far as to drive an overadventurous adolescent back to school.

It was simply easier to accept it than argue.

Of Van there was no sign. Judith had merely glanced into his room when they had returned early that morning, but now she took a closer, puzzled look. It appeared emptier than usual, although in the chaos it was hard to tell. The curtains obscuring the light were drawn. Pulling them back, her eyes searched the once-attractive bedroom. The bed was unmade – nothing unusual in that. She crossed to the closets and pulled them open. Empty hangers swung between what remained of his clothes. His suitcase was gone.

Relief swept over her. Maybe he wouldn't come back. But even as she fantasized about such a wonderful prospect, she could see there were enough of his belongings still hanging around to rob her of that comfort.

Much as she disliked having him around, it made her uneasy not to know where he was. Gritting her teeth, she called Shade's flat. Vinny answered. She lied effortlessly. 'Where is he, Vinny? The police have been looking for him.'

'No idea,' he said rudely. 'Why should I tell you?'

'No reason, Vinny. Shall I tell them to ask you instead?'

'Bitch,' he breathed.

Judith felt herself start to shake. 'Vinny, I don't give a damn where he is. You're his friend. Either I tell him not to come near here for a while, or you do. Or when the police find him, they may not be very reasonable.'

'All right, all right. He's in Scotland for a few days. Left last night. Shade's gone to join him.' While he was still laughing at what he imagined would be her fury, she replaced the phone.

Here was the space she needed. There was a God.

Judith followed Alice's example just as soon as she had packed Alice's clothes into her suitcases. She also rang her father, who had had an idyllic week working without interruption on his new book, breaking off only to eat the meals that the faithful Janey Woolcross had prepared and left for him. Laura had sent him a card saying she was being spoilt rotten. Thank God, neither of them need ever know about Alice's narrow escape in London.

236

Another secret. More protection. When would it ever stop? Lies beget lies. Secrets spin their own suffocating web.

Judith had taken the precaution of bolting the door to the flat while they slept so that she would know if Van returned. Even Vinny claiming he was in Scotland failed to reassure her. She didn't allow herself the luxury of hoping he would drown in a loch, choosing instead the bliss of sleep until it was time to take Alice back.

Alice clung to Judith when she left her at school. Judith whispered comfortingly into her ear. Gray took her cases up to her dormitory, drawing curious stares from teachers and Alice's classmates, two at least of whom earned immediate detention for emitting piercing wolf whistles as he walked by.

It wasn't like Alice to be so clinging but she had been through a lot and she was after all still not much more than a child herself. However, with the promise of being allowed to stay with Melissa on her next weekend exeat, she cheered up considerably and let Judith go.

She came with Judith to the door to wave her goodbye and treated Gray to a hug as well. He laughed and swung her around.

'Bye, angel,' he said, kissing her cheek. 'Life's going to be very dull without you around.' Alice was pink with pleasure and as they got into the car, could be heard telling Melissa, 'Useful guy to have on your side in a fight,' with the nonchalance of one used to being arraigned on a Friday night.

Judith made a mental note to check the school fees. What *were* they paying for?

She and Gray drove back from Oxford in silence, and it was only as they reached the centre of London that Gray suggested dinner and swung the car round so that they were heading towards his home.

'My housekeeper is cooking,' he explained. 'I just needed a night eating at home. Do you mind?'

She didn't. Not at all. She had been in his company now for almost eighteen hours and was reluctant to break the thread that was keeping them together. Nor did she want to be on her own. Rosie away, Carey presumably away, Libby in the country. The thought that if every friend she possessed had been available for the entire evening, she would still have felt the same, was pushed unblushingly to the back of her mind.

'I promise to have you home by midnight,' he added, taking her silence for indecision.

As early as that. Oh well.

This time Judith found herself eating in the kitchen. It was silly, but the easy way in which he just presumed it would suit her, pleased her. The housekeeper offered to stay but Gray assured her that between them he was certain they wouldn't ruin her culinary creation.

Judith rang her flat to be on the safe side, but there was no answer. Van was so cowardly, setting Alice up and now disappearing until the flak settled. Well, this time she was going to tell him to move out. Living elsewhere would not make his hold over her any less threatening, but after Friday's dreadful interviews with Stella Frankenheim and then Spencer, she was now fearful for her professional reputation.

They sat in the drawing room by the fire after dinner. Gray sprawled full-length on one of the sofas, Judith sat on the floor, her back propped against the other sofa, enjoying the warmth of the fire, the hauntingly beautiful strains of Bruch's Violin Concerto in G reducing them both to companionable silence. For a while at least, Judith was at peace, knowing that Alice was safe and she herself was temporarily protected from the world.

She let her gaze wander to Gray, who was lying with his eyes closed, a glass of brandy lightly resting on his chest. She knew he wasn't asleep, simply enjoying the music.

Warning bells began to ring. It was too seductive, too easy to fall into the trap of wanting a man to look after her. No, not *any* man. At least she was no longer pretending that. But would she be sacrificing all she had worked for? For a brief relationship that clearly had nothing going for it but physical attraction? A voice in her head said, get out now.

But Gray's voice was the one she listened to.

'Okay,' he murmured, as though he could feel her looking at him. 'You first. Tell me the dark secrets of your soul.' He twisted his head and opened one eye. 'It's only fair,' he pointed out. 'I provided dinner, wine and music. Oh, and that fire that's been transfixing you for the past half hour. Now I think you should reward me by telling me all about yourself.'

'What do you want to know?'

'What do you want to tell me?'

She took a deep breath. 'Not the deepest secrets of my soul. I'm saving those to sell when I'm old. A girl's got to have something to live on,' she joked.

'I'm listening.'

'Okay. It isn't what you or anyone else think. Van is neither my boyfriend, my lover or . . .' She paused. 'Friend.'

She expected him to say something but he waited. Silence was his greatest weapon. She noticed he didn't waste words. He was practised in out-nerving the opposition into revealing more than they should.

'Do you want me to go on?' she asked politely.

'What do you think?'

'That this conversation is one I will regret.'

Then Gray did open his eyes and slowly swung around until he was facing her, impatience written all over him. Alice was quite right: he did look sexy in jeans. Not that the wearing of them improved the bluntness of his manner.

'Tell me something. Is your life really one long regret? You are young, beautiful and clever. You are also funny – not many women are – and I have long ago understood why Howard went to such lengths to keep you.

'But what are you doing letting that guy leech off you? Good God, you must see he does. You have everything on your side. You just don't add up, there's another agenda going on and I wish you'd let me know what it is.'

He stopped. Waited.

This wasn't how she had envisaged the conversation. She had seen it as an exploration of their feelings, and the opportunity to unload some emotional debris from both their lives.

Gray had an unnerving habit of cutting out foreplay and getting to the heart of the matter. He also made her answer in a way that made her seem like a street fighter, and not the sophisticated vision she was currently presenting in a cream baggy sweater and narrow black trousers, with loose tendrils of hair falling from a coiled knot on top of her head.

'Look, buster,' she snapped, matching his bluntness in a way that belied her expensive schooling. 'I'm not on trial here. We don't all have the skill to skip the foothills before we get busy with the mountain. Okay? Now if you want to hear what I have to say, fine. If not, go back to sleep and I will see myself out.'

He nodded approvingly as she clambered to her feet and put her glass down on the nearest table with a snap.

'That's better. Much more you. We're not talking about a major war, just a couple of regular lives that need sorting out. And if you go, we can't even do that.'

Judith wasn't surprised Lisa had left him. Trying to make him react to feelings instead of facts was about as easy as trying to open a tin with your teeth.

'And for the record,' he went on, reaching out and taking her wrist as she moved past him, halting her progress towards the door, 'just because I don't get off on soul-baring doesn't mean I'm insensitive. It's just that I'm not into all that walks on the beach stuff. I don't think your Mr Kingsley is either. He's such a wanker.'

Gray's clasp on her wrist tightened. Gently he drew her back so that she was facing him. He reached out and took her other hand, looking up at her with genuine bewilderment.

'Howard, I can understand. But God, not him.'

Granite, she decided, had more feeling than he did. Here she was with an emotional agenda to keep a posse of counsellors occupied for a year, and he had to look at her like that. He hadn't the smallest clue that her biggest problem was sitting in front of her, quietly waiting for her to make a decision.

'There's nothing to understand,' she said stiffly, wriggling her hands so that he was obliged to release them. 'He was a client. I got too friendly with him. When he quit his job, he had nowhere to live. What else do you want to know?'

'Anything you want to tell me,' he replied. 'Shall I stand up too, or will you sit down again?'

'Don't be ridiculous,' she scoffed, sitting at the far end of the sofa.

'Tell me about Howard,' he said, nothing if not direct. And she did. Gray seemed to know quite a lot already, obviously gleaned from the man himself. To justify her relationship with Howard, she told him about Roland.

So they sat and talked, and she forgot that she had threatened to leave and he seemed not to have remembered that he had promised to have her home by midnight. Occasionally she would sip her wine and he would pour some more brandy. Once he got up and slipped another CD on the player and on the way back he snapped off one of the lamps.

Judith told him about Howard and the accidental affair they had embarked on. Gray laughed and said he doubted it was an accident where Howard was concerned. She curled her legs under her and said she didn't agree. But it had been on the rebound for her; she had thought she would die after splitting up with Roland.

He moved nearer to pour some more wine and stayed there, resting his arm comfortably along the back of the sofa just above her head, his body half turned towards her, and asked her about her father and Alice and how they all managed.

It was strange talking about things she had almost forgotten, but she made him laugh about her schooldays and how going to Washington with her parents when she was sixteen was the only thing that prevented her being thrown out. The presence of Libby Westhope in her life regrettably made it impossible to draw a veil over it all.

And Washington? Mmm, a difficult time. If he noticed she chose her words carefully, he didn't say so. And her mother? She said it was just something that had happened, cancer. Swift, merciless. Judith missed her. But she coped. Sure? Well, she gave a small jerky smile, nearly sure.

It was an unsafe topic. Gray leaned forward and kissed her lightly on the cheek. Poor baby, he said.

Confess. He'd understand. He would, he would. He might not. Not yet. Instead, she told him Laura had been her tower of strength and that her father was a wonderful, gentle man, but of the old school. Yes, Gray agreed, Alice had said as much.

Later he told her that his parents now lived in Paris. When his father, who had been a banker, had retired they went to live there to be near his younger sister who, to his mother's joy, had married a Frenchman and had obligingly produced two grandchildren for his mother to dote on. He was god-father to the little girl.

Quite naturally he moved onto Lisa. Beautiful, accomplished, the perfect corporate wife. They'd met at a house party and were married six months later.

'She was – is – dazzling,' he said. 'Really dazzling.' He stopped and thought for a while. Judith held her breath and stared fixedly at her drink. She didn't want to hear that Lisa had broken his heart.

'And you still care about her, don't you?'

He looked surprised. 'Of course. She never did me real harm. But I nearly wrecked her. I didn't know it, though. Lisa needs attention, lots of it. I can't give that to anyone. I work, my job is demanding. I'm not in an insurance office, working nine to five.

'Sometimes she would have been organizing a dinner party all day and I would ring from the airport to say I wouldn't be home, or a meeting would take longer than I planned, or we might have arranged to go down to the country for the weekend and at the last minute I would have to invite a client. It was hard on her.'

If they compared definitions of hardship, she knew that Lisa wouldn't just be in a different ballgame, she wouldn't even be on the park. How could men be so stupid? Lisa was a spoilt brat.

'No relationship in the world can survive such different lifestyles unless one of you gives a bit more than the other.'

Judith just listened. She wanted to ask him what the difference was between soul-baring, which he had insisted he wasn't into, and this voluntary intimate insight into what was the most profound event of his life. She twisted round so that her elbow rested on the back of the sofa just in front of his arm, and leaned her face against her hand so that she could see his face.

'In the end she had an affair. I didn't know, didn't suspect.

There were clues everywhere, but it just didn't occur to me that it would happen.'

'How did you find out?'

'The guy's wife rang me. Lisa said it was my fault, I neglected her. Stupid of me. We might have been happy. Who knows?'

'How did it affect you?'

For a long while Gray gazed up at the ceiling, his head resting against the back of the sofa. Judith waited. He turned sideways to look at her.

'At the time it nearly killed me. I'm amazed my clients never caught on. I slugged back whisky every morning for nearly two months to get me to work. For a whole year I believed I would be left with this black pit inside me . . . but it's been three years now. You know, it's strange, I have no difficulty recalling the pain, but I no longer feel it.'

'And now?' Judith stared into her glass, gently rolling it around.

'Now? I want to see her happy. She's part of my life. We have dinner. It's civilized. Then she meets someone she thinks is going to be "the one" and the same old syndrome starts. She usually ends up here, broken-hearted and blaming me.'

'Blaming you for what?'

'Not making her happy while we were together. If I had, apparently, she wouldn't be as vulnerable. But that isn't true. She doesn't see the difference between loving someone for themselves and loving someone who can make her happy. You must have noticed, she's very spoilt. But then she's easy to spoil.'

Judith felt like grinding her teeth.

'Look, you asked me about Van. Let me ask you something. Why do you feel so guilty about her? She's the one who had the affair, not you. Are you . . . are you still in love with her? Is that why you're there for her, always with her?'

Gray looked surprised. 'I don't remember falling out of love with her, there was too much pain and angst going on. I just know that a long while ago, I stopped waking up with a hangover and she didn't have the power to hurt me any more. Does that make sense?

'There wasn't a day or a moment when I realized it had happened. It's just moved on. No big deal, and if it helps for me to be there for her, then why not? I haven't remarried. Like you, I'm not even involved with anyone. There's no-one to hurt, is there?'

Yes, there bloody was, she thought. A lot he knew. All she could think of was Charles MacIntyre banging on the door of the ladies'. If Gray knew all about Lisa's affairs, why did it matter so much that they kept it a secret from him?

'Umm, I know,' he grinned. 'Charles MacIntyre.' He laughed outright at her startled face. 'I don't know how you know, but Lisa plays games. They'll never marry. Partly because he doesn't want to leave his family, but mostly because I pay her too much alimony for her to sacrifice for a married man who earns half what I do, and would still have to support three children at private school. Also she likes to think she can still make me jealous.'

'And can she?'

'No, Lisa can't,' he said, deliberately emphasizing the name. Judith dropped her eyes first.

'So why . . . ?'

'Easy. He pays her the kind of attention I never could.'

'Never?' she teased, arching an eyebrow. 'Surely sometimes?'

He looked at her in silence. No laughing now. 'Not to Lisa,' he said quietly. She held her breath. They were staring straight at each other, both searching for the clue, the one that said you've read the right signals. She had to be sure.

'But I could pay a lot of attention to you, you must know that.'

Judith shook her head. 'I know you made me think you could . . . once. But I'm not into games any more. You never got in touch with me again . . .'

'You were living with . . . all right, sorry, sharing a flat with, Van. What did you expect?'

Nothing. Even now she expected nothing from him. And she didn't want it to be a one-night stand, or something casual, nor did she want it to rob her of her freedom, or to find herself involved with someone who would eventually want to know too much and, oh God, she didn't want to end up looking for him everywhere she went. She didn't want to walk with ghosts. Not again.

'It's late,' he said, taking her glass from her. 'Do you remember what I said in that note? "What happens next?"'

She nodded.

Gray reached over and took both her hands in one of his, running the other up through her hair from her neck, holding her head very still so that she couldn't look away and the decision had to be theirs together.

'I think we should find out, don't you?' he said, leaning forward and very gently brushing her lips with his.

'You promised to have me home by midnight,' Judith reminded him, helpfully moving closer as his lips moved to her ear, not wanting to appear to be impeding her host's progress.

'So I did,' he said, pulling her to her feet, slipping his hand under the hem of her sweater and gently stroking her back. 'But you will also remember,' he said, moving them both towards the door, 'that I'm a lawyer and I carefully didn't specify whose home, did I?'

So unfair, he could make her laugh, and God knows what he had done to her brain, which she knew had ceased to function rationally because as sure as hell what he was doing to her body had deprived her of the ability to do anything other than give him every encouragement to persist.

She knew when she was outclassed as he pulled her sweater over her head and she impatiently dragged his sweater over his and jeans and trousers somehow lay in a tangled heap on the floor by the green canopied bed. And then the intense pleasure of limbs entwining and stroking and the mutual craving of deep and powerful ecstasy took over and she had to admit that she really had been given no option but to stay.

Chapter Twenty-Four

It had been a long time since Judith had stayed in bed for nearly the whole of Sunday. By the time Gray dropped her home late on Sunday night wearing one of his sweaters and the trousers of one of his track suits, belted in to keep them up, she thought she would keel over with happiness.

'Stay,' he'd said over and over. 'Get your clothes and stay here.'

But she had kissed him and said she was a working girl, although if it weren't for Premier needing her mentally alert the next day she would willingly move in forever. But did he really want her to attend a breakfast meeting with Stella Frankenheim hung over, with a silly grin on her face?

Gray said Stella Frankenheim was so vain she would assume the look was one of admiration for everything she'd ever said or thought.

So he unwillingly left her and phoned as soon as he got back. When they had talked for nearly an hour and he'd threatened to drive back and get her, she insisted he put the phone down.

At Premier the next morning, eyebrows were raised at the very evident change in Judith's manner. The downbeat, heavy-eyed young woman who'd been driving them to exasperation had come in like a whirlwind, supercharged and urging everyone into action.

Camilla reeled. Annie and Clark, meeting at the coffee machine, raised eyebrows at each other as Judith sailed past, laughing over her shoulder to a grumbling Spencer.

'Tell Rik Bannerman I appreciate his views but he's punching above his weight telling me what to do.'

'But Judith,' Spencer called as she disappeared into the lift. He shrugged and turned to see Clark and Annie taking in the scene.

'All I said was that Rik and I had dinner together and he had some great ideas that Judith might want to use. What's wrong with that? That bloke of hers must have given her a good seeing to at the weekend,' he slyly murmured to Clark, not thinking Annie could hear. Annie indignantly opened her mouth to protest but Clark shot her a warning look.

'Spencer's answer to anything he doesn't understand,' Clark whispered, apparently engrossed in a file he was carrying. He waited for Spencer to close his office door and turned back to the seething Annie.

'But between me and you, he might be right.' He threw his arms across his face to protect himself as Annie hurled a tube of paper cups after him.

Just before lunch while Judith was in a meeting, Gray called but when she returned the call he was with a client. He was with another client when she called again at five o'clock.

Maybe there wasn't time between meetings to call, maybe there was something wrong with the switchboard and he couldn't get through. She picked up the phone and started to dial British Telecom engineers, but banged the phone down before they answered. Stop it. Stop it now.

When the phone rang in the outer office she would look up expectantly and tried hard not to feel too disappointed when it wasn't him.

Her own day ricocheted from one meeting to another, but undoubtedly the de Vries ball dominated the office. Libby had called more than once purely to shriek 'never again' down the phone. Stella Frankenheim had been partly placated over breakfast at Colby's; the guest list had now been adjusted, a simple error, explained Judith.

Lisa Hamilton and Libby had attended the meeting. But Judith and Lisa, for their own quite separate reasons, avoided each other's eyes. The meeting had wound up and all four were moving towards the lobby when Lisa uttered a small exclamation.

'Do go on,' she said to Libby and Mrs Frankenheim as they all stopped. 'I meant to ask Judith for a telephone number.'

Libby and Stella Frankenheim strolled off together.

Lisa waited until they were out of earshot. 'I expect you're wondering why I was with Charles at the hotel. It wasn't what you imagined, although I admit Charles does have a thing about me . . .'

Judith listened with amazement and awe to the quite extraordinary lies, proclaimed with the insulting belief that she could con anyone she cared to. 'It's just that I know Gray would love Charles as a client, and I agreed to meet him for breakfast. Unfortunately he chose that moment to confess how he felt about me.'

This was too much. 'Lisa,' Judith began. 'You don't owe me any explanations, really . . .'

'Oh, but I do, because I would not like anyone to think I would do anything that would hurt Gray or indeed Charles's sweet little wife.'

Judith thought she was outrageous. How could Gray have been so blind? 'Of course not.' This conversation had to be curtailed. 'Why not tell Gray just in case anyone else gets the same impression and tells him first? Now, I really must dash or Stella won't get her list.'

Annoyance and suspicion competed on Lisa's face. 'Of course. Gray and I have a table. Will you be with your American friend?'

As body blows went, it was well-aimed. Judith felt her stomach lurch. She mumbled something about not being sure, more than likely, long time to go to make that decision.

A sigh of relief escaped her when just after seven she could finally switch off for the day. No word from Gray, but Judith was confident he would ring as soon as she reached home.

Of Van there was, thankfully, still no sign. She let herself into the apartment and checked the machine, jotting down names and the occasional number. To be on the safe side she took the phone into the bathroom while she had a bath.

When it rang, she grabbed it only to fight off an irrational wave of disappointment when it turned out to be Rosie.

'I've just got in. Fancy supper?'

'Hi. Oh, Rosie, I'd love to, but I think I'm having supper with someone.'

'Think? It's nearly eight now.'

This was ridiculous. Why didn't she just go with Rosie? After all, how long did it take to make a phone call to tell someone if you were seeing them or not?

The effort of fighting down a sense of panic that he wasn't going to call was getting to her. Her rational side said, he's just busy. The insecure side said, not another Roland. Please.

'Tell you what, Rosie, give me five minutes. I'll make a phone call and call you right back.'

The phone in his house switched to the machine. It didn't even have his voice on it; it was his secretary. Too late she realized that she didn't have the number to his second private line. A day lolling, or more accurately rolling, around in bed had driven such details from both their minds.

The idea of leaving a message made her wince. She tried the office, but it was now after eight thirty. No. No. No. Never again would she be left waiting around for someone to call. Stop right now while you still have the strength.

Without pausing, she rang Rosie back and arranged to meet her at a favourite wine bar off Sloane Square. Rosie said she would call Carey to see if he could join them.

'Great, I haven't heard from him for weeks, have you?'

'He called Piers a couple of times but had to cancel at the last minute. Some exclusive or other he's working on.'

Judith remembered he had sounded evasive the last couple of times she'd spoken to him. So maybe it wasn't Van at all. But in the event it was just Rosie who arrived. Carey's phone had been answered by his friend Josh, who told her he was house-sitting while Carey was away.

So, sitting in a candlelit booth sharing a bottle of wine and not having much appetite for the fettucini she'd ordered, Judith confided to Rosie the whole story of Alice and Gray.

'But why would Van involve Alice?'

Judith did a mental somersault. 'Thought it would be a treat. It went wrong when Shade was raided. Anyway, when he gets back I'm going to tell him to go.'

'Brilliant,' approved Rosie. 'And . . . um . . . you said you had dinner with Gray? How come?'

Judith looked at her and smiled sheepishly. 'Bit more than dinner . . .'

Rosie clapped her hand across her mouth to stop the squeal of laughter and delight from being heard at the next table. 'I knew it, I knew it. I knew something was up. When did all this start? You never told me and we're not leaving this table until you do.'

So she did. Well, nearly everything, right up to the fact that he hadn't phoned and she didn't want to be just sitting there when he did.

'Ring him,' said Rosie, bewildered. 'He's a terrific guy. Busy one too. How often have I called you at the office or you called me and we haven't got back to each other till the evening? Why should he be any different?'

'Because, old thing, I'm not in love with you,' Judith remarked dryly. 'And also because he told me how Lisa used to nag him to be there for her. I don't want him to think that I'm just the same.'

Rosie eyed her shrewdly. 'But you think he should drop everything and be there because it's you and that's different?'

'Don't be ridiculous,' protested Judith, knowing perfectly well it was true. Surely if he felt like she did, he couldn't have let a whole day pass without talking to her?

But he had.

It was after ten when they left the wine bar and Judith got a taxi home, pondering on Rosie's advice. As she pushed open the doors to the lobby she had more or less decided that she would do nothing, simply have an early night and wait.

There was a message on the machine when she arrived, so at least Gray knew she hadn't been sitting tamely by the phone. No matter how hard she tried to convey this when she called back, sitting on the edge of the bed, her coat still on, this idea did not seem to have occurred to him.

But coming over to see her had. Torn between exasperation that he had failed to recognize how independent she was and longing to see him, she hesitated, waiting for him to persuade her.

'I have some papers to run through . . .' she said.

Gray did sound concerned at that. 'Tough day, eh? I know the feeling. The penalty for falling for a career girl, I suppose,' he said with such disappointment in his voice that all her defences collapsed.

'But they shouldn't take long.'

'I'll be there in twenty minutes.'

They went to Paris for the weekend, staying at the apartment belonging to his parents, who were away in the South of France. Strictly speaking, it was a business trip for Gray but he pointed out they could have dinner each night, which would make up for the fact that they had only been able to manage it once all week.

Dinner at the breathtakingly beautiful Le Grand Vefour in the Palais Royal Gardens was almost perfection. Sitting across a candlelit table from the one man in the world she couldn't get enough of, in the oldest and most fashionable of restaurants where everyone from Colette to Cocteau once dined, the food ambrosial, the wine flawless, only the presence of the two French lawyers, the impossibly chic wife of one and the sultry mistress of the other, prevented her happiness from being complete. And really, she had to be fair, it was the reason Gray was there.

Judith flew back alone on Sunday night, after a blissful day strolling around Paris, but feeling guilty that she should really have spent the weekend on neglected paperwork. Gray stayed on for an early-morning court hearing at the courts of appeal, and wouldn't be back in London until Wednesday.

Lying in bed, drowsy with sleep and wrapped in love in the late afternoon before she had to leave for the airport, they discussed the impossibility of their situation. It was too soon, but too important to rush. It would, they agreed, sharing a last lingering kiss, sort itself out.

Van was there when Judith arrived home. So much had happened in the last week that the thought of him in her flat, using her things, sleeping under the same roof, made her feel unwell. He had to go.

She stood in the doorway of his bedroom. Stretched out on the bed, wearing just boxer shorts and white sports socks, she could not recall why she ever thought he was attractive. In his hand he was holding a letter.

'I want you to leave, Van,' she announced quietly, leaning against the door frame. 'What you did to Alice was contemptible. Do whatever you like but just get out.'

He looked at her with interest. She waited. 'I mean it, Van. I've had enough. Alice could have been wrecked.'

What was the matter with him, just staring like that? 'Van, are you listening to me?'

Not only was he listening but he was beginning to laugh, languidly rolling off the bed and moving towards her. 'Get out?' he echoed as he drew level with her. 'New house rule, honey. I'm not going anywhere, but your boyfriend is.'

Gray. How did Van know? Of course, the answer machine. She hadn't wiped it before she left. Gray had called to say he would meet her at the airport instead of picking her up at the flat. Van laughed again. It was a peculiarly high-pitched laugh, and when he was excited it was tinged with hysteria. It was then that the possibility that he might be mentally unstable took a grip.

'What do you mean?' she asked quietly, trying not to look at his grinning face.

'I mean,' he said, placing one finger lightly under her chin, 'that you cool it with the lawyer. If you don't,' he yawned, cutting across her protest, 'his clients get to know all about the dame he's screwing.'

'Leave Gray out of this. He's done nothing to you . . .'

'That's right,' he said softly. 'And that's the way we keep it. Drop him. Got it?'

Just having Van near her made Judith feel physically ill. She brushed his hand away.

'Don't touch me, Van, okay?'

There was a silence as they gazed at each other. His hand dropped. He shrugged.

'I don't need to touch you,' he taunted. 'I'm not joining the queue to get between your legs. My women pay me for the pleasure. I don't have to buy them and besides, I know where the bodies are buried.'

'Get out,' she breathed. 'Get out now.'

Her fury amused him. 'Your ears playing you up, sweetheart? I said, I make that decision.'

Judith watched as he strolled into the shower and in full view stripped off his shorts, turned the jet on and let the water bubble and slide down his tanned body.

She remained where she was. Anger, frustration, fear of having no aces left to play, vied for attention in her brain. Van was watching her as he massaged soap into his arms. Suddenly he stopped and reached out to close the shower door.

'Seen enough?' he asked. His voice was insultingly suggestive. She turned and, as she headed for her own room, heard the click of the glass door shut behind him.

Gray rang later that evening. 'So when's he moving out?'

The phone felt clammy in her hand. Van was lounging against the opposite wall, listening. 'He's just going to be here for a bit longer . . .'

'I see,' Gray said. There was a pause. 'It's what you want?'

A scream rose up in her throat but what came out was, 'Not particularly, but I'm sure Van wants to find his own flat as soon as he can. He's busy. Time is a bit pressured . . . you know how it is.'

Van was chewing the side of his thumb. She was convinced he was mad.

'I see,' Gray said, clearly not seeing at all. 'Call you when I get back.'

The argument that justified the decision she made later as dawn inched its way through the crack in the curtains in her bedroom, was simple.

For the moment she would no longer be safe seeing Gray, based on the fact that she was scared of what Van now knew and because she was irrationally hurt that Gray hadn't said, 'Look, move in with me, until he finds somewhere else.' Like he hadn't said when she left his bed in Paris, 'Stay. Take the day off.' Or that he didn't seem in a hurry to leave the restaurant so that they could be on their own.

Just how much did he need her? What other man who was crazy about her would tolerate her sharing a flat with a man he detested?

But the reasonable voice in her head said, 'You've been

sleeping with him for one week. That's enough time to feel committed but nowhere near long enough for him to burn all his bridges.'

It was a sobering thought that he would only have had to suggest she packed all her belongings that night, and she wouldn't have hesitated to throw a match to hers and not look back. But that freedom was not yet hers. Maybe it never would be unless she could stop Van Kingsley blackmailing her.

The night seemed endless. At four she went into the kitchen and by five she was huddled in her bed sipping strong black coffee, hoping in vain that some other solution would present itself.

At ten o'clock, having been behind her desk for two hours and wondering if she would stay awake another two minutes, all necessity to make decisions was taken from her.

Camilla had opened the post and got the day started. Ten minutes later, carrying a steaming cup of coffee for Judith, she came in studying her notepad.

'On Friday, after you'd left, let's see, yes, here we are, your bank manager phoned personally, and also Marjorie Fulton and Circe wanted you rather urgently.'

'Circe must mean Annie,' yawned Judith, wondering if it was worth just calling Paris on the off-chance that Gray might be able to talk.

She was still pondering the thought when Annie checked back to say it was Judith herself Circe wanted.

'Get her on the phone, will you, Camilla? See if you can find out what she wants.'

Camilla buzzed through to say Circe had 'that' voice on.

Judith picked up the phone, automatically removing an earring and ready for the usual catalogue of complaints from the most famous florist in England.

'I wanted to tell you personally that I'm moving my account,' Circe announced.

At first Judith didn't register what she was saying.

'Where to?' she asked in a near normal voice.

'That is something I would prefer not to discuss with you.

I know you like plain speaking and I'm a great believer in that myself.'

Judith sat bolt upright. What the hell had gone wrong? She was automatically reaching out to buzz Annie when Circe's next words froze her.

'I have a very exclusive clientele. As a courteous gesture to you, I allowed your personal bill . . .'

Personal bill? What *was* she talking about?

'. . . to run up a little higher than most. But I really am not going to have my name associated with little trollops like Shade Morgan. If I had known your fiancé – and believe me, your private life is your own and I don't want to suggest for a moment that anything is going on between them – if I had known the team I put in at that restaurant party was for her, believe me, I would have most certainly declined the order.

'Judith, I don't need that kind of business. But that is your affair. I simply don't want it to be mine. I feel you have abused your position and once you've settled the account, I will say no more.'

Judith didn't have to be told. Van had been using her name. Dear God, when would it stop? It was useless trying to get Circe to change her mind. The phone went dead.

Camilla had of course heard and came in, shutting the door behind her. 'Judith, I'm so sorry. I really thought you had given Van permission and he told me that you wanted to thank Shade for . . .'

'*Thank* Shade?' she breathed. '*Thank* Shade? My God, are you mad? Why do you listen to him? Why don't you tell him to ask me? Surely you don't think . . .' She stopped.

Camilla was gazing at her in a mixture of horror and anger. Why should Camilla have asked her? Not a word, not a syllable of criticism had ever publicly passed Judith's lips about Van Kingsley. Why should Camilla have doubted what he said? Judith sunk her head in her hands.

'Sorry,' she said softly, looking up at the shaken woman. 'Sorry. A bad weekend. Van doesn't always understand. I'm always so busy. I expect he didn't want to bother me. I'll speak to him.'

Puzzled, Camilla turned away. In her opinion Van wasn't

the person Judith had to speak to, it was Annie. And worse, Spencer.

Annie was despatched by Spencer to visit Circe personally. He didn't look as perturbed as Judith thought he might and she was grateful that he hadn't gone completely over the top; he seemed strangely confident that they would get the erratic florist back.

Marjorie Fulton was next. This time a sixth sense warned Judith to shut the door between her and Camilla. 'How are you?' Marjorie asked.

'Okay-ish,' said Judith lightly. 'Lost a client this morning. Bit of a nuisance. How are you?'

There was the briefest of pauses. 'Judith, my dear, please don't take this the wrong way, but I've known you since you were a little girl and Lizzie – your mother I mean – would understand.'

'Good God, Marjorie,' Judith exclaimed. 'Don't scare me. What is it?'

Van, of course. Her husband was a bit concerned. They'd discussed it. Not Van so much as his friends.

'Really Judith, charming man and all that, but the bill from the golf club was outstanding. Restaurant, bar, lessons, green fees . . . We love doing good deals with Premier for client lunches, weekends, that kind of thing, but the club secretary has closed the Premier account.'

Marjorie went on but Judith wasn't listening. She promised to talk to him, asked Marjorie to have the club send a bill. But she knew while her name was linked with Van's she was also off limits. 'And of course you would like me to stop him showing up at the golf course?'

Marjorie was hideously embarrassed. Not her, you understand, must see her point, understand her position. And of course Judith did.

She didn't need to call her bank manager to know what was going to happen. Her credit card bill had arrived that morning; the only way she could pay it was to overdraw at the bank. But she had done that before.

Then it had been a loan to Van for no more than a week while he sorted out his banking arrangements. By the time she had seen the bill for his visit to the States he had already outlined his unwelcome plans for their future.

Future? What future? Certainly not one with Gray. How could she even think of letting all this garbage tarnish his reputation? If they had any remote hope of a future together, she had to sort it out.

Her phone call to Gray that evening was short. Not because she didn't want to talk to him, never that. But she returned his call to find he was on his way out to dinner with the French Minister of Justice and his wife, and his parents were going to be there.

They'd asked who their house guest had been. He was going to keep them guessing for a while. Thank God for that.

They would talk tomorrow. Dinner?

'Yes . . . Yes . . . Wish I was there, too.'

There was no point in confronting Van with any of it. That night she sat in the corner of the lounge and watched him. Her silence, curiously enough, unnerved him.

He jeered at her. Mocked her. Threatened and finally slammed out of the flat. For once Judith felt a faint sense of victory. But since he knew the intimate details of her teenage years in Washington, she could not change the fact that he retained the upper hand.

Chapter Twenty-Five

Judith could not bring herself to break it to Gray in person, so she told him over the phone. Space, she said, a bit of space to think. It was all going too fast.

The shock in his voice was undisguised, but the calmness of his acceptance of what she said nearly killed her.

He asked only one question. 'Is Van going to continue living with you?'

To which she answered a whispered, 'Yes. For the moment. But, it isn't that . . . truly.'

'I see,' is all he said.

Alice and Ginny were given leave to go to London for their appointment with the police. Judith waited silently while the duty officer said that the prosecution had brought no evidence to implicate the girls and therefore no charges would be brought. A relieved Alice fervently promised to be careful about the company she kept in the future and that was the end of the matter.

Shade had been fined and cautioned but thanks to Gray, Arnold had advised her to save her colourful story for another time and the tabloids soon lost interest in her.

Judith dropped Alice back at school and tried to focus her attention on an increasingly fragile lifestyle.

The de Vries ball held at the end of May was every bit the glittering affair Judith had hoped it would be. The money raised reached six figures and Libby had tears in her eyes when Jacob Frankenheim brought the Duchess to the dais to present her with the cheque.

Judith arrived alone, and was beyond feeling anything other than a deep desire to either get very drunk or leave immediately. Neither was an option. She was coping by moving through each day automatically, reacting to what she was required to do but initiating no more. Before the ball, Libby had taken her out to dinner and found that it was like talking to a machine.

An extra table had been included at the last minute after Judith had personally taken responsibility for squaring it with Stella Frankenheim. She asked for it to be placed as far to the back of the room as possible, and just prayed it would not attract too much attention.

Van was not pleased with the placing but once the dancing commenced he and his entourage would be free to check out the names they needed to be seen with. Shade and Vinny, Maurice Allton and a dreadful nightclub singer were included on their table, as well as a photographer and a columnist from the *Planet*, who had filed his copy linking complete strangers with each other before he sat down to dinner. Judith stayed with them just long enough to realize that after this evening her credibility was zero, and any report linking her with Van's name could only be forgiven.

Gray was seated on Jacob Frankenheim's table, between Stella and the Duchess. It had been two months since she had last seen him or spoken to him. She knew from Libby that he and Lisa were rumoured to be getting together again, since she herself was no longer around to distract him. Now that Charles MacIntyre had made it plain he would not be leaving his wife, and having heard rumours of her ex-husband's interest in that Craven Smith girl, Lisa's own interest in securing Gray had revived.

Every weekend, Judith had been going to Yorkshire to walk across the moors for hours on end. Laura tried to get Andrew to talk to her, but, engrossed in the final draft of his book, he was inclined to dismiss Laura's worries as overreaction.

And now Lisa, looking ravishing, was sitting between Jacob and the Duke, fully aware that she was without a doubt one of the most stared-at women in the room. The MacIntyres were seated on the top table too, while Libby was being escorted by Carey, who looked strained and ill-at-ease when he saw Judith.

Carey, aiding and abetting Van. How deep did friendships

go? She gazed at him without speaking and then dropped her head and let him walk by without a word. Spencer was hosting a table for Premier with Annie and Clark valiantly trying to fill the gap that Judith should have occupied. Rik Bannerman, a last-minute addition to the party, smiled a great deal and was kind to Judith when he stopped by her table.

It was more insulting than if he had been derogatory.

She left as the dancing started, unable to bear for one more moment the mortifying sight of Shade and Vinny quite openly touting their pet photographer from table to table to be photographed with every celebrity in the room, or the spectacle of Maurice Allton attempting to get past the bodyguards surrounding the Duke and Duchess to have his picture taken with the guests of honour.

But it was seeing Gray dancing with Lisa, smiling at her and kissing her temple as the music finished and they left the floor, that finally defeated her.

Judith reached the office later than usual the next morning to find Camilla anxiously waiting for her.

'Spencer wants to see you the minute you get here.'

Judith drew her breath in and tried to concentrate. 'Black coffee, Cam, and then I'll go down. Tell him, ten minutes.'

At first she didn't notice Rik Bannerman sitting in Spencer's office when she pushed the door open. It was only when he rose from his seat in the corner alcove of the window that she saw him. What was he doing here?

'Hi,' she said politely as he rose and came over to kiss her on both cheeks, and to Spencer: 'Shall I come back?'

Spencer waved her to a chair. 'No, not at all. I think I mentioned that Rik had some ideas that might be good for Premier.'

She remembered. An unpleasant thought flickered in her mind. Rik was looking awfully at home, smiling winningly at her. The earnest, helpful look. The I-just-want-to-be-your-friend look. The hell he did. Now what?

On any other day, backed by a night's sleep and confident of outmanoeuvring anything thrown at her, Judith would have been a match for them. As it was, haunted by the memory of Gray and Lisa, her eyelids feeling as though stone weights were on them, unfit even to be at work let alone at a meeting, it took less than fifteen minutes for Spencer to describe the changes he was making in the company without a word of protest from her.

Phrases like 'extra workload' and 'tremendous input' and 'the burden of carrying the weight of the company was proving too much' filtered through the one fact that she could hang on to. No matter how many ways Spencer put it, it came down to the same thing: Rik's appointment as Consultant Director to Premier meant Rik was taking over.

Spencer poured champagne to welcome Rik back. Annie and Clark and the rest of the staff were invited in to join in the brief, uncomfortable little ceremony. Since Judith's face was chalk-white, no-one had to guess how she felt and no-one for a second believed it was a move that had her blessing. But what did she expect?

When they had all gone and Judith had recovered sufficiently to realize just how humiliated she had been, she detained Spencer. He didn't want to talk. 'You owe me this,' she said quietly, so he shut the door and they faced each other.

His tone was all the proof she needed that his generosity in front of Rik had been a gesture to her former hard work. His anger was just under control and made her wince.

'I think we can hang on to de Vries, but only just. Stella Frankenheim wants you off the account and last night it was only because Rik spent so much time with her that she relented and told Jacob not to remove their business altogether.

'It's my fault,' he said bluntly as she started to speak. 'I should have known a young, attractive woman would have other things on her mind. Companies like this need a strong hand on the tiller.'

Judith listened to what he had to say. She hadn't been too young or too attractive a year ago when he had practically begged her to join them. The burden of a huge operation like Premier had not been so weighty then.

'I knew that Kingsley account went to you because he fancied you and it was obvious you two were more interested in each other . . .'

She was on her feet. 'I have never been interested in Van Kingsley other than as a client. I got that account because . . . because . . .' She stopped. Honesty prevented her from saying, because she was the best person for the job. It wasn't true.

'What about Circe, Farley, Harcourt, Masters and de Vries? I suppose I got all of those because I was young and pretty?' She almost spat the words out.

Spencer closed his eyes in exasperation and shook his head. 'De Vries and Masters were already here,' he said, ignoring the fact that they were on the point of departure until Judith had reinvented their image. 'Annie got Circe and Clark brought in Harcourt,' he went on, rewriting events to suit his decision. They may well have suggested them, but it was Judith who'd drawn up their profile, Judith who'd got them to sign.

Spencer had not finished. 'Kingsley's set up his own company – which in itself has left you open to question – and we almost lost Circe.'

'Almost?'

'Yes, almost.' He looked her straight in the eyes. 'She's decided to stay. Rik spoke to her. Provided he handles the account she'll stay.'

Spencer moved around to sit behind his desk, glancing briefly at his watch, a gesture that did not go unnoticed. It was the one movement Judith needed to help her get a grip on the proceedings.

He spoke more kindly but to Judith's ears it was even more damning. 'Look, you're a great kid. Let's take the weight off you for a bit. I gather Van is trying to get that agency off the ground and look . . . hell . . . I understand these things. He needs you there for him. Men do. Fact of life, but we can't jeopardize Premier with half your attention on someone else's company and until you can sort out the dividing line between your clients and his . . .' He paused, then said bluntly: 'Premier's clients do not want to be involved with him and last night was out of order.'

The miracle was she had a job at all. What did it look like? A boyfriend who dominated her life, helping his clients by milking her own.

Her mind trailed back over the last dreadful months. Where once Premier boasted only the best and the most distinguished accounts, it was becoming accepted that hookers and crooks, shady figures from nightclubs and showbiz could be guaranteed on the guest list.

And she had done it.

In the eyes of the world Judith Craven Smith, diplomat's daughter, high-flying career girl, who had laid such store by independence, had sacrificed her own career for her man's.

Game, set and match.

Rik was already installed in a spare office near Spencer. As she passed Judith glanced through the door and saw Fenny standing with a clipboard feverishly taking down his instructions.

Camilla had been briefed to assist Rik in any way that she could. Clearly she wasn't happy with the arrangement, but with a supreme effort of will Judith looked encouraging and said she thought Rik would be okay to work with.

The rest of the day passed in a haze. Spencer's decision to bring Rik back in was generally accepted as right. Clark and Annie, uncertain where their allegiances should lie, suggested they took her to lunch.

Smilingly Judith declined, saying she needed to dash over to Marks & Spencer in Oxford Street. Instead she went for a long walk, not noticing or particularly caring where she went. The list of things she had lost since Van Kingsley had come into her life was the stuff of which cheap melodramas were made: her reputation, her lover, her career. The alternative was to sacrifice her family's happiness and in doing so she would probably have lost everything but her job. And what was the point of running Premier if everyone's lives were in ruins?

In this mood she turned corners, crossed streets and strolled through leafy squares, for once knowing she wasn't needed so urgently back at the office.

Van was out when she arrived back at the flat. Evidence that he had only just got up was all around; a stale smell of tobacco mixed with the muskiness that comes from windows that haven't been opened and doors that have been kept closed clung to her once-comforting and comfortable home.

The evening stretched ahead. For the first time in a long while, she was home before seven. Rosie was working on a night shoot. Libby was having dinner with the Frankenheims. Majorie Fulton's opera gala would be well under way without Judith. She could have gone, but she knew Gray would be there, probably with Lisa. She couldn't have stood that. Better to be here.

The phone rang as she was stepping into the shower. Nervous that it might be Rosie or Libby, trying to get her to have supper, she let it ring. On the sixth ring it switched to the machine.

The voice stopped her. 'Judith. This is Josh. I'll ring again. Please don't go out until you've heard from me. Please.' He rang off. Reaching for her robe, she hurried to the phone and called Carey's number since Josh had been house-sitting. Why would he ring her? She replayed the message. No mistake, Josh's voice was racked with desperation.

Once again she tried Carey's house. No answer.

She rang Carey's office and asked for him, but they hadn't heard from him all day. No, he wasn't out of the country. Had she tried his house?

Something was wrong. Something was badly wrong with Carey, she knew it. He had looked so ill last night and she had avoided him because she couldn't bear the thought that one of her closest friends actually liked, no, fancied the man she most wanted to hear had fallen into a river.

Josh would ring back. She'd find out then. The phone stared silently back at her. She stood biting the corner of her thumb. It was only a phone call, but it was the first one in a long time.

Maybe if she just went over to his house? Just to make sure, nothing more. And she needed to get out of here or she would go mad.

Carey lived in a double-fronted Edwardian house in a cloistered square in Battersea, which attracted young media celebrities and artists. Judith left the taxi at the black entrance gates and walked across the cobbled square to Carey's house. It was in darkness and clearly no-one was at home. Nor did it look as if there had been a break-in.

Feeling rather foolish that she had obviously overreacted, she stepped back onto the pavement and scanned the upper windows but they too were in darkness. Rummaging in her bag, she fished out a piece of paper and a pencil and scribbled a note for Josh to say she had called and that she was going straight home and would wait in to hear from him.

She didn't know Josh all that well, so it was odd that he had phoned her sounding so panicky. Why would he ring her in particular? With a last backward glance she started to walk away when a woman in the next house, who had been eyeing her through the latticed blinds, threw open her window and called out.

'Are you looking for next door?'

Judith whirled round and looked up. 'Yes, I am. Do you know where they are?'

''Ang on,' she called. 'I'm coming down.'

Seconds later the front door opened and a middle-aged woman wearing a track suit and pink fluffy slippers appeared in the doorway. Judith walked over to her.

'I clean for 'er.' She indicated the house from which she had just emerged with a nod of her head, folding her arms across her chest. 'She's away, so's he. Which is why I'm here. 'Ouse-sitting, know what I mean?'

Judith nodded, wondering where all this was going. The woman was clearly bursting to tell her something she regarded as important.

'Well, about six o'clock . . . no, I tell a lie, it was ten to, because I switched over for the news . . . or was it the end of "Neighbours"? No, I was right first time. It was the news. Anyway, I saw that young man who's been staying there go in and then about half an hour later an ambulance arrived and they brought that Mr Templeton out on a stretcher . . .'

'Stretcher?' Judith grabbed the woman's arm. 'Are you sure it was Carey? What was wrong with him? Where have they taken him?'

'Well, that's what I was going to tell you. I don't know,

only you was knocking and I thought you might not have heard.'

'Which hospital?' Judith asked rapidly, moving towards the gates. 'Did you hear which hospital?'

'No, but the nearest casualty is St Dominic's, over by the harbour.'

But Judith was already off. She sprinted to the main road and turned onto the bridge. Roadworks were clogging one lane but she spotted a taxi struggling through and raced to get in it.

What on earth was wrong? That was why Josh was in such a panic. He must have called from the hospital.

Judith hated hospitals. It brought so much back: the night Alice was born in Washington, her mother's white, strained face and then the long, dreadful daily trek to see her when she finally succumbed to cancer. Now she hurried down the white-walled corridors, lights blurring overhead, arrows signalling the way to unfamiliar territories of x-rays, cardiac units, emergency; the faded, worn-out chairs, peeling paint and brave attempts by staff to disguise the neglect with green trailing plants and bright posters.

Judith grabbed a nurse as she hastily scoured the crowded casualty department for Josh.

'Mr Templeton? Templeton? Oh yes,' the nurse said, consulting her list. 'He's been admitted. Oh, about two hours ago. The ward sister will advise you.'

Judith took the crowded lift to the fourth floor and pushed her way out into the long, wide, bleak corridor. Ahead of her was an empty bed pushed against a wall, oxygen tanks flanked the sides, black plastic bin liners were piled haphazardly in a heap. There were no seats.

An old man shuffled towards her, pushing himself forward on a frame, his dressing gown hanging loosely open over striped pyjamas. Behind him an elderly woman attached to a saline drip was easing herself into a wheelchair, encouraged in a gratingly brisk voice by a nurse to be a 'good girl' and buck up.

'Judith, Jude.' She wheeled round. Josh was walking rapidly down the corridor. She ran towards him and they caught each other, both talking at once.

'Josh, what's happened?' she demanded, searching his face anxiously. 'Where's Carey? Josh, oh please don't cry . . . He isn't . . . he's not . . . ?'

'No, no,' Josh wept. 'He's alive. Just. Jude, come away from here. We mustn't be seen.' Glancing over his shoulder back down the corridor, he pulled her around a corner.

'Carey tried to kill himself.'

Judith froze. 'What? Why? Josh, what's happening? No, no, take your time. I'm here now, take it easy.'

Her arms were around him, cuddling him. Josh's body was shaking with fear. Through broken sobs he told her that he had arrived home to find Carey unconscious, a note saying he couldn't stand it any more left beside him.

Judith was horrified. 'Josh, why didn't you tell me? Why was Carey so depressed?'

Josh took a cautious look around and gave a low gasp as he spotted a small knot of people emerging from a side ward.

'Jude, I'll tell you everything. Please just help. Do as I say. Pretend you're my girlfriend. Please? Carey's parents are here, they don't know . . .'

'Don't know what?' she said urgently, her back flat against the wall, Josh alongside her peering anxiously into the main corridor. 'What, Josh?'

He twisted his head, pleading with her to understand. 'They don't know he's gay. They don't know about . . . me . . . us. Please, Jude. It would kill his father.'

Carey's father, a high court judge, was known to be fiercely proud of his only son. Judith didn't have to be told the rest. Anyway, there wasn't time. Josh had slung his arm around her shoulder and walked her quickly back down the corridor.

Mrs Templeton, a slim, elegant woman in her late fifties, was grey with shock. The judge, with one arm around his wife, was listening intently to a young woman doctor. They glanced up as Josh approached.

'This is Judith, my girlfriend and close friend of Carey's,' he told them. Mrs Templeton nodded wearily, trying to smile. 'Yes, Carey mentions you a lot,' she said. Her husband looked dazed and just nodded.

Judith took Carey's mother's hand. 'Is he all right? You poor thing. This is dreadful.'

Mrs Templeton's reserve went. Shoulders hunched, she began to weep softly. Judith and Josh both moved to her and wrapped their arms around her, all three standing holding each other in the corridor.

'I should have known something was wrong,' the older woman was sobbing into Josh's shoulder. 'He never said. So depressed and yet he couldn't tell me.'

Over her head Judith's eyes met Josh's, urgently seeking guidance.

'He was working so hard. He was tired, as well,' Josh was saying in a voice that was far from steady. 'It's just that he wasn't sleeping either and he took too many pills.'

Mrs Templeton blew her nose and gave Judith a watery smile. 'So sorry, my dear. How good of you to come. Carey has such kind friends,' and she began to weep again.

The group was broken up by a nurse arriving to tell Carey's parents that they could see him for a few minutes. Alone with Josh, Judith turned to him.

'Carey's never been afraid of hard work in his life,' she stated deliberately. 'Has he?'

Josh shook his head. 'No. He couldn't take any more.' She waited, guessing what was coming. It all made perfect sense now.

'Carey didn't want you to be hurt.'

'Van,' she said. 'Van, isn't it?'

Numbly he shook his head.

'Dumped him?'

Josh's eyes flew to her face, hurt and anger mixed up together. 'Van dumped him? Carey was never with him, you have to believe that. He just wouldn't let go of him. Everyone thought Carey was involved with him, but he wasn't.'

'And you and Carey think Van and I are together?'

Josh hesitated. 'Well, yes. Van said . . . I mean, you and him . . .'

'You're wrong,' Judith said gently. 'So wrong. I loathe him.'

She'd said it. The freedom, the blissful release of voicing her hatred swept over her. She was never going back. Never.

'Loathe him?' Josh looked at her in amazement. 'But why is he still with you?'

'It's a long story. Tell me about Carey. Surely to God he hasn't tried to end himself over that little shit?'

With no chairs to sit on in the bleakly furnished corridor, Judith had to rely on the wall for support when Josh next spoke.

'Never,' he said vehemently. 'He was blackmailing Carey.'

Her stomach did a somersault, her heart began to beat a tattoo. Why hadn't she realized? Carey, of all people, Carey who was discreet and charming, with a vulgar little sod like Van – impossible. Blindingly clear now. But blackmail? Over what?

'Because he's gay? Nonsense, no-one would take a blind bit of notice.'

Behind her Josh saw the Templetons returning. He slipped an arm round Judith. Mrs Templeton seemed better; Carey had spoken a few words. It was an accident. He hadn't meant to scare anyone. Poor, poor boy. She couldn't wait to get him home. He'd like to see them both for a few minutes, she'd told him that Josh's girlfriend, Judith, was outside.

Carey was lying in a narrow bed in a small side ward. A drip was attached to his arm and there was one in his nose. The sight of him made Josh give a convulsive sob.

'Hi, Jude,' Carey said weakly. She went to him and kissed his forehead. He tried to explain but his voice was a mere croak, his speech a slur. 'Don't,' she admonished him gently. 'Just get better. I need you around.' She could see him trying to focus on Josh, who was stroking his hand.

'Don't worry,' she whispered to Carey. 'I'll take care of him, until you're out of here. Promise. And Carey . . . forgive me? I didn't know . . . I thought . . .'

Carey smiled weakly at her. 'Stupid of me. Should have told you.'

Judith stroked his hair and told him not to speak. Josh was still holding Carey's hand; the pain on his face wrenched at her heart.

'Josh? I'll wait outside, okay?'

She stood in the alcove to the side ward so that Carey's

parents would not know that Josh had remained privately with their son. This was too incredible for words.

Carey was thirty-three, a grown man. It was years since he had lived at home. He was successful and still afraid of his father. God, another reputation to save. And the ideal setup for blackmail.

Josh joined her, a bit red-eyed, but more in control of himself now that he knew Carey was out of danger.

It was arranged Judith and Josh would come back briefly later on to make sure the Templetons had some back-up. The press would be told that Carey had gone down with a virus but that he would be back at work in a few days. Mr Templeton looked relieved. Mrs Templeton was watching Judith closely.

As they left she hugged her and whispered, 'Thank you. I know you think I'm stupid, but I've always known. It's difficult for his father. I made Carey promise he wouldn't tell. Not yet. Will you ring me?'

She stepped back, only she and Judith aware of that murmured exchange. In the confusion of goodbyes and departures, Judith could only catch Mrs Templeton's eye, smile her understanding and nod.

Josh's description of Carey's last few months left her feeling ashamed. Ashamed that she had not made more effort to find Carey, ashamed that she had brought Van into his life and ashamed that because she was so bound up in her own fears, so many other people were being hurt – Carey, Gray, Alice. And she had not tried to fight back. Just given in.

Now she understood why poor Carey had agreed to be photographed with Shade and Vinny Perrereo. It wasn't infatuation after all.

'Carey can be stupid at times,' sighed Josh wearily as they sat in a pub near the hospital. 'So discreet, and then wham, someone like that prick Kingsley comes along and he's flattered and attracted all at once.'

Judith listened. It was a familiar story, and not one that particularly surprised her. Carey had quite obviously found Van attractive, and let him get too close. She'd been there, seen it. How she wished she had stopped it. But she couldn't

270

have. Won over by his undeniable charm, quick wit and winning smile, like her, like Alice, Carey had believed in it.

Van had stayed for a couple of days with Carey just as a change from hotel life. Neither of them had told her, the one because it didn't suit him for her to know, the other to protect her from what he thought would hurt her.

'He must have waited until Carey was out filming and then went through his letters and stuff. Anyway, he found a note from Brendan Harman, remember?'

Remember? Of course. What was this?

'The note Van found was fairly loaded. Carey and Brendan had been lovers for nearly a year, but when they discovered Brendan was HIV positive they broke up.'

Judith's hand flew to her mouth. Brendan, eccentric, dynamic, clever and bitchy, the winner of so many fashion awards his friends would joke the only thing he hadn't won this year was Cruft's. It was the first she had heard that Carey was anything more than just another member of Brendan's huge circle of friends.

'Carey hasn't been infected?'

Josh shook his head. 'We won't know for certain for another three months. He was tested straight away but the clinic won't give him the all clear until he's had a third test that's negative. But Carey knows that if their affair was discovered he'd be out of that job in seconds and the shock would kill his father.'

Judith was less concerned about Carey's father. But Brendan's reputation was well-established. Rock stars and actors, models and photographers, his name had been linked with them all. Wild and reckless, he had made no secret of his lifestyle, but he had also been intensely loyal to those of his lovers who preferred to be discreet. Carey had been one such person.

Van had simply found another meal ticket. Just as he had helped himself to a free ride on the back of Judith's reputation.

Van was waiting for her when she got home. As usual she ignored him. The effort was paralysing her. But she had to think. The door to her room was open, her belongings scattered everywhere.

Turning, she faced him, letting her eyes flick over him with a contempt that was always destined, she realized later, to tip him over the edge.

'Just checking,' he smirked, lighting a cigarette and hurling the match into the base of a plant near the door.

Pathetic. Evil. She had no time for him now; Josh needed her back at the hospital. Quietly she went to close her door.

'Dead, is he?'

Something snapped and before she had time to think she walked back and smacked him hard across the face. It was instinctive. The livid marks of her hand stood out on his cheek.

With lightning speed he spun her round and pushed her against the wall. The breath was knocked out of her. With his face inches from hers, his body pressed against her, features contorted, sickeningly, Judith could feel he was aroused.

'So you want it rough, do you?' he breathed, thrusting his body against her with an obscenity that made her recoil.

Fear gripped her, immobilized her. He was grinding his body into her as she struggled to push him away. But her resistance urged him on, exciting him, his face flushed, his breathing growing uneven. Laughing hysterically, he was driving himself harder and harder against her terrified body.

Much later, Judith wondered how she remembered – no, not remembered, even *knew* – what to do. Van's hand had tightened on her chin, the other leaned heavily against the door frame, and he was using the weight of his body to push her against the wall. It took the briefest of seconds but it was all she needed. Her elbows pushed against his body, her left knee came up and hit him hard between his legs, and again, and again.

The force shook him. For a split second he couldn't breathe, his eyes rounded in shock and with a scream he fell backwards, sliding to the floor, bent double, his hands ineffectually clutching his groin, leaving Judith horrified and feeling sick.

'Bitch,' he screamed. 'You fucking bitch.'

He rolled in agony on the floor. She backed away, panting, not quite believing what she had done, knowing she'd had no option and glad, watching him in fascinated terror as he writhed in front of her, a stream of abuse pouring from him, glad she had.

'Stay away from me, Van,' she warned as he tried to pull himself up against the wall. 'Nothing, nothing, do you hear, is worth having to put up with that kind of shit from you, okay?'

But still he dragged himself towards her. Judith grabbed a wicker chair and pointed its four cane legs at him. She was panting hard and scared. 'If you touch me, Van, if there is a mark on me, everyone will know it was you. You've linked our names, you live here . . . stay where you are . . .'

On all fours he was slowly getting closer. She raced on, frantically glancing behind her for escape. 'One mark, one injury, one day missing at work, you'll be done for blackmail and assault. Are you listening to me?'

He was on his feet, naked hatred written on his face. Judith's nerve began to crumble. Throwing the chair at him, she lurched towards the door, but was not quick enough.

The speed with which he hit her gave her time only to jerk her head sideways. The thud landed between her left eye and her ear, and she slumped to the floor with waves of nausea sweeping over her.

The room was spinning. She could hear a roaring in her ears and she couldn't focus. Van's legs were the only things she could see standing over her as she tried to push herself up, her body convulsing.

As she did he lunged at her and pushed her down again.

'You get my point, sweetheart?' he panted. She lay in silence, trying not to vomit. 'Understand?' he repeated. 'And if you try any cute tricks like that again, I might be forced to demonstrate just what else I can do,' and then she heard him turn and slam out of the flat.

For a few minutes Judith stayed where she was, sitting hunched against the wall. Slowly she turned over and on all fours pushed her hands against the wall, wishing the room would stop spinning.

Swaying sickeningly, she made her way to the bathroom, and ran both taps into the sink, splashing water on her face.

273

Sitting on the edge of the bath, she pulled a towel from the rail and held it to her throbbing face.

That's where she stayed until the room stood still and she was able to pull herself carefully up to peer at her face in the mirror over the sink. It wasn't bleeding, but the red swollen side of her eye shocked her.

Briefly she closed her eyes and then pushed herself upright, holding the towel to her face as she walked unsteadily into the kitchen. She poured cold water into a tumbler, and pulled a bag of ice from the fridge to crack some into the towel. Holding both, she went to her bedroom, locked the door and sank down on her bed.

In God's name, what was happening? Was it worth it? The answer was obviously no. No, not for a second.

Judith hadn't cried for a very long time. But she did now. Tears ran down her cheeks and mingled with the drops of ice from the freezing pack on her face. Sobs racked her body, engulfing her until finally exhausted she fell asleep fully clothed, clutching the towel, and for a few merciful hours knew nothing about her poor swollen face turning into hideous evidence that she would find very difficult to explain.

Chapter Twenty-Six

Two days later Carey came home and found not only Josh to care for him, but Judith too.

'This is more like the casualty department at St Dominic's,' he joked, seeing Judith's eye, and because they were so relieved to be home and safe, they hugged each other and laughed and wept at the same time.

'I could be HIV positive, you've got a black eye and we're both being blackmailed. You're going to tell me everything, aren't you?' he insisted. 'I'm not going to let you end up like me.'

Josh and Carey were both waiting for her to agree. And she did, slowly nodding her head. Carey's arm was still around her as much for support as comfort.

Her bruised and swollen face had told Josh everything when she had arrived at the hospital to meet him to visit Carey a few hours after Van's savage attack.

'He knew,' she said as Josh hugged her fiercely. 'He heard it on the news. He wasn't fooled. No, no. Please don't say anything. You don't understand, I can't go to the police, but I could probably find out from casualty if my eye is okay. It feels so blurred. Josh, can I come back with you? Just for a few days?'

It was strange how one got used to hospitals and the swift transition into a twilight world until now inhabited only by other people in Judith's life. Ten o'clock at night in a busy casualty department was not, she decided, the most fertile ground for sympathetic attention.

Josh had gone back to sit with Carey, who had been transferred at his father's insistence to a private ward. Judith took her place on the end of a row of chairs and waited. Next to her an old man was asleep, snoring noisily, his head bouncing gently up and down on his chest. A young stick-thin blonde was ignoring every notice and dragging heavily on a cigarette and regarding Judith with idle curiosity.

Judith caught her eye and looked quickly away, but not quickly enough.

''Ad 'im arrested, did you?'

'Who?' asked Judith nervously.

'The bloke what done that,' said the blonde, jerking her hand towards Judith's cheek with her cigarette.

'No, nothing like that. I hit myself against the door,' Judith lied, knowing it sounded like a cliché.

The girl sighed and dropped her cigarette on the worn linoleum floor, extinguishing the stub with the sole of her shoe as an angry young nurse approached. 'Everyone says that. Makes no difference, they don't care about "domestics" down 'ere. You'd be wastin' your time.'

The young doctor who looked at her eye didn't believe her either. He moved round and sat beside her on the edge of the examination table taking her chin in his hand. 'Does it hurt much?'

Judith shook her head. 'Looks worse than it is.'

He nodded. 'You'll have a bit of a headache, but no eye damage as far as I can see. Ice packs and a real shiner for the next few days. Come back if your vision doesn't stabilize in the next twenty-four hours.'

It could have been worse. Easing herself off the edge of the table, she smiled her thanks. The weary young doctor had a roomful of drug addicts and road accidents, drunks and assaults to deal with. And a beautiful young woman whose life was in a mess.

'Look,' he said, pausing by the curtained cubicle, 'it's your own business how you got this. But you don't strike me as someone who would tolerate being abused in this way.'

The bluntness of his opinion took her by surprise. Automatically she lied – it was becoming second nature to her. 'You're kind but honestly, this was an accident. Stupid of me. I just panicked when I got the phone call about my friend and in the rush to get out I was pulling on my boots and slipped over. Crashed straight against the bedside table.'

He pulled the curtain aside and shrugged.

'I thought you said it was a door.' He held up both hands to stop her as she opened her mouth to explain the discrepancy. 'As I said, your business.'

The bruise on the side of her face was slowly turning yellow and Judith was only too thankful that no-one could see her hip and the top of her thigh, which looked even worse.

The shock of the beating Van had given her was more forceful than she would have believed. Everything had changed. Where once she had feared a sexual assault might be in his mind, she had never envisaged how savage he could be.

When she left the flat she had taken only a suitcase of clothes, her passport, bankbooks and a small attaché case in which details of her personal accounts were stored.

Carey's house was the one place Van would avoid. He'd pushed him too far. So it was now the safest place for her to be.

That night, after she and Josh had sat talking long into the small hours, she had promised that just as soon as Carey got back she would tell them both why Van had such a hold over her. Curled up in the small spare room, she turned over in the narrow bed and gazed at the suitcase behind the door, lit by a shaft of moonlight from a crack in the curtains.

For a long time she just lay there looking at it, a silent symbol of all that her life had become. Somewhere outside a dog was barking; occasionally she heard the swish of a car as it swept past in the road beyond the black iron gates and below her window the gentle rustling of the trees resisting each gust of wind that swept the silent square.

She was too troubled to sleep. Twisting, she pulled herself up into a sitting position and reached out to draw the curtains back to the sides of the square sashed window. Moonlight flooded across her bed. She folded her arms behind her head and in this way confronted a number of uncomfortable truths.

Somewhere in the carefully constructed life she had led since her mother's death there was a flaw. In the last few weeks and days and hours she had begun to recognize what it was.

It lay not in her family history, nor in a sequence of events best forgotten, but in something more fundamental. Strange, once she would not have hesitated to say her life was full of risks.

But in truth she had never taken a risk in her life. The bold, feisty, glamorous woman who had pulled Premier back into shape was a myth.

Not once had she known the courage to fight back at what life threw at her. She negotiated, she bargained, she listened and accepted. But when had she ever said what she wanted, what her terms were, how she would like things done? It was a habit she had got in to and it had controlled her.

Roland Whittington, married and using her, dangling her on a string, had called the shots. Why hadn't she confronted him with her own needs in the deeply unfair and unequal relationship? Too scared to take the risk in case she lost him. And she lost him and her job anyway.

What about Howard? Hadn't he been a risk? Not in a lifetime. What risk was there in being the love object of a randy millionaire? When David Corrolla had been appointed over her, she had said it was unfair, protested. But she hadn't fought back. She'd gritted her teeth and allowed Howard to try and talk her into remaining with him, more money, less power, a new title. Oh please. All because of a stupid affair, sleeping with him because he was sexy and she felt lonely. Risk? Get out of here.

She groaned and rolled over, pulling the pillow over her face. Did she have any brains at all?

After Howard, Spencer. Where was the gamble when she had no option? Talked into a job that Rik Bannerman had rejected, half London had rejected. And now that Premier was on its feet, he was back seizing control. Even if Van hadn't handed Spencer the reasons on a plate, what would she have done if he had pulled Rik in anyway?

All that would have happened, she realized, was that she would have been indignant, created a fuss, believed Spencer held her in great affection and she'd have returned to her desk locked into an uneasy alliance with a man, knowing that she once again had the boss's heart but not his serious respect.

And Van. Where was the risk in that? Too scared, too nervous about the consequences of taking her life into her own hands, she had allowed him to pluck the joy from it while she sat pathetically by.

She was kneeling on the bed, staring out into the silent square below, hugging a pillow to her chest, gently rocking to and fro. After a while she swung round and padded over to the narrow dressing table where her handbag was slung over the back of a chair. Without turning on the small lamp, she felt around in the zip pocket and pulled out the small square card Gray had sent her so long ago. The light from the street lamp picked out the scrawled message written in black ink.

'What happens next?'

Lowering the card, she held it in her lap and sat contemplating the dark sky, the trees moving restlessly in the night wind, and knew with a certainty and a strength she had never experienced before that it wasn't just her flat she could never go back to.

It was also the deception, which she had called her life, that must never be revisited.

Chapter Twenty-Seven

It was obvious on Carey's first evening home that he was still weak, but would soon recover under Josh's tender ministrations. Both he and Judith had found to their surprise that knowing of each other's misery at the hands of Van had given them an odd kind of strength and sense of purpose.

'If nothing else, Josh's cooking isn't going to waste,' she grinned as she and Carey both reached to spoon up the last of the sauce in the dish in front of them.

Josh beamed delightedly. His devotion to Carey, a friend for a year before recently becoming his lover, was absolute. Tall, thin, with owlish glasses and a shock of blond hair that fell forward into his eyes, he looked every inch the academic. Who knows if Carey would ever have chosen someone so opposite to him in every way if Josh had come along at another time in his life?

Carey was witty and stylish; Josh was quiet and donnish. Carey would sit up half the night fiercely debating any issue from feminism to Spurs' chances in the cup. Josh preferred Keats or Milton. There was nothing camp about their relationship; no histrionics, seldom waspish, rarely did they let bitchiness intrude. No overt affection in front of Judith. They could have been any reserved couple in love, preferring privacy to public displays of affection.

The following morning Judith called Spencer. Making an effort to sound confident, she said she was taking a few days' leave.

Only weeks before she would have felt guilt-stricken at taking a long lunch break, let alone an unscheduled vacation. As she replaced the phone it was hard not to feel depressed that Spencer had agreed to her absence with such alacrity. Rik would be happy to take over until she felt well enough to come back.

I bet he bloody will, she thought. It was only after she put the phone down that she realized she had never said she was unwell. They had simply assumed she was cracking up.

Then she called Laura and said she would be with Carey for a while because he had just come out of hospital.

Thankfully Rosie and Piers were away on a fashion shoot for a couple of weeks and didn't have to be lied to. Not for a second would Rosie, who loved her, and Piers, who had known Carey since they were both thirteen years old, have believed a word of it.

And Gray?

Yes, well, Gray.

After that with nothing to disturb them, Carey, Josh and Judith closed the doors to the world and Judith, knowing the time had come, put her future on the line.

'Van discovered that while we were living in Washington when Dad was posted there, I got caught up with a boy called Harry Jardine. Easy to do, he was nineteen, terrific looking, rich parents and . . . well, straight from England and a repressed boarding school, the freedom and the lifestyle of those rich kids just went to my head.'

It was strange sitting in Carey's pleasantly cluttered kitchen, early summer sunlight filtering through the casement doors that led to a small sheltered garden, talking about Harry.

Harry Jardine. If he had lived what would have become of him? Rich, spoilt and drug-addicted, who knows if all Seth Jardine's money would in the end have been capable of curing an instability in his only son that had its roots in a lethal combination of parental excess and neglect.

Certainly Seth thought money could buy everything and the memory of his terrifying rage when it didn't still haunted her. His passion for Judith's mother had made it erupt. Sometimes she wondered what would have happened if her mother had run off with Seth as he had pleaded with her to do. What would have happened if Harry had not been killed?

It was such a relief to have Josh and Carey to tell the story to, so easy to talk to them. So easy to explain why Van had controlled her for so long.

'If my relationship with Harry had reached the papers, Dad would have been discredited. Well, when he was in Washington, the post he had was regarded as top security and he simply never spoke about what he did. Still doesn't, you know. Talks about his books, but not his work. There would have been an enormous question mark over his judgement, the sort that would make the difference to the rest of his career, if any of our family had a breath of scandal attached to us.

'Mum was terrific, I often thought half the reason Dad got the posting was because she was so brilliant with people. Actually she found the life there terribly oppressive so she did what she was good at and started working on charity committees.

'She also found us a house up in Ridge Harbour, Greenwich, so that we could get away from that Georgetown set. Dad would fly up at weekends and stuff, and that's where we met the Jardines.'

Those first few weeks, she told them, had been the happiest in one sense, because in the eighteen months she was there, her life had turned upside down.

'Dad was hardly ever there. I was the new kid on the block, it was only Mum who really got me organized. There was this guy Seth Jardine, a mega-rich industrialist that Mum got to know through one of her committees. They met at some party or other. I remember Dad forbidding both of us to have anything to do with the family, he just couldn't afford to have his name linked with the Jardines.'

'But why?' asked Josh. 'What was wrong with him?'

'Because everyone knew that Seth Jardine was associated with organized crime, drugs and that kind of stuff. No-one ever proved a thing against Seth because he was so staggeringly wealthy he had everyone tied up. Also,' she hesitated and then said in a rush, 'Dad hated the way he hung around my mother.'

It wasn't hard to remember her mother all those years ago, dark like Judith, a strong woman, one who made people feel good just to be around her. And she was fun. Whenever she thought of her mother, Judith thought of her smile.

Harry Jardine was another matter. She'd known almost from the first that he had deliberately set out to shock her.

'I was game for it. I understood Harry. He was wild because no-one thought to replace toys with attention. He was a kindred spirit. We recognized it in each other. Harry was into drugs, I was dazzled by it all and no way was I going to split on him.'

The light outside had faded. Josh got up, pulled the blinds and switched on a couple of lamps, sending a soft yellow glow across the kitchen. Judith looked across at where Carey was sitting with a small frown on his face.

'I can stop if you're tired, Carey,' she said anxiously.

Carey shook his head. 'No, I'm not, not at all. I was just thinking, you're the last person in the world I would have said had been doing drugs as a kid . . .'

'Oh I wasn't, I wasn't,' she said earnestly. 'Maybe a drag on a joint but nothing serious. Harry was doing anything that came his way. Suck, blow, sniff. I sometimes see that wild manic behaviour in Van.

'All those rich kids hung around Harry because he could make things happen, but only because his parents left him alone in a house with a pool and a jacuzzi and unlimited booze.

'The house was amazing. It was a half-mile drive from the gates to the main house, security guys everywhere. Now I'd find it intimidating, then I hadn't quite grasped the plot. I just wanted a good time.

'Van knows, God knows how, that Harry was killed in a car crash on his way back from picking up some drugs from his regular supplier. I was in the car when it crashed. Harry wouldn't listen to me that night. Why should he? He'd never listened to anyone in his life. He'd only known me for a short time and I had what no-one else around him had.'

'What was that?' asked Josh.

Judith laughed. 'A very English accent. Otherwise I don't think I would have rated with him at all.'

But she had, and it had all ended in the chaos of the blue

flashing lights of the ambulances, Harry's lifeless body hanging through his own windscreen. The terrible scream that she was told later had come from her, although she couldn't remember. And then the silence, worse than the noise.

A young wasted life. Leaving terror. Pure terror.

Silence hung over the room as Josh and Carey waited for her to continue. Judith was still in a country road with blood all over her skirt, her hands cut and bleeding from trying to drag Harry from the car, sobbing wildly as Seth's bodyguards pulled her away from the wreckage.

It was Josh who got her attention, moving around the table to slide an arm around her shoulders.

'Sorry,' she said, shaking her head. 'Sorry. It's so long since I've allowed myself to think of it.'

Josh held her hand. 'Have you ever told anyone this before?'

She shook her head. 'No, apart from my mother . . . I couldn't. It's why Van has kept a grip on me. You see, I was with the son of a man linked to crime who had been killed high on drugs with more stuffed into his pockets.

'Harry's mother was in LA and they contacted her, but no-one could find Seth and those security guys were frantic. Someone guessed he might be with my mother and . . . and he was. That's where they broke the news to him. Sitting in my mother's drawing room, in the home of an army diplomat who loathed him.

'Harry dead. Me in hospital, drugs all over the shop. Seth collapsed and Mum was the only one who could deal with him.'

Josh and Carey looked at each other. Neither could see the cause for blackmail all these years later.

The question Judith faced was how much more to reveal. She chose her words carefully.

'Mum knew that Dad's credibility would never survive his daughter being involved in a car crash in which Seth Jardine's son had died. Too many questions would have been asked. Seth pulled every string imaginable and Dad, in a total panic, let him.

'Harry's death was reported as a tragic car crash. No drugs

were found on him or, according to the doctor's report, in him. But then the doctor they employed was paid by Seth Jardine. The kind of guy who would swear Michael Jackson was Madonna if he was paid enough.

'I wasn't even mentioned. I was transferred that night to another hospital, a private one, under another name. You know,' she added sadly, 'I wasn't even allowed to go to Harry's funeral.'

'Were you in love with Harry?' asked Carey gently.

'In love?' Judith repeated the question slowly. 'In love? I thought I was. But it was just teenage infatuation. It's a terrible thing, but I can hardly recall his face now.'

Carey made them coffee while Judith talked on: her father's fury, which seemed more directed at Seth for being in his house; her mother trying to keep everyone calm; the urgent instructions to wipe from her mind anything she had ever heard or seen that would connect Harry with drugs or her father with Seth Jardine.

Seth, who had sewn his empire up to the point where a team of frustrated drug enforcement officers could not touch him, knew his son's death would destroy him completely if the truth were told. Judith remembered Seth's grief-stricken face and his broken voice warning her, frightening her.

'And Van somehow knows all this.'

Judith nodded wearily. 'God knows how. I've racked my brains to try and recall who else knew, but it was just a handful of people. Seth's dead now. Harry's mother wasn't even around, they'd been divorced for years. A year later just when . . . just when we were getting back on our feet, Mum died.'

She gave herself a shake. It wouldn't do to dwell on all that. So she looked up quickly and said, 'But Van also knew all the gossip about Alice.'

'Alice?'

Judith stopped. She hadn't meant to go that far.

'There was a lot of gossip about my parents' marriage. At one point it was rocky, which is the only reason Mum ever had time for Seth. He used to listen to her, you see, talk to her. He had time for her. Dad didn't.

'Anyway, there was some fairly vicious stuff about Mum and Seth. But the point is Van could wreck Dad. You can see it now, can't you? Diplomat in drugs cover-up, diplomat linked to organized crime. What's it going to do to him? And Alice . . . she . . . she knows none of this. And all because of me.'

She knew what they were thinking. 'No,' she said quickly. 'You're wrong. It's never mattered to me about my reputation. It might matter to other people. It could damage other people if they were too closely associated with me.'

'Like Gray?' asked Carey pointedly.

Judith looked at him. Carey had his spies.

'Yes,' she agreed lightly. 'Just like Gray.'

Carey argued that Gray wouldn't give a damn. Judith said it wasn't what he thought but what his clients would think. It was a moot point. The relationship had gone nowhere. She needed someone to be there for her, and for a while he had been – but usually only on the end of a phone.

'So now what?' asked Josh. 'Do you go on letting Van put the screws on you? For that matter, do you?' He turned to Carey.

Carey ran his hand across his jaw. 'In another month it might not matter,' he said lightly, looking at their shocked faces. 'But even if the test's okay, there will always be a doubt hanging over me if Van lets it out about Brendan.'

Josh busied himself clearing cups and glasses away. Poor Josh, thought Judith. It must be terrible for him.

Carey was also anxious to change the subject, watching Josh's retreating back as he went to lock up.

'You're right, I can't let it go on. Neither of us can. But what do we do? Going to the police is all very well, but these things leak out.'

The problem was, thought Judith, that all their plans were defensive. Did they have the courage to fight back?

Probably.

What did they need?

Weapons.

And did they have any?

Judith sat very still. Stupid, stupid people. Why hadn't she or they thought of it before? To fight back you need to know the strength of the opposition.

She began to laugh.

'What's funny?'

'We are. Listen, Josh. Take care of Carey. I'll be back in a week or so, maybe sooner.'

'Back?' they chorused, looking at her as though she had finally flipped.

'That's right. I'm going to New York. You see, absolutely no-one in this country could have given Van that information. It must be in Connecticut. It must be. I'm going back.'

Judith managed to get a flight the following evening. Laura was told it was a business trip. Carey and Josh drove her to the airport and watched her as she disappeared through the departure lounge before making their way back across the concourse.

'Do you think she'll find anything?' asked Josh as they crossed the road to the car park walking slowly, Carey still not quite steady on his feet.

Carey pursed his lips and squinted up at the sky. 'Maybe. It's worth a try, we haven't got anything else. I've drawn blanks every time I tried to find out where he came from. But she hasn't got a lot of time.'

Josh halted, and stared across the top of the car roof at Carey.

'You mean, if she's to get herself back on course at Premier?'

'Premier? Oh no. Not that.'

'Not that?'

Carey was looking thoughtfully into the distance. 'Last night when Jude was telling us about Harry and Seth and all that? It didn't make absolute sense to me. I had the feeling she was keeping something back.'

Josh, who didn't know Judith as well as Carey, looked surprised.

'She fudged all that stuff about her mother and Seth Jardine. Jude adored her mother and she loves her father, but it is possible that it's what she *didn't* tell us that is at the root of all this.'

By now they were in the car heading up the M4 towards London. As Josh said afterwards, it was just as well he'd had forty-eight hours of dealing with shocks, otherwise the result of Carey's next words might have had an unhappy conclusion.

'So, my clever one, what do *you* think it is?'

'I think,' said Carey calmly, 'that Judith is going to have a hell of a job telling her father that Alice isn't his daughter.'

Chapter Twenty-Eight

From her window seat Judith watched the yellow streaks of light slicing across the suburbs of New York. As the aircraft banked to make its approach to the landing strip she adjusted her watch to nine P.M. and longed only for her hotel room.

In her head it was now two in the morning. With luck, she worked out, she could be through customs and heading into New York within an hour. The plane bumped onto the tarmac and with a final roar of its engines, landed on time at JFK.

For once Judith was glad that there was no Howard to meet her. This was one journey she did on her own. Carey and Josh would simply sit tight until she called. Carey had wanted to go with her, but with newspapers still reporting his 'virus', it would attract attention if he took off for New York, accompanied by Judith sporting a black eye. If there was a problem he had Jed's number in New York, Howard's in an emergency.

Reluctantly they let her go alone.

The temperature had been in the eighties all day in Manhattan, and had dropped very little as the evening wore on. The hotel Judith had chosen to stay in on Sixth Avenue was large, international and anonymous. None of her New York friends was likely to dine there and she only needed a night's sleep before driving up to Connecticut, beyond Greenwich to the small country town of Ridge Harbour.

There surely she must find what Van had found? Someone might remember him. She was certain Dr Bradley Wallace would remember *her*.

Until she could answer that question, she wanted nothing but a shower and somewhere to sleep. It was with a groan of relief that she finally sank onto her bed in the air-conditioned room high above Manhattan, caring nothing that within walking distance the most exciting city in the world was just moving into action, and knew no more until a deep buzzer pulled her out of a dreamless sleep at eight the next morning.

She reached Ridge Harbour at noon, driving a hire car that she had picked up from the rental bureau just around the corner from the hotel. The route was a familiar one. Once she was on the New England Thruway, place names rose up and swept by, the urban decay of New York giving way to more socially acceptable suburbs and gentler lifestyles.

The last time she had seen the small town of Ridge Harbour, surrounded by the twin attractions of rolling countryside and a breathtakingly beautiful harbour, which had become the exclusive province of wealth and influence, was a month after her mother had been cremated. After that there had been no need to see it ever again.

She never thought she would have to.

Lizzie's ashes had been taken back to her native Yorkshire six months later when Judith's father had briefly joined her and Alice at Laura's house to try and pick up the pieces of their sad and shattered lives. For that she was grateful. Only memories remained, nothing more tangible.

The house they had lived in on Hunting Street on the far side of Ridge Harbour was not on her route. Nor did she want to see it. Her goal was the home of Dr Bradley Wallace.

Chestnut Drive was one of the prettiest roads in the town. White colonial- or federal-style houses vied with each other for timeless charm, each surrounded by deep velvet lawns, all bathed in sunlight trickling through the thick oak and plane trees that were everywhere.

Wide wooden porches surrounded most of the houses. Dr Bradley's was on the corner of Chestnut and Cooper Street. There had been no need for Judith to go inside on the one occasion when she had seen it; Harry had told her to wait in the car. It had been a long time ago, but Chestnut Drive was still the same.

She drew a deep breath, climbed out of the car and walked to the front porch. She knew instantly the journey had been wasted. An elderly white-haired man wearing a baseball cap was sitting lazily in a well-upholstered garden chair on the front lawn, browsing through the morning paper. As Judith approached he glanced up and laid his paper aside.

No, young lady, Dr Wallace had moved and moved again. Not sure where to, certainly out of the area. All he knew was that he now owned a private clinic over at Coniston Point.

Owned it? My God, he had done well out of Seth Jardine.

Judith thanked him and drove back into Ridge Harbour, parked her car on the main street and walked back past the rows of shops, past the dog parlour and the small Japanese restaurant, the interior design shops and the small cinema. Banks of gleaming Range Rovers and sleek BMWs that had brought the leaders of the ladies who lunch into town were parked on either side of the road, a further testimony to the town's affluence and its view of life, one that years before had been so familiar to her.

The street was almost deserted; the lunch break and the heat had driven most people to cooler spots inside.

The Post Office was empty except for a couple of counter clerks who did no more than glance fleetingly in her direction as she thumbed through the local phone book looking in vain for Dr Bradley Wallace. To double check she rang information, but they had no listing for him. Without an address they could tell her nothing.

Damn. She wandered back into the street, gazing each way, hoping for inspiration. Across the street she spotted Main Street News, a stack of local papers on a rack outside. Maybe he had his papers delivered. It was worth a try.

The store keeper shook his head. No, Dr Wallace was not on his list. Anyway, he explained, he was new here. Try the Post Office. She smiled her thanks.

Drawing attention to herself was not a good idea. Retracing her steps, Judith unlocked her car and considered her options. There really was only one.

Coniston was a similar town to Ridge Harbour but on a busier, more commercial scale. It was not difficult finding the clinic, but getting to see Dr Wallace was.

The simplest thing was to ask to see him. So she did. The receptionist asked her what time her appointment was.

'I don't have one, but could you ask if he would see me? I was once a patient of his.'

The receptionist stared pointedly at Judith's eye, which was still noticeable.

'I'm sorry, I thought . . .' Her voice tailed off. She must think I'm one of his face lifts, grimaced Judith, who had forgotten the bruise.

Her name noted, the woman indicated to her to wait in the reception area before the desk. Judith thought the arrangement of turquoise and deep blue armchairs grouped informally around a centrepiece of a copy of the Venus de Milo was gross.

Dr Wallace had clearly moved on to more lucrative pastures since the glossy expensive literature lying on the individual tables beside each armchair, on which were also bowls of rose petals floating in sparkling water, was a menu of body reshaping and resculpturing available at the clinic. A more serious-looking document mentioned everything from heart bypass to traction that could be carried out in the state-of-the-art clinic.

'Ms Craven Smith?' The receptionist beckoned her over. 'I'm so sorry but Dr Wallace isn't available.'

'Can I make an appointment to see him?'

The white-coated woman looked uncertain. 'Well, I don't think that would be possible. He's very busy . . .'

'But he must have an appointment free sometime,' insisted Judith pleasantly. 'Would you please find out for me?'

The receptionist seemed about to say something but changed her mind, instead picking up the phone spoke to someone in another department.

'I see. I see. Yes. I have explained that. Okay. Thank you.'

She replaced the receiver. 'I'm afraid Dr Wallace thinks there must be some mistake. He does not recall you as a patient. Have you got the right Dr Wallace?'

He knew her all right. He couldn't have forgotten. Just how many seventeen-year-old English girls get involved in fatal car accidents late at night and have the obliging doctor take care of them and all the subsequent problems?

Judith thought rapidly. This was her only lead. She smiled at the receptionist.

'You know, maybe I have made a mistake. Do you think

you could just check the records and see? It was a long time ago and I may have mistaken the name. It was certainly this hospital.'

'Certainly, ma'am. Take this slip over to records,' she said, scribbling on a docket and ripping it off the pad. 'Second floor, turn right out of the lift. They'll help you.'

Records were computerized now. But they had made a careful transcription of all old files. They looked for the name and the date, but there was no mention of the name she had been booked in under. Judith asked them to try her own name. Nothing.

'Maybe you didn't transfer all the files?' she suggested.

The records clerk was adamant. 'No, ma'am. If you'd been in this hospital any time in the last twenty years we would have your records.'

Then how did Van know who to find? Maybe the hospital hadn't been his source after all. But where else? Who else? She tried again.

'Has anybody else asked about either name in the last few months, maybe a year?'

The clerk was quite adamant. 'Ma'am, you've got the wrong doctor and the wrong hospital. Is there anyone who can maybe refresh your memory?'

Only Dr Wallace. One last chance.

Judith shook her head as though she was genuinely confused, pulling her bag over her shoulder, giving the receptionist the impression the interview was over.

'Dr Wallace will sort it out, I'm sure. I have to go over to his house later.' She pulled her diary from her shoulder bag. 'Reception said his address was . . . oh damn, where is that slip of paper? It was right here in my hand, oh don't say I've lost it already.'

She made a big play of turning out her bag, watched by the clerk. Looking up, Judith smiled helplessly and, she hoped, sheepishly. 'This is so embarrassing. Dr Wallace will think I'm so incompetent. I've lost the address.'

The clerk shook her head sympathetically. ''Fraid I can only tell you he lives out on Eagle Heights somewhere. Would you like me to ask his secretary?'

293

Quit while you're ahead was a maxim Judith had respect for.

'No, don't worry. I've just remembered I left the file on the desk in reception. It must be in there. Thanks a lot.'

She reached the lift before she allowed herself to draw breath.

The rest was simple. In the car she searched the map for Eagle Heights. There it was, roughly five miles from the hospital. Once there a man like Dr Wallace could not be hard to find.

And he wasn't. The local florist knew him. She also knew that he lived with a lady who wasn't his wife and that his daughter had married and no longer lived there.

Bradley Wallace had indeed done well out of Seth Jardine. His home was in a private road guarded by a security officer, who occupied a sentry box painted white, surrounded by banks of flowers and an American flag.

Judith watched as he checked the credentials of anyone attempting to turn down the wide lane flanked by tall, well-cultivated hedges protecting the homes behind them from curious eyes.

She drove on past the lane to a point in the main road where she could see anyone arriving but be of no immediate interest to the occupant of the guardhouse, who had given no more than a passing glance at her car as she had driven past. She parked and waited. Wallace would have to come home sometime. After an hour of sheer boredom she was rewarded.

A black Porsche drove slowly up the main street and pulled into the lane. She had a glimpse of a silver-haired man in his middle years at the wheel. It had to be him.

Ten minutes later Judith drove her car into the lane behind him.

The guard noted her number, asked for her driving licence and her destination, handed back her documents and waved her through. She knew he would be phoning ahead to the house to warn them of her arrival.

Dr Wallace's house was built on prosperous if obvious lines. A wide gravel drive led to an imposing Jacobean frontage, bordered on one side by a vast sweep of lawn, relieved only by an oak tree and on the other by a high perimeter hedge. Away to the left of the house Judith could see a row of garages surrounded by thickly-wooded trees.

She turned off the engine and waited for signs of life. There were none.

Wide but shallow stone steps flanked by tubs of geraniums led up to the heavy oak door. She pulled the bell and waited. After a pause she heard sounds inside and the entry phone rattled into life.

Judith cleared her throat and spoke into the microphone.

'I've come to see Dr Wallace. Delivering some flowers,' she finished, thankful that she had taken the trouble to arrive with an excuse.

The door was opened by a middle-aged woman who said she was Dr Wallace's housekeeper. She held out her hands for the flowers.

'Oh, I'm so sorry,' Judith said innocently. 'I meant I was delivering them personally. My family are old friends of Dr Wallace.'

The housekeeper, not surprisingly, looked puzzled.

'Is he expecting you?'

Judith smiled with a finger against her lips. 'It's meant to be a surprise.'

The housekeeper hesitated, uncertain. But this young woman didn't look like a maniac. She was obviously educated and well-bred in spite of that nasty bruise on the side of her face.

'Can you wait a moment? I'll see if Dr Wallace can see you.'

Judith stood in a large oak-panelled hallway and marvelled at how all the money in the world couldn't buy taste. The rooms she could see either side of a central staircase appeared to be crammed with reproduction furniture, heavy velvet drapes and portraits of people who she would have bet her life had never borne the name Wallace.

Through a door to the left of the staircase she could see a vast drawing room with a grand piano positioned in the window, which in turn looked down over the hills to the county line and beyond that to the water of Long Island Sound.

This was where Bradley Wallace found her. She recognized him instantly. His hair was now grey, his body a little thinner, but his eyes and jawline were surprisingly youthful. Judith's arrival so soon after his return from the hospital had not given him time to change; he was still wearing a beige linen suit, and a small brown bow tie hung loose around his neck. But it was him – the doctor who'd instructed her firmly that if she was a good girl and did what she was told, no-one would get hurt.

For a brief second their gaze held, his shocked, angry, blustering, defensive.

'Just who do you think you are?' he stormed. 'Impersonating your way into my house? You were at the clinic this afternoon, weren't you? You knew then I couldn't see you. This is outrageous.'

Judith let him rant on, staring quietly at him, wondering how a man with the ability to cure and treat could be as corrupt as he was. There was something about him that told her, like Coniston, like Ridge Harbour, he too had simply grown a little older, a lot richer, but nothing had fundamentally changed.

'What's outrageous about coming to see you? I only want the answers to a couple of questions and then, like you, I hope we never have to meet again,' she said quietly.

'Questions? What questions? I've never seen you before in my life.'

Judith laughed, a stunned surprised laugh. He couldn't be serious.

'Then why are you so angry, accusing me of impersonating someone? I have yet to give your housekeeper my name. Of course you know me,' she said. 'How could you forget me? How could you forget Harry, Seth or ... or my mother?'

His face was now twitching nervously. 'Are you telling me,' she continued, 'that you don't know who the Jardines are? If so, you must be the only person in the whole of Connecticut who doesn't.'

Dr Wallace was not a man easily cowed, certainly not by a slim chit of a girl. But he wasn't stupid either.

A woman appeared in the doorway, having heard raised voices. She was somewhere in her early forties, nut brown, saronged, manicured and tailored to within an inch of her streaked blonde hair.

'Honey, are you okay?' she drawled, taking his arm, looking coldly at Judith. 'I didn't know we had visitors.'

'This young lady has made a mistake,' the doctor said, his temper switching unnervingly from blind fury to smooth reason. 'I'll be with you in a moment. Could you send Marty in to show her out?'

With a final suspicious look at Judith, the woman left them.

Alone again, Dr Wallace's voice took on a hissed urgency. 'If you try and see me again, I will have you arrested.'

Judith's temper snapped. 'Arrest me? Who are you kidding? I know enough about you to put you away for years,' she pointed out. 'Don't threaten me, Dr Wallace. I didn't come here to threaten you or to make your life difficult. I came to ask just a couple of questions.'

'Like what?' he asked stiffly.

'Like, have you ever heard of a man called Van Kingsley? Does the name mean anything to you?'

'Van Kingsley? Van Kingsley?' he repeated. 'No. In what context?'

For a reason she couldn't quite fathom she knew he was telling the truth. All his other denials had come without pause.

'He seems to know a lot about me. Things that happened here at the time. Things that happened to Harry and Seth.'

The mention of the Jardines' names affected him. He licked his lips, and was back on the defensive. 'I've told you, young lady, I have no idea what you're talking about. I certainly knew the Jardine family but Harry is dead and Seth too. And all my memories of my association with them.'

The point was not lost on Judith. She tried one last time.

'Van Kingsley is a dangerous man. He's wrecking lives. Trying to wreck mine. I'll describe him to you. Blonde, tall, athletic. East Coast accent, educated. Women find him attractive . . .'

'Please stop this,' he interrupted impatiently, moving towards the door. 'I don't know the man and all the descriptions in the world aren't going to help. If he is giving you problems I suggest you tell the police, not me. Ah, there you are, Marty. Please show this young woman out and don't let her back in again.'

The housekeeper stood uncertainly in the doorway. Judith looked at the retreating figure of Dr Wallace, so safe in his denials, cocooned in lies. What a way to live, never quite knowing when your past might catch up with you.

The irony of it was not lost on her.

He disappeared through a door at the far side of the hall. The housekeeper coughed.

'This way please, ma'am.'

There was nothing for it but to go. It would be a while before her disappointment surfaced, a few hours before she had to admit defeat. Was this really where all hope ended? In this man's drawing room filled with bad taste?

The housekeeper was waiting. Judith shrugged. As she walked towards the door she glanced at a large round table covered in silver frames.

A wedding-day picture, on the doctor's boat. Several of small children, some taken at parties. None of his benefactor, Seth Jardine. One with his arm around a young girl . . .

Judith stopped. There was something about the girl that looked familiar.

'Excuse me,' she said to the housekeeper. 'Who is that?'

The housekeeper paused uncertainly.

'Who?' she asked, moving closer. She glanced at the picture Judith was indicating and seemed relieved that she was able to answer her.

'Oh that. That's Dr Wallace and his daughter,' she said. 'When she was much younger. That was taken when she was home from college, the last time before the boy she was to marry was killed.'

'Killed?'

'Yes. I wasn't around then, of course. I came when they moved here. So I didn't know her. She was never really at

298

home much after this boy she was just wild about was killed in a car crash.'

'Car crash?' Judith asked sharply.

'So I gather. She was so distraught she never really came back to live here. After a while she married, but I believe she's now divorced.'

'What was his name? The boy in the car crash?'

'Harry. Harry Jardine.'

Judith wasn't even surprised. Most girls had been crazy about him; he'd had everything going for him, good looks, money. A wild, exciting boy to be around. She'd felt that way herself. Strange she had never heard about Bradley Wallace's daughter. But then she had lived rather than listened in those days.

She replaced the frame and followed the housekeeper across the hall to the door, down the stone steps and across the drive to her car. She felt rather than knew someone was watching her from a window on the first floor.

The knowledge made her take her time. Only at the very last moment as she unlocked the car door did she turn and look directly at the window, where she was just in time to see Bradley Wallace step back into the dim interior of the room.

Not know her indeed. But now what?

Chapter Twenty-Nine

The house was still there, just as she knew it would be. The ten-foot-high electrically operated gates were firmly shut. Judith had left the hire car in the lane and walked along the short gravel drive until she reached them, just the way she used to do when she had gone there as a teenager.

Only this time she didn't press the gate control, or expect to hear guard dogs barking or a disembodied voice ask for identification before the gates swung open.

Then small security cameras monitored the gates and grounds from a control room situated right inside the door of the office block during daylight and from a control panel that triggered a monitor in every main room of the house once it grew dark.

Through the gates she could see a little of the drive leading to the imposing frontage of a house built a mere thirty years before, but in a style of a grander, more Colonial era. Clipped yew hedges ran along both sides of the drive until it opened out into undulating lawns, which eventually curved around a circular courtyard in front of the house in which a stone fountain occupied the central position.

If she stood still and closed her eyes, she could see it, hear it as it used to be. The noise from transistors blaring from the poolside, Harry racing along the edge, plunging in, not surfacing until he reached the other end of the pool, his hair flattened, gasping for breath. Cheering teenagers applauding his daring.

She saw herself at seventeen, her bikini revealing a pale tan that marked her out for an English girl against the mahogany glow of the others, laughing and admiring along with them, and not knowing the tragedy that lay in store.

And the evenings when Seth entertained. Fairy lights strung through the trees, along the terrace, white-jacketed servants moving swiftly through knots of people who would not be seen dead together in public. But in the safety and security of the Jardine compound and protected by Seth's wealth, politicians mixed with movie stars, crooks with lawyers, mistresses with married men.

'If a lawyer and crook got hit by the same car, how could you tell which was which?' Seth would ask. 'The skid marks stop at the crook.' He would bellow with laughter, bending double the easier to cope with the spasm that such wit inflicted on his body. He loved the joke, he loved entertaining and proclaiming that there were more honest crooks than lawyers, smarter actors than senators, mistresses were better than wives.

No-one disagreed, at least not within his hearing. Power exuded from him. But it did not extend to control over his son, the mother of whom, the second of his four wives, had not been seen there since Harry was four.

Judith could see her mother arguing with Seth in a small summerhouse by the pool, pulling away from him and running across the paved pool terrace through the gate to her car in the drive.

Of course he loved her – everyone did. But Lizzie had remained utterly loyal to her husband. Her dismay and fury at the way she had finally been lured to the house, compromising her position, had left Seth Jardine shaken.

In the first five of the thirty minutes between her arrival and abrupt departure, the very shrewd Lizzie Craven Smith had figured it out that the interest of the people assembled did not extend to any of the fund-raising she had in mind. For once Seth had found someone whose price exceeded his wealth and power. Over the years, whenever Judith remembered that raging man she was convinced, as she suspected her mother had been, that his passion for Lizzie came from knowing he could never have her completely.

She thought of Howard. Like mother, like daughter.

The sun was high overhead, the temperature already soaring into the eighties. Judith's hands were clammy where she had been holding the white railings of the gate, but it was not entirely due to the heat.

But now there was a silence that hung in the air, and a deserted house with an air of neglect, not from overgrown gardens or peeling paint, but from lack of people. It had been that way for a long time.

At least that's what the girl at the real estate office had said in town. Her boss would meet Judith at the house at three, she'd said. Judith glanced at her watch and strolled slowly back to her car, wondering what seeing inside was going to achieve.

The night before, she had driven back through Ridge Harbour. She didn't want to let go, not yet. Just retracing her steps might trigger something. Too late and too tired to drive into New York, she'd booked into the Harbour Hotel.

A solitary evening going over and over the minimal conversation she'd had with Wallace produced nothing. She called home to check in with Carey, and they both hung up feeling gloomy. The morning tabloids had reported that Shade and Vinny were being considered to star in a new game show called 'Intimate Moments' in which unsuspecting members of the public would be lured into revealing their sexiest secrets. Their agent, Van Kingsley, was confident that the TV company would select the tacky duo.

'Who's he got the dirt on there?' Judith asked as Carey laughed mirthlessly.

Any news from anyone else?

'No, love,' said Carey sympathetically. 'Nothing, I'm afraid.'

Well, what could she expect? Trying to get Gray on the end of a phone during their brief time together had been hard enough. It wasn't likely he'd find time now.

After a dinner that she barely touched, she wandered down to the small jetty and strolled along the boardwalk between the boats moored either side until she decided that a one-sided conversation taking place in her head with a dark-haired, high-powered lawyer was not very fulfilling and strode rather more briskly back to her room.

By morning, breakfasting alone, she knew she was being driven towards revisiting Seth's old home.

The early-morning drive had found the house shut up and

empty, without visible signs of life, no guards, no cars. There was no point in trying to see if the back of the house, which overlooked the ocean, was any different. There was no way visitors could get to it except from the jetty where Seth had moored his yacht, and such men do not leave their doors unlocked or their landing stages unguarded. She didn't need to be told it was for sale.

Judith didn't expect a local realtor to be handling the sale of the place, but she was right in that they might be acting as agents for a bigger company in New York. The young girl at the office in Main Street, Ridge Harbour, excited by the prospect of an unexpected client, had happily explained that the executors had maintained it to keep the investment sound. The house had received much interest, but they were only now able to place it on the market for sale at the executors' request.

Judith told her that she was buying for a client. She had made sure she looked the part: short-sleeved white linen jacket, cool rust silk skirt that skimmed her calves and flat canvas pumps that matched her skirt.

Now, waiting outside the Jardine compound, she still didn't know what she was expecting to find. The one thing Wallace had said that was true was that once Seth had died, all association with that time died with him.

Almost.

A car rounding the bend caught her attention. She watched its progress as it slowed and pulled in behind her. The top of the convertible was down, the driver whipped off dark sunglasses and was already extending her hand before the sound of the engine had died away.

'Miss Craven Smith? Carolann T. Flannagan.' She pumped Judith's hand and never stopped talking. 'Please call me Carolann. We have several other properties if you are not entirely satisfied that the Jardine property is what your client wants. Although I think you are going to be very surprised. Shall we take my car? I have the code to the gates, right here.'

She politely refrained from mentioning Judith's bruise, but her eyes had flicked to the yellow and green contusion.

'Car in front stopped too quickly,' Judith lied smoothly. The door story was lunacy.

'Oh, what a shock,' gasped Carolann, who had been trained to react positively to anything her clients had to say.

In this fashion she guided Judith through the house that had been so instrumental in shaping her life. Carolann's information seemed inexhaustible, inaccurate and derived from far too many readings of *Tender is the Night*.

Parties of every imaginable kind had taken place there, and still could. 'Tennis, swimming, golf, riding . . .' Carolann swanned ahead, reeling off events that existed only in her sales pitch.

And drugs and vice, Judith muttered to herself. Carolann had forgotten those. The stables were in immaculate condition, the office block coped easily with a staff of ten . . .

'Is your client a sporting person, Judith? No? Well, this house is perfect for someone who does not want to exert themselves to entertain their guests, but can provide everything for them to amuse themselves.

'But then what would you expect from the owner of Jardine Leisure?' she laughed, hoping it might rouse this calm and unresponsive English woman into giving her a clue how the pitch was going. 'Dancing, swimming, the entertainment area is in a class of its own . . .'

Judith wasn't even listening any more. She wandered behind Carolann seeing things that the vociferous saleswoman did not know existed: lives, passions, deaths.

'Carolann,' Judith interrupted. 'Who is selling the house for the Jardine estate? One of Se . . . I mean, Mr Jardine's former companies?'

'Er . . . no, I don't think so,' said Carolann, once again flicking rapidly and loudly through her notes. 'Let me see here. O-kay, I have it. It's the lawyers representing Mrs Jardine.'

Judith stopped. 'Mrs Jardine? Which Mrs Jardine?' Seth had never remarried after his fourth wife had been paid off. All the others had been divorced and relinquished all claims on his estate. Harry had been his only child.

Carolann was busily running a finger down her notes,

flicking the pages over. 'Mrs Jardine of Dune Point, Black Hollow Road, East Hampton, Long Island.'

'Which Mrs Jardine is she? I believe he had four wives.'

'Well, it doesn't say,' said Carolann reasonably. 'We only have the owner's name or the executors of the estate. Do you particularly want to know?'

It was crucial. Judith nodded. Carolann did not miss a beat, so out came her mobile phone. They were standing by the pool. A lone maintenance man was tinkering with the pump. Judith sat on a low wall and waited. She could see Carolann, who had retreated to the shade of the house to make the call, 'uh-huhing' into the phone.

Judith knew Jardine Leisure had been the subject of a takeover because Howard had made preliminary bids for control, but pulled out. For all his dissolute lifestyle, he would not have so obviously involved himself in drugs. She had looked up Seth's death in the obituary files at the New York Public Library when she'd arrived in that city three years ago.

There had been no Mrs Jardine mentioned; simply a man who had divorced four wives, with an only son who died in a tragic car accident.

Bradley Wallace had never mentioned a current Mrs Jardine. But he must have known all of the wives. Bradley knew all there was to know about Seth. When a man pays you that kind of money you'd have to be a fool not to, and Bradley was no-one's fool.

'Here we are,' Carolann called, her high heels clipping the stone terrace as she hurried towards Judith. 'It's Mrs Jardine Senior, mother of Mr Seth Jardine.'

Judith wheeled around. 'Mother?'

Carolann lowered her notes and stared at Judith. She was clearly beginning to feel uneasy. 'Yes, his mother. I don't want to pry, but are you acquainted with the family?'

This lying business was a doddle. 'No, but I understand that my client is. He never mentioned any relatives. The attorney . . . is it still Webster Conway?' she asked, mentioning the first set of American lawyers who came into her head.

'No, Simmons Ziegler Brindell.'
Judith committed it to memory.
'Thank you, shall we move on?'
Dune Point, East Hampton. She could be there next day.

Chapter Thirty

The Hampton Jitney left 41st Street across the street from Woolworths, just after eleven thirty on Sunday morning.

Judith knew she wasn't concentrating enough to handle the three-hour drive out of New York and the attraction of just sitting back as the air-conditioned bus pulled out of the nearly deserted city streets, across the Triboro bridge and out onto the Long Island Expressway, was too strong to resist.

The phone call from Carey the night before had unnerved her enough to cover her tracks even more thoroughly, and to arrange to leave for Long Island by bus. The fewer people she met or who knew her plans the better. Howard would start trying to locate her by checking car rental firms and once started he wouldn't stop. He would systematically work his way through her friends, starting with Jed, moving onto Ellie, until half New York would be looking for her.

She had called Simmons Ziegler Brindell before she left Ridge Harbour on Saturday afternoon and finally managed to get Todd Simmons himself.

It was not encouraging. The name Jardine coupled with a call from Ridge Harbour had an instant effect, but the message was dismissive. Mrs Jardine was a valued client. She saw no-one she was not acquainted with unless advised by her lawyers it was necessary. She had not, he said brusquely, spoken to any remaining members of her family for years, and so it was unlikely she would see a complete stranger turning up from England.

'Can you just ask?' Judith pressed on. 'The worst that can happen is she will say no. But I am determined with or without help to see Mrs Jardine.'

The lawyer gave an impatient sigh. 'Young lady, give me the number where you'll be staying. But I think it's a wild

307

goose chase. And now, with respect, my time is valuable and I am not being paid for this.'

Bloody lawyers, she thought as she put the phone down after giving him the number of the Hampton Lodge, where she had booked a room for a couple of days. Everyone of them. None excepted.

Judith reached the Jitney with just a few minutes to spare and made her way to the back to the only available free window seat.

A long-legged tawny-haired blonde wearing minuscule shorts boarded after her with a great deal of shrieking and helplessness that saw two men immediately leap to their feet to relieve her of the not-terribly-heavy-looking bag. Judith thought sourly that her thanks, accompanied by much eye contact and flirtatiousness, was a little excessive. Leaning back in her seat, she hooked her foot around the bar under the seat ahead, and settled down to do nothing more than relax for the next few hours.

The expressway, however, was boring and the traffic heavy. It was now June and most New Yorkers were getting ready to decamp with their families to Long Island for the summer, or at the very least were trekking up and down the Long Island Expressway going to or returning from their summer retreats in the Hamptons for the weekend.

Somewhere out there in East Hampton Mrs Jardine could be waiting, maybe with solutions, but it would be much easier, thought Judith as the bus rolled patiently on, if she knew what it was she was looking for, what exactly it was she had to find out.

Her mind went back to last night's conversation with Carey. How could he have been so careless? Oh, that wasn't fair. He didn't know Howard, didn't know just how adept he was at smelling a rat.

'He called the office and Camilla said you were in York for a few days, then Laura said no, you were in *New* York and that I had the number. I had to do something, because he finally said if I didn't tell him where you were he would call Gray to have you listed as a missing person. What was I supposed to do?'

Damn, damn, damn. Why hadn't she thought of Howard? She wasn't expecting him to ring, and had not for a moment thought he would call Yorkshire. Oh what a tangled web she had nearly hung herself with.

She did make one phone call to Ellie, the one person she knew would not question her if she asked her not to, the person she could trust to ward off Howard.

'Will you say I'm staying with you? Just for a couple of days?'

'I'll say anything you want me to, but not if you don't promise to stay totally in touch with me,' Ellie replied calmly. Judith heard her hesitate. 'Jude? I know you. There's something more to all this than not wanting to see Howard, isn't there?'

Sitting in her hotel room, the temptation to pour out the lot to one of her closest friends was almost overwhelming. She had been three days on her own with only Carey to check in with. Ellie's voice began to topple her resolve.

'Yes,' she admitted simply. 'But I'd rather tell you when I see you. Trust me?'

There was a pause. Ellie gave a deep sigh.

'No. But I'm going to have to. Just remember, if I don't hear from you by midday tomorrow I'm coming out there myself, okay? Take care and leave Howard to me. I might even enjoy it.'

Judith smiled to herself, wishing she could see the battle of wits between her former lover and a fiercely determined friend who'd cheered when Judith had refused to give up her own life for the tycoon, and whose success as a TV film producer annoyed Howard intensely.

Just before two o'clock having, well over an hour before, consumed the complimentary orange juice and peanuts the Jitney courier had smilingly handed over to her, the effects of no breakfast began to take its toll. In fact almost the entire bus seemed to have conspired to keep her aware of her fragile state.

She watched enviously as a mother and daughter shared a cooling bunch of grapes and wished she had thought of something as practical, particularly when they fed an equal portion to their pet cat meowing in its basket on the next seat. Ignoring a young couple sharing a chicken salad sandwich was a lot easier, particularly as they seemed unable to resist turning to nuzzle each other's noses, which they did with increasingly irritating and, in Judith's opinion, quite unnecessary frequency. Why an elderly couple on the opposite side of the bus was smiling indulgently at them was a mystery. God, all you need when you're in an emotional mess and likely to end up losing everything is a happy couple and nothing to eat.

Judith gazed out of the window, wishing the bus wouldn't bump quite so much, and refusing to acknowledge that if Gray had been with her, she would not have noticed if the entire engine fell out before they reached the Hicksville turnoff.

The sight of the first white clapboard houses and neatly pruned gardens of Bridgehampton sitting serenely under near-perfect blue skies, and then East Hampton with its manicured green lawns and white picket fences, the sun dappling through the trees, the tiny white clapboard churches with their self-important spires and the gentle wit of the local clergy solemnly proclaiming, 'Thou shalt not park here', raised a ghost of a smile and a sigh of relief that even in this impossibly flawless example of American affluence, the social pressures of twentieth-century life had made their mark.

The Jitney finally pulled into the bus station at East Hampton just after two o'clock, by which time Judith's confidence in her plan had undergone a radical shift.

You must be mad, she panicked as she watched the passengers ahead of her start to alight. Why would an elderly woman agree to see a total stranger if she had ignored her own family for years? And how do you get to her without her lawyers? Oh, bugger it, she thought viciously, something will turn up. You're here now. Get on with it.

Laura had always remarked that Judith would never make a success of feigning helplessness, but there were times, she thought grimly as she began to lug her bag down the aisle, when she fervently wished she had cultivated a little of the art.

The tawny blonde was helped from her seat, luggage restored to her by just about every eligible man on the bus, while Judith waited, tapping her fingers impatiently on the overhead rack to signal her irritation.

The heat after the air-conditioning of the bus was oppressive. Judith dumped her bag on the sidewalk, made a mild attempt to straighten the creases out of her shorts, untucked her shirt and, leaving her midriff bare, tied the ends in a knot.

Across the street she saw what she wanted. Slinging her holdall across her shoulder, she made her way over to the car rental office. It was manned by a plump middle-aged gentleman with an overhanging stomach that had prevented him from viewing his feet for years. Behind him a young girl sitting at a computer glanced up idly as Judith came in and then returned to punching in the letter that had been occupying her. The owner came forward, pushing a baseball cap back from his eyes.

He spread his hands and rested them on the counter, smiling genially at Judith. 'And how can I help you, young lady?'

Judith dropped her bag on the floor and explained she needed a car for a few days and that she would be staying at the East Hampton Lodge.

'Making a long stay, Miss?'

Judith feigned a bigger interest in the leasing leaflet than it deserved and said vaguely, 'Um . . . Three or four days, maybe a week.'

Formalities over, he called to the girl to get the keys of a white Mercury Sable and turned back to Judith to extol its virtues. But Judith was not listening. The girl behind the desk was looking sharply at her. For a split second their eyes met. Judith, on the alert, dropped her gaze first.

'Take Miss . . .' He consulted the contract Judith had just signed. 'Craven Smith to the car, Pearl,' and with a smile he ripped off the top sheet of the pad and handed it to Judith.

Judith looked back at Pearl who was regarding her with a puzzled expression. Alarm bells began to sound faintly in her head.

'Don't I know you?' demanded Pearl. 'I seem to recognize something about you.'

Judith swallowed hard, trying to recall if she had ever seen this girl. Nothing. She smiled pleasantly, denied ever having been in East Hampton before and began to follow her out of the door, watching nervously as Pearl, still shaking her head, tried to establish where she had come across her.

'You weren't working here for the summer or something? Waitressing? It's just I can't figure out what it is. You know that feeling, when you just know, you know something . . .'

Judith, following her around the corner of the building, prayed she would get away before this girl clicked who she was. What *was* it that she recognized about her? Throwing her bag in the back seat, Judith slid behind the wheel, pressed the button for the electric windows and was about to start the engine when Pearl suddenly shrieked.

'Got it,' she said triumphantly. 'You're right, I've never met you before.'

Judith almost screamed with relief. It was short-lived.

'It's the name,' Pearl crowed. 'I did all the staff cars for Dorfman Industries a couple of years back and I remember the name. You signed for them. Not a name you hear in the States too often, know what I mean? A real classy name. So English. I mean my name is Lieberholtzen and that's not very common, I mean it *is* common, not classy, doesn't have that kind of Englishness about it . . . sometimes I think of changing it, but then . . .'

Pearl, who had learned about England and the English from the school of Merchant Ivory, was in full flow.

Judith almost had a stroke. Shit. Of course. Howard had brought two secretaries and a couple of executives down with him to his East Hampton house. Being Manhattan dwellers, they didn't have cars, and Judith had signed the expense sheets for them to hire.

'Sorry,' she smiled, with what she fervently hoped was a convincing expression. 'Such a common name in England. I'm afraid it must have been someone else.'

Fifteen minutes later she pulled out of the car rental outlet, leaving behind a disappointed Pearl who had been compensated by a long and entirely fictitious account of Judith's background, and was heading out of East Hampton towards Montauk.

Forget East Hampton. Forget the Hampton Lodge. She

would call later and make some excuse. Montauk, not nearly so fashionable but to Judith more agreeable, would not remember anything about her. Unlike the prattling Pearl, who remembered a little but in Judith's opinion a great deal too much. The last thing she wanted was Howard to find her and start interfering.

Before she reached the village itself, Judith turned off the main road and onto the old Montauk Highway. Slowly she drove along the winding roads that led to the small hotel where she had once had dinner with Howard. Along here somewhere, she muttered, leaning forward to catch the names of the narrower side roads that punctuated the smooth line of the highway. In less than ten minutes she found what she was looking for and turned the car sharply into the car park that fronted the small wooden inn.

The room she booked into was simple, comfortable and commanded a view of the dramatic Atlantic coastline where white foaming waves rolled and crashed onto the stretch of beach that disappeared in a haze of foam and heat in either direction.

Pulling open the sliding door, she stepped out onto the slatted sun deck into the unrelenting heat of the late afternoon and stood gazing out at the rolling waves, the near-deserted beach, allowing the memories to come flooding back.

The summer Sunday morning when she had laughingly teased Howard that he was so unfit he wouldn't make it one mile up the beach without telephoning for assistance. She smiled, and almost laughed out loud when she recalled how he had desperately tried to hide his mobile phone which betrayed him before they had even hit the sand with an urgent call from his office.

This time there was no Howard. This time she was alone and facing an uncertain future. But frankly when had she had any other kind? She looked wistfully at the beach. If only things had been different. She saw herself strolling there, the spray from the foaming waves rushing around her feet, arms entwined . . . she stopped and gave herself a mental shake. Remember what he said, all that walk-on-the-beach-stuff was not for him?

And neither, it seemed, was she.

The problem with you, my girl, she told herself sternly, turning her back on the view, is that you think too much. Concentrate on what matters now. Out there at Dune Point, Mrs Jardine is waiting.

Chapter Thirty-One

The early morning sun woke Judith long before she wanted it to. Even the strain of knowing what lay ahead had not prevented her from having an uninterrupted night. Lulled to sleep by the sound of the ocean a few feet from her door, she had found it more therapeutic than disturbing.

It was not yet six thirty. She stirred, stretched and in one movement rolled out of bed and pulled aside the mosquito shield from the door. Blinking in the already strong sunlight, she gazed along the beach to where East Hampton lay securely tucked into the coastline.

Well, maybe in a few hours it'll be over, she muttered, yawning. Turning back into her room, she had a quick shower before pulling on a T-shirt, shorts and white canvas sneakers.

The small breakfast room was empty but for a couple of waitresses stacking cereal packets and bowls of fresh fruit onto snowy white cloths already laden with plates and crockery. It looked good, but the heat and the surroundings and what lay ahead was not conducive to the idea of food. A vending machine in the lobby dispensed cartons of orange and with one of those in hand, Judith asked the receptionist for a local phone book.

She checked for a number but, like Dr Wallace, Mrs Jardine preferred to remain anonymous. Judith didn't even waste time ringing information. It was too early to expect a call from Todd Simmons; last night she'd left a message for him to say she'd switched hotels. Handing the directory back with a smile she wandered out into the sun and, shading her eyes, surveyed the beach.

Maybe she should take a drive out to the house anyway. Just look. But it was too early. A lone car and even more noticeable a lone female viewing the house at such an hour would attract too much attention. Better to wait until the beaches began to fill up, more cars were on the move, so that she could melt quite naturally into the background of the slow-moving but captivating life of the Hamptons.

Anyway, by then she might have a proper appointment to see Seth Jardine's elderly mother. She could not admit that, having come so far, her nerves were now arguing her into delaying the interview; delaying the moment when the trail might go completely cold.

Judith slipped down the rough wooden steps to the private beach that fronted the small hotel. This time there was no Howard, no anyone. Reaching down, she slipped off her shoes and stacked them at the foot of the steps. The carton of juice she pushed into her waistband under her T-shirt.

The long uninterrupted stretch of beach, the white foam bouncing off the waves, was too inviting to be ignored. Slowly she began to run, the wind whipping in off the sea pushing pleasantly against her body, the rushing and plunging swell of the tide smashing against her legs, spraying foam, drenching her shirt until, panting and perspiring, she turned away from the shoreline, flung herself down into one of the sandy dunes well back from the tide and sipped her orange juice.

It was the first taste of freedom she had had in well over a year. Seductive, beguiling, the headiness of it filled her brain with escape. Out here she was safe. Alone, uncomplicated.

Somewhere thousands of miles away Spencer and Rik and Annie and the dreadful Stella Frankenheim were struggling to work, arguing, stressed. Van Kingsley was leading his corrupt existence and Rosie was in all probability fretting about the next weekend and staving off the conflicting demands of her son and Piers.

It all seemed so ridiculous. Her thoughts strayed to Gray – when did they not? – also somewhere in London, and doing what? She thought of him in his office, tie loosened, phone tucked under his chin, the sun from the leafy square outside sending a shaft of light across his desk.

Who would really care if she just stayed? Never went back? Free. Lost. Safe. She remained like that, her eyes on the distant horizon, not wanting to move, knowing she must.

It was in the end the image of Alice laughing, Laura holding out her arms to welcome her home, her father smiling with pleasure as they met for lunch, that got her reluctantly, guiltily, to her feet and moved her back towards the hotel, towards the questions that still had to be answered. Towards an old lady who never received visitors.

She had reached the lobby when the receptionist called out to her.

'Ms Craven Smith? Oh, there you are. We're trying to put a call through to your room. You can take it in one of the cabins.'

Judith acknowledged her thanks and went into a small booth at the other side of the lobby, now bustling with other early risers making their way into the breakfast room. She pushed her damp hair aside. This was it.

The phone shrilled. 'Hello. This is Judith Craven Smith.'

'Hello yourself,' said the familiar drawl of Howard's voice.

Judith was silent.

She heard him laugh. 'Don't hang up, that's pointless. I can find you. Now, either you tell me what's going on or I get some of my guys up there to find out for me.'

Judith's mind was in overdrive. 'I wasn't going to hang up. How did you know where I was?'

He sighed. 'You should know by now that I have two careers, both of which I excel at. One is running Dorfman Industries and the other is finding you.'

She couldn't help laughing. When she had wistfully told herself that no-one would know or care where she was, she had forgotten Howard. 'Okay, but I know it wasn't Ellie.'

This made him snort in derision. 'Ellie? God. She is a nightmare. What did you pay her? She treats me like I'm your father checking up on you. No, it wasn't Ellie. You goddamn English women. What is it with you?'

Judith ignored him, familiar with the quarrels he regularly got into with her friend.

'Then who?'

'The guy at the car rental,' he admitted sulkily. 'When you gave the car back three days before you needed to, you said you were going to take the bus out to Long Island.'

Judith swore softly down the phone.

'Tsk, tsk,' he mocked. 'All that trouble, too.'

'And the hotel? Don't tell me. You remembered I liked it here?'

She was an amateur at getting lost. Why hadn't she just put neon signs all the way out on the Long Island Expressway?

'No. I just got you checked out by the police department. You have to register at the hotel. It wasn't hard. So what's the problem? What are you doing?'

'Howard, don't ask me, help me.'

'Anything.'

Judith took a deep breath. It was a risk but he might be able to sway Todd Simmons.

'Do you know a woman called Arabella Jardine, lives at East Hampton, Dune Point, mother of Seth Jardine who died a few years ago?'

Howard was puzzled. 'Sure, I knew Seth. Not well, he was a lot older. But I never knew his family. Why?'

'I need to see her, Howard. It's so long and complicated, but she might remember my family when we lived in Connecticut all those years ago. It's really important that I know.'

'My God, you sound desperate. Now I really am coming up there.'

'No, really, there's no need. I can handle it. Only I rang her lawyers to see if she would see me and they said it was unlikely. She never sees anyone.'

'Are you sure you don't want to tell me what all this is about?'

'Sure. Quite sure. I mean I will, but it isn't something that I want to go into now.'

Twenty minutes later she hung up. In return for Howard calling up Todd Simmons and seeing what he could find out, even better get her into Mrs Jardine's, she had promised to stay put for a couple of days and not even attempt to get in touch with the old lady.

She didn't say so, but the relief of having someone on her side was enormous.

All day she stayed close to the hotel. Not so long ago the prospect of nothing more demanding than sitting on a sun-drenched verandah reading magazines would have been her idea of bliss. But by the time dinner came round, she had exhausted every magazine she could find, checked so often with reception for any calls they took to ringing her to save her the trouble, and was now mentally screaming with boredom and frustration.

Finally at ten she rang Howard's apartment only to find he was out for the evening. Out? How could he go without calling her? She just hoped he was taking her request seriously.

The next day, Judith made her escape from the hotel for a couple of hours. Having been accosted at dinner the night before and then at breakfast that morning by a determined tennis coach who had more than improving her service in mind, she disappeared to the beach.

At least it distracted her from listening for the phone she told herself grimly, as she finally gave up hoping to hear from Howard that day and fell into bed.

There had been no messages for her overnight when she emerged next morning from her room, but then only Ellie knew where to find her. No word had come from Howard. That made her uneasy. Common sense told her that it was less than forty-eight hours since he had phoned her, but total silence was unnerving.

I'll give him until ten, she decided, and then I'll ring him. She spent two hours on the beach composing a letter to Gray which she then tore up and chucked away.

Dead on ten she called Howard's office. His secretary Nancy took her call. Howard had gone out of town. No, he hadn't left a message for her. Yes, she was quite sure.

Don't panic. Give him until midday. Howard was selfish but Judith couldn't believe he would just ignore her. By two o'clock she didn't know what to think, except that she would go mad if she just sat around doing nothing.

Fifteen minutes later, showered and with her hair still damp, she paused only long enough to slip into a sleeveless white T-shirt, a fresh pair of shorts and sneakers and scooping up a canvas bag, went on a visit.

The car purred into life as she pulled out, taking the road

that led back onto the main highway for a straight run of about twenty minutes before she reached East Hampton.

Finding Dune Point was harder than she had imagined. The Hamptons might well have been familiar territory to Howard but weekends out here for Judith had been rare. Not until they had embarked on their brief, stormy affair had Long Island been part of her social life. Now, slowly touring the wide avenues looking for the one home that mattered, Judith wished she had paid more attention to where she was on the occasions when she had come with him.

Outside the temperature was creeping up into the eighties once more. The DJ on the local radio station forecast the high eighties before the end of the afternoon.

Judith realized she had come full circle as she saw the main highway once more ahead of her. Cursing, she took a left and to her relief saw Black Hollow Cove ahead of her.

Right at the end was a small grey wood sign with 'Dune Point' picked out roughly. She drove past the entrance and turned into the next road leading up to the car park at the head of the beach.

Sideways on, the house was half hidden by trees and shrubbery, but she could still feel the power of the place. Even on a sweltering day on one of the most beautiful stretches of coastline in America, Dune Point was not a welcoming sight.

The house which stood defiantly alone, facing out to sea on top of a steep cliff path rising out of sand dunes, was like a fortress, seemingly impenetrable. Its nearest neighbour was at least half a mile along the coast and the entrance was accessible only to the most intrepid of unexpected visitors.

Grey stone walls protected the house from winter storms and summer heat. Mullioned windows in groups of twos and threes punctuated the walls, tall chimneys reaching up into a blue sky only added to its austere and forbidding appearance.

Judith was in no mood to go knocking on the door before she had got the measure of the place, or at least tried to. Locking the car, she set off down the rough path that led to the beach. In the distance she could see a woman with two children romping in the surf; a lone jogger ran past. She began to make her way down to where the soft shingle gave way to the firmer sand that the tide had given up and the sun had baked hard, her feet sinking into the surface.

Walking near the tide's edge was a lot easier. She slipped off her sneakers, emptied the sand from them and continued until she was standing right in front of the house. It was still formidable, undeniably stately but seemingly deserted. The question of wealth was not even up for debate. For a long while Judith stared up at it, searching for signs of life. Children's voices floated shrilly up from the beach as they raced each wave to the shore, but from the house there was not a murmur.

Okay, let's take a closer look, she thought, and made her way back up the beach to the car. Turning it round, she drove a few hundred yards to the road and swung the car to a halt just beyond the narrow lane that led up to the house, where her nerve finally failed her. Or perhaps it was common sense prevailing.

Howard would have called her dilemma option paralysis. Judith called it pushing too far. Now what? Suppose Howard had managed to arrange for her to talk to Mrs Jardine's lawyers? Storming the house would fuck up all of that and no mistake. But suppose she had missed him?

Prudence got the better of impatience. One more try to see if there were any messages at the hotel and she would then call Carey for advice.

Judith arrived back at her hotel less than twenty minutes later.

'Any messages for me?' she asked the receptionist.

'No, ma'am. But you do have a visitor. Waiting out on the terrace.'

Howard. Typical, just turning up. Swiftly she walked through the cool, dimly lit bar that led on to the terrace. Through the mesh door she could see the white chairs and blue-striped umbrellas stirring gently in the sea breeze.

Momentarily blinded by the sun as she swung the door outwards, she put up her hand to shield her eyes against the light. The man who had been lounging in a wicker chair, white cotton trousers rolled up to show bare tanned feet, dark glasses pushed up into his hair, face turned up to the sun, the shirt he had been wearing slung across the next chair, swung his legs to the floor and stood up.

'Hi,' he said. 'God, you do find the most awkward places to stay in, don't you?'

Judith stared in disbelief. Not Howard. Gray.

'Didn't you know it's rude to stare?' he went on, sitting easily on the edge of the terrace while Judith stood transfixed in front of him. 'Enlighten me a little here. Were you hiding or running this time? Neither? Okay, how about you've decided you are the only person on the planet capable of solving whatever it is that's going on and you don't mind who you turn over . . .'

'Stop it. That isn't true,' Judith shot at him, finally recovering sufficiently to speak. 'Typical lawyer, aren't you? Doesn't it ever occur to you that it's no-one's business but mine?'

'Or Howard's,' he said curtly.

'No, not Howard's. It's got nothing to do with Howard. I just thought he could help, and he will. That's all.'

'And you don't think I would help you? Can't help you? Not capable of . . .'

'Oh, grow up,' she snapped, slumping into the nearest chair partly because of the heat and mostly because the shock of seeing him had made standing suddenly very difficult. 'What are you *doing* here? I thought you were in London, how did you know . . .'

Gray gazed out to sea and then back at Judith. 'I know because Howard told me.'

'Howard?'

'Yes, Howard. You know my client, your . . . whatever it is he was or is to you.'

'You know perfectly well Howard is nothing more to me than a dear friend – yes, that's right, friend. What he once was has nothing to do with what's happening now. Now he's helping me.

'I needed some information, a bit of influence. In spite of what you believe, I do know when I need help. The difference is I don't ask for it unless I know it's possible. Why waste everyone's time? Howard had the means to help me.

Incidentally, where is he and why hasn't he got in touch? And come to that, why are you here?'

'I've just told you,' Gray said, like one addressing a particularly dim child. 'Howard asked me to help out. I have a few days in between meetings and Howard called me to see if I knew why you had done a bunk to New York.'

For a few ecstatic seconds she had thought he might have come to find her because he wanted to see her. But Howard had sent him. Sick with disappointment, she turned on him.

'*You* to help out? What does that mean?' Judith was incredulous and fearful. What had Howard told him?

Gray sighed and pulled the chair nearest to him round so that he was sitting astride it, facing her. 'Howard is my client. He knew I was coming out here for a few days – even lawyers take time to walk on the beach. See, I even came prepared.'

He lifted one foot and wiggled it at her.

'Don't be sarcastic,' snapped Judith. 'What are you doing here?'

'I've told you,' he repeated. 'Howard has asked me to plead your case with Arabella Jardine's lawyers. It so happens we have a reciprocal arrangement. I act for them in London.'

'You know her?'

'Never met her in my life. I said I work with her lawyers, not her.'

The reason for Howard's silence was now clear. She might have known what she'd told him wouldn't be enough. He had called Gray in London and got him out here because he knew Todd Simmons.

Judith stared back at him.

'My brief is to act as broker in getting you in to see Mrs Jardine.'

'Do you think you can?' she asked cautiously.

'Who knows? I can try. She's got no reason to see you . . . has she?'

The deliberate pause was not lost on Judith.

'Yes, she has,' she said quietly, no longer wanting to lie to him. 'Whether she sees it that way is something else.'

Gray's patience was almost at breaking point as he gazed at Judith. To anyone else his expression would have seemed inscrutable, almost bored. But she knew him well enough to recognize the anger in his eyes. It was almost more than she could bear.

'I hope Howard is paying this bill?' she said lightly, striving for humour. 'Because I can't afford you.'

He pushed his chair aside, grabbed her and hauled her to her feet.

'Stop being so fucking rude, will you?' he fumed, shaking her. 'What is it with you? You regard help, advice, friendship as being conditional the whole time. Don't accept anything in case it costs, is your creed. Haven't you ever heard of people just wanting to help because they l . . . like you?

'I don't know who matters enough to you to make sense of what you do. Howard, Van . . . anyone. When it doesn't suit you, you take off. You ran out on Howard, you ran out on me.'

He stopped, dropped his hands from her shoulders and turned away from her.

If he only knew how she longed to unload all this. Just enough to get Van off her back, enough to give her space to deal with the rest of the problem in her own way, in her own time.

The means to do it was standing with his bare back to her, hands thrust into the pockets of his trousers. Suddenly it was all so easy. Reaching out, she put her hand on his arm.

'Gray . . . I am so fed up. I want to stop all this. I hate the way I live. Will you help me?'

Slowly he turned towards her, searching her face. Finally he balanced on the wooden barrier surrounding the sun deck, hands pressed either side taking his weight.

'Please?' she asked, and waited.

'The truth,' he said bluntly. 'The truth. All of it. Okay?'

Judith hesitated.

'Enough to make sense,' she agreed.

The sun was well down and the first of the guests had started to saunter out onto the sundeck for a pre-dinner drink before she'd finished.

The anger had been replaced by concentration. Her

narrative, punctuated by his precise questions, was coherent. The insanity of isolation was replaced by the strength that came from finally sharing the burden she'd carried alone for so many years.

Judith knew she wanted nothing more than to wrap her arms around Gray and let the world take care of itself while she took care of her own feelings. How good it felt being with him after so many weeks apart, so near she could reach out and stroke his arm as he scribbled notes and frowned down at what he read back. But he hadn't tried to reach out to her. She found it necessary to quickly sit on her hands as he looked up.

'Is that it?'

Judith nodded.

'Okay, check this back with me. Van Kingsley somehow knows that when you were seventeen you were in a car crash that killed Harry Jardine, the drug taking son of a wealthy racketeer, with whom you were experiencing a teenage infatuation. Seth Jardine did not want it to be known that his son was buying drugs although he himself was a dealer, because it would have put him at risk from the drug enforcement agency.

'Seth Jardine's minders, who were first on the scene of the crash, removed all traces of drugs from Harry and by the time the police arrived, you, the only witness, had been spirited away.

'On Seth's orders, you were transferred by Dr Wallace, his Mr Fixit, to Coniston County Hospital and treated under another name. That way you couldn't be questioned by the police and the fact that Seth Jardine was with your mother at the time would not be revealed.

'Your father's position as an army diplomat would have been seriously compromised if it had been known that his daughter and . . . his wife were involved with this family. Your father's reputation is still sensitive. This information, although it is fifteen years old, could raise serious questions about his judgement. And . . .' He paused and looked thoughtfully at her.

Judith held her breath.

'And perhaps a very unwise relationship between your mother and Seth Jardine?'

'Friendship,' she said, too quickly. 'Friendship, not relationship.'

'Of course,' he said. 'That's what I meant.'

'It's not what you said,' she laughed shakily, recalling another occasion when the precise definition of a word had come into question and because she wanted to divert him.

Gray gave her a brief smile and a memory they had both been avoiding was evident in their locked gaze.

But he was not easily diverted. 'I have a couple of questions,' he persisted, tapping the sheaf of papers in front of him. 'I can see your father might not be very happy with any of this coming out, but although it was traumatic for you at the time, no-one would hold it against you now, would they?

'So,' he went on without waiting for a reply. 'We're talking here about protecting your father. Of course his reputation being damaged would not be pleasant for you or . . . Alice?'

Her throat felt dry. This was what it must feel like to be in court. 'Naturally. And the second question?'

'Did your father know about your mother's friendship with Seth Jardine?'

Dear God. 'My mother was on a number of committees – fund-raising, lobbying, that kind of thing. She was introduced to Seth at a fund-raising lunch and yes, he did find her attractive and yes, he did pursue her.

'My father was aware of Seth's presence from the word go. While it remained unpublicized he wasn't worried. Quite a lot of the people who give vast sums of money to charity are total crooks looking for respectability to cover up what they do. Seth was just one more.'

The well-rehearsed speech was spoken with a note of defiance. She expected him to argue, but instead he simply remarked, 'Alice was born some time later. Did your mother know then that she had cancer? Is that when it was detected?'

Judith could feel tears welling up in her eyes. Poor, poor Mum. Struggling not to let her voice go, she gripped the side of her chair, waited a moment.

'Alice was three months old when . . . it was diagnosed,

nine months old when she died. Please,' she whispered, not looking at him. 'Please, it's not something I find . . . easy.'

If she had expected gentle and immediate sympathy she was disappointed. Gray made no comment, merely flashed a look at his watch, reached out for his shirt, and slipped it over his head in one easy movement.

'No,' he agreed. 'None of this is easy for you. But you do make life unnecessarily difficult for yourself. You could have told me all this in England . . . and what have you done to your eye?'

In the mirror that morning it had been barely noticeable.

'Van,' she said briefly. 'I got in the way.'

'And you let him get away with it?'

'I didn't have much choice.'

It was hard to read his expression. But it wasn't sympathetic.

'Don't tell me off,' she whispered. 'Carey suffered, I did too. How could I tell you without implicating you? Van would have had a field day with your reputation. It seemed the best way of dealing with him – find the source and stop it.

'Dr Wallace doesn't want to know. I've only got Harry's grandmother left, don't you see? I started all this, I've got to do something. So what shall I do?' she asked anxiously.

'Stay here until I arrange something. It could take a few days. Or come and stay down at Howard's house in East Hampton. He'll be there soon, as he has friends coming to stay. I'll be there myself. Meanwhile, you could at least ask me if I wanted to stay for dinner.'

'Do I have a choice?' she asked, not looking at him.

'Every time,' he said, indicating the maitre d' who was weaving his way among the tables towards them brandishing huge menus.

No choice at all.

The spirited rendition of the theme from 'Sunset Boulevard' from an energetic trio hired by the hotel to entertain their dinner guests made conversation impossible and drove Gray and Judith to a quieter spot once they had completed their meal. The bar was crowded as Judith followed him through the dimly lit recess and made no protest when he took her hand and led her through the double glass doors onto the wooden-slatted terrace.

Gray was wary, she nervous.

'If you're tired,' he said politely as he guided her to the railing, 'I can easily go back to Howard's house. You've had quite a day.'

'Thank you,' she replied politely. 'I'm fine.'

'I mean it,' he said, studying her profile as she stared fixedly ahead watching the light from the moon rippling across the bay, the warm night air gently gusting stray tendrils of hair around her face.

He turned her round so that she faced him, lightly holding her shoulders so that she couldn't move. Something in his tone stopped the protest she was about to make. Instead she looked up at him silently, and he wasn't smiling, just looking questioningly at her.

There was no mistaking what Gray had in mind. For heaven's sake, she remonstrated inwardly, you can't, you mustn't. No more hurt, no more being let down. Too much was happening in her life.

Where Judith got the steel to refuse she did not know.

She shook her head wordlessly. 'No, please, I'm okay. I've got a lot on my mind, I'm better off with . . . with a crowd, than on my own.'

'You don't have to be on your own.'

It was too much, her resolve was evaporating. She tried one last time. 'But you see,' she said, pleading with her eyes for him to understand. 'I have to be.'

'Why?'

The body language was unnerving. There was an economy of movement about him that betrayed little. His hands were thrust into his trouser pockets, his eyes rarely left her face. To him it was obviously so simple.

But the answer could not be found in sex; it only complicated things, and who knows if in the end he would see it as compromising him? Silence hung between them.

At last he spoke. 'I asked you this afternoon, if that was everything. The whole truth, remember?'

She nodded.

'You're an odd girl. I'd hate to have you on a witness stand.'

Witness stand?

'I don't know what you mean.'

Clouds scudded across the moon, momentarily screening the expression on her face. Otherwise, he would have seen the fear there. Her lips felt dry.

'I think you do.' He studied the ground for a moment and then looked straight at her. 'Why did you lie to me?'

'I didn't,' she protested. 'Nothing I said was a lie. I told you the truth. I wouldn't lie . . . not to you.'

He tucked his hand under her arm and began to lead her back inside. Panic had taken hold of her. She pulled back, stopping him.

'Did you hear what I said?'

His glance flicked over her and then he gave a small resigned smile. 'I heard you. As usual you didn't hear me. I never said what you told me was a lie. It's what you didn't tell me that interests me. Haven't you ever heard of lying by omission?'

He didn't know. He would have said by now. He was guessing. Please let him be guessing.

'It's not what you think . . .'

'No,' he interrupted. 'It never is. Shall we go back?'

Chapter Thirty-Two

East Hampton was nearly deserted. Shoppers and the last of the holiday-makers were down to a trickle. The hurricane warning was being taken seriously. Shops were selling special provisions in case the eye of the storm should hit the Long Island coastline and the residents had to sit it out.

In such circumstances Judith was taking a huge risk trying to get to Mrs Jardine but desperation was urging her on. Van Kingsley mustn't get to her first. Carey had sounded desperate when he'd finally got through to her on the phone the following morning.

'Don't know, Jude. He's disappeared. Josh and I were trying to keep an eye on him, but you've been gone for days so he was bound to be suspicious. He followed the same track as Howard. He phoned Camilla yesterday and then Laura who confirmed you were in New York. But we've only just found out that he left for New York this morning, or at least that's what Shade says. Josh phoned her saying he was someone else of course. What will you do?'

Do?

She slipped out, bundling her bag into the car, got into the driver's seat and started the engine. Appointment or not, there was no longer any time to wait to see if Todd Simmons could do anything for her.

The day had started with a thick sea mist but while that had mostly evaporated, the sky had been getting steadily greyer, the wind was beginning to whip up and the rain was not far off.

Warnings had been broadcast on radio stations every few minutes since dawn and TV stations were obsessed with tracking the hurricane, which was currently hammering the North Carolina coast.

Fire Island, the thin strip of land at the tip of Long Island packed with holiday-makers at this time of year, had already been evacuated. A siege mentality had gripped the town. Boats had been pulled inland, the docks were strangely empty and the main highway holding the sudden exodus of tourists cutting short their stay to return to New York was jammed. Heading towards the coastline, Judith was through East Hampton in a few minutes.

Gray didn't deserve this. He would guess where she had gone, and would be hurt and furious that she hadn't confided in him. *Run out on him, that's what you've done, what you always do. Dear God, when will it ever be all right?*

Howard had arrived at his East Hampton home the morning after Gray's evening at the Montauk hotel. The latest news was that Todd Simmons was going to phone Gray later that day. Nothing concrete, but Mrs Jardine only ever saw her lawyers by appointment and they too had to line up for her attention. But at least she hadn't said no.

'So what do you make of Jude's story?' Howard asked, settling himself back into his hammock, rubbing his damp hair with a towel and squinting over to where Gray was reading a copy of the Wall Street Journal.

'Unfinished,' he replied.

Howard propped himself up. 'How so?'

Gray lowered the paper and pushed his sunglasses up into his hair. 'There's something about her that I don't get . . .'

Howard roared with laughter. '*One* thing? With Jude? Hell, man, I've never understood anything about her. What do you mean?'

'It's not making any sense the way she tells it,' Gray said, ignoring Howard's mirth. 'All the principal people are now dead. So my advice would be that she simply denies any of it happened. Her father denies it and Wallace is not going to say anything, is he? So Van Kingsley's story is stone dead. A few photographs showing what? As far as I can make out, a group at a party. Could be any fund-raising event.

'But she still comes all this way to visit Arabella Jardine, who doesn't want to see her, to find out who told the little schmuck something she did when she was just a kid. There has to be more to all this than she's admitting. But every time I get close to it, she clams up.'

Howard was watching him with interest. 'Is this why the big chill comes down when she's around?'

'You mean she avoids talking to me? No, that's something else. She's protecting someone. Her father, Alice, her mother, I don't know which. Maybe all three.'

He stood up and leaned against one of the columns supporting the ornate trellis-work around the terrace. 'I've asked Todd Simmons to dig out some papers around the time when Harry Jardine died. Maybe I'll find what I'm looking for there. Sure as hell I'm getting nowhere with her.'

Howard's eyes narrowed. A thought so blindingly obvious occurred to him. He laughed softly to himself.

'Poor bastard,' he said. Gray just looked back at him with a resigned shrug.

'You should talk,' was all he said.

Don't think, just drive. Dune Point was at the far end of a small narrow track off Feather Lane. The maze of long, straight blocks of lawn-edged, tree-lined avenues bordered on either side by the extravagant, covetable houses that were home to Wall Street bankers, socialites and the finest names on the New York social register, left Judith unmoved.

Dune Point and Mrs Jardine was all she cared about. She rehearsed for the hundredth time what she would say. Each time it sounded less convincing than the last. She hit the steering wheel with a clenched fist and tried again.

'I would like to see Mrs Jardine for just a few moments . . .'

Oh purleese.

'I wonder if it would be possible . . .'

Forget it. How about:

'Mrs Jardine isn't expecting me but I know once she knows why I'm here, she will see me . . .' In this way she arrived as dusk and a high wind met head on at the bottom of the long drive up to Dune Point.

Judith stopped and turned the engine off. She could hear the Atlantic breakers already slamming the beach with unnatural force. The roar as each successive wave gathered strength to

332

pound even further towards the dunes seemed to sap her own.

This is your only hope. It is only a storm. Okay, a hurricane. But this woman cannot harm you, whereas Van Kingsley has, and will continue to do so. Just get on with it.

Slipping the car into gear, she eased her way in the gathering gloom to the front of the house. The crunch of wheels on the gravel drive was drowned out by the noise of the wind and the waves. The house loomed up, grey, imposing, awesome. Any minute Norman Bates will appear and say his mother's in the attic, she muttered, turning off the engine and opening the car door as her progress was halted by a pair of black iron gates. The rush of wind caught her off guard and for a second she staggered against the door. Head down, she half ran to the entry phone and pressed the buzzer. Through the gates she could see just one half of the house. Close to, it looked no friendlier than it had from the safety of the East Hampton Beach.

There were lights on already in some of the upper windows, which was a small comfort as she waited for a response from the house. No matter, she told herself sternly, no matter how terrifying these people are, you are not to run away. It's all you have left.

Within seconds a voice on the outer intercom asked what she wanted.

'I want to see Mrs Jardine,' she blurted and fleetingly wondered why she had bothered rehearsing anything. As openings went it was not award-winning.

'Do you have an appointment? I don't believe Mrs Jardine is aware of one,' came the woman's voice, distorted and crackling competing against the increasingly high wind.

'No she isn't, I mean she doesn't know,' Judith shouted back through the speaker. 'Look, I know this sounds mad and I wouldn't blame you for not letting me in, it *is* odd, but I've come all the way from London and . . .' The sentence was finished with a scream as a rogue squall flattened her against the railings.

Gasping for breath she pulled herself back to hear an anxious voice repeating, 'Hello, are you there, are you all right?'

'It's the wind,' shouted Judith. 'I can hardly hear you. *Please* let me come in and speak to you.'

There was a second's pause and the voice ordered her to stay where she was. Judith dived for her car. A set of wavering headlights suddenly pierced the gloom. She screwed up her eyes against the glare. At least someone was coming to see her.

The lights stopped. The vehicle they were attached to didn't seem to be that big. Judith saw that it was little more than a small motorized buggy.

A masculine shape heaved itself out and came as far as the gates.

'For a start you have to be crazy,' came an exasperated voice. 'And for seconds, who are you?'

Judith walked as steadily as she could to the gates and saw a middle-aged man with grey hair and a round pleasant face staring not unkindly but very cautiously back at her.

'My name is Judith Craven Smith,' she said. 'I don't know whether Mrs Jardine will have heard of me or not. But if she has I know she will see me, and if she hasn't she must realize that I wouldn't have come this far or even come out on a night like this unless it was important. Couldn't you just ask?'

The man looked past her to her car which was taking a severe battering from the storm as the first lash of what promised to be torrential rain started to fall on them both.

'Please,' Judith pleaded. 'I am so scared you'll all say no. I'm not a crank either,' she added with a small trace of indignation as the man's face clearly showed his thoughts.

He surveyed her for a brief moment. Shrugged to himself.

'Young lady, I should send you straight back to where you've come from, but I'm not sure you'll make it in all of this. But I also think the chances of this storm being a figment of our imagination is greater than Mrs Jardine agreeing to see you. Okay, come up to the house. You can't stay out here, that's for sure. Just follow me and let's get that car out of the way.'

'Oh, thank you so much,' Judith yelled and raced back to her car before he could change his mind.

The black iron gates opened and Judith drove through,

noticing in her rear view mirror that the gates had automatically closed after her. Following closely, she inched the car towards the far end of the house, through a wide stone archway where ahead of her she could make out the outline of what appeared to be a set of garages. Her escort signalled her to drive her car into the nearest one, so she edged it up alongside a limousine with blacked out windows and just behind a white Astra Coupe.

Switching off the engine, she grabbed her bag, locked the door and turned to find her escort standing in the doorway waiting for her, with the motorized buggy parked behind her.

'Buck up, I want to batten this down,' he said as Judith ducked under the already descending door. 'Through here.' He indicated a side door which evidently bypassed the main entrance.

Judith found herself in a small lobby. Parquet flooring and dark oak-panelled walls housed a collection of walking sticks. On the wall was fixed a wooden board hung with bunches of keys. She turned as her companion closed the door after both of them and indicated the one ahead for Judith to go first.

'I'm Jackson Searway, Mrs Jardine's butler. My wife Melly is housekeeper – she answered the buzzer. Through here.'

Judith looked around as she followed him across a well-polished floor through a pleasant morning room, richly furnished and clearly little used, where a small grey-haired woman somewhere in her early sixties, she guessed, was standing waiting to meet them.

'My dear girl,' she said, coming forward. 'This really isn't very sensible of you.'

Judith almost laughed with relief. Far from being terrifying, they were concerned and charming. Maybe Mrs Jardine might be less forbidding than everyone claimed.

Her hope was short-lived. 'Mrs Jardine won't see you, my dear,' said the woman who was evidently Melly as she ushered Judith into a smaller drawing room, cosier and obviously designated for the Searways' own. 'This is a pointless journey. She hasn't received any visitors other than half a dozen old friends, her attorney and her accountants for the last ten years, not counting her doctor of course and me and Jackson.'

'But why?' asked Judith. 'Why won't she see anyone? I'm not going to harm her. I just want to ask her a couple of questions that are terribly important to me and she's the last person I can try. She's not ill, is she?'

The Searways looked at each other.

Jackson spoke first, sending a fleeting frown at his wife, who went off to make some coffee.

'Why should she see you? As far as I know you're a complete stranger to her, aren't you?'

He let the words trail off. Tricky.

'I am, sort of. I've never met her. I knew her grandson, Harry, years ago, and I knew his father, her son, Seth. My mother . . . my mother knew him better than I did. They were on committees together. We lived in Ridge Harbour for a while.'

Jackson eyed her uncertainly. 'So how do I know you aren't going to upset Mrs Jardine? Why do you want to see her? You could have written, telephoned.'

Put like that, it seemed like madness to have travelled three thousand miles at enormous cost when a telephone call would have solved the issue. But then, when Judith had left London she hadn't known Mrs Jardine existed. She hadn't known what it was she was looking for; she still didn't. Mrs Jardine might not know anything at all. The ramblings of someone who had slept too many nights on a park bench might have made more sense. It wouldn't be too smart to tell all this to Jackson, who would have had justice on his side if he locked her in the garage with her car until the storm abated.

Instead she just said lamely, 'I thought if I phoned she wouldn't see me, or even get the message. In person I had more chance. You see, she might be able to resolve a problem that's come into my life in London. Look, frankly, I don't know that she can help, it's just that I have nothing else left to try.'

'My dear,' he said, indicating a blue-flowered easy chair for Judith to sit in as Melly returned with a tray of coffee. 'She has no family to speak of. Her son and grandson died a long time ago in tragic circumstances. Did you know that?'

Judith felt her stomach lurch. This couple clearly had nothing to hide. She did.

'Most of her friends, as you would expect, are no longer around. Some have died, others moved out to Florida. Maybe once a year, she might go up to Connecticut for a few days to see one friend, but she's old too.'

'Doesn't she ever go out, go away, do anything?' asked Judith, accepting the coffee Melly handed to her.

'Very occasionally she has a dinner party and sometimes she goes to dinner here or over at Bridgehampton. But that's all. A couple of times a year I drive her to New York to see her lawyers but she says it's a heathen city and there's nothing there now but arrivistes. Mind you,' he added with a chuckle, 'she thinks the same about everyone on Long Island.

'The world hasn't been kind to her, now has it? So you see, she doesn't need to give anyone an explanation, does she? She's rich and old. She's paid her dues and owes nothing to anyone. Melly and I look after her and she's content with that. We've been with her for nearly fifteen years. Now we will just stay with her until she doesn't need us any more. But that doesn't help you, does it?'

Judith couldn't have agreed more.

All this way. For what? She *had* to see her. The storm was now raging around the house and the wind was pounding remorselessly against the old granite building. Getting home was out of the question. She tried once more and finally, after much exchanging of worried looks, Jackson agreed to let Mrs Jardine know that she was in the house but he urged her to think only of the house as a port literally in a storm and nothing else.

After he'd disappeared Melly collected up the coffee cups and led Judith to a drawing room at the back of the house. The windows were taped and some had been boarded up to withstand the force of the hurricane that was whirling its way along the coastline.

'Let's pray it pushes out to sea before it gets here,' said Melly as she excused herself to return the tray to the kitchen.

Judith glanced around the room, rather wishing that she hadn't been left alone. The noise of the wind was unsettling. The furniture was comfortable and elegant. Chintz and stripes

337

with needlepoint cushions, bowls of gardenias and roses filled the room. The style reflected a period when the owner must have been the belle of East Hampton and possibly even the toast of New York.

Scattered around the room were black-and-white photographs in silver frames, of family groups and of scenes that recorded the social life of a bygone time.

A group of young people in tennis whites, inscribed underneath with the year 1934; a laughing group on the beach in front of this very house, taken about the same time, girls in front, the young men with arms slung casually across each other's shoulders, standing behind.

Another group showed a couple now considerably older, middle-aged, one with a young boy sitting on the terrace outside this house, another a group of Ivy League young bucks horsing around in a swimming pool.

And there was a young man Judith recognized. Harry. So long ago, she could hardly remember his face. There was Seth Jardine with his arm around Harry's mother, so secure and confident and without a clue about what lay ahead for all of them.

Judith wondered why she didn't react more strongly when she saw Harry. The wild passion she had felt for him was difficult to recall. She could not even understand it, looking at him now; she saw him for what he had always been, charming, feckless and spoilt. She never noticed any of those things at the time. But at seventeen, someone paying her attention was heady stuff. Irresistible to a young girl caught up in her first love.

Above the open fireplace there was a portrait of a young woman, not exactly beautiful but with a bone structure that meant her looks were assured for life. The eyes were warm, but the smile slight, perfectly in keeping with the owner of this house. Judith recognized with a jolt to her heart the expression on her face. A strong family likeness.

A movement as the door behind her opened made Judith glance round. Standing in the doorway, small, thin, perfectly groomed but white-haired and leaning on a stick was the portrait on the wall.

Judith held her breath. Shock kept her rigid. Her eyes were riveted on the elderly woman in the doorway.

'Good evening,' the woman said coldly, making no attempt to come any further into the room. 'I am Arabella Jardine. I've been expecting you.'

Chapter Thirty-Three

'I hope you're not always this neurotic,' said Arabella Jardine, walking stiffly to the fireplace where she turned and faced Judith, who was still transfixed by the portrait on the wall.

'Neurotic? Why is coming to see you neurotic?'

Arabella Jardine looked her up and down. Arrogance and disdain were mixed and it was hard to say which triumphed. 'All this drama, pressurizing my staff. Couldn't you have waited until the morning? Why arrive in a storm? Or did you think that way you couldn't be turned away?'

The scorn in her voice lashed Judith. It was some time before she could speak. Jackson knocked on the door and brought in a tumbler of whisky on a tray, and placed it on a small table near Mrs Jardine.

Slowly the old lady lowered herself into a high-backed armchair, placed her stick by her side and reached for the glass. 'Don't just stand there,' she snapped. 'I have ten minutes before I plan to retire for the evening. This storm is going nowhere, just a lot of noise and fuss and bother for something that won't last.'

'How do you know?' Judith asked. 'It sounds quite serious. The weather reports . . .'

'Hogwash.' Mrs Jardine dismissed the idea with a wave of her free hand. 'I've lived here for forty years. I know when to expect trouble.'

The significance of the remark was not lost on Judith, who was still gripping the chair in front of her. Sit, stand, run. Someone tell her what to do? Jackson came to her rescue by gesturing to Judith to sit down. She shook her head at his offer of a drink. Mrs Jardine just shrugged.

'Well, get on with it,' she urged Judith impatiently. 'What is it that you want that's so urgent?'

'You said you were expecting me,' Judith reminded her. 'Did Mr Simmons . . .'

'Simmons? Todd Simmons? What's he to say to anything? Did he send you?'

Bewilderment swept over her. If not Todd Simmons, then who? Howard, Gray?

'I know the names. Don't wish to know the faces. Dorfman's a disgrace to the family name. Charles was a good man.'

If she hadn't been so shocked by the swiftness of events, Judith would have smiled at this assessment of the head of Dorfman Industries.

'As for Hamilton! The arrogance of you English. Thinks he knows best all the time. Whippersnapper.'

Judith gaped at her. 'What did he do?' she asked.

'Do? Nothing. It's what he didn't do. No concern of yours, but I don't like having my instructions overturned.'

The question raised by that remark would have to wait. Mrs Jardine had already glanced twice at the clock. The roar of the wind had not abated, but now she was here, Judith was not going to waste time.

'Then what do you mean, you've been expecting me?'

Mrs Jardine shot her a shrewd, sharp look.

'I knew one day you'd turn up. Money brings everyone out of the woodwork. How much are you looking for? Because you won't get it.'

'Money?' Judith repeated incredulously. 'You think I want money from you? I don't want your bloody money. How dare you!' Her eyes narrowed in fury. 'You know exactly who I am, don't you? But you don't really know me at all. Money? My God.'

She was on her feet, gripping the ledge that ran the length of the open fireplace, gasping out the words in her rage. 'Do you think I would take a penny from anyone with the name of Jardine? Do you? After all I went through? I never wanted to hear or see the name or have anything to do with it ever again. What did any of you ever do for me that didn't cause me grief? Harry, Seth . . . I didn't know you existed until a few days ago. They never mentioned you and I'm not

341

surprised. You talk about other people's arrogance but in just a few minutes you have presumed on no evidence at all that I am here for money, that for years I have been planning this moment.

'Believe me, Mrs Jardine, I am here only *because* the very idea of being linked with the Jardine name sickens me and the last, very last place I want to be is here with you.'

Mrs Jardine took a sip of the whisky. Judith stopped, trying to get her breath. After she'd come all this way, she had no option now but to leave.

'I make allowances for the fact that you are neurotic . . .'

'I am not,' exploded Judith. 'I am at the end of my tether with just trying to get someone in this godforsaken country to answer some questions, that's all. You'd be at screaming pitch too if the boot were on the other foot.'

Mrs Jardine gazed impassively back. Fifty years of weathering the storms of marriage to a man incapable of being faithful to her yet who'd left her a widow too soon had inured her to anyone else's grief. But the greater agony of being forced to take her only son to court to stop him recklessly squandering the Jardine fortune, and a year later to hear her only grandson had been killed, had made her what she was.

Resolute, unmoved, untouched by the outside world. A grasping set of ex-daughters-in-law who each wrote separately but regularly for money had become her yardstick by which to judge women.

'What do you want then?' she asked suspiciously. 'What can I possibly have to interest you unless it's money? And much as I hate to disappoint you, I don't have that much. Enough to pay Jackson and to keep that pack of lawyers happy, but Seth ruined the company. In the end his only real asset is that house at Ridge Harbour, and most of that will go in death duties. Like you, my dear, the Jardine name has brought me only grief. So if it's not money you want, what is it?'

'Information.'

They stared at each other, neither much liking what she saw. But one was desperate and the other curious. It was a combination that Judith could see was chipping away at the old lady's abrupt manners. Not sympathy, shock or sentiment; just curiosity. It was better than nothing.

'You'd better tell me. But first ring that bell next to you for Jackson.'

There was silence until the butler appeared. He raised his eyebrows enquiringly at Judith but his expression did not alter, accepting Mrs Jardine's instructions without question. He would bring her another whisky and her guest – at least she was now acknowledged as a guest – whatever she wanted.

'Why were you expecting me?' Judith asked when he had gone.

Mrs Jardine waved a hand vaguely. 'Oh, everyone else Seth was involved with has turned up. You perhaps had more reason than most. It was a shocking business about Harry. Shocking.' The old lady briefly closed her eyes and put her fingers against her mouth as though to steady her voice as much as to subdue the memory that fleetingly gripped her.

It was over in seconds. She cleared her throat, and with a sip of whisky, she recovered.

'I assumed you had come to extract money. More Jardine skeletons to rattle.'

Judith almost laughed. She was here because she was being blackmailed, and now she was suspected of the same thing. 'What reason could I have to do that?' she asked. 'I'm being blackmailed myself.'

The button-bright eyes in the worn face looked startled. 'Blackmailed? How?'

'I'll start from the beginning,' said Judith. 'I don't want to upset you but I think you need to know the whole truth.' She hesitated. This was going to be hard, not only for her but for this elderly woman. Did she have a right to ask her to confront the painful facts of a relationship that she had never been party to, had not encouraged and did not even know had existed until it was all over?

Mrs Jardine interrupted the silence. 'You'd better tell me everything. There isn't much I can't cope with. I might look frail but life has given me strength in return for taking my peace of mind.'

Judith was certain she and this old lady would have little

343

in common but a shared belief that truth was the only salvation for them all in the end.

'Okay. First, do you know someone called Van Kingsley?'

The old lady shook her head. 'Should I?'

'No. But he's the person blackmailing me and, apart from you, I can't think who could know about me and your family. Except Bradley Wallace.'

'Well, he would,' remarked Mrs Jardine. 'He arranged everything, didn't he?'

Judith nodded. 'I've been to see him. He says he doesn't even remember me, let alone know Van Kingsley. I found out about you by chance when I went back to the house. I don't know why I went, but there was nothing else to do. You were my last hope.'

Mrs Jardine's voice was less gruff.

'You said you would start from the beginning. Why don't you?'

So she did.

It was only when she got to the part about Alice that Mrs Jardine looked genuinely shocked. Judith could have cursed herself. This woman was elderly; it was too much to ask of her.

'Shall I call Jackson?' she asked anxiously. 'Let me get you something.'

A frail hand waved her back to her seat. 'Nonsense, nonsense, I'm fine, just trying to get used to the idea. But you never got in touch with me or Seth and I never knew Lizzie had died. I thought Seth had arranged an abortion?'

Judith shook her head. 'He did, but Mum wouldn't hear of it. What Seth never knew was that Mum asked Bradley Wallace to arrange for Alice to be born well away from Coniston or Ridge Harbour. Bradley Wallace was so terrified of Seth that he told him that he had carried out the abortion.

'But in fact Alice was born very healthily a few months later. You see, Mrs Jardine, neither Mum or I wanted anything to do with Seth. I'm sorry if it hurts you to hear that about your son, but he ordered people's lives to suit him.

'He cared more for Harry after Harry had died than all the

time he was alive and that isn't saying much. I was dragged from a scene of absolute carnage, shaken, terrified and distraught about Harry, and all he cared about was that drugs shouldn't be found on either of us. And he was . . . well, he could have ruined my father if it had got around that Mum was a friend of his.'

Mrs Jardine sat staring at Judith. 'I don't defend my son. But your mother was not an innocent, she must have known what he was like. She was, after all, already married and aware of the effect her association with Seth would have on your father.'

It was true. But it wasn't like that, never like that. Her father had been totally immersed in his career, so blindly confident that her mother could not possibly be attracted to anyone else. He simply didn't know her. It would not be untrue to say that even now, lost in his fading world of gallant generals and pointless battles, he was still no further forward in understanding a modern world.

Her mother had said at the time: 'It doesn't matter what decision is made, everyone will believe the worst anyway. So cheer up, the baby is wanted and welcome and will be loved.'

And indeed Alice was. It was that which sustained her in the face of the inescapable truth of what Mrs Jardine was saying.

'After Mum died, Dad sent Alice and me back to England to live with my grandmother and somehow over the years, between her and Dad and me, Alice has grown up quite normally and all that stuff in Ridge Harbour has been left behind. At least I thought it was until six months ago.'

'But you must have known that at some point you would have to tell Alice who her father was. You had no right to keep it secret from her . . . or me.'

'I've told you, I didn't know of your existence. You said yourself you and Seth had not spoken for years. And Alice is going to be told. Yes,' she said, seeing Mrs Jardine's face full of disbelief. 'I just wanted to find the right moment, but it never seemed to happen. She loves Dad so much. And I didn't want his name dragged through the mud when none of it was his fault.

'But don't worry, Alice won't be after your money either. I'll only tell her about you, if you want me to.'

'Don't be ridiculous.' Mrs Jardine was becoming angry. Bright spots of red had appeared in her powdered white cheeks. 'My son might have wanted to disown her. But I don't. Or you. Now,' she said briskly. 'How can I help with this blackmailer?'

'I'm not sure you can,' Judith said glumly. 'You've never heard of him. I just thought there might be some mention of him or a name . . . something that would jog my memory that only you would know.'

'My dear.' Mrs Jardine spread her hands helplessly. 'I never saw or heard from Seth, Harry or Harry's mother, or even that last one he married – what was she called, oh, it doesn't matter – while Seth was alive. When he died, the lawyers went in and took out business papers and family letters and we went through everything. Believe me, there was no reference at all to Alice. Don't you think I would have got in touch, if I had heard about her?'

The thought had not even occurred to Judith. So used was she to the indifference shown her by the only two Jardines she'd ever known, the notion that one of their family might actually care enough to be interested in her wellbeing, in Alice's, was a novelty. Her surprise was written on her face.

Mrs Jardine smiled, a thin smile but not without warmth. It would be too much to say the news of Alice's birth had changed her from flint to velvet, but without a doubt she was affected.

'Yes, I'm sure you would have got in touch,' said Judith gently. 'But once we have talked, I promise you won't be disturbed again, truly.'

There was a hesitancy in Mrs Jardine's expression. Part of her didn't believe that anyone could not want something from her, the other part was struggling to summon affection for a child she didn't even know existed until today. Her most immediate desire was simply for the moment to be back in control. Later, when this strange girl had gone, she would examine her feelings.

'Well, let's see,' she said, not wanting to be too precise or

346

to make a promise she could not keep. But then, Judith did not seem to be asking for any to be made.

Mrs Jardine was not a stupid woman. She knew her irritation was irrational, but she had grown to like the feeling of power that she had learned to exercise over Seth's dependants in the years following his death.

It didn't make up for the years of estrangement; nothing could do that. But it was good to be able to refuse access ever again to any part of his life to those dreadful people who had influenced him, encouraged him, all coming to her, all loaded with reasons why they should benefit from his largesse. Judith wouldn't understand that. But this girl stealing out of the past had upset that control. The English girl had slipped through the carefully constructed barrier the old woman had erected around the last of the Jardines.

'There was nothing among Seth's papers?' Judith was asking.

Mrs Jardine shook her head. 'There was only one box full of personal mementoes. I kept it, God knows why, but there's nothing in it. You can look if you like.'

She reached over and tugged the bell. Jackson appeared and was despatched to bring it.

Jackson placed a rather elegant case on a low table within reach of the old lady. It was rather like a travelling desk, in black leather with a gold trim. And locked. Mrs Jardine opened it and Judith could see from where she was sitting that the inside in pale fawn suede was divided neatly into compartments. Within those compartments were carefully stacked letters, documents, photographs.

'Come over here. Jackson, move Judith's seat. You can't see from there.'

Jackson shot Judith a look that was clearly meant to convey 'well done'. Briefly she smiled and took her place at Arabella Jardine's knee.

Letters were shared between them to sift through. Old friends thanking Seth for weekend visits, acrimonious ones from his previous wives that were meant to bypass lawyers and speed up the process for getting their share of his wealth. Letters to Seth from Harry at school, which were heartbreaking in their formality, and confined totally to events and not feelings. It was odd seeing his handwriting. Judith wasn't sure that she had ever come across it before, so briefly had she known him, and these were written when he was fourteen and fifteen years old.

There were photographs of Harry as a child with his mother, Seth entertaining friends on the terrace, all facing the camera, glasses raised.

Mrs Jardine leaned back in her chair. 'My dear, I don't think there is anything here.'

Judith sighed with disappointment and slumped visibly. She looked up at Mrs. Jardine. 'What next?' she asked forlornly.

The old lady began to replace the documents in their compartments, ready to be locked away. Financially they were worthless, but she saw no reason to tell Judith that they were the most valuable possessions she had.

She reached out to take the photographs from Judith, who was still idly flicking through them. 'If only I knew what I was looking for. Who I was looking for,' she said. And stopped. On the top of the pile there was a snap of Seth and his last wife, Harry, and a group of their friends by the pool.

Sitting two away from Harry was the girl she had seen in the photograph in Dr Wallace's house.

'Bradley's daughter,' confirmed Mrs Jardine, peering over the top of her glasses at the photograph. 'Everyone wanted her to marry Harry, but she ended up marrying someone else on the rebound after he died and it didn't work out. Candida Wallace was not rich in the way the Jardines were, but wealthy all right. It was a match everyone wanted – although I gather Seth was going off the idea because she had a drug problem. Tragic, really.'

Judith was staring intently at the girl's face. She knew her. But from where? 'What happened to her?'

Mrs Jardine was packing up the boxes and losing interest in the subject. 'Oh, I don't remember too much about it. It took her a long time to get over Harry's death. After all, she was the first on the scene when the crash happened . . .'

Judith froze. The security men were first on the scene, surely? She tried to sound calm. 'Mrs Jardine, Candida was not at the accident. No-one came except Seth's men . . .'

'Oh but she was,' Mrs Jardine interrupted firmly. 'I know it was worse for you, but Candida was already on her way to meet Harry – he was late or something and so she had set off to meet him – and came around the bend to find the car in flames, Harry lying in the road and you unconscious.'

The room wasn't quite steady. Judith shut her eyes, summoning up that sickening scene. A girl screaming. They'd said it was her, but she'd always been puzzled by that. But it wasn't her, it was Candida. Hysterical screaming. She looked closely at the girl and felt as though a ghost had passed through the room.

Harry had said he was going to meet someone who gave him his stuff. Who else would find it that easy to get prescriptions but a doctor's daughter? A doctor's daughter who was crazy about him.

In a bizarre twist of thinking, Seth would have sent Harry away if he had tried to score from the dealers he himself used. And Harry knew that, Harry who would solemnly declare quite truthfully that he wouldn't go near his father's dealers. She could hear Harry's voice, laughing derisively, boasting about conning his old man.

That's where Judith had seen her. Not at Seth's house, but much more recently than that. In New York, working for Howard. Candida. *Connie. Connie Mayerson.* Connie, who so disapproved of her, who must have known her the minute they shook hands. Connie, who had access to her father's notes, would have known about Judith and Harry and Lizzie and Seth. And about Alice. Everything.

Judith could hardly speak. Shock and relief were all mixed up. 'Mrs Jardine,' she said, trying not to sound breathless. 'Candida Wallace is someone I know, only she's called Connie Mayerson.'

'Of course she is. Mayerson is her married name. She married a young man called Carl Mayerson, but it didn't last. Someone she met a few years after Harry died. I gather they were all pleased because she was a very highly strung young woman. Don't ask me about her husband because I don't know anything about him.

'You have to remember I was not invited to these things. And I don't know where the "Connie" came from. But if you know Candida, why didn't you ask her all of this?'

'You don't understand. I know who she is now. She's mixed up in this . . . she knew everything. I met her in New York when I was working for Howard and she never let on. But she must have known me.'

Mrs Jardine looked doubtful. 'I never knew her, my dear. I just heard about her when Harry died. But I do have some family albums that she's in. That might help. Let me see.'

She pointed to the far side of the room to a shelf of books and picture albums.

'The blue one, I think. Can you get it for me?'

Judith was almost screaming with frustration. She had to be right. She handed the blue album to Mrs Jardine, who leafed through it.

'Here we are, Candida on her wedding day. See, there's Seth and his last wife. There's Bradley Wallace and his wife – only she left him the same year, probably because Candida no longer needed her at home.'

But Judith wasn't listening. There he was, laughing into young Mrs Jardine's face, slightly turned away from his bride, self-assured, handsome, so at ease with all that wealth.

Not Carl Mayerson, but Van Kingsley.

Chapter Thirty-Four

The Queens midtown tunnel was solid. All the way back from Long Island Judith had gone from sheer rage to fright to bewilderment. Connie. Connie bloody Mayerson.

Why? Why? And Van, not Van at all, but Carl. The traffic eased forward and for once Judith remained unmoved by the sight of the Manhattan skyline as she headed for the toll. No wonder Van knew all about her. Connie must have alerted him that she was in New York. Where the hell was he? She had to get to Connie now before he did.

Nine in the morning was not the best time to be hitting midtown Manhattan. It was not the best time to have run out on Gray. But common sense told her it was over. The kind of history she had was not what futures were about. Reputations had to be considered, and trust established. She had given him no reason to trust her. But then he had made no effort to find room for her in his life as it was, let alone with all the emotional debris that she was now dealing with.

If he'd stayed that night, he might have talked her into confiding in him. Might? No doubt about it. So it was better to just go. Anyway, he had made no attempt to call her at Mrs Jardine's. And he was no longer at Howard's house in East Hampton.

The instincts of a woman who had lived for over forty summers in a house staring out over the Atlantic had triumphed over all the predictions of the weather men and the noisy threats of the hurricane that had kept them all guessing had finally veered out to sea. A phone call to Howard's house assuaged Judith's conscience; that Gray must have been concerned for her safety was something she would deal with another time.

It was just after midnight when she'd called. The maid said Mr Dorfman and the other guests were still at dinner, but Mr

Hamilton had left to go back to New York. Judith refused to allow her to call Howard to the phone, simply asked her to tell him she was safe.

Arabella Jardine insisted she spent the night with them. The old lady in the end had succumbed to age and bewilderment and allowed Judith to gently bully her into going to bed.

But not before she had extracted a promise from her to stay in touch. 'If you want Todd Simmons to help, tell him I sent you. No, better still, I'll tell him myself,' she decided.

'Thank you,' Judith said, pressing her hand. 'But I've had quite enough of lawyers one way or another. And I've imposed on you enough. I'll leave as soon as it gets light. I have a lot to do.'

Mrs Jardine moved slowly to the doorway, stopped and turned. Her voice was gruff, abrupt. It took an effort to say what she had to say.

'I should like to see Alice. I should like to . . .' She paused and glanced uncertainly at Judith, who had made no attempt to move their relationship onto different ground. She was talking with great difficulty. 'I should like,' she repeated, 'to help.'

For the first time since Judith had arrived out of the storm, Mrs Jardine really looked at her, standing in her crumpled cotton dress, barelegged and her hair pulled untidily back where she had hastily tied it that morning. There was a calmness about her now that touched the old woman, a dignity that came from the kind of pride Arabella Jardine recognized so well. She had a strong suspicion that Judith was going to be very hard to help.

Half an hour after she was engulfed in the crosstown mayhem of early-morning New York, Judith dumped the car at the car rental on 54th Street and booked herself into her safe, anonymous hotel on Sixth.

Throwing her cases onto the spare bed, she picked up the phone and called London. No answer from Carey. She left a message on his machine and called the museum where Josh worked. He was out for the day.

Laura was at home and delighted to hear from her. The

effort it took to sound cheerful, busy and gossipy nearly killed her, but she replaced the phone ten minutes later satisfied that Laura didn't suspect a thing. Alice was coming home for the weekend and Andrew had been persuaded to accompany Janey Woolcross to a friend's wedding reception at a hotel in York.

In spite of her anxiety Judith laughed. 'Poor Janey, short of turning up for dinner wearing a white veil, Dad will never take the hint.'

Connie too was out at a conference for the day. The girl on the switchboard checked and suggested Judith rang back after five.

A whole day stretched ahead. Only Connie was keeping her here, but a whole day meant Van could track her movements. But what could he do, except get to Connie first and warn her not to say a thing? Her only hope was that he would go tearing out to Long Island trying to find her, and waste time discovering that she had already flown. She knew she should call Ellie or Jed, but her nerves were now too stretched to talk sensibly to anyone except Connie.

Rik Bannerman's insidious manoeuvring to unseat her seemed unconnected with her life. They were all still there, still working, still lunching, meeting, negotiating. But she wasn't. It was a sobering thought.

After several forays wandering aimlessly around the shops, finally Judith took a cab to the Metropolitan Museum of Art. At least that way she didn't risk being seen by anyone she knew, since it was in the middle of a working day, and it might just help to restore some sanity to her feverish brain.

When she realized that she had viewed an entire gallery of impressionists without remembering one picture, any further attempt to concentrate was abandoned and she walked out onto the wide, steep, imposing steps and sat among the students and tourists just gazing at New York life as it swept by.

'Connie Mayerson,' she snapped into the phone. 'Tell her it's Judith. Judith Craven Smith.'

There was a silence. Then the switchboard operator's voice came on. 'Judith? I'm so sorry, Connie's not here right now,'

353

she said with an excuse that sounded completely bogus. 'Can I get her to call you? Where are you?'

Judith knew that Connie was there. The pause had been nearly a minute too long to discover if someone was there or not. Either Connie was practising her usual arrogant indifference, or alarm bells had started to ring. And why shouldn't they? Somewhere in this city Van Kingsley was lurking, alerted by Connie to Judith's presence.

'Tell you what,' said Judith smoothly. 'I'll just drop by the office and wait for her, how about that?'

The New York sangfroid vanished.

'I'm not sure . . . I mean, what a waste of time . . . I'll get Connie to call you . . .'

'No trouble,' Judith countered. 'Unless of course you want to have another go at finding her?'

There was a silence. If she hadn't been in a rage, Judith might have smiled. 'I know,' she said helpfully. 'Why don't you try her office again, she may just have gone to the rest room.'

Seconds later Connie's voice came on the line.

'Okay, Connie, where do you want to meet?'

'Meet? Well, of course I'd love to meet you, Judith, only . . .'

'Only I might have something to say you don't want to hear. Right?'

'What?'

'Listen to me, Connie. Either we have a civilized meeting or I blow the whistle on you and your father.'

'My father? I don't understand.' Shock made Connie whisper. 'How dare you threaten me?'

Judith clenched her teeth. The time for games was over.

'Connie. I'll be at the Royalton at seven. I'll see you there. If you're not there by seven oh five, I'll make life very uncomfortable for you, okay? It's up to you. Listen to me and listen good. I have nothing left to worry about, but believe me, you have. Oh, and Connie, don't even think about calling London or Howard or anyone else, understand?'

She replaced the phone. For a few seconds she stood staring at the wall, trying to regain control over her breath. Her heart was thudding. She was taking a risk; Connie was tougher than old leather. Nearly six. C'mon, get going. A quick shower and a change into something that would not attract attention among the cocktail crowd at the Royalton.

Carey had left a message for her at the hotel to say he had picked up her call and please call soonest.

'It's Gray,' he said. 'He left a message when I was out. He wants to speak to me in the morning. What's happening?'

'I don't know. I left him in Long Island. No-one could help me, so I just took off on my own. Carey, listen. Van's not Van Kingsley. His name is Carl Mayerson.'

Briefly she told him about her visit to Mrs Jardine, glancing at her watch. Having had all day to talk, she now had no time at all. 'Connie will know more. I'm going to see her. Sure, I'll be careful. I'll call tomorrow. Carey?'

'Yes?'

'Did Gray sound angry . . . or anything?'

'It wasn't him in person. It was his secretary.'

'I see.'

An hour later, changed into linen trousers and a crisp white T-shirt, Judith was being dropped onto the narrow crowded sidewalk outside the anonymous double steel doors that led to the foyer of the hotel on West 44th Street. Inside it was already crowded, but the discreet low lighting suited her mood. She made her way to a small white-clothed table against the wall, sat down and ordered a drink.

Five to seven. From Dorfman Industries downtown on Wall Street it could take up to forty minutes in this traffic to get here. Connie would not even think of the subway.

Judith sat in the well of the reception area where she could see everyone who came in. She recognized the art director of an international fashion magazine, an English rock star being interviewed by a gossip columnist, and sitting moodily alone was a stick insect who was currently the model every magazine was pursuing and the rage of New York.

She herself was greeted with screams of delight from two girls, both account executives who had not seen her since she'd left New York. Judith was becoming practised in the

355

art of deception. A brief business trip, she explained. The tan? Oh that, well, the business included checking out Long Island, and they laughed and said, *some* business. Smiling, she enquired about their lives, although she knew there was no need.

Not much changed in New York. Single, successful but not always satisfied, working hard on it though with the help of a fashionable shrink, the girls were prepared to practise what he taught at every opportunity. Being in touch with their feelings, promoting their self-esteem was high on the agenda and they wanted to share this ambition with everyone.

At any other time Judith would have loved catching up, but all the while her attention was focused on the door. It occurred to her, too late, that in spite of the dim lighting that made instant recognition difficult, the Royalton was not exactly the most discreet place to meet someone who was going to put the final pieces into the jigsaw of her life. Mid-sentence, barely concentrating, not really needing to, she saw Connie walk in.

'Excuse me,' said Judith. 'Look, let me call, maybe we can fix lunch before I go back ... terrific ... lovely ...'

She rose as she spoke and, taking her glass, made her way to where Connie had just sat down at a recently vacated table.

For a moment they stared at each other. Connie looked uneasily around her.

'What is all this, Judith?' she asked clearly nervous but retaining her usual position of regarding the other girl with bored disdain. Judith waited until she had ordered a drink, which also gave her a chance to take stock.

'All this, Connie,' she said pleasantly, smiling so that anyone glancing their way would not suspect that anything other than two business friends having a pre-dinner drink was taking place, 'all this is to ask you what you know about Van, sorry, Carl trying to blackmail me. But more to the point, Connie, what have I or my family ever done to harm you? I didn't even know you until I met you at Dorfman's. Why?'

For the first time Judith really studied the young woman opposite her. Every time Judith had met her when they both worked for Howard, Connie had said little to her. Judith couldn't recall a time when they had voluntarily had lunch together. Always business, always with Howard there. Not once had Connie ever indicated that she had heard of Judith or, more accurately, knew anything about her and her family. Judith was on her guard and spoke more gently.

'Connie, whatever the reasons, you have already done so much harm, for your own sake, tell me the truth, so that I can try to protect my family and stop any more hurt. Please? Van, I mean, Carl is looking for me. You must know that. You must realize how dangerous he is . . .'

She had half expected Connie to be defensive or to lie. But she did neither. Between Judith's phone call and arriving at the Royalton, Connie had clearly decided to bluff it out. However, faced with the reality of Judith sitting across the table, the aggressive arrogance that had been part of her image began to evaporate.

In its place was a bitter girl weary of life, beyond really caring much what happened to her. She glared angrily at Judith, whispering fiercely.

'Protect your family? What about mine? Okay, okay,' she mumbled seeing Judith stiffen, 'I actually really don't care any more what happens to me. It's just that I need to protect my father. It would be awful for him, the clinic . . .'

Judith hadn't expected such an easy conquest. 'Why your father? I would have thought you needed more protection than he does.'

'Me? Oh, I guess in some ways. Maybe you're right, but now I haven't the energy to care. If I had I wouldn't be sitting here. You see, Judith, you haven't forced me into anything. I don't know what you know, but it's plainly enough for me to want to end all this too.'

'Enough?'

Connie tossed back the rest of her drink and signalled to the waiter to refill her glass. Judith asked for mineral water. Connie looked thoughtfully at the ceiling and closed her eyes.

'Enough of pretending,' she said bluntly.

'Connie,' Judith said urgently. 'Where is Carl? Is he here? You must tell me.'

'Carl?' Connie's expression went blank. 'I don't know. He

never tells me a thing. Just does what he wants. Yeah, I told him you were in New York. That's all I know.'

There was a pause. Across the room, one of the account executives was coming on strong to the rock star and the other was holding the gaze of the gossip columnist just a fraction longer than was decent. The crowd at the next table burst out laughing. The waiter arrived with Connie's refill.

'Tell me about Carl,' Judith invited.

Connie eyed Judith with a small cynical smile. 'It's a long story,' she warned, pausing as she raised the glass to her lips.

'I'm not in a hurry,' returned Judith, leaning back in her chair.

'Maybe we should go somewhere where we won't be interrupted,' said Connie. 'I can't talk here.'

Judith spread her hands and shrugged her agreement as Connie finished her drink and called for the check.

Connie's apartment, a rambling, disorganized set of rooms on Central Park West, was well above the usual area affordable by even a reasonably well-paid Manhattan PA. Clearly Connie's private wealth was paying the rent.

Inside it was perfectly neat and tidy and terribly soulless. The room into which she indicated Judith should sit overlooked a small square yard. Tubs of flowers were dotted strategically around to relieve the starkness of the grey flagstones, but not with care, more because it seemed appropriate, in the same way that the room itself had the required amount of furniture to provide its occupants with somewhere to sit and somewhere to eat.

It bordered not so much on the minimalist but upon the purely functional. Two deep red armchairs faced each other across a wide expanse of a richly patterned kelim rug which Judith thought was the only evidence that the owner didn't count the cost.

What it needs, she decided as Connie disappeared to get them a drink, was a touch of identity. It was only then that she noticed that in spite of a fitted white-slatted cupboard that ran the length of the wall, there was not a single personal photograph anywhere.

A Tiffany lamp, a carved wooden box inlaid with mother-of-pearl squares, above the shelf a totally impersonal abstract by an artist Judith had never heard of. Not a flower, no letters, no invitations. None of the detritus that piles so companionably into living rooms and kitchens.

Nothing revealing here, except perhaps that Connie's life was not in this apartment. But it was hard to say where Connie felt her life was conducted. Her appearance gave nothing away either, except that she clearly didn't lack money.

Judith silently watched her as she returned preoccupied with pulling a small table between the armchairs on which she had placed a tray carrying two glasses.

She handed one filled with white wine to Judith. She herself was into yet another very generous measure of vodka, into which she splashed a token jet of tonic.

In smart bars, in the upscale stores, Connie would merge effortlessly, anonymously into a crowd. Wrapover skirt, white sleeveless shirt tucked into a cinched waist. Safe. Hair well cut, falling just to her chin. Unmemorable.

Fleetingly Judith thought that without her money this girl would not have attracted a man like Carl Mayerson. But this same girl had become indispensable to Howard Dorfman, which was a mystery given Howard's taste in women.

Difficult to believe she could attract anyone now. Connie looked emotionally crumpled and rather lost, not at all the walking exercise in efficiency and coldly distant formality that Judith had so often witnessed. But it was that memory rather than the forlorn figure in front of her that Judith kept at the front of her mind. Connie was no-one's fool.

No-one's fool opened negotiations by insisting that while she was prepared to describe what she knew, it was a conversation that she would deny had ever taken place. After all, what proof had Judith got that her father was implicated in anything? None at all.

Judith had come too far and sacrificed too much to lose it all now. Bluff. Block all the loopholes. Lie.

'You know, Connie,' she said calmly, holding her glass in both hands and twirling it gently around. 'I would never have been able to implicate you – or your father – if it hadn't been for Harry's last letter to me. Silly thing to keep. But you know how it is. First love, always treasured.

'You see, he mentioned you in it. But he referred to you as Wallace not Mayerson, that's why your name meant nothing to me when I met you at Dorfman's. But it does now.'

The colour drained from Connie's face.

'Odd that,' Judith went on, retaining the ground she had won from her opponent. 'He scribbled the note because he wanted to pick me up earlier than planned. He said, let me see if I can remember exactly . . . oh yes, he said, "I have to see Connie Wallace. She gets all my stuff for me."'

Judith paused, waiting for Connie's reaction. It didn't seem to matter to Connie whether it was true or not. Her face was white with strain. She pressed her fingers into her eyes and rocked painfully backwards and forwards. It was a long time before she spoke and when she did she needed no prompting; the words came out as though she had been rehearsing this moment for years.

'After Harry died, I was sent away to friends of my family out at Bridgehampton. Oh, not so far that it was banishment, but enough to convince everyone that I was simply going away for the summer. I was too distraught to be kept around at home.

'Carl was one of those good-looking guys, usually charming but penniless, who hang around on the fringes, at tennis parties, at the pool, you know the kind of life that happens in the Hamptons. No-one quite knows who they are or who invited them, no-one questions it either. You may have noticed that good-looking single men are at a premium on the East Coast,' she said with a sardonic flash of humour.

Judith just shook her head and motioned to her to go on. Connie refilled her glass and continued.

'I was vulnerable, traumatized too. My parents wanted to get me away, so that I couldn't be implicated. I wanted to get away too. So I lived out at Bridgehampton almost permanently for the next few years, watching the seasons come and go and finding no-one to replace Harry.

'I met Carl there. Being half English gave him an added

charm. I suppose I was looking for comfort. I found someone who was apparently interested in meeting that need. It sounds boring now, it's all so classic. But he courted me, listened to me, then eventually – at least three weeks later – said he loved me and that my money was meaningless. Looking back, I know now that he had tried to stalk richer girls than me, but they either had sensible fathers or could see right through him. You know what Harry was like . . . if he didn't get what he wanted, he went elsewhere. Carl was like that too. Only with Harry it was sex and drugs, not money.'

The implication of the remark was not lost on Judith. She stared stonily back at Connie who, having shot the barb, had gone back to her former tone.

'I couldn't see past the charm. I was isolated. Do you know,' she said with a self-deprecating humourless laugh, 'he even said that he wanted my father to sign all my money into a special trust so that he could never use it. Puleeese.' She looked at Judith. 'I believed him,' she said simply. 'When you are that unhappy, that despairing, you will believe anything. I know that now. Too late of course.'

Judith found it hard to imagine the self-controlled, disciplined Connie feeling passionate about anything. It was even harder to imagine that for years she had carried a torch for a teenage infatuation, but she found no difficulty at all in believing the woman in front of her was now telling the truth as she saw it. She suspected the drink was doing most of the talking.

'So I married him. As terrifyingly simple as that. And of course I confided in him. Do you know what it's like carrying a secret around with you for all those years, blaming yourself for someone's death? It stops you working, getting on with your life. I just had to tell someone. Yes, I gave Harry the drugs and yes, I stole the prescriptions from my father. Satisfied?'

Judith swiftly shook her head. 'Don't be absurd, why should that please me? I feel sorry for you.'

A flash of annoyance crossed Connie's face. 'I don't want your sympathy. I've never wanted that. I just want you to understand.'

'Forget it,' Judith interrupted. 'It's not important what our private reasons are for this conversation. Let's get it over with and maybe even get on with our lives.'

Connie drained her glass and refilled it. Judith hoped she hadn't decided to get drunk. That's all she needed.

'So, okay, I carried this burden around with me until I married Carl and I thought, now I can finally share those terrible hours in the night, knowing that I can reach out and have someone to hold me when I was frightened . . . never betray me . . .'

Big tears began to roll down Connie's face. Judith was alarmed. The drink was going to Connie's head. She had asked for facts, not a soul-baring scene. This might be tricky. Better get her to the point before the vodka left her incapable of walking, let alone talking.

'And what went wrong?' she asked, raising her voice slightly to make sure that Connie's wits were kept in reasonable working order.

Connie wiped her wet cheeks with the back of her hand. 'Wrong? Oh God, everything. At first he had set out to find a short-term meal ticket, someone who would introduce him to the right people, provide cars, holidays, introductions. His life was going to be shored up by being married to Candida Wallace, he was going to take everything he could until my patience ran out and my common sense came back. Oh yes,' she said, correctly interpreting Judith's mild protest. 'Oh yes, he knew his charm and my infatuation had a sell-by date.

'But what did I go and do? Instead of the cheap day return, I handed him a ticket for life. I told him my secret and he simply blackmailed me. My money, my friends, my life, became his until the money started to run out and I couldn't pay the bills without attracting my father's attention.

'I'd caused him so much trouble already. He had never wanted me to marry Carl, but he'd had enough and wanted normality back. We all did.'

Judith recognized the scenario. Carl, Van, whatever he called himself, spent his life working the same routine. She felt a rush of humiliation as she recalled how easily she too had fallen for the charm, but, thank God, not the man.

Connie hardly noticed Judith any more. Her story unfolded

in a sickeningly familiar vein and a measure of misery to rival the vodka in her glass. Connie had taken off for New York, hoping that Carl would think she wasn't worth the effort of following and would get off her back.

For a while it worked. The Hamptons still had a lot of heiresses to investigate. But eventually even the social life there began to pall as did the tolerance of the socialites who were beginning to get touchy about a freeloader. Five years later, he tracked Connie down. Still married to her, she was still his meal-ticket. And he loved Connie's job.

She was bright, bi-lingual, and had an air of breeding that had impressed Howard Dorfman when she applied for a job as his Personal Assistant. It was she who had persuaded the very few people who had employed Carl to do so, in any job that might take him away, all expenses paid. But none of them had warmed to Carl Mayerson.

One man, a friend of Bradley Wallace, had given him a job in their office in Geneva, but the commission to check out a couple of companies in Switzerland lasted barely three months. Carl came back to New York and once again made Connie's life unbearable.

Anyway, Connie explained, splashing more vodka into her glass, Carl wasn't looking for work to make money but he had sussed that Howard's penchant for low life made him a vulnerable target.

'But I wouldn't help him there. Howard was off limits. I knew Carl would blackmail him if he could.' The vodka was working its inevitable effect. 'Howard's not that bad,' she went on, letting her head loll back on the cushions. 'Call girls, not toy boys, hash not trash.'

She began to giggle weakly at her own joke.

Two things were now concerning Judith. One was that Connie was rapidly getting very drunk and the second would have to wait until she sobered her up. Finding out why Connie had once deliberately misled her about Howard was a mystery. But for the moment it would remain so.

She asked Connie if she could make herself a coffee. Connie waved a limp arm towards the kitchen and with a yawn invited Judith to help herself.

'After all,' she said with such bitterness in her voice it halted Judith in the doorway, 'you've helped yourself to everything else in my life.'

For a moment Judith stood where she was, half tempted to turn and demand an explanation, but her other half overpowered the temptation. She needed Connie sober.

Ten minutes later she reappeared to find Connie was drowsy and not so inclined to talk. Bored now with recounting the past, she obviously found greater comfort in silently dwelling on it.

Judith was having none of it. Taking the nearly empty vodka bottle off the table, she poured hot black strong coffee and ordered Connie to drink. Protesting that she was fine, Connie refused. Judith stared intently at the slouching girl. She'd certainly been knocking back the vodka, but not at such a rate to have rendered her this comatose.

A look of pure fear crossed Judith's face. Reaching down, she wrenched the glass from Connie's hands and as she did so some small yellow tablets fell onto the slumbering girl's lap. Judith dropped to her knees and began shaking Connie and calling her name. Getting no response, she slapped her face, not hard, just enough to get her alert.

'Connie,' she shouted. 'Connie, what are these? Connie, listen to me, do you hear? What are they? Sleeping pills? Pain killers? What . . .'

'Stop it,' slurred Connie. 'Stop it. Wanna sleep.'

Cursing her own negligence for not heeding the warning signals, Judith swiftly put both arms under the sagging Connie's armpits and hauled her to her feet.

'C'mon, Connie, walkies,' she said grimly.

'No walkies, no talkies,' Connie protested as Judith, with one arm around her waist, dragged her left arm around her shoulders.

Judith ignored her. Half carrying, half walking, she hauled the stupefied girl out of the living room, across the passage to the bedroom and dumped her on the bed. Panting for breath, convinced she'd wrecked her muscles for life, Judith reached for the telephone to dial 911 for an ambulance. A low moan from Connie changed her mind.

Frantically her eyes swept the spacious bedroom, past the rows of built-in wardrobes, an elegant chaise longue in the same dusky pink as the swagged curtains and velvet-smooth carpet, a dressing table that ran the length of one wall, but apart from an air of expense it was as lacking in warmth as the living room. A door opposite led, to Judith's relief, to an en suite bathroom.

Back to Connie. Gritted teeth, deep breath. God, what a weight for someone so slight. C'mon, keep going. Shut up, Connie. Two more yards, nearly there . . . made it. With a last desperate heave she pushed Connie's head over the basin.

Supporting the nearly lifeless form of Connie with one arm, Judith splashed water into a glass and then forced her to drink.

'You've got to, Connie, come on. It'll be over in a few minutes. C'mon, c'mon . . .' It was hopeless.

Snatches of how to make someone vomit came floating back to Judith. Grabbing a small hand towel, she lowered Connie to the floor with her head resting on the rim of the lavatory.

Dear God, the things I have to do, she muttered, wrapping the end of the towel around two fingers as she forced her hand into Connie's mouth.

The action sent a shudder through Connie and that in itself brought her momentarily back to consciousness. Again and again, Judith pressed her fingers into Connie's mouth, pushing her tongue down, almost faint with relief when Connie began to gag and then . . . then it was over.

For nearly fifteen minutes, Judith held the other girl's convulsing and retching body. Finally satisfied that the immediate danger to her life was past now that the poisonous mess she had poured into herself had been dealt with, Judith pushed her gently against the side of the bath and ran back into the bedroom for pillows and a blanket.

Connie, eyes closed but breathing more normally, still had a ghastly grey pallor and she was shivering uncontrollably. Judith wrapped her as warmly as she could and then headed for the phone. Rapidly she punched out the number of Howard's private doctor, the only one she knew would come to her aid and ask questions afterwards, and begged him to come.

Dr Bryn Walters didn't fail her. He ordered her to keep Connie still and warm and most importantly awake, and said he was on his way.

Judith raced back to the bathroom, and squatting on the floor next to the exhausted girl, talked urgently about anything.

'Sorry, Connie. I had to do it. What were those pills? Dr Walters is on the way. Connie, speak to me. Answer . . .'

'Oh no. Howard . . . You should have let me go.' Connie's whisper was so faint Judith had to put her ear nearly against her mouth to hear her.

'Don't worry about a thing, Connie. He's the person you need. So do I. Just keep saying your name. C'mon, say it after me. Connie. Connie. Connie Mayerson . . .'

The response was weak but at least Connie was talking. Where was the doctor? For almost thirty minutes Judith bullied, cajoled and pleaded with Connie to keep responding until she thought she would scream with fright and exhaustion. Worst of all, she couldn't rid herself of the suspicion that Connie's blatant attempt on her life was the result of the threat to expose what had happened one summer so long ago.

Chapter Thirty-Five

Judith stirred and stared up into the face of someone vaguely familiar. Oh, of course, the *nurse*. Judith struggled up in the bed.

'Connie? Is she all right?'

'Yes, yes. Fine. Still asleep. I've brought you some coffee. I'll be off in a few minutes, just as soon as my relief comes.'

The coffee was black and strong. Judith's head swam uncomfortably, the events of the night before crowding back before she was even conscious enough to cope with them.

Within forty minutes of Judith's frantic phone call, Dr Walters had arrived and gave her a swift hug as he followed her into the bathroom where the now conscious but weak Connie was propped up with pillows against the side of the bath.

Crouched in the small space between her and the door, he rapidly got to work checking Connie's blood pressure, temperature, and responses, throwing questions as he went at Judith, who was crouching next to him holding Connie's hand.

Connie's answers were muddled and confusing.

'I couldn't ... bear it ... Judith hates ... m ... m ... me ... I couldn't take ... any ... more ... everyone blames me ...' she tailed off, sobbing uncontrollably.

The doctor, still busy examining her, didn't seem to hear the string of self-pitying justifications for such a dramatic act, simply confining himself to cheerful, soothing platitudes.

Judith, on the other hand, froze. What had she done to Connie to bring all that on? If anyone should be slitting her wrists it was Judith herself, not this slumped girl on the floor of the bathroom.

But even as the thoughts raced through her head, she was relieved if puzzled by Connie's ability to speak reasonably coherently to the doctor while she had remained so senseless with Judith. After a few minutes he pronounced Connie fit to be moved and together they carried the weak and by now softly weeping young woman back to her bed.

Dr Walters had stayed for nearly an hour, making no discernible judgement or displaying any real curiosity in Judith's description of the events leading up to Connie's attempted suicide. The details of her conversation with Connie she omitted, simply confining herself to the fact that Connie had been living under dreadful pressure for the last few years and that Judith's arrival and confronting her with a few unpalatable details from both their pasts had been too much for her.

'I doubt that's why she did it,' he said dryly. 'I know Connie reasonably well. Howard sent her to me once or twice.'

Judith was startled.

'Howard?'

'Yes, Howard. By the way, does he know you're here?' he asked as he wrote up his notes in the living room out of earshot from a now-sleeping Connie.

'No,' said Judith. 'Just for the moment it might be better if I can keep it from him exactly where I am. My problems and Connie's are nothing to do with him directly.'

'Aren't they?'

Judith looked at him in surprise. 'Why should they be? What I was discussing with Connie happened years ago.'

He gave her a thoughtful look. 'How do things stand between you and Howard?' he asked, draining his coffee and nodding as Judith held out her hand to refill it.

The question caught her off guard. 'Fine. I mean, we're friends.'

'Howard was pretty cut up when you left for England.'

Relieved that she was able to say quite truthfully that they had both recovered from a match out of hell and were truly friends, Judith was glad she had already passed him his refilled cup when he next spoke.

'Good, because I don't mind telling you that the reason Connie has been sent to me is because she is so infatuated with Howard.'

'Infatuated with Howard?' The coffee jug she was holding wobbled precariously. Judith dumped it down on the table in front of her with a bang. And he'd never said a word to her about it?

'But when? How?'

He shrugged. 'It's been an ongoing thing for about five years. Frankly I thought that was the problem tonight . . . but if you tell me it's something else, I believe you. Only fair you should know.'

'Does Howard know how she feels?'

He seemed genuinely surprised.

'Know? Of course he knows.' He paused and studied her carefully.

Judith sensed his hesitation. 'Bryn, please tell me the truth, whatever it is. Connie could have died. You owe me this one.'

Bryn sighed. 'Between us? Okay?'

She nodded. 'I'm good with secrets.'

Bryn gave a wry grin. 'Howard is amoral, you must know that? Women are not a serious part of his life. I always applauded you for going the way you did. I had you marked down as another patient in time, but you cheated me out of that one.'

Judith couldn't even smile. 'Are you saying Connie and Howard were . . . ?'

'Having an affair? I wouldn't call it that. She was sleeping with him, still does I think. In between his other relationships. Sex is what he'd call it, goes with the job. Sorry, Judith,' he apologized. 'I didn't mean you.'

She waved a dismissive hand. What else did it look like?

'Connie of course has to shroud it in something else. It can't be sex with an attractive man, straightforward, good fun, she has to load it with all kinds of emotional junk.'

'Maybe she is in love with him?' protested Judith.

He looked scornful. 'Women like Connie are love freaks. They're victims. But they set themselves up for it. A long time ago Connie decided, maybe not consciously, that the death of some teenage sweetheart was going to rule her forever. It was going to be the weapon that she would use to make everyone pay her attention for the rest of her life.'

Dear God, he could only mean Harry. Silently she listened. His voice was bored. Connie wasn't a big interest of his. But Howard was. And Howard was a generous man, who had helped push Bryn into the realms of fashionable doctors who ended up nearly as wealthy as their clients. Bryn had shrewdly guessed that the less publicity there was, the better for all concerned. Keeping Howard Dorfman's secretary out of the public gaze was one thing, the woman he was crazy about was quite another.

New York was full of people like Connie; she wouldn't in herself attract any attention. However, Judith's name would, if she were to involve the police and they questioned her. So Bryn made one of his decisions that had made him indispensable to Howard. He planned to file a report, keep everything above board and hope for the best, but as a precaution he knew that Judith must be aware of the risk if she insisted on taking Connie to hospital. A discreet nurse was what he needed to keep an eye on the situation. Meanwhile, Judith was waiting for what he had to say. And it was, to Judith, riveting.

'Failing her college exams? Harry's death. Connie's bad marriage? Rebound from Harry. Connie's unwise affair with Howard? On the rebound from her marriage because her husband didn't understand about Harry. Howard didn't want to sit and listen to all this, so he sent her to me. Of course, he's never happier than when he's got some woman wound up to a pitch. His passion wanes when they start sounding stable again. He and Connie talk about love, but I doubt either of them knows what it is.'

What was it La Rochefoucauld had said? 'True love is like seeing a ghost: we talk about it, few of us have seen one.' How could Judith disagree? The evidence was overwhelming. Even in her own life.

Harry, a teenage infatuation that would have burnt itself out in weeks if he'd lived. Roland, a passion that was unwise, unstable and undeniably unreal. Howard? She remembered that day in the park when she had felt their relationship moving into calmer waters. His interest had been kept fuelled while he was capable of rousing her passions in every way, but once she stopped taking him seriously, he had thrown in the towel.

But Howard and Connie? No wonder she had hated Judith. Poor Connie. First Harry and now Howard. For a brief second Judith could almost understand why she had pointed Van in her direction, but almost immediately she felt rage at what the consequences could have been.

Because of Connie's ill-judged interference and sense of revenge – and Judith had no trouble deciding it was revenge – her life was now in tatters. Any sympathy she had felt was fleeting. Bewilderment that she'd never guessed Connie's feelings for Howard was stronger. And why hadn't Howard told her?

'What's she still doing there? How on earth can it work?'

'It's not uncommon. Secretaries fall for their bosses. In Connie's case I think he finds her useful.'

'Howard's not that selfish,' Judith said sharply. 'What man would have a besotted woman around and have relationships with other women?'

Her voice tailed off. It was only too true. If the doctor noticed the warm flush in her cheeks she would say it was the heat.

Only the agreement that he could send a nurse in to sit with Connie overnight and that Judith would supervise her for the next day or two stopped him sending her into hospital.

'And you,' he said bluntly, 'need a rest too. How did you know what to do?'

Judith stared blankly at him. Suddenly she had no idea. She shook her head.

'I must have read it somewhere. All I know is that she hadn't swallowed anything corrosive, just sleeping pills. She muttered what they were, although I couldn't get it out of her how many. But she could only have taken them while I was out of the room which was for no more than ten minutes.

'I just thought they couldn't have had time to do any real damage, but if I'd waited for an ambulance they might have. God, I couldn't have killed her, could I?'

He laughed. 'Bit late now for doubts. No, she wasn't unconscious, you knew what she'd taken. On balance the risk was worth it.'

He glanced up at her alarmed expression and snapped his case shut. 'Take it from me. Otherwise I would have had her hospitalized.'

Having collected her luggage and checked out of her hotel, Judith spent most of the day in Connie's spare room trying not to think about Gray and succeeding in doing little else.

Once she had reached for the phone and dialled his number in London, but when the receptionist's voice answered the phone, she lost her nerve and hastily replaced the receiver.

At three o'clock the doctor called again and pronounced that Connie was progressing satisfactorily.

'I've persuaded her to see a counsellor when she's back on her feet,' he told Judith as she saw him to the door. 'And Howard does know about all this. The nurse told me his office called this morning to find out where Connie was.'

Damn it. Why hadn't she thought of that? If Annie didn't turn up or Camilla had failed to materialize it would be the first thing she would do.

'And presumably he knows I'm with her?'

'Of course. When the nurse called me, I rang Howard myself. It seemed safer. He's told the office he forgot to mention that he had given Connie a few days' leave. But he isn't a man I would try to fob off under any circumstances.

'He wanted to know why you were here and I said I didn't know. Don't worry, I've persuaded him it wouldn't do any good to turn up here but I said you would call him.'

Judith tried to keep her voice steady and to sound casual.

'Did he mention Gray Hamilton to you, you know, his lawyer?'

'Yes, he did. He said he'd gone back to London.'

And Lisa, she thought dully.

Just how much time did she have to talk to Connie before Van or Howard got here? Before she could broach the subject, the nurse came to say that Connie had been asking for her. 'Do you feel like talking to her?'

'Is she strong enough? The last conversation we had nearly tipped her over the edge.'

'I think you'll find it will be a help for her. Go on, I'll bring you some coffee in a while.'

Judith tapped lightly on Connie's door and went in. Connie did indeed look better; her face was still pale, her eyes looked heavy but her voice sounded stronger.

'Where were we?' she said weakly, almost resentfully. 'I'm not sure I want to thank you, I didn't want to live.'

Judith just shook her head. 'I'd rather you didn't thank me, I had no idea what effect it would all have on you. But I'll tell you one thing, Connie, if you want help to get Carl off your back, I'll be right behind you. I'm not daft enough to believe it was me did all that to you, and you're not that daft either, just don't do it again, you hear? I was terrified.'

Connie looked surprised.

'You? You're not the sort. Howard always said that if a ship was going down you'd be the one conducting the band to keep everyone from noticing.'

Judith felt exasperated. 'There are times when I wish I had grown up knowing how to flutter my eyelashes and sound helpless. It would have got me a great deal further in the world. Try and believe me when I say that I'm not tough, just capable. I'm not immune to flattery, charm, being pampered, spoilt and having the troubles of the world removed from my shoulders. But I have a horror of regarding men as a meal ticket, and I don't see why I have to give up me to be loved by all of them.'

Connie gazed blankly back at her. Clearly she didn't believe a word.

'You've always got what you wanted ... you, your mother ...'

Judith politely but firmly stopped her. She certainly was not going to discuss her mother with Connie, who had obviously made her mind up about them both already. She was dimly aware that even after all they had been through, Connie's view of her didn't matter. Only one person's did and she'd fucked that up.

'Listen, Connie, we can talk about me another time. But right now, do you think Van, I mean Carl, will come here?'

Connie turned her head away. Judith tried again.

'He'll get nowhere going to Mrs Jardine. But he's in New York, you know he is, and I'm frightened. He's already beaten me up. If he gets his way and gets to Alice before I do, or goes to a newspaper in England, I'm ruined, but believe me you'll go down with him – you're still his wife, the source of all his information.'

'How do I know where he'll go?' Connie retorted angrily. 'But Howard will come.'

'You know? For sure?'

Connie turned back and for a moment looked silently at Judith.

'For sure. But not for me. For you. Always for you, Judith. Always you,' with which she turned her head away and closed her eyes.

As though life weren't complicated enough. In the few seconds during which it became blindingly clear why Connie had gone on resenting Judith, Judith tried to recall a moment, a scene, a conversation in which clues to Connie's feelings for Howard could have been dropped. None came.

She thought Connie was pathetic. Howard's passion for her had been aroused because she was new in his life. If she had not made herself available to him, he would have ceased to find her interesting. Surely Connie could see that?

Bryn had said that she needed help and Judith agreed. Not because Connie lacked self-esteem, but because until Carl had come into her life she had been spoilt rotten. Connie was driving herself to such a low ebb, and her revenge on Judith was as immature as it was vicious.

Even her dramatic attempt at suicide, designed to make Judith feel guilty and to get Howard's attention, was childish. Like Harry, she was a rich spoilt kid so protected from life that when adversity struck, she threw a tantrum. Compared with Connie, Lisa Hamilton was a walking model of reason.

God knows whether her feelings for Harry sprang from real emotion but at seventeen surely like Judith it had been a teenage passion as swiftly spent as it had been ignited? Judith looked grimly down at the girl quietly weeping. Feelings might

374

well have altered, but the legacy of a few weeks of madness so many summers ago had lived on in all of them.

'Connie, if we are to help each other we've got to be honest,' she said patiently. 'I have no emotional interest in Howard, I never did have. He was only interested in me because I was different and because he always wants something he can't have. He didn't really love me and he never said he did.'

Connie turned back and looked at her.

'You know that's not true. You're just saying it to make me feel good about you. Well, I won't, you've caused me too much hurt.'

Judith gritted her teeth.

'I'm sorry for that, Connie,' she said. 'It wasn't deliberate. Since I've never even known of your existence in Harry's life until yesterday, you must see that's true.'

Connie gazed sulkily at her. Judith was so rational, it was hard to argue. But years of quite irrationally blaming Judith for all her problems was difficult to erase.

Judith pressed on.

'You were telling me that Carl was threatening to blackmail Howard. What did you do?'

Connie gave a mirthless laugh and pulled herself a little way up in the bed.

'I wanted a decent life. I wanted Howard,' she said bluntly, manoeuvring a pillow behind her head. 'Carl was going to wreck it all again by telling him we were married. I'd always kept that from Howard. I knew the only way I would do that would be to give Carl something else to think about. You gave me the chance.'

Judith listened fascinated as Connie described how she had first heard her name at a board meeting. She had recognized the name immediately, guessed it was Judith and when she saw her, she was convinced. She hadn't changed much at all.

In fact nothing had changed. To Connie, Judith led a charmed life. Her past was well-buried; her future was bright. How much brighter could it get in Connie's eyes when she saw what was happening between Judith and Howard?

Howard seemed mesmerized by this cool English girl. Where an entire board failed to get him to mend his ways,

Judith had simply shrugged when he questioned her advice. Intrigued by her calm acceptance of his wealth, the courteous but unmoved response to his raised voice, the rapidly established shared sense of humour, his need for Connie had evaporated.

'I had no idea you and Howard had a relationship,' Judith interrupted. 'You never gave any indication, no-one mentioned it, certainly Howard never did.'

'Why should you? Howard moves rapidly from one toy to another. Oh, for sure I was never publicly acknowledged, but just before you came along we were moving towards it. You'd better believe it . . . and no, I'm not imagining it,' she said fiercely as Judith's expression clearly betrayed what she was thinking.

Judith was not convinced. Howard made everyone around him feel like the centre of his universe, but equally he could be ruthless. Only someone as self-absorbed as Connie could have mistaken his feelings.

'So one afternoon he calls through to my office to say he wants me to make reservations for him to take you to Aspen for the weekend to ski, because you needed a break. You? What about me? Working all the hours God invented, always there. What about me?'

Judith could cheerfully have killed Howard for his cruelty. Typical of him to try and defuse the situation by openly parading another interest – Judith. Thanks a bunch, Howard, she inwardly raged.

'I went home and found a message from Carl saying he wanted to see me. So I met him for a drink. In fact several. I was sick of the whole world, and I told him why. Told him how every time I turned around you were there, wrecking my life.'

Judith clenched her arms tightly around her waist. What a dreadful person Connie was.

'So I told him all about you. Oh, don't worry, my father didn't tell me, my mother did.'

'Your mother?'

'Sure. She loathed the hold the Jardines had over Dad. Although the money was good, there was I falling apart over

Harry Jardine. The name just drove her wild in the end. They broke up over the Jardines. Mother just couldn't take it any more. I think she told me to try and make me see what a lucky escape I'd had, not marrying Harry. He would have turned out just like Seth.'

No such thing as a secret, Judith thought bitterly. Someone always knows.

'I told Carl that you were going to be the next Mrs Howard Dorfman. I don't remember clearly what I said, but I swear I never told him to blackmail you. I was too drunk for all of that. Next thing I know he's lost interest in me and is setting his sights on you. Do you know,' said Connie as though the thought had just occurred to her, 'for once I was glad to unload someone on to you.'

Shortly after that conversation Judith had inexplicably left for England. Connie had told Carl it must be because they were trying to distract attention from their relationship.

'Carl left shortly afterwards and I guessed why. He thought what I said was true and that you would shortly have more money than I could ever drum up. The very last cheque I gave him was to pay you. The big time loomed. Bonanza.'

Judith couldn't make up her mind whose grip on reality was the most tenuous, Connie's or Van's. But then she had read somewhere that blackmailers live in a fantasy world. Dear God.

'But why when you knew the truth, didn't you tell him?'

Connie shrugged. 'He was gone. The divorce papers could go ahead. If I had told him, he would have dropped you and concentrated on me again. While he was around I couldn't get on with my life. While you were around, Howard was distracted.'

For a brief moment Judith considered asking Connie what on earth made her think that she could make someone love her just by removing the debris of another life? Considered it, dismissed it. Wealth had spoiled Connie, self-pity had wrecked her.

'What about your father, Connie? When he found out you were giving drugs to Harry, why didn't he stop it?'

For the first time a look of pure fright came over Connie's face. 'Judith, look. I've not played it absolutely straight. But my father mustn't come into this.'

'You mean you need protecting from him?' interjected Judith.

Connie looked down and whispered. 'Yes, no. Who knows? His reputation would be wrecked and all he ever did was to make sure all of us came out of it clean. Yes, all of us, Judith,' she said, glaring defiantly at her. 'You and your mother and your father too, don't pretend it wasn't useful at the time. Your father's career would have been destroyed if it had emerged that a diplomat's family were involved with a racketeer. Everyone knew Seth Jardine was nuts about your mother and as for you . . .' She trailed off.

There was no denying it. No denying either that there was a curious bond between them. Both had loved the same wild and reckless teenage boy. Both had fathers to protect, both were being blackmailed by the same man.

The nurse, arriving with coffee and to do a routine check on Connie's pulse and blood pressure, relieved Judith of the need to reply. By the time she had departed, pleased with the patient's progress, the counter accusations she wanted to fire seemed pointless.

'How much do you know about Van's – I mean Carl's – background?' she asked a still smouldering Connie.

'Not much. He lied about it. He said he had no family, but one day I came across part of a letter from his mother stuffed in between some other papers he had. It was while we were moving I got the impression she was really worried about him. When I challenged him, he just said the letter was sent years before and she was now dead. But I think he just didn't want anything to do with her.'

'Where was it from?' asked Judith.

Connie frowned, trying to recall the address, but failed.

'Somewhere in Wales, I think.'

Judith gasped. '*Wales*? He told me his parents came to the States when he was a baby, that they were still here. Chicago, I think he said.'

Connie laughed contemptuously. 'Bullshit. He'd only been

378

here a year or two when I met him. I can't remember where he said his home was, but he lied the whole time.'

It was their only chance. Van had lied about his family: he must have had something to hide. Otherwise why deny their existence? Carl's mother had to be found before he got to her.

The sound of the door buzzing cut across their conversation. They exchanged a swift, silent glance. Connie's hand shot out, gripping Judith's wrist, Judith stared silently at the door, straining to hear the nurse's voice.

Neither needed to be told who it was.

Chapter Thirty-Six

Judith lifted a warning finger to her lips. Silently she moved to the door. No mistake. Van, Carl, was already moving past the nurse.

'Connie,' she whispered urgently. 'Can I get to my room out of one of these windows?'

Connie was sitting bolt upright in bed. Her face wore a look of horror. 'You can't, he'll know.'

Van's voice was floating down the hall assuring the nurse his wife would see him.

'Quick,' hissed Judith. 'Say nothing. I was never here. Anyone but me . . . tell him anything. Connie, if you don't we'll never either of us be free of him. Lie, Connie, it's our only chance.'

'The bathroom window,' whispered Connie, her face ashen. 'There's a flat ledge a couple of feet wide. Right at the end you can drop down into the garden. Come in through the garden room. Oh for God's sake be careful, quick quick.'

The bathroom door shut behind Judith as the door to Connie's bedroom opened and the nurse ushered in Van Kingsley.

Her hands were shaking, and she bit her bottom lip with the effort of trying to slide the bolt off the window above the vanity unit without anyone hearing. A window rarely opened for safety's sake was not going to be easily dislodged.

Judith tried again. Straining every muscle, she pushed upwards, upwards, until her arms gave way and her elbows cracked with a sickening crash against the pane.

She froze. They must have heard. Almost immediately she heard Connie weeping loudly, incredibly loudly.

Judith hesitated. Connie was beginning to scream hysterically. She could hear the nurse and Van trying to calm her. For a second her instinct was to race back to protect Connie, but as she reached for the door handle she heard Connie sobbing, 'If you've brought that bitch with you, you can get out. I don't want Judith Craven Smith in my house, ever, ever. Do you understand?'

Van's voice was raised, trying to be heard above the din.

'Bring her? Jee-sus. Are you crazy? I thought she was here. For God's sake, Connie, get a grip. Connie . . . ?'

Suddenly it hit her. She stifled a laugh. Connie was covering for her, distracting them, keeping them occupied until she was clear. With a grunt she pushed the small window once more and without warning it suddenly spiralled out of her hands and shot up. Turning, she heaved herself onto the unit and wriggled forwards on her stomach through the window out onto the ledge that Connie had described.

The space was not designed for a girl, even one as slender as Judith, who thanked God that Connie had bought an apartment at ground level. Even so, the drop below the ledge looked uncomfortably high.

Taking a deep breath, she set off on all fours towards the corner of the building. Once there she inspected the drop. Not too bad. Bruising at best, a cracked rib at most if she fell. One foot on a drainpipe, holding on for dear life, with a thud and a stifled yelp she slipped and fell onto the concrete below, her hands grazed, her knees throbbing painfully from the jarring contact with the wall as she tumbled.

Breath knocked out of her, she rolled into a ball up against the wall. Panting, shaking, listening. Nothing. The windows of the garden room were ajar. Bent double, keeping close to the wall of the house, she scrambled to the entrance to the garden room and, inching her way inside and around the perimeter, reached the doorway that led into the hallway.

Judith almost laughed aloud as she heard Connie's sobs grow more desperate and more piercing.

In the hallway ahead, she could see the back of the nurse clutching the telephone, stabbing out a number she had no doubt was Bryn Walters's. Under cover of the noise she slipped unseen and unheard into the room she had been occupying for the last twenty-four hours.

The Gucci holdall was lying on the bed. Into it she threw

her purse and the few belongings she had with her, zipped it and waited.

The nurse did not immediately go back to Connie's room but ran into the kitchen, emerging seconds later with something to calm her patient's sudden hysteria.

Poor Connie.

As the nurse disappeared into Connie's room leaving the door slightly ajar, Judith caught a fleeting glimpse of Van, his hand pressed against his forehead, glaring at Connie, urging her to calm down.

'I can't!' screamed Connie. 'I don't know where anyone is. I've told you. I never want to see either of you ever again in my life. Why don't you ask Howard? Why me?' And she was off again into a screaming tirade as Judith edged her way out of her room, raced for the front door, squeezed the lock open and was gone, leaving the door ajar.

The plane landed at Heathrow at ten o'clock in the morning. As she emerged bleary-eyed and feeling crumpled, Judith realized that her life was never going to be the same again. Sleep on the flight had been impossible; her brain was racing, fretting about her enforced inactivity, frantically wondering if Carey had made any progress.

Once Van knew she had left New York, he would come straight back. One thing about him was that he wasn't stupid. You don't beat up someone like that and then not care where they've gone. He must have known he'd gone too far, must have realized that once she raced off to America he had to find her and stop her from getting at the truth.

Van's power lay in the fear generated by the unknown and the power to control events. How long Connie would hold out against his insistent questioning was uncertain. Keeping one step ahead was Judith's only chance.

Carey and Josh were there to meet her, reaching out to hug her across the barrier as she came through arrivals clutching her holdall, her bag slung carelessly over her shoulder. She could see straight away they were full of news.

'We know where to find her,' Carey said gleefully as they walked rapidly along either side of the steel barrier. 'Listen to this. Olwen Mayerson, that's her name. Small village, just outside Abergavenny. Easy.'

Judith was jet-lagged and exhausted. She had phoned Carey from the concourse at JFK once she had got a seat on the last flight out. The noise around her made conversation almost impossible.

Finally she'd shouted down the phone. 'Carey I can hardly hear you. But this is important. Check Van's, I mean Carl's, mother. Connie thinks she's in Wales. Can't be that many. I'm on my way. Carey? Can you hear? I'm on the next flight.'

Now she gazed excitedly at Carey. 'God, you were quick. How did you do it?'

'A cinch,' he called as the barrier creating an entrance to the concourse forced them to part as they reached the end of the arrivals area. Judith hugged Josh who took her bags and urged Carey to get on with the story.

'Couple of minor offences years ago. One short jail term for fraud.'

Judith's eyes rounded in amazement. 'Fraud? What kind?'

Carey waved her question aside. 'Oh, who cares, cheques I think. But this is the best bit, the guy who checked him out went to see Olwen Mayerson and guess what?'

'Tell me, tell me,' she begged impatiently. 'What? What?'

Carey shot Josh a triumphant look. Josh was practically hugging himself with glee.

'Please.' Judith shook Carey's arm. 'What is it? What have you found out?'

He took a deep breath. 'Not his mother.'

'Not his mother?' Judith said blankly. 'Then who's Olwen Mayerson?'

'His wife.'

'*His wife?*' Passers-by pushing to get towards the car park stared curiously as Judith stopped in her tracks, blocking their way. 'I don't believe this. He never mentioned he'd been married. When was he divorced?'

'That's the best bit of all,' said Carey, pulling her away from the crowd. 'He wasn't . . . he isn't. He was never divorced. His marriage to Connie is bigamous.'

'A *bigamist?*'

'Judith,' said Josh nervously. 'Try not to shout. Everyone's looking.'

'But this is incredible,' said Judith, all traces of fatigue gone. 'You two have been brilliant. How did you do it so quickly?'

For the first time they glanced uneasily at each other. Judith waited. Now what?

'C'mon, how did you do it? It's the best break we've had. Who told you?'

It was Carey who found the nerve to speak first.

'Now don't go mad, will you? We had no choice, and honestly, Judith, I'm very glad we didn't have a choice.'

Judith turned impatiently away from him.

'Josh, tell me what he's going on about, will you?'

Josh cleared his throat. 'Well, actually we didn't find her. We tried to tell you last night before you got on the plane, but you couldn't hear. It was Gray.'

Chapter Thirty-Seven

Of course. Who else? But how?

'When did you see him?' she asked, starting to move towards the car. 'He left Long Island shortly after me. I thought that he had given up on the case.'

Carey slipped an arm around her shoulders and hugged her. 'I can't make him out either, love. He told us yesterday. That's why he wanted to know where you were. I think he wanted you to come straight home not bother with Connie, to leave her to Todd Simmons.'

Carey closed the passenger door and slipped into the back. Judith was trying to do some calculations in her head. While she had been with Mrs Jardine and Connie, and risking life and limb escaping from Connie's flat, Gray had flown home and got to work.

But didn't he understand, she'd had to see Connie. It had been like living in a fog and every now and then it would clear just enough to glimpse the truth. She didn't want glimpses any more. She didn't want anyone ever again controlling her life.

Carey and Josh looked quickly at each other through the rear-view mirror as Josh pulled the car out of the terminal and headed for the M4.

'It turns out that Van or Carl whatever he's called lived in Swansea,' he ploughed on, pretending not to have noticed her stony face. 'He was terribly hard up, and he lived in a dream world. Everyone who knew him at the time said he behaved as though he lived in a palace and not an ordinary 1930s semi.

'Olwen – who came from a much wealthier family – said they met in a pub and she just fell for him. You have to remember she was so young, only about eighteen at the time, and no-one could make her see he was no good.'

Judith felt a sense of déjà-vu. 'So what happened?'

Carey was relieved the rigid look had gone from her face.

'Well, the inevitable happened. He ran off and left behind all kinds of debts for her to settle once he knew her father wasn't going to give her a penny. She isn't poor by any means, but she was in love with him for a long time, couldn't face the fact that he married her for her money and kept hoping he would come back.

'Gray says her own lawyers will now pursue him through the US courts, but it's unlikely she'll get anything. Apparently she's just glad she's found him and now she'll divorce him.'

'Where is he?' she asked as Josh turned the car off the M4 to head towards South London. 'Gray, I mean.'

'Not sure. Said he was going to be out of town for a while. Asked when you were coming back and said to tell you what he had found out and . . .'

She turned to look at him in the back seat.

'And what?'

'Well, he said to tell you to leave everything to him. You were not to do anything else about Van, I mean Carl.' Carey sounded as uncomfortable as he looked. 'He said, if you preferred I could talk to him for you.'

'I see,' she said and sat in silence or giving mechanical answers to their questions until forty minutes later they reached Carey's house and went inside.

Gray's office said he was out of town for a few days. Camilla welcomed her call as though she had been away for a fortnight's holiday in Greece.

'Are you feeling rested, now?' she asked solicitously.

Judith almost laughed. She had been beaten up, flown the Atlantic, caught in a hurricane, escaped from Connie's flat, had only just made it onto the last flight home. Rested? Would she ever be again?

'I'll be back in a couple of days,' she promised. 'Ask Spencer to see me when I get in, won't you?'

Camilla hesitated. 'Jude, you aren't going to do anything you'll regret?' she asked. 'I mean, Rik's fine, but . . . oh, damn it, Jude. We all miss you. It isn't the same.'

Judith was touched but realistic. It would take a small

miracle to change Spencer's view of her, even if he knew the truth. In fact, the truth might nail the lid on her career at Premier – whatever sliver of career remained. Rik Bannerman was not going to relinquish his role now that he was back.

She replaced the phone. So what? A far bigger hazard lay ahead.

However, Rosie was barely speaking to her.

'Don't, Rosie,' whispered Judith. 'I can't take any more.'

'And what about me?' demanded Rosie. 'I have to hear it from Ellie, not from you. Ellie, frantic with worry because you promised to call and never did. Me, sounding like an idiot not knowing my own friend was in dead trouble. Oh, I knew something was up, but not on that scale.

'I got it out of Carey and Josh. That fucking little creep, Kingsley. Oh, *why* didn't you tell me, I would have told him where to go, helped you. Ellie wants me to phone the minute I hear from you.'

Judith clamped a hand to her head. Ellie. Oh God, she'd meant to call. Was there anyone left she could call a friend?

The weariness in her voice softened Rosie. 'I'll make you pay for this,' she muttered gruffly. 'Are you all right? Am I to be told about all of this? What's going on?'

'Yes,' said Judith blankly. 'Yes, I'll tell you. Truly I will. You'll be the first because Rosie, Rosie, I'm going to need you so much. But first I have something to do. I'm going home for a few days, to see Laura and Dad . . . and Alice.'

Laura was expecting her. Judith saw her waiting in the doorway before she had even paid off the driver who had brought her the five miles from York.

Silently she wrapped her arms around her grandmother and together they stood in the hallway just hugging, and knowing without words that whatever lay ahead they would be there for each other. No judgements, no explanations. Just there.

'Where's Dad?' Judith asked finally, breaking gently away. The house seemed strangely silent. 'And Alice?'

Laura linked her arm in her granddaughter's and led her out onto the back porch, pushing her gently but firmly into the big old armchair that she loved to sit in herself. She settled into the big wicker chair that Alice loved to sit in, legs stretched out, gazing out across the field by the barn and beyond to the moors.

Taking Judith's hand, stroking it with her own, she reached out and pushed a strand of hair back from her face.

'I blame myself, you know,' she said in a voice that was strangely distant. 'I should have stopped you.'

'Stopped what?'

Her grandmother sighed. 'Keeping Alice from knowing the truth. But looking back, what else could have been done?'

'What do you mean? Why are you saying all this? What have you found out? Where's Dad and Alice?'

Sighing, Laura pulled herself up. 'They're both here. And so is a friend of yours.'

Judith felt a tug, a tight little vice grip her heart. 'A friend of mine?' she asked faintly. He couldn't have got here from New York. Not so quickly.

'Where's Alice? I must see her. I've got to tell her. No-one else must.' She was panting, white, already on her feet and striding towards the garden.

Laura just nodded. 'She's over in the barn.'

It was a good hour before sunset, the sun was still warm, but a gusting wind was whipping off the moors. Judith didn't bother with a jacket, running across the lawn in her jeans and cotton shirt, calling to Alice before she had even crossed the narrow lane that ran past their house, rapidly climbing over the barred gate and dropping down into the field ahead to where Alice's favourite retreat was to be found.

The path that ran through the field was dry and dusty; without rain it kicked up small clouds of dust as Judith raced towards the barn, frantically twisting her gaze to right and left as she went.

'Alice?' she called. 'Alice, where are you?' Please God, don't let him have told her. Not this way. Not like this. Please.

She reached the point in the path where it raised its uneven surface and badly hewn sides to roll over and down into the hollow beyond.

And then she saw her, climbing up from the dip that dropped away from the barn down to the small hollow: Alice, in torn jeans, a T-shirt that she had bought when they went to see Smashing Pumpkins, those much-loved aggressive boots, her hair hanging uncombed around her face.

Judith's heart lurched. Both hands linked through his arm, talking earnestly, Alice was engrossed with Gray walking beside her, hands pushed into the pockets of his jeans, listening carefully to the young girl beside him.

They both saw her at the same time. All three silently surveyed each other. Gray bent and whispered something to Alice, who nodded and punched him playfully on his arm.

'Jude,' she called. 'Isn't it great? Gray's come all this way to see us. Make him stay for dinner?'

Gray was walking ahead of Alice, striding easily towards the house, a jumper slung loosely around his neck. As he drew level with Judith he paused. They were standing three feet apart. Judith gazed at him, then at Alice bending to tie a lace, and back at Gray, a questioning, apprehensive look in her eyes that needed no explanation.

He knew. Of course he knew. He'd known for a long time. She could see that now.

'Go on,' he said quietly. 'You have a lot to talk about.'

She nodded. 'Alice,' she said, catching her hand as she drew near and was going to continue up to the house with Gray. 'Come with me, I have to tell you something.'

Leaning with his shoulder against a tree that shielded him from their gaze, Gray watched them walking hand in hand towards a cluster of trees surrounding a fallen log that had been a favourite playground for Judith as a child.

He saw Judith sit down and look up into Alice's face, patting the log beside her. Alice declined, jumping up to pull a branch down, swinging on it, listening to Judith.

And then he saw her slowly stop swinging, letting her feet touch the ground, still holding the branch above her as she just stood there. Motionless, she gazed at Judith, letting the branch she had been playing with slide out of her hands and rock aimlessly up and down behind her.

He could see Judith was talking quietly, gently and only once did she briefly put her head in her hands before looking up once more. Alice seemed to be shaking her head. Judith scrambled up and tried to hold her.

For a moment they stood frozen against the skyline. He knew without being close enough to see that one of them was stunned, shaking her tousled head in disbelief, and the other was crying.

And then Alice pulled away, one hand held out in a gesture that clearly said she wanted to be alone. He waited until the girl had disappeared, half running, half walking over the brow of the hill, saw Judith slump back onto the log. Then he turned and walked back to the house.

The air was chilly, the wind gaining in strength as the sun dipped, exploded and disappeared from sight.

This wasn't the moment. She needed time. They both did. In the end she couldn't go on running. In the end Judith had to tell Alice that Harry Jardine, the wild, drug-taking son of an American racketeer, was her father and that she herself was her mother.

Chapter Thirty-Eight

Laura bade Gray goodbye a few minutes after he reached the farmhouse. She longed for this thoughtful man to stay and support her, but she knew he was right. At this moment the Craven Smiths had to be together. Andrew had gone in search of Alice. Judith they knew would not appreciate anyone going in search of her.

'When you came this morning,' said Laura, holding one of his hands in both of hers, 'I didn't want you here, but you've made us face what inevitably had to be faced, and I'm glad. Yes, really. But my poor, precious Judith. Whatever you believe, she has never given herself a thought. You don't know her as I do. Much of this is my fault, Andrew's and even Lizzie's and, God knows, I wouldn't have a word said against her either.'

Gray stopped her. 'I doubt anyone would attempt such a thing. Certainly not me. I must go. If you need me you know where to find me.'

Laura nodded, walking with him towards the front of the house and across the lawn to where his car was parked at the end of the driveway.

'And Arabella Jardine? Will she want to see Alice? She is her great grandmother, just like me.'

'Todd says she'd like to see you all. When you feel ready, no rush. Give yourselves time to adjust to the changes here first.'

Laura nodded. 'I'm just relieved that revolting man has been stopped. Will he be arrested when he comes back?'

Gray paused. 'I doubt he'll be back. My colleagues in the US will pick him up and charges will be brought there. His marriage to Olwen is valid, he married Candida Wallace in the States, so that's where the offence was committed. If he has any sense he will keep quiet about Bradley Wallace. There

391

is not a scrap of evidence other than his word against theirs and adding blackmail to his sins isn't going to help. Todd Simmons will tell his lawyers the facts.

'It was only Alice that was his weapon. And it doesn't matter now what he says, because she knows. I imagine it will be a ten-day wonder in this country and as Andrew says, even if a tabloid or two do pick up the full story, he's retired now, his books won't be affected. Who knows, they might even benefit from a colourful past.'

For the first time Laura allowed herself the glimmer of a smile. She knew he was trying to comfort her. 'And what about poor Carey?'

They were standing by his car. Gray had opened the boot and slung his briefcase in the back. He glanced at his watch. He could be in London before midnight.

'Todd has instructions to tell Mr Mayerson that charges of blackmail, extortion and assault are waiting for him in England. I'm not Carey's lawyer. But if he asks me I will strongly advise him to find the courage to tell his parents. After all he's thirty-two and his own man. Besides, as Judith has discovered, there's no such thing as a secret, and no life's worth living constantly looking over your shoulder.'

Laura nodded. It was impossible to argue with that. But then they hadn't meant to live that way; it had just seemed so much easier at the time. Just as she had explained to Gray that very morning, when he had arrived to see her and Andrew.

'It was Lizzie's idea,' she said as Andrew Craven Smith went to pour drinks for their guest. 'Just like Judith trying to protect all of them.'

Sitting in the sun-filled drawing room, the doors to the garden wide open, Laura was glad she had insisted this quiet, courteous young man should come to them and not meet them in York as he had offered. It was a dreadful shock hearing what Judith had gone through, without a word to them. Brave, silly, wretched, dear girl.

For a while Laura had thought Andrew would clam up, refuse to see Mr Hamilton, but for once she had stepped in and put herself on the side of Gray, who had simply pointed out what lay in store if they continued to let Judith keep on running.

'And that's what she does,' he said quietly. 'The minute she thinks the scenario she has mapped out for you, all of you, her, starts to go wrong, she doesn't wait to confront it. She simply moves on and recreates another life for herself. Is that what you want?'

There had not been a moment since he had agreed to Lizzie's plan all those years ago when Andrew Craven Smith had felt entirely comfortable with the deception. Although no-one but them would be affected by it, and at some stage Alice would have been told the truth, it had seemed all wrong. But while they lived in Washington, it was important that no scandal attached to their name. So much easier to create a smokescreen than clear the air.

With a resigned sigh, Andrew allowed Laura to tell Gray much of what he already knew.

'I can't say that Andrew and Lizzie had given Judith the stability she needed as a child. She was always wild and headstrong, just like Alice. But where in many ways Alice is probably overprotected, Judith had a more unsettled upbringing.

'Andrew's career was soaring, Lizzie made sure of that, but in the process Judith was not given as much attention as she needed – they were frequently abroad and her holidays were spent with me or with Libby Westhope's family.

'Frankly if they hadn't taken her out of school, the head-mistress was going to ask for her to go anyway. Playing silly tricks, truant trips into town with her cronies. I think it was because they knew she was really bright that her behaviour angered them, but what she wanted was someone to take notice of her.

'Harry did. It isn't particularly unusual, but it had more far-reaching results. You may have noticed, Judith is anxious to please . . .'

For the first time Gray intervened. 'Actually, I hadn't,' he said dryly. 'But then you know her better than I do. Do go on.'

Laura regarded him doubtfully. But he smiled in a way that made her want to smile back.

'Where was I? Oh, yes. Lizzie also knew that she had allowed her friendship with Seth to become a little too public and so engrossed was she in her own dilemma of how to persuade this crook to bow quietly out of her life, she failed to see that Judith was getting involved with his son.

'Then came the crash. Dreadful business. Judith survived. The boy didn't. It was all hushed up and that would have been that, except that about six weeks after Judith and Lizzie returned from Ridge Harbour, Judith finally admitted to Lizzie that she was pregnant.'

Gray glanced up at Andrew Craven Smith, who was standing by the open door staring silently out over the hills. Laura followed his gaze.

'Andrew, isn't it time you went to meet Alice from the train? Why don't you take her to lunch and by that time I will have told Mr Hamilton all he needs to know.'

He turned stiffly and put his drink down. 'If you think that would be best. Mr Hamilton?'

'Of course.' Gray stood up. 'Take your time. Alice mustn't be allowed to guess anything is wrong until Judith gets here. What time are you expecting her?'

'About five,' he said and Gray could see he was relieved that he had a legitimate excuse not to have to listen to a story of which he was not terribly proud, but helpless to deny.

When they were alone, Laura resumed. Terrified of being associated with the Jardines which would have certainly placed a question mark over his career, Andrew had at first insisted that Judith had an abortion.

In this he found an unlikely ally in Seth Jardine. Shaken to the core by his only son's death, horrified to find his involvement in drugs was extensive and now this pregnancy, he agreed to fix up an abortion in return for Judith's silence.

So it was arranged. Her father's all-important reputation was to be kept intact and Judith and her mother went to Coniston and to Dr Wallace.

But it was there that Judith, on the one hand relieved that she had been able to unload her secret but on the other hating the pressure that was forcing her into a decision she had not even had time to consider, upset all their plans.

'She refused to have the abortion. I remember Lizzie telling me that it was the first time she had seen herself reflected in Judith's face.'

Gray smiled. 'You don't have to convince me. I've seen the look.'

Judith's decision, she said, had sent panic waves through both Andrew and Seth. Andrew could not tolerate the thought of sharing a grandchild with a man who could ruin him and Seth did not want the burden of a grandchild without his son. Like most men who ruled by force, his morality for his family was inflexible. Harry fathering an illegitimate child was not to be considered.

In the middle was Judith, terrified and clinging obstinately to one fact. It was her baby.

'In the end it was Lizzie who came to her rescue. She ranged herself on Judith's side, but at a price. She suggested that Judith had the baby, but for Andrew's sake, they would pretend that the baby was hers, a "surprise". Not only would it confound the gossips who had been openly linking her name with Seth's, but it would enable Judith, still little more than a child herself, to finish her education and to keep Alice.'

'And she agreed?' Gray asked.

'Well, not entirely. But Judith has a sensible head on her shoulders and even she could see that in a foreign country, she would need the support of her parents trying to raise a baby, and it seemed a good compromise.'

So Judith and her mother had left Washington when Judith's pregnancy could no longer be kept a secret and disappeared into the country. Andrew visited at weekends.

Lizzie had quietly called in Dr Wallace. Too terrified to tell Seth that his instructions had been disregarded, and that he, Bradley Wallace, had failed to convince this awkward English girl to see sense, he could be relied on to stay silent. A secret deal was struck with him: arrange for Judith's baby to be born privately and without fuss and she would never tell Seth that the birth had gone ahead.

That way the Jardines would have no access to the baby, should Seth in his old age change his mind, and the Craven Smiths would simply bring Alice up as their own, planning of course to tell her the truth when she was old enough to understand.

And then tragedy struck. Gray spared Laura the ordeal of repeating the painful details.

'I'd always thought it was odd,' he said. 'Judith's reaction to Alice was not that of an older sister. She cared about her, really cared. And then the likeness between them was extra-ordinary. What made me even more suspicious was the fact that Lizzie had been diagnosed as having cancer, and extensive cancer at that, so soon after Alice's birth.

'It was doubtful but not impossible that such a condition could have gone unnoticed, with all those routine ante-natal checks. When Howard phoned me to tell me Judith was in America, I started to investigate. I got someone to look up Lizzie's records at the hospital against Alice's birthdate.

'Alice was born a month after Lizzie was diagnosed. I could not believe that any doctor would have allowed such a drastic treatment at an advanced stage of pregnancy.'

Pausing, he leaned forward and took Laura's hand. 'Nor could I equate Judith's description of her mother with a woman who would permit it, even if it was possible.

'By the time I reached Long Island I was very sure. But you know what Judith is like. She wouldn't tell me the truth. Is everything in her life done on a need-to-know basis?'

'No, of course not. But Lizzie didn't tell anyone that she had cancer until after Alice was born because she couldn't see what good it would do. Maybe that's why Judith does what she does. You're not angry with her, are you?' she asked anxiously. 'Howard isn't cross, is he?'

'No,' said Gray grimly, finishing his drink. 'No, Howard isn't angry. Ask me another time how I feel. So tell me, how did Alice get passed off in Washington?'

'Easily. A lot of ribbing went on, but Judith started back at college and only finished her studies when it was evident that her mother did not have long to live.'

When Lizzie died, Andrew, too shattered to think of anyone

but himself, sent a grief-stricken Judith home to Laura with Alice, who was then just a few months old.

'The trouble was Judith getting a job, to support herself and Alice. At first she thought it wouldn't matter if they knew Alice was her daughter, but I'm afraid I'm responsible for the myth continuing.'

'Why?' Gray asked sharply. 'You don't strike me as someone who would care two hoots about what people think.'

'I'm not,' Laura replied candidly. 'But I do know this is a censorious old world and the minute Judith, who was barely eighteen, said she was living with her grandmother and a tiny baby, the shutters came down. Andrew supported us reasonably well, but Judith is very proud and determined and she knew it was what Lizzie would have expected.

'So one day I sat her down and said, "Stop telling everyone about Alice. Say she's your baby sister." There were no miracles but eventually she got a job, researching for a local writer, and then through him, a research assistant at a library and from that to a marketing company.

'All local, so that she could be near Alice. Why else would someone as bright as Judith not try her luck in London? With her contacts, her education, her sheer determination? How many other young girls would do as she has done? Never whined, never asked for help. Simply got on with it the best way she knew how.

'Eventually when Alice was old enough to go to weekly boarding school, Judith did take a job in the capital. By that time Andrew had had a heart attack and come home. Judith was virtually the breadwinner. An army pension is not great, let me tell you. We are not poor, but Judith has made it possible for all of us to stay together. So don't you or anyone else start berating her, you hear?'

'As if I would,' said Gray with an odd almost exasperated smile that made Laura wonder if somewhere along the line her granddaughter had not been entirely frank with her. 'Perish the thought.'

Chapter Thirty-Nine

The flat in Kensington was cold, silent and musty. Even the warmth of a July morning warming the windows of the drawing room and flooding the kitchen with sunlight could not stop her shivering as she closed the door after her, stepping over the clutter of mail that had accumulated for the last month.

That's all it had been. A month. When she left she had been pushed to the brink of defeat, knowing that her life would never be the same again. But now she was back.

The place bore all the signs of Carl's hasty departure; the drawing room was awash with old newspapers and magazines. Ashtrays were overflowing and glasses and cups were strewn unappetizingly on any flat surface she could see. It took all her courage to look into her own bedroom, which surprisingly appeared to be untouched by Van — or Carl as she now thought of him — or any of his friends.

Carl's room defied description.

She had not removed her jacket, but just stood staring hopelessly around her at her once charming and welcoming flat. It was inevitable that it would soon become part of her history; the idea of staying there was now unthinkable.

It was also unreasonable to expect anyone to want to buy it looking like this. In the kitchen she ran her finger down the list of telephone numbers that she had on the board and dialled a cleaning agency. They would be there in the morning, said the girl. Meanwhile, scooping up the post, Judith binned everything that bore Van's name or the dreaded words 'Starlite Promotions' and stuffed everything else into her bag to be read later. The answer machine was silent. Nothing for her or Carl.

Later, she dialled Rosie and asked if she could stay the night.

'Can't wait,' said Rosie. 'Come over now. Instantly. Do you hear?'

'And how did Alice take it?' asked Rosie, pouring more coffee for Judith as she sat curled up in an armchair in Rosie's comfortingly familiar sitting room.

'Who knows?' sighed Judith, briefly closing her eyes. 'At first she asked for Gray but he'd left. Then for a day or two she wouldn't talk to any of us. Then she just stayed close to Laura.

'I think she finds it easier to make the leap from grandmother to great-grandmother, rather than father to grandfather and sister . . . to mother.'

'And Andrew?'

Judith gave her a faint smile. 'Poor Dad. Not as bad as I feared. Fortunately not that many people over here have heard of Seth Jardine and it's given Janey Woolcross much more scope to drag him off for long comforting talks. She'll get him yet.'

'Why don't you ask Gray's advice?' Rosie suggested, trying to sound casual.

The look in her eyes told Rosie all she needed to know. Judith shook her head. 'He knows where to find me,' she said quietly. 'And he hasn't, so . . .'

It had been a shock for Rosie and Piers to discover that Judith had a fourteen-year-old daughter. But the shock had been at their own failure to guess.

Of them all Carey had at least realized that Alice's paternity was in question, but that, he told them, was easy.

'It seemed more probable from what she was saying that her mother had been playing away from home and Judith was protecting her father. But when you look back,' he had said to Rosie and Piers as he and Josh discussed the truth with them while Judith was still in York, 'Judith has never done anything that didn't centre around Alice.

'Coming back from New York every couple of months or having Alice brought over. Remember Spencer taking her that time? We should have guessed.'

'And come to think of it,' said Piers, 'I don't think I ever heard her refer to Alice as her "sister". She just never contradicted any of us when we said it. Did you ever notice that?'

But they hadn't.

'Was there never a moment when you could have told us?' Rosie asked as they sat late into the night as they once had when Judith had first returned from New York, before Premier, before Van Kingsley. Before Gray. 'No-one would have cared a jot.'

'Plenty of moments, but I conditioned myself not to mention it. I always vowed Alice would know first and the moment never presented itself. Rosie, it just got more and more difficult, not easier. She adores Dad . . . oh, I know she thinks he's a dinosaur but what teenager doesn't think that of their parents?

'And while I truly did want to protect Dad, Alice was first. I must give her time to get used to all of this. She's back at school and we've told her headmistress, but I'm afraid of so many things now.'

'Like what?'

'Oh, of her not being able to come to terms with it – God, Rosie, I'm having a helluva time myself. I mean, what do I do now? How do I behave? I've got to be a mother figure, not a sister. And I'm so terribly afraid she will reject me . . . all of us.'

Rosie looked thoughtfully at her friend. Rejection was at the root of all Judith's thinking. Or fear of it.

'And has she?' she asked gently.

Judith looked at her, her eyes brimming over with tears. 'I don't know,' she whispered. 'I just don't know.'

There was a definite shift in the way Judith was now regarded in London. Excited whispers usually preceded her in restaurants and colleagues she had not heard from in a year found the weakest of excuses to ring her.

Most people thought she didn't look old enough to have a four-year-old daughter, let alone one of fourteen, while others reliably told each other that the father was an unnamed married man. Even one normally sane diary editor mooted the

400

possibility it could be Spencer's child, only to shift his ground when someone pointed out it was more likely to be Roland's. Truth collapsed, outmanoeuvred by fantasy, and Judith hated it. But for Alice's sake she put the record straight.

For once Judith had applied the advice she gave to all her clients to herself. If the world knows the truth, admit it. Get it out of the way. Denial or refusing to comment simply fuelled imaginations weaned on the demands of news editors who regard any story which included the phrase 'no comment' as fair game for speculation.

The first public acknowledgement that Judith had a 'secret' daughter came in the diary pages of the *Comet* and was followed up by the *Daily Mail* and the *Express*.

To each Judith gave a candid reply. 'I've never denied having a daughter. No-one ever asked me. Alice is hardly a secret, she is known to all my friends and frequently stays with me in London when she's out of school. We spend most weekends together.'

And Alice's father. Was she married to him?

Deep breath. 'No. It was a relationship I had when I was seventeen years old and living in the US. He died very tragically in a car crash before Alice was born. His name was Harry Jardine, son of Seth Jardine, one time chief executive of Jardine Leisure. All of which was well documented in the American press at the time.'

And would she be marrying Howard Dorfman?

'Mr Dorfman remains a good, loyal and dear friend. But marriage has never been an option in our relationship and, yes, he knows Alice.'

What about Van Kingsley?

'Mr Kingsley has not been a client for months and is now back in the US.'

God, she sounded like a tart.

Faced with such candid replies, all delivered in a slightly perplexed voice as though she were amazed they were unaware of Alice's existence, interest in Judith Craven Smith's daughter soon abated.

Arabella Jardine phoned her on her return to London. After Judith's departure she had contacted Todd Simmons and

401

ordered him to have Carl Mayerson arrested. After that she told him that she wanted to discuss some alterations to her will. To Judith she simply requested if she might be permitted to meet her great-granddaughter.

'Of course,' Judith agreed. 'I'll bring her on a visit soon. She's naturally curious about you as well. And Mrs Jardine . . . ?'

'Perhaps you could call me Belle. After all you are the mother of my grandson's daughter. Mrs Jardine sounds so silly.'

At the other end of the phone Judith smiled. How hard it must have been for the old lady. 'Belle, of course. Thank you for everything.'

Premier was more of a problem. Outwardly Spencer welcomed her back with a hug and a table at Ciccione's for lunch. But since Rik joined them, his efforts to convince her that her return was welcome, and that nothing had changed, sounded hollow.

Throughout lunch they kept up a steady stream of news about Masters and de Vries, Circe and Farley Cottenham, some admin problems which Camilla had sorted out but of future plans very little was said. In fact, nothing at all.

Either there weren't any or they didn't want her to know. Later in the quiet of her own office – and it was uncharacteristically quiet – she knew she would have to make a decision about her role. Before Spencer did.

Of them all Clark was the one who found Rik's presence the most irritating and frustrating. He tried to tell Judith as much when he stopped by her office later on in the afternoon on her first day back.

'Now that you've returned,' he said casually but she detected the hope, 'maybe we can get some new ideas under way.'

'Sure,' she smiled at him, reaching for the phone as a way to end what she found an uncomfortable discussion. 'A think tank later this week, okay?'

Each day she steeled herself not to ring Gray's office. Each day she tried not to grab the post, and to quell the tide of disappointment that swept over her when the familiar handwriting could not be seen as she rapidly sorted through it. She grew to hate her answer machine.

Thanks to the cleaners, the apartment was once again habitable. Ellie rang for a conversation that lasted nearly two hours and next day sent her a basket of flowers. Jed called to ask if he could be an honorary godfather.

'We should do the christening all over again,' he said excitedly. 'I haven't got a godchild. It might even make me less selfish and just think, finally a legitimate excuse to spend my free time in FAO Schwartz. And of course Alice likes me better than Carey, in case you were planning on asking him.'

Judith wasn't planning on asking anyone but she remembered when she had taken Alice to the big toy store in the centre of New York. They could still go again, no-one was ever too old for such a treat.

However, Alice was still not communicating. Speaking, yes. But when Judith tried to raise the subject of their relationship, she would get up and shake her head impatiently or listen without comment until Judith had finished and then silently, politely ask if she might go to her room.

For the first time any of them could remember, Alice claimed she wanted to work. Laura begged Judith to be patient. 'In the circumstances I think she's behaving remarkably well. Give her time.'

So they did. Summer began to give way to autumn and Judith's life in London took on a semblance of normality. Through Libby she heard that Gray was immersed in a libel case and was expected to win record damages. Lisa was letting it drop that they were once again an item, but Libby thought it was more to annoy Charles MacIntyre than in any real belief that Gray could mean it.

'Trouble is,' she said to Judith who listened dully, 'the stupid cow usually gets what she wants. If only someone would come along and give her a run for her money.'

Since Judith seemed unmoved by the possibility of being a contestant, Libby simply sighed and got on with her meal.

Howard made a flying visit to London. A different Howard, less sure of himself. Connie's attempt on her life had frightened him more than he would admit.

'She wasn't really going to do it,' Judith told him wearily as they sat over dinner at her flat. 'Just wanted attention.'

'In a way that you never did,' he said sombrely.

Judith shook her head. 'No. Not that kind of attention. How is she?'

'Back home with her old man. Says she'll give evidence against Carl if they ask her, but they won't. Meanwhile she's resigned and I've accepted her resignation. She was just crazy, really screwed up. Honest to God, I had no idea. You know about me and women . . . I just don't understand them.'

They were sitting in the drawing room, Judith curled up beside him on the sofa, Howard stroking her feet which were resting on his lap.

She swilled the wine around in her glass. 'It doesn't matter now. What's happening to Carl? How long do you think he'll get?'

Howard shrugged. 'Who cares? For ever I hope, the little jerk. Jude, why didn't you tell me? Did you think that would come between us? Hell, I would have had you on any terms. A daughter might even have been my salvation. And Alice would just love living in New York and I could take her to FAO Schwartz . . .'

Judith laughed. 'Not you as well. Jed thought that's the ultimate in happiness, but neither of you would have got Alice past the Village Cobbler. She's into boots, not toys.'

'Well,' he said, leaning over to refill his glass from the bottle standing beside him on the carpet, 'at least she has to like me better than Jed.'

'Go on,' she teased, tickling his ribs with her toe. 'Admit it, we're better as friends, aren't we?'

'Yeah, I guess. No fun chasing someone when you know you've been outclassed.'

They looked steadily at each other. 'Am I that transparent?' she asked ruefully.

'Hell, not you. There was a time when I thought Gray was . . . but I don't understand it, I saw him this morning before he left the house and even suggested we all had dinner and he just said he was busy.'

'Really,' she said coldly, swinging her feet to the ground. 'How about coffee?'

On the surface Spencer publicly and consistently enthused about their luck in having her on the team. But it was Rik who could be found late in the evening sharing a drink in Spencer's office, Rik who was roped in for dinners with clients and finally Rik who was offered a partnership.

It came at the end of a particularly trying week for Judith, who was desperately trying to complete a difficult project so that she could go down to Oxford to spend a weekend with Alice, just the two of them. The offer on her flat had come as a welcome surprise, but she still had to find somewhere else to live.

Spencer had twice referred her suggestions to Rik for approval and since she thought it more likely that Howard would embrace feminism than Rik recognize a good idea, she had laughed disbelievingly when Camilla showed her the memo announcing Rik's promotion.

An uncomfortable atmosphere hung over the offices. Since Judith's return from New York both Annie and Clark had felt much more motivated. Circe had taken the unprecedented step of sending her a 'personal arrangement' as she called it. Through an artless remark of Beth's she learned that Rik's day started after ten, encompassed a three-hour lunch and sometimes a game of squash, and that he had taken to handing over clients such as Circe rather than have to listen to their concerns.

Clark had suggested to him they both approached a theatre chain to take on short-term promotion for individual shows, and had even set up a meeting, only to find that Rik was on a freebie to Paris organized by a magazine with whose features editor he was currently sleeping.

Judith, en route to lunch with Rosie, had encountered Clark fuming in the hallway and instantly changed her own plans. They won the account.

Enough was enough. 'Excuse me, Cam,' she said, grabbing the memo, and brushed past her. Followed by apprehensive glances as she swept past, she arrived at Spencer's office, ignored Fenny, walked calmly in and closed the door behind her.

Spencer, talking on the phone, looked startled. 'Can I call you back?' he asked the person on the other end of the line and replaced the receiver.

He didn't need to ask what was the problem but he tried to bluff it out anyway.

'You have every right to offer a partnership to whoever you like,' Judith cut across him, leaning with both hands on his desk so that he couldn't avoid staring her straight in the eyes. Spencer pushed his chair back so that it was wedged up against the wall behind, trying to make some distance. Tears he understood. Hysteria was his forte. Rational and reasonable behaviour defeated him.

'But I think it would be helpful to know why you've reached this decision. I admit for a while I was off course, but it was a temporary lapse in an otherwise near-faultless performance. You've said so yourself. Since I've been back, Circe has asked to have her account switched to me . . .'

'But that's because Rik can't handle everything,' he protested, trying in vain to rally his defences. 'You used to delegate to Annie and Clark . . .'

'Used to? *Used* to, Spencer?' She stood upright and gently tapped the memo she was still holding. 'Are you saying you've come to another decision? I thought my job had remained unchanged?'

Spencer would have liked to throttle her. He had known she would be in and he had prepared his speech which would have been on the lines of a fatherly talk about family responsibilities leaving less time for the kind of commitment he needed, followed by an invitation to lunch and a new title which would have meant little but encouraged her not to make a fuss.

Faced with her cold enquiry it all came out in a rush.

'Well, now that you're a mother . . . I mean, we know about Alice, I mean, I really understand the demands of working mothers and while I would not rule out a partnership in a couple of years at the moment you wouldn't want such a responsibility and I don't see how you could give it . . .'

Judith was laughing. Helplessly, disbelievingly. Had he really said all that?

'Spencer,' she gasped. 'No wonder you went down the tubes. My problem is not Alice, it never has been. I put this company back on its feet and gave you back credibility. You never thought my commitment to Alice was a problem then, did you? So what's changed?'

Flushed and furious, Spencer scraped back his chair and stood up. '*You* gave me credibility? I never lost it. I gave you a chance. You might think you did all the work, but I was here to guide and ratify every decision you made. You people think all you need to get and keep clients is to come up with grandiose schemes. Well, let me tell you, it is and always has been my own personality, keeping them happy, using charm instead of aggression that has kept Prem . . .'

Judith didn't want to hear any more so she stopped him simply by raising her hand. 'Spencer, if you had bothered to look, Camilla has kept the administration of this company going, I've pulled in the clients. You and now Rik are the ones who dispense the charm. If you think you can run this company while you are being charming and Rik is playing squash, then I congratulate you.

'Meanwhile I'll bow out of your life. It was fun, Spencer. Sorry it didn't work out.'

Leaving him silently fuming, she closed the door behind her but not before she heard him press the intercom for Rik.

One look at her face told Camilla all she needed to know. She put a cup of tea in front of her and sat down.

'You've done it, haven't you?'

Judith nodded. She felt nothing except the realization that this moment had been coming for months. Long before Carl had made life a misery for her, Rik had started courting Spencer. Rik was more fun; Rik made a middle-aged man who had survived a triple bypass feel like one of the boys.

Judith made him feel his age.

The phone on her desk buzzed furiously. Camilla picked it up. Spencer's voice was audible, clearly asking her about Judith. Camilla said she would go down to his office.

'He wants to know if you've walked out or are intending to go today. Sounds panicky.'

Judith gave an exasperated sigh. 'Would I be that immature? Ridiculous man. Of course I'm not walking out. I'll leave when I've tied up all loose ends here. A couple of weeks should do it.'

Working mother indeed.

Chapter Forty

A weekend with Alice helped Judith make the final decision. Her flat sold, her job gone, not exactly penniless, she would take a whole month off over Christmas and take Alice away somewhere.

Alice did not sound thrilled. 'Whatever you like. Will Gran come too? Oh I see, just us. Yeah. Fine, whatever.'

Judith could have shaken her. It was now several months since Alice had been told. Months of trying to establish a bridge, a link that would ease them all into the new family structure. Her efforts were met with blank looks and no attempt at all to help meet her halfway.

The following week Alice would be fifteen. This was the landmark Judith had kept her sights on, maybe a milestone for both of them. Alice's birthday, and then Christmas. Surely something would change?

But Alice was having none of it. Her headmistress had said that Alice's behaviour and attitude in the light of this revelation of history had been subdued and Melissa, who had openly and excitedly said it was better than anything she had ever watched on 'Neighbours', did little to shift Alice's mood.

There was of course some good news. Carey's test showed he was HIV negative and his parents had taken the news of his sexuality with typical fortitude. They had, however, arrived at a tacit agreement with their only son that until they had become more used to the idea that they would never be grandparents, he would be discreet about who he was seen with.

'But then I've always, I hope, behaved discreetly,' he told Judith as they strolled back from lunch one day shortly before she was due to leave Premier.

'What about Josh? Does he mind not being publicly acknowledged?'

Carey shook his head. 'Not for the moment. It's just a relief not having to lie. Don't you agree?'

She did, but occasionally, when she was house-hunting, she looked to a time back before Carl, before Gray, when weekends with Alice and Laura had been a wonderful mix of laughter and gossip and warmth and love. What were they now?

About a week before she was due to leave Premier, Clark asked if they could have a quick drink after work. Judith shrugged. Why not?

He came straight to the point. 'If you decide to set up on your own, I'd like to come with you.'

She gazed at him in amazement. On her own? 'Clark, I haven't decided what I'm going to do but I promise you, I'll ring you first. Are you unhappy at Premier?'

He was. Annie, on the other hand, was flourishing under Rik's patronage. Judith almost choked.

'Which means his power base is extending. Annie is good. And Rik knows it. Haven't you seen the way she just glows when he congratulates her? Stupid woman doesn't see she's doing his work for him.'

Start on her own? Why not? Judith's bank manager was cautious but a week spending every evening working on a business plan had impressed him enough to arrange a second meeting, once she had found a house that would double as an office.

Her own boss. It sounded good. And it wasn't as though she was poaching Clark; he was going to leave anyway. The house, of course, would need to be more central than she had planned, but then if you're going to succeed, you have to be brave.

Bill Jefferson invited her to an early drinks party he was giving before leaving to spend Christmas in Gstaad, but she declined when she knew Gray would also be a guest.

Of them all she had thought Gray would be the least affected by all the changes in her life. But she could not deny it was not the fact of who Alice was, but that she had lied so constantly to him, that had alienated him.

Strange that Harry, who'd cared nothing for her beyond

the excitement of an easy seduction, Roland, who'd seen her as a way of adding glamour to his life, Howard, who'd wanted her to be both powerful and submissive, and Carl, who had fooled her into believing her own fantasy existed, had all had fed her loneliness.

But not Gray. He had been the reverse, making her stand up for herself, not taking the responsibility for her decisions away from her, making her face life. But in the process she had lost him.

She, who had spent a lifetime accusing men of letting her down, had done it herself to the one man who had never asked anything of her, respected her space and let her guide their relationship. No pressure, no pain. No commitment either. Nor would there be.

It did not help to read in most of the morning papers that after winning record damages in an out-of-court settlement, Mr Hamilton and his client had enjoyed a quiet celebration dinner at the Belfry. Mr Hamilton was accompanied by a mystery brunette who declined to give her name as they left at midnight ahead of their companions.

The school phoned at five o'clock two days before Judith was due to leave Premier, just as Camilla was asking her seriously if she started up on her own, would she consider taking her on?

It was an hour after they had persuaded a reluctant Melissa to tell them what she knew that they rang Judith to say they were calling in the police. Alice had run away.

'What do you mean, run away?' Panic swept over her. The questions tumbled out, falling over each other unanswered, frenzied. 'Why? Are you sure? Yes, yes, the police. I'll be there in,' she glanced frantically at her watch, 'two hours . . . what? Yes, of course. Stupid of me. I can't think straight. Give me a moment.'

Camilla took the phone out of her hand as Judith sank into her chair, trembling and white.

A series of quick, concise questions established that Alice had told Melissa she needed to get away and was going to see a friend. The problem was she refused to tell anyone, even

Melissa, who the friend was or where she could be found.

The school thought Judith should stay in London. Andrew Craven Smith had been told and was convinced Alice would be trying to get there to see Judith, even though Melissa said she hadn't got that impression. He was on his way and would be there by eight. It didn't make any sense. She didn't have to run away to see her. She simply had to phone.

Nothing else mattered but to get home. The rush hour was a nightmare. Everything was stacked against her. London was awash with Christmas shoppers. Schoolchildren lustily singing 'See Amid The Winter Snow' were packed into the entrance of the tube station. Bright lights shaped like holly and reindeer and mistletoe swung crazily in the wind, neon signs flashed merriment at her from shop windows as she half ran, half walked, searching for a cab to get her through the chaos to her flat.

But Alice wasn't there.

Her father arrived minutes after her. Wordlessly they hugged each other, each hoping the other would have news. There was none.

'There's no point in both of us going out,' insisted Judith. 'You stay in case she turns up here. Call the school. Stay in touch with everyone. If she was coming to London she would be here by now. Melissa said she went during the lunch break. You just don't know, she could be wandering around Covent Garden – she loved it there. Oh God, Dad, where *is* she?'

Reluctantly Andrew let her go. Threading her way through the bustle of shoppers, searching over their heads, Judith craned her neck for the sight of a heart-shaped face with a mop of uncombed hair. It was nearly nine by the time she realized her exercise was pointless. The phone in the flat was engaged. Impatiently she redialled, but the busy signal droned on. She slammed the receiver back and without bothering to retrieve the coins, flagged a cab to take her home. Ignoring the lift, she mounted the two flights of stairs and before her key was even in the lock she was calling to her father.

'Dad . . . Dad? Any news? Da . . . What?' She stopped, seeing the drawing room door open and a tall familiar figure appear.

'How did you get in?' she asked sharply. 'Where's my father? Oh my God, not Alice . . . please . . . not Alice?' She ran to him, tugging at his lapels, her eyes wide with fright.

Gray was still wearing his coat, a scarf hung loosely round his neck. He took her wrists and held them to stop them shaking. He looked tired and drawn but watchful. 'Take it easy,' he said gently. 'Alice is fine. She's at my house.'

'*Your* house?' Judith's legs felt weak. She groped behind her for a chair. Safe. 'Oh, thank God,' she whispered brokenly, and tears began to pour down her cheeks.

'Please, can I go to her? Will you take me?' The door was still open. He simply nodded and followed her out. Afterwards she never recalled exactly how she got to his car or the journey across London; shock and terror and overwhelming relief made her questions incoherent and his answers sound incomprehensible.

'She needed to talk to someone. I truly don't think she thought her vanishing act would start such a commotion. She said Melissa was a prat.'

Gray was glancing each way as they crossed Oxford Street and headed north to Baker Street and then St John's Wood.

'What time did she get to you?' Judith asked, trying to make sense of the jumble of figures in her head. 'And why you?'

'She arrived just before you left to go looking for her. She got lost on the tube trying to find the right stop, otherwise she would have been there sooner. I rang your flat straight away. Your father came over and he's been with her since about eight.

'We simply swapped places. And the answer to "why me" is simple. She needed someone to listen to what she had to say. I'm flattered she thought I would be that person. She seemed to think we were . . . well, friends, and that you might listen to me.'

He glanced briefly at her as he drove. Huddled in the passenger seat she remained silent, staring fixedly ahead. Friends? Even that would do.

He pulled the car into the side of the road, switched off the engine and turned towards her.

'Judith, let me talk to you, before you see Alice. Please?

She's fine, she's safe,' he insisted. 'Believe me, ten more minutes won't harm but what I have to say might also be worth considering. Just this once, will you listen to me?'

The road they were parked in was one street away from his house, but was busier. Car headlamps flashed eerily across their faces, the curious looks thrown their way by the odd lone walker out late exercising their dog left her unmoved.

For the first time since she had seen him walk through the door of the drawing room, she became conscious of who she was with. Last time she had seen him was on a warm day at Torfell when he had simply gazed at her and walked on past and, she had assumed, out of her life.

She thought he looked thinner, wearier, and she had to ask him to repeat his first sentence because so busy was she drinking in his nearness she had not understood what he said.

'I said, Alice doesn't know how to react to you. For as long as she can remember, you have been her older, glamorous – yes, that's what she said – sister who made life exciting for her. Andrew has always been Dad. And suddenly everyone expects her to start reacting differently to you all. Now you want to be her mother, but to Alice her mother is dead. She's never had a mother – she doesn't know what you're supposed to say to them.'

Judith listened in silence, not quite believing that Alice wouldn't have told her all this. He must be mistaken. Reading her thoughts, Gray shook his head.

'Don't you see? She was so overwhelmed that all she could take in was that all of you – you, Andrew and even in her own way Laura – kept looking at her and trying to make her talk when she didn't know what it was she wanted to say and worse, what it was you wanted her to say.

'All of you have been rehearsing that moment for years. Whether you like it or not, you were prepared for it. She wasn't. She didn't know what the next line was meant to be. She might seem street-wise, a terror in tough boots, but you know she's just a little kid still. She just wants everything to stay as it is. And frankly, I think she has a point.'

Judith had been staring straight ahead through the windscreen watching a flurry of leaves whipping across the bonnet of Gray's car, skimming the surface and falling to the ground. She looked down at her hands clasped in her lap and wondered why she had got it all so wrong.

'You know,' she half whispered, 'I've spent all this time telling myself that I was protecting Alice, Dad. But do you want the truth?' He waited. 'The truth is that I was terrified that I would lose her. Lose her love, her need for me. The longer she didn't know, the longer I didn't have to put it to the test. You see,' she gave him a faint smile, 'I might look as though I know what I'm doing. But I lose more than I gain.'

They sat in silence. The car was growing cold. Finally she turned to him. 'What shall I do?' she whispered. 'I just want her to be happy.'

His voice was matter of fact. 'I expect you do. Alice has come to the conclusion – quite wrongly, you don't have to tell me – that she is responsible for all this upheaval. But what else could she think? All around her, everyone telling her that all anyone wants is her happiness but she *was* happy. She always has been. You all made her the centre of your lives, so why shouldn't she have been? All she wants is for everything to be as it was.'

'But that's not possible,' Judith protested. 'How can it be? I'm her mother, not her sister. I have to get used to that as well, remember.'

'Do you?' he asked gently. 'Do you really mean that? Why can't you be like Alice and accept things for what they are? You've never thought of Alice as anything but your daughter, have you?'

She didn't answer, just continued staring at her hands. 'Hey,' he said, softly brushing her cheek with his finger to get her attention. 'Want my advice?'

'Can't afford it,' she said automatically, reviving an old, shared joke, but knowing that everything he said was true and wondering if she kept her eyes closed he wouldn't guess how much she longed to be wrapped in his arms and rocked the way she had so longed to hold Alice.

He chuckled in the darkness, softly, and she turned and smiled at him.

'This is free,' he replied. 'Most of us just want to be accepted for what we are. Not to have to conform to someone else's idea of how we should be. An idea that suits their notion of happiness but maybe not ours. Be like Alice. Accept life as it is, not how you would like it to be.'

'You mean I just leave her to go on living at Torfell with Laura and Dad? Where do I come in?'

Gray looked exasperated. 'Where you have always come in. First in her life. So what if she doesn't call you "Mummy" or "Mother". Is that really going to change how you both feel about each other? I doubt it. But then that's just my view,' he finished.

'Why are you bothering with all this?' Judith asked abruptly. 'You could have phoned Dad and had him collect her.'

'True,' he said carefully. 'But then Alice had the good sense to come and find me.'

For a moment he stared ahead and then turned to look at her. 'One of you had to.'

'Can I see Alice now?' she asked quickly.

Clark told Judith on the quiet that Farley Cottenham was horrified to hear that she was leaving and had told Spencer in a very forthright letter that he had given his account to Judith, not Premier, and would be rethinking his future.

'Just thought you'd like to know,' he said with an air of innocence that deceived no one, least of all Judith. She wasn't into poaching clients. Farley would have to come to her.

Libby had been headhunted by the finance committee of Country Heritage. 'ChildLife stays with Premier, but I could do with your expertise in this new job. Not much money, but me and plenty of prestige, can't say fairer than that, can I?'

It was a start. Rosie said go for it and Jed was so excited at the prospect he couldn't believe she was hesitating. Carey and Josh thought she would be crazy not to do it. Ellie called from New York and said she could do with a short-term publicist in London to promote her films when they were shown on British TV.

'Don't turn me down,' she pleaded. 'I can't tell you what a

relief it would be to know you're there. No-one understands what I do better than you.'

Alice had said it would save her getting a job in the holidays. 'I'll be your Gofer,' she volunteered as Judith drove her back to school late in the afternoon the day following her escape. A night of tears and hugs at Judith's apartment had done much to restore their old ways.

Andrew left early in the morning to return to Yorkshire and Judith had taken Alice shopping, then lunch before finally heading back to Oxford.

'Mel says there aren't any Saturday jobs for fifteen-year-olds and I'm too young to get a national insurance number and I won't charge much.'

'Thank you, Alice,' Judith said meekly. 'I'm very moved.'

'I thought you would be,' said Alice. 'Anyway, just wait until I tell that stuck-up cow Sarah . . .'

'Still as bad, eh?' Judith asked, throwing her a sympathetic glance.

'Gross,' groaned Alice. 'Anyway, wait until she hears that you've got your own company. Her mother does nothing.'

Only Judith knew what an effort it took to stop herself from hugging the young girl beside her, or crying, or both. But Gray's advice was uppermost in her mind. She gripped the wheel and tried to sound convincing.

'Alice,' she said sternly. 'That is a very sexist remark.'

And Then What . . .

Twice she walked away and once she even got as far as hailing
a cab. This is ridiculous, Judith told herself, having hastily
dismissed an annoyed cabby who had carved up a motorbike
and a Porsche to get to her.

All you're doing is – as any normal, courteous person would
do – thanking someone for helping Alice. Now get on with
it. If Lisa is there, so what? Or the unnamed brunette. He said
. . . didn't he . . . that Alice thought they were friends. And
friends is what she would settle for.

Liar, she told herself.

This time she made it as far as the gate in front of the steep
white stone steps leading up to the black door with its brass
knocker. Which was a vast improvement on the three phone
calls that had been curtailed the minute she got through and
the pile of screwed-up paper strewn beneath her desk, evidence
of the carefully composed and impatiently discarded letters of
thanks she had thought of sending.

The festively wrapped present under her arm, a silk-lined
plaid scarf to add to his collection, carefully chosen and
bought by her and Alice earlier in the day, was now her excuse.
The stiff white card – the sixth attempt – bore a simple message. 'From Alice and Judith. Thank you and happy Christmas.' Alice had signed her own name and put two kisses
underneath.

This time Judith closed her eyes and rapped firmly on the
knocker. The housekeeper opened the door and did not seem
in the least surprised to see her.

'Oh do come in,' she greeted her, ushering her into the
hallway. 'Gray will be with you directly. You must be cold,
come in by the fire. I'll just tell him you're here, and see to
dinner. Will you be all right for a moment?'

Removing Judith's coat she bustled out, leaving her guest

standing awkwardly in front of the fire. The calf-length maroon flared wool skirt and pale grey cashmere sweater suddenly seemed all wrong. Judith wished she had worn shoes instead of these boots, and her hair was well overdue for a cut.

'Hi,' he said from the doorway. 'You're late.'

Late?

'I'm sorry,' she said blankly, looking embarrassed. 'You mean this is too late to call? I'm so sorry, I've only just dropped by to give you this from Alice . . . and me of course . . . but Alice wanted you to have it tonight.'

He strolled into the room and she wondered if it was her imagination but was he looking uncomfortable, trying not to smile? The familiar jeans and navy sweater suggested he had been home for some time and as it was now eight o'clock he couldn't possibly be going out.

Oh God. He was having guests. 'Please, don't stop for me, I'm just going . . . a silly present . . . nothing much. Just, you know, thanks.'

She thrust the box at him with a small self-conscious smile and shrug, and then looked around for somewhere to leave it.

'How kind,' he said, reaching out to take it from her. She watched as he glanced at the label. 'Can I open it now, or must I save it for Christmas Day?'

Even to her ears her laugh sounded forced. 'Whatever. Now I really must go.'

This had been a *big* mistake. What on earth had possessed her? Tomorrow she would learn to live with the humiliation. What the hell must he think?

'What a shame,' he said calmly. 'Alice said you would almost certainly stay for dinner.' *Alice?* Halfway to the door she wheeled round to face him. 'And I'm so hopeless about presents that I can't wait for Christmas,' he said with a sheepish smile.

She swallowed hard. 'What do you mean, Alice?'

'Hey,' he said, dropping the wrapping paper to the floor and holding the scarf admiringly in his hands, and came towards her. 'This is terrific . . . thank you.' He leaned

419

forward and kissed her on the cheek. She couldn't move. 'Oh, that's for Alice,' he said. 'Of course I would have kissed you too, only you haven't put any crosses under your name.

'Sorry, you asked about Alice? Well, she called my office this afternoon – you know I adore that girl and she likes me much better than Howard – and said you were coming to see me. She said you would be hungry so I arranged dinner . . . only it got later and later.'

Judith eyed him with a look that spelt danger for someone. 'And what else did Alice say . . . ?'

He frowned as though trying to recollect exactly what else her enterprising daughter had relayed.

'Let me see. Oh yes, she said if I wasn't really set on going to Paris for Christmas, she and Laura wanted me to come to Torfell.'

The housekeeper appearing in the hallway, pulling on her coat as she spoke, stopped her replying.

'I think that's all, Gray. It's ready whenever you are. I'll do the dishes in the morning, so just leave them. Goodnight, Judith.'

Judith? Morning? Christmas in Torfell? The door closed, and the plot was now spinning wildly away from her. She felt like one of those people sitting in a train who can't understand why everyone else in the carriage suddenly disembarks without telling them the reason.

She stood in silence. Alice might possibly be found murdered in her bed . . . Gray gave a discreet cough.

'Don't you think you could just stay and have dinner? I'm getting so bored hearing all about you from your friends. Libby tells me you're starting your own company, Carey says you've sold your flat, John Imber tells me you're spending New Year with Rosie and Piers at his place and Alice has to let me know when you're coming to dinner.'

The space between them was small. Now she came to think of it, they were standing much too close considering the size of the room and they were the only two people in it.

'You're not expecting anyone else?'

He shook his head.

'Not Lisa . . . ?'

'Certainly not Lisa. She has a new interest, thank God, and it would help to discourage her from dropping around here quite so much if she thought I was entertaining someone else . . . and if you think I need thanks it's the very least you can do.'

This was difficult. She kept her tone light and only succeeded in sounding suspicious.

'Or the er . . . unnamed brunette?'

'Oh dear,' he grinned. 'Me being knight in shining armour. Barbara MacIntyre. Got fed up with Lisa monopolizing Charles and asked me to take her home.'

Of course. How stupid. 'Are they staying together?'

He nodded. 'Always were. Charles just needed a bit of a shake-up and Barbara walking out did it. I . . . er . . . hope you're not going to walk out, not until you've had dinner at any rate.'

'No, no. I mean yes, well I mean, of course. Thank you, dinner would be lovely. I'm sorry about Alice, but I expect she meant well. And she does like you.'

'And what about you?' he said, leaning inside the door frame, not taking his eyes from her face. 'You did once . . .'

'So did you,' she reminded him. 'I mean, liked me.'

'I never stopped,' he said quietly, reaching out and gently stroking the side of her face.

'But you've stayed away. It doesn't sound much like that to me.'

'One day,' he said, clearly choosing his words carefully, 'one day you will stop running away. I thought you would trust me to tell me what was the matter. I am not a mind reader. I can guess but I have no right to make decisions for someone, unless they invite me to do it.

'You never asked me to help. That hurts. Oh yes, it does. Maybe in time you might learn the difference between shutting someone out of your life and retaining your independence.'

Her boots were now utterly wrong. She stared down at them. Why on earth had she ever bought them? For no other reason than she now hated the sight of them and the idea of

421

sitting through dinner wearing them was a nightmare, she took them off.

'What are you doing?'

Count to three and tell him.

'My boots hurt. No, that's not true. I just wanted some of your time,' she said, raising her eyes to his.

'I asked you to stay in Paris with me,' he pointed out. 'It was you who insisted on going home. You who put work first. You didn't hear me complain . . .'

She rounded on him, indignation flashing in her eyes, in her voice. 'All I wanted was for you to *ask*. Don't you understand? I just wanted to feel you cared enough. Just to know that you wanted to be with me, even if you couldn't . . .'

He dropped his head and shook it in disbelief. 'Oh Christ, you're not going to start all that walking on the beach stuff again, are you?'

'I am not starting anything at all,' she flared back at him, picking up her boots and making for the front door. 'I have better things to do than stand here while you . . . while you . . . what are you doing?'

He was bending down and stripping off his socks, solemnly rolling up the bottom of his jeans.

'I'm getting ready to go for a walk on the beach, any fucking beach you like. I'll do anything. Whatever it is that makes you happy . . . Brighton? Monte Carlo, East Hampton? You name it . . .'

They glared at each other, both furious, both wanting to win, and then Gray's mouth began to twitch and slowly they started to laugh, giggling helplessly. Two grown people, one barefoot, the other halfway out of the door on a freezing December evening, carrying a stout pair of boots with only rage to keep her warm.

'Gray . . .' She tried to speak, but it was too funny for words and she subsided into laughter that left her half crying at the absurdity of it all.

It was hard to concentrate but there was something she had to tell him. 'Gray,' she started again but, in a more advanced state of recovery, he pulled her into his arms and kissed her.

'Gray,' she tried again a few minutes later. 'I wanted to

explain about Van and Howard and why I behaved like I did because I think you need to know.'

He gave a muttered oath. 'Come here,' he said, leading her to the phone by the stairs. He picked it up and held it out to her. 'If you want to tell someone how you feel, tell Carey, or Rosie, or even call Ellie in New York. But if you want to know how I feel, you know where to find me.'

Dizziness was making her breathless. A feeling of relief swept over her. He was waiting, knowing what she was going to say, impatient to hear it, prepared to wait . . . but not for much longer.

She took the receiver out of his hand and replaced it carefully in its cradle. Then she studied the machine next to it and switched it to 'answer'.

'Ten to one,' she called out after him as he started up the stairs, 'they'll be out anyway. Er . . . where are you going? I thought you invited me to dinner?'

He stopped and came back down the stairs. Taking her hand firmly in his, he pulled her after him. 'I did invite you to dinner,' he said as they reached the top of the stairs. 'But I don't recall specifying a particular time, do you?'

And indeed, she had to admit, as she sank down onto the blue-canopied bed, that now she came to think of it, she couldn't.